CRITICAL ACCLAIM FOR
TALES OF MUSIC, MURDER, AND MAYHEM

"An anthology that gives an entirely new meaning to the phrase 'killer beat.' An exceptional work, and a grand homage to Music City, USA." —Joel W. Barrows, author of the Deep Cover thrillers

"You may know Nashville as the land of Rhinestone Cowboys and Hee Haw Honeys, but Music City has a darker side and it is on full display in these twenty-four *Tales of Music, Murder, and Mayhem* featuring some of the top names in contemporary crime writing, is more entertaining than a rowdy Outlaw Country Cruise. I took to these stories like a cold hog to warm mud and I reckon you will too." —Chris Orlet, author of *So Many Things to Bury*

"Stories so rich in detail that it's like getting twenty-four novels for the price of one." —Stephen D. Rogers, crime fiction author

"*Tales of Music, Murder, and Mayhem* is a thoroughly enjoyable volume certain to top the charts with a platinum collection of 25 original crime fiction stories written by some of today's finest maestros of mystery." —Andrew McAleer, co-editor of *Edgar & Shamus Go Golden*, and author of the Henry von Stray mysteries

"*Tales of Music, Murder and Mayhem* captures the essence of the south, so enjoy these fresh picks from the new American literary frontier. Down & Out Books has long been known as the home of the best mystery and crime talent in the land. This year's anthology is no exception." —Elaine Ash, *Bestseller Metrics*, Editor, Author & Book Marketer

"Music is the throbbing heart of the stories in this collection— the obsession that drives characters up to, and over, the edge. From lonely pop stars to juke joint owners to the least reliable narrator ever, these stories shake, rattle, and roll." —Mysti Berry, writer and Anthony-nominated editor

"If music be the food of murder, read on with this masterful collection of mayhem." —Gray Basnight, author of *Madness of the Q*

"Talent doesn't guarantee success in Nashville. Killer instinct helps...plus a good alibi. 24 unique and varied stories that hit the mark! An absolutely stunning collection of powerful have-to-read-the-next-one stories." —G. Miki Hayden, author of *Dry Bones*

"The music and the passion flows through these terrific crime stories. Music from Bach to rock to bagpipes and more. Stories from the swamp to the dance floor to the juke joint and everywhere in between. Get set for a platinum performance!" — Kaye George, national bestselling author

"Just as the 'Nashville sound' covers the range of human emotion, so do these stories—amusing, thrilling and heartbreaking. Like good country songs, you'll want to revisit them again and again." —R.J. Koreto, author of the Historic Homes series

"Music has a dark side. Yet it binds everything together. Nowhere is that truer than the country music capital of the world. And nowhere is that better illustrated than the stories of *Tales of Music, Murder, and Mayhem*." —Jim Winter, author of the Holland Bay series

"Good ol' Nashville, aka Music City, music capital of the world. Now, with the publication of *Tales of Music, Murder and Mayhem*, we learn that Nashville and its environs have also given birth to some of the most ingenious murders and acts of mayhem that this writer has ever encountered." —Patrick H. Moore, author of *27 Days* and *Rogues & Patriots*

"A brilliant array of tales; all killer, no filler, and with a glorious thread of musicality running throughout." —Tom Mead, author of *Death and the Conjuror* and *The Murder Wheel*

"These stories of cheating hearts, hard times and heartache, all the country music classics, make this a killer anthology." — Elaine Viets, author of *A Scarlet Death*, an Angela Richman, Death Investigator mystery

"*Tales of Music, Murder and Mayhem*, the 2024 Bouchercon anthology, lives up to the promise of its title. The varied stories, all having a tie to Nashville, reflect the good and bad tales that provide the twang of country music." —Debra H. Goldstein, award-winning author

TALES OF MUSIC, MURDER, AND MAYHEM

BOUCHERCON ANTHOLOGIES

EDITED BY HEATHER GRAHAM

TALES OF MUSIC, MURDER, AND MAYHEM

BOUCHERCON ANTHOLOGY 2024

DOWN&OUT
BOOKS

Down & Out Books
3959 Van Dyke Road, Suite 265
Lutz, FL 33558
DownAndOutBooks.com

The characters and events in this book are fictitious. Any similarity to real persons, living or dead, is coincidental and not intended by the author.

Cover design by JT Lindroos

ISBN: 1-64396-379-1
ISBN-13: 978-1-64396-379-2

TABLE OF CONTENTS

FOREWORD
Heather Graham

Welcome to *Tales of Music, Murder and Mayhem*!

All of these stories are inspired by Nashville, a city that is synonymous with music.

From our earliest days—imagine cave drawing and rocks knocking against stone for a musical beat—we, as human beings, have needed to tell stories, in one form or another. Some stories are told through art, a progression from those cave drawings, some are told through the beauty of dance, many come to us through the written word, and many through music!

Because, of course, the arts complement the arts! The written word has given flight to the creations of musicians zillions of times, just as a song has stirred in the heart or soul of writers, instigating some of our most classic written tales. And what is dance without the music behind it, or a touching song without incredible lyrics?

But, of course, Bouchercon *is* "The World Mystery Convention!" So, these tales of murder and mayhem—filled with music and more—are...mysteries!

We give our deepest thanks to the authors you'll read in this anthology, all who believe in the power of reading no matter where we want to go in life, or what we want to do! Our charity this year is one near and dear to all our hearts as writers and readers—the Nashville Public Library Foundation! Many of

1

us "grew up" in libraries and to this day, I love being in the library, exploring books that cover the world and often give special attention to the city in which they're located. We all love books; libraries are about books—and they will always need all the assistance we can give!

We'd also like to thank those who so willingly gave their time and efforts to this collection, starting with our judges: Yasmin Angoe, Michael Bracken, Jonathan Brown, David Dean, John Floyd, and SJ Rozan, Eric and Lance of Down & Out Books for their incredible support and patience, and finally the amazing and talented people who spent countless hours to bring this anthology together—Susan and Kevin Cella, Connie Perry, and Mike "Mystery Mike" Bursaw.

And, as always, to Anthony Boucher, and all who throughout many years have kept Bouchercon going as an amazing place for readers, writers, publishers, editors, and all who have laughed, cried, and been taught and touched by the written word!

THE BIRTH OF THE LONGTOOTH BLUES

Eric Beckstrom

They say a person makes thousands of decisions a day. I don't know. Is flipping your pillow over to get the cool side a decision, or is it just a thing you do? Is having beans and franks instead of hamburgers for dinner a decision, or just the mood you're in?

Killing a person. What's that? Maybe that's a decision. I guess for some people it's a mood. For others, just a thing they do.

Maybe it depends on where you've been and where you're going, or where you are, the timing of when you're there, and why you're there. Maybe it depends on who you are.

For me, the killing was out of necessity.

I used to know who I was, and what kind of person, but I'm having to refigure some of that.

There are, in case you didn't know, 20 Nashvilles in the United States. I had moved from Nashville to Nashville, before going to *the* Nashville after my friend Jed asked for my help. I simply *had* to go to Nashville, Tennessee.

Let me start over. Let me be more honest.

Funny how that sounds like a plea, or a prayer.

That "simply"—I *simply* had to go to Nashville, Tennessee—is, as my late Uncle Jonathan might have said, carrying enough weight to stagger a dray horse. It's covering up my incaution. Covering up death.

That *simply* is a morgue sheet. Four of them, actually.

Under two sheets are my friend Jed and his son, both of whom I got killed.

Under the third is another guy I got killed. A public records employee.

The guy under the fourth sheet…well, if I'm honest, him I murdered. Not manslaughter. Murder.

This story starts out weird and gets weirder, with more coincidences than you'd think could be swept into such a tiny corner of the universe. Somewhere there must be some folks who didn't get their fair share. I was born in a tiny California town called Nashville, named after *the* Nashville, the one in Tennessee. Jed grew up in a tiny Oregon town called Nashville, named after some English guy. That's just the first coincidence. Jung would have interpreted the convergence of these Nashvilles and everything that followed as synchronicity. With everything that's happened, I can't help but think the same.

I loved my little life in Nashville, California, but the closest Black family to ours must have been in Sacramento. I had casual friends at Indian Creek Elementary, some white, some Miwok from Shingle Springs. But my mom and Uncle Jonathan ran the Christmas tree farm that had been in the family for a couple of generations, and it was really the trees that kept me company while they and I grew up together from saplings. Aside from the rare day with a school friend, it was just my mom, her brother, me, and the trees.

And then, one day, the trees and Uncle Jonathan were gone, taken by a wildfire started by a man who was vacationing from Tennessee. He was playing with his Rolex, burning ants alive on the forest floor by reflecting sunlight off the glass.

The trees burned, the insurance company underpaid, and my mom had to sell the family land because it and the business were ash. A trucker who would haul our Christmas trees to box stores and grocery chains in nearby towns got her a line on a job managing the Rattleberry Tree Farm near Nashville.

Meaning, Nashville, Oregon, where I met Jed Longtooth.

Jed and I shared the fourth grade classroom of a charter school. Kids were bussed 25 minutes each way from all over that part of Lincoln county. The first time I stepped onto that bus all I saw were army-green, vinyl-covered seats and the white faces sitting in them. I sat alone, the new kid—the Black kid— and lost my eyes in the Douglas firs on either side of the road. The trees were blurred by rain. They thinned here and there to accommodate the Yaquina River, which is really just a glorified creek.

I felt the side of the seat next to me depress. It exhaled its foam padding breath. I turned and looked into a face the same hue as mine. I was shocked. The Black *kids*, it turned out. He had walked the length of the bus just to sit next to me. He later told me he felt the same way, and of course he did. How long had he been *the* Black kid?

"I'm Jed, what's your name?"

"My name's Pearl because my mom says pearls cover sand and suffering and make them into something pretty and I'm also named after Pearl Bailey who was a singer and an actress and a writer and won the Presidential Metal of Freedom."

Caught off guard, nervous and excited, I rattled all that off and even forgot the punctuation.

"I'm named after my Longago Grandad, Jedidiah. He was a slave, but he escaped."

As we got to know each other, I learned he often put it that way when he claimed to be talking about his ancestors, like a formal title, because he never knew how many "greats" to put in front of a name. It was always his Longago Aunt or his Longago Grandma.

"Hey Pearl, why'd you move here?"

"Our tree farm in California burned," was all I could bear to say.

"Well, I'm glad you didn't get hurt! Hey, lemmee tell you about my Longago Uncle. He used to hunt for gold in California!

He was a real miner forty-niner at Sutter's Mill where the Gold Rush happened."

For a few seconds I couldn't hear the wheels on the pavement, the other kids, or my own breathing. In the distance I heard myself say, "He couldn't have been. He'd a been a slave, too." But in my head I was pondering the coincidence that Sutter's Mill is 30 minutes north of our ashed tree farm in Nashville, California.

"I don't know," said Jed. "Maybe he got away, too. Or maybe he was white. My mom said some of our Longagoes were white."

Each day on the bus ride I revealed more about the old tree farm and he'd tell me about his Longagoes. Sometimes I got tired of his stories, but maybe that's because it made me think about my uncle and how I had no real extended family. My parents divorced when I was two and my dad had gone back East to be near his parents, whom I'd met twice. My mom's parents had both died relatively young, and I didn't know a thing about my Longagoes.

But mostly I liked Jed's stories. I even believed some of them. It was his family lore and history that germinated and became my career as a genealogist. I started looking stuff up in libraries when my mom and I visited Salem or Portland. I even learned how to access public records, which at the time were either microfilm, microfiche, or paper. I'm sure part of me just wanted to prove to Jed that his grandma hadn't worked in Area 51 studying alien corpses, as he claimed. But mostly I wanted to learn about my own great-great-greats.

We went to school together until college but attended different universities. I triple-majored in Folklore & Ethnomusicology, American Studies, and African American and Diaspora Studies. Jed majored in English and became, unsurprisingly, a writer and a very good creative writing teacher. We kept in touch and when email came about in the 90s we kept in even closer touch.

I took a job at a not-for-profit called the African American Heritage Restoration Initiative based in Portland. For years I expected Jed to ask me to research his family tree. Finally, one day he did. He wanted to see if any of the stories he'd told me were true. What I discovered compounded the Nashville synchronicity and turned the whole thing into a genealogical X-File.

Jed's great-great-great grandfather, Jedidiah Longtooth, was born into slavery in 1845. From what I could tell, he escaped around 1860, but nothing online revealed where he'd been enslaved. Along the trail to the Free Territory of Oregon he met Josa. In 1870, at age 25, with the country already un-reconstructing, Jedidiah and Josa Longtooth welcomed Jed's great-great-grandfather, Honor, into the world. Both Jedediah and Great-Great-Great-Grandmother Josa died in 1920 at age 75.

In 1895, at age 25, Honor and Sefi Longtooth welcomed Jed's great-grandfather, Frederick Douglass Longtooth, right around the time Jim Crow moved in. Both Honor and Great-Great-Grandma Sefi died in 1945 at age 75.

In 1920, at age 25, Frederick and Sophie Longtooth welcomed Jed's grandfather, Fortune. Both Frederick and Great-Grandmother Sophie died in 1970 at age 75.

In 1945, at age 25, Fortune and Jo Longtooth welcomed Jed's father, Elijah. That was the same year Fortune returned home from serving with the 332nd Fighter Group—the famed Tuskegee Airmen. Exactly 20 years later, Jo became the first Longtooth woman to vote. Both Fortune and Grandma Jo died in 1995 at age 75.

In 1970, at age 25, Elijah and Ina Longtooth welcomed Jed, named after Great-Great-Great-Grandfather Jedidiah, who had been enslaved just 125 years prior. Jed's parents, Elijah and Ina, both died in 2020 at age 75.

You see it, of course. Each Longtooth couple was the same age and each welcomed a son at the same age. The names of the

Longtooth women? All nicknames for Josephine. Each Longtooth man and woman from Jed's lineage lived to be 75.

If twice is a coincidence and three times is a pattern, what are a half dozen coincidences spread across generations? Synchronicity? Destiny? Something written in the stars?

What happens to the man who chooses to end with fire and glass something that is written in the stars?

That's what I'm doing. Telling you what happens to a man like that.

Jed was delighted when I shared the Longtooth family tree with him, but I wasn't satisfied. I wanted to know more about Jedidiah. Where had he been enslaved? How did he become free?

I'd been to the Portland city archives hundreds of times. I found original documents supporting what I'd read online, and exhausted every source I could think of. It's standard practice for me to check with my archive contacts in case I've missed something, but both my Portland people had recently retired.

Which left me with Pete.

Every genealogist, folklorist, or historian is part detective. My detective instincts kicked in the moment I mentioned the name Longtooth to Pete, the New Guy. Pete was scared.

I acted with more authority than I had, flashed my laminated genealogist credentials and employee IDs, and mentioned the network of attorneys my organization has on retainer.

"Alright, alright. Freedom papers," he said.

I gaped.

Jed had told me his namesake had escaped slavery. It was sacred family lore. But freedom papers meant he had been granted or somehow bought his freedom.

"Jedediah Longtooth had freedom papers?"

"Yes. I came across them when we were digitizing everything."

He paused.

"What aren't you telling me?"

He sighed. "The papers had some lyrics or something on them. I thought they seemed kinda good. I know a guy who knows a guy whose in Bobby Bob Ferrell's band. I sent a picture—just a corner of one page to give a hint. Ferrell was interested. I got fifty bucks, he got the papers, I got screwed. No one knew Bobby Bob Ferrell until a few months after he got his hands on those papers, and now he's the latest filthy rich country star."

"I don't understand. How could Ferrell's songs be on free-dom papers from 150 years ago?"

"There were words on the papers. Lyrics. Bobby Bob changed 'em around, put in new words, took stuff out. But you can tell his hits—his only hits—came from those papers."

I got the address Pete had sent the papers to. It was Ferrell's office suite in Nashville, Tennessee, in a high-rise right on Broadway. The rent must have been astronomical.

In 1995, at age 25, Jed and Posie Longtooth welcomed their son, Jed III—JJ.

Two months after JJ's 25th birthday and the day after my conversation with Pete, Jed and JJ Longtooth were on their way to Rattleberry Tree Farm to join my mom and Posie for lunch when their car was firebombed on Logsden Road a few miles north of Nashville. Chunks of glass and burning plastic landed among the trees. Pieces landed in the Yaquina River. Probably some landed among the tall trunks, through which Jed and I had run 15 years before, chasing each other into the water. Probably some pieces splashed right where we had.

To this day—every day—I hear our footfalls and our teasing voices echo like needles through the forest and the narrow riverbed. Like needles, they blur my vision.

Je-ed, I'm gonna get you! Right behind you!

Pear-al, you're never gonna catch me! I am looong gone!

I didn't wait for the funerals. I left Posie in my mom's hands and took the next flight to Nashville, Tennessee. *The* Nashville, according to everyone.

Having no other leads—listen to me, sounding more and more like a detective—I drove my rented car past the Broadway high-rise with Bobby Bob Ferrell's upper-floor office. Honky-tonk was already stomping its way through every other doorway up and down the street. I had to figure out how to get a peek inside that office. I noticed a reception-slash-security kiosk. People came and went. Occasionally someone was stopped briefly before being waved on. Security monitors were ignored. Custodians entered and exited elevators.

I decided there was no point in waiting. It seemed unlikely Ferrell would be around. How many singers spend their time hanging out in an office? I parked my car in a garage and found an upscale club. In a restroom stall, I changed into my uber-professional suit skirt, blouse, and heels. I'm a plain-looking Black woman, so people don't often give me a second glance. It's rare for me to get a first glance. It's one of my distinguishing features, that I'm indistinguishable. It's a bit sad, but sometimes useful.

You can also get people to miss you by looking like someone who knows where they're going and what they're about, or by blending in the way service staff like custodians blend in with the walls because few people want to see them. I didn't have a custodian's outfit, so I camouflaged myself with confidence and my indistinguishableness. With my head high and nose up, my briefcase held with ease, I breezed passed the security kiosk, heels clicking with self-possession. The security guard looked about to say something, but my breezy passing had already ruffled his bangs and someone else was asking a question.

I'm not used to winging it, and don't rely on luck, but I had no choice. I wasn't really a detective. Just a rather hapless genealogist.

But I did get lucky. Several more times. More stuff swept into this one little corner of the universe, I guess.

I hopped on board the elevator with a custodian, a Black woman, who swiped a keycard and pressed floor 26. She raised her eyebrows at me.

"Oh, thank you. 25, please."

She swiped again and pressed 25.

I tried the knob on 2506, hoping the lack of attention to the security monitors held.

Locked. Well, of course it was. The light on the key swipe above the knob was steady red.

The light on the key swipe on the custodial closet door down the hall, on the other hand, was steady green.

In it, were several hooks. On one hung a janitorial smock. The tail had gotten caught between the back of the door and the jam, preventing it from closing tight enough for the lock to engage. On the breast pocket was a large ketchup stain. It had been half-heartedly dabbed, but was still wet, presumably abandoned until the next day.

Behind the stain, in the pocket, was a keycard.

Several lights came on when I entered Bobby Bob Ferrell's office. A motion detector. Just for the illumination, I guessed, since no alarm sounded. The man just couldn't be bothered to flick a switch. I did, and the office went mostly dark again.

The space was expansive in both size and tastelessness. Everything was glass, stainless steel, vinyl, and the kind of plastic that's expensive but still plastic. I didn't think there was a single piece of wood in the place. On the walls were photos of peach trees, single ones and rows of them. Some pictures were obviously very old, but originals. Daguerreotypes, tintypes, photos printed from film, and others obviously digital. It was an accidental history of photographic technology. All were framed in black metal. Beneath each was a little parchment label sandwiched behind clear plastic. Each label said Peach Haven Plantation in fancy script, and each had a quaint location name and year. With my penlight I read River Bend Way, 1859. Shadiest Acre, 1930. African Breeze Veranda, 2023.

The wall of windows overlooked Broadway and the curva-ceous Cumberland River. The view was a cataclysm of neon, red-lighted cell towers, and echoing light of all kinds. I think it would have melted the trees my mom tended back in the other Nashville. The night wasn't so much lit up as beaten off. Over the square of window glass aligned with Ferrell's desk hung four records framed behind more glass. Two gold, two plati-num.

Usually, desks face away from windows so the person seated there has a commanding view of the room and whoever enters. That wasn't enough for Bobby Bob Ferrell. His desk—a monstrous amalgam of stainless steel and acrylic—faced the windows. Except for the chunk of Nashville obscured by the records, he had a commanding view of the town he figured he'd conquered. It might sound like I was reading too much into things, but you'll see I was right about his sense of himself. You'll also see that I was wrong about two things.

On his desk lay two pieces of paper. One was common, lined note paper. The other was made from rag paper, circa 1861. It was surprisingly white given its age, but rag pulp doesn't brown the way wood pulp does. The words written on it were perfectly clear. They stated that the Clerk of the Davidson County Court certified in Nashville, Tennessee on the 25th day of August 1861 a Deed of Emancipation for the freedom of one negro man named Jedidiah, having taken the name Longtooth, aged about fifteen years, the owner having been fairly compensated by the local abolitionists society.

On the back of the sheet, there they were: the lyrics. The first set, initialed J.L., was comprised of five spirituals, none of which I'd ever encountered. The briefest skim brought tears to my eyes. Jedidiah's spirituals drew from his experiences in bondage and his plans to escape any way he could.

The second set was comprised of blues lyrics signed by Fred-erick Douglass Longtooth, 1935. He had transformed Jedidiah's spirituals into soul-wrenching blues, which, to my ear and knowledge, seemed ahead of their time.

Above the first of Frederick's adaptations was the title, "Woke Up This Morning Blues." Those four words begin countless blues songs. They're usually followed by commas and periods, and in between the commas and periods are laments, lists of things lost or never had, and litigious descriptions of deals made with the devil. But sometimes just those words are enough: Woke up this morning. Period. Frederick Douglass Longtooth said this in a way no one had before and no one has since. All this I could tell because that brief skim hit me so hard.

I looked at the framed records. One of the platinums was titled "Woke Up This Morning Blues." I knew that song. I'd heard it countless times. It was hard to avoid. It was a pop country cross-over "hit" but that's all it was. On the modern paper sitting next to the freedom papers, Bobby Bob Ferrell had begun transforming the fifth and final example of Jedidiah and Frederick's creative life into another piece of Top Ten plastic.

I said I'd been wrong about two things.

First, the office wasn't all metal, glass, and plastic. There was, in fact, one piece of wood. A black, #2 pencil lay next to the papers. It wasn't yellow and the barrel wasn't hexagonal like most. It was black and cylindrical, like the barrel of a gun. I guess Ferrell was supremely confident a pencil wouldn't dare roll away from him.

Secondly, I was wrong about him not being in the office that night. If I'd realized the obvious when I saw the papers on the desk, there'd be one less dead man on my conscience.

In that moment, a wedge of light bathed the room. Bobby Bob Ferrell emerged from a bathroom.

"Who the hell are you?"

"Uh. I'm cleaning. I'm the custodian."

"No. You aren't. I know who cleans my office. It isn't you."

"Well, they're sick tonight, so…"

Lame. I had no Plan B. "Overconfident is unprepared" Uncle Jonathon would tell me when I climbed too high up a tree and couldn't get back down.

"This is Monday. He cleans my office on Fridays."

He. Wow. I wasn't just up too high, I was clinging to the top in a strong gale.

He walked to the desk and looked at the papers. Then he looked at me.

"Ha." He laughed the word. "I got a call from Portland. You're the one who's been poking around. It was you, not Longtooth. You got Longtooth and his kid killed. You got that archive guy killed."

"What..." My God. Another death my fault.

"*You* had Jed killed, and JJ. *You* had them all killed."

I spoke through gritted teeth, but his expression said he saw the guilt of failure on my face.

"Ha!" He barked again.

"What you stole from that family—"

"I stole nothing. They didn't even know the papers existed. I plucked them from obscurity and made those words worth something. I made them hits. Don't you know who I am? I'm the new soul of this town. If anything, I *gave* that family something."

He spat every "I" like a bullet.

Bobby Bob Ferrell. He was the soul of Nashville, Tennessee. Not Hank Sr. Not Patsy, Johnny, or Dolly. By his estimation, certainly not Charley Pride or Robert Johnson. Sure the hell not Linda Martell.

He grabbed me by the throat and drove me the ten feet to the windows. My head smashed the records that hung there, sending glass and gold and platinum-tinted vinyl in every direction. Still throttling me—he was a big man—he dragged me back to the desk, knocking my penlight to the floor beneath it, and threw me to the carpet. I could smell cigars and bourbon in the fibers. His fingers pressed into my throat, into bundles of veins and nerves. Plastic and glass crackled under my back and his knees.

Over his shoulder I caught site of the pencil. It had rolled when he had knocked me against the desk. The eraser end was suspended over the edge. The tip with a freshly-sharpened spike of graphite was visible in dark silhouette through the clear acrylic of the desktop, lit from below by my penlight.

My vision went dark and my ears went deaf. My left hand was pinned beneath me, but the desk was to my right and that arm was free. I aimed my hand for the spot where I thought the pencil must be.

I clutched it, only half feeling the smooth barrel, and, unable to see, on the verge of unconsciousness, plunged it in his direction.

He gurgled. Something wet pattered my face.

My eyes cleared. He was above me on his knees, his body at a 90 degree angle, holding his neck much as he'd been squeezing mine. Three inches of pencil protruded from between the middle and index fingers of his right hand, the pink eraser bobbing in the neon glow from Broadway. The rest of the pencil was buried in the left side of his throat.

He fell over with a dull crunch-thud. A nasty shard of gold-tinted vinyl buried itself in the other side of his neck.

Litigation is still underway, but the record company will have to pay up, and the copyright will go to Posie. She already has a handshake deal with a Black record label and a young blues prodigy who just might be the next B.B. King or Buddy Guy. She won't need to worry about the mortgage or whether she'll have something to leave her twin daughters.

I didn't mention that before, did I? They were born one month after Jed and JJ were murdered.

Because the copyright dispute is technically not settled, I can't share the lyrics written on Jedidiah Longtooth's freedom papers. But I wouldn't if I could. The grief, exaltation, despair, and hope in the original words Jedidiah wrote down from memory, and which Frederick Douglass Longtooth adapted to embody his and Sefi's experiences, are not mine to share. The renditions that made Bobby Bob Ferrell rich and dead are vapid and uninspired. How could they be otherwise? He stole Frederick's lyrics—there's enough in the four hit singles he released to prove that—but he couldn't comprehend them, so he changed them by removing their soul.

Jed had simply asked me to look into the stories he'd been told when he was a kid, and which he'd told me. That was the research problem. Were any of those stories true?

Jed simply asked me. There's that word again. *Simply* comes from the Latin *simplus*, a medicine made from one ingredient, usually a plant. But plants aren't simple. They have roots, branches, lineage, history. Just like family trees.

Jedidiah's freedom papers authenticate the Longtooth lineage and their connection with the lyrics. They will, yes, provide economic freedom through revenue from the songs, which Posie and her and Jed's daughters need. But those papers also reclaim what was stolen from that family going back generations. Not just intellectual property, but spiritual property. They reclaim stolen memories, stolen blood and sorrow, stolen triumph.

My story isn't important here, but I will say this: I'm a better historian and a better genealogist for all of this. Until now, I didn't truly understand to my core the way I do now that family trees aren't just beautiful in their intricacy. They're also beautiful because they are restorative. Among other things, they restore truth.

I also understand now that genealogy can be dangerous. Digging can be deadly. It was deadly for Jed and JJ. Deadly for Bobby Bob Ferrell. For Pete the New Guy. I don't know if I'm a better person or a worse person for all of this. I killed someone. Murdered him. I didn't do it in cold blood, as they say. My blood was boiling. That's what made it murder.

I was arrested for criminal trespass, attempted burglary, and second-degree murder. I'm out on bond. My lawyer, John

Smith, is a competent and very nice white man from the Davidson County public defenders office. Tochi Onyebuchi said white people—all generations of white people since Manifest Destiny, genocide, slavery—are an "aftermath." I've met good white people, kind white people, generous white people; but since this business it's hard for me not to think of every white person I meet as an aftermath, no matter what else they might be. A stone is a stone. Whether it's poised in a slingshot, part of a building's foundation, or set into a piece of jewelry, a stone is a stone. My mom taught me that. I don't know, maybe she was wrong too.

But Mr. Smith has been a blessing. He tells me that while Tennessee law includes the castle doctrine, the strangle marks on my neck—obviously inflicted at great effort over time—and the fact that I had no weapons with me, are points in my favor. The charges have already been reduced to involuntary manslaughter. The prosecution, he hopes (he doesn't say he believes, but that he hopes—a difference that doesn't escape me) will have a hard time proving Bobby Bob Ferrell could have believed he was in "reasonable and real imminent danger" from a 110 pound woman armed with nothing more than a penlight. He hopes the jury sees the same thing. So I guess my future depends on, as they also say, a hope and a prayer.

During my subsequent research into Peach Haven Plantation, I remembered something. I remembered the name of the man who burned our trees.

Jimmy James. The same name that came up when I researched the Ferrell family tree.

Jimmy James Ferrell was Bobby Bob's father. What goes around comes around, and, it would seem, goes around again. Even Jung might shudder.

If the pop country star's daddy burning my family's tree farm to cinders was a poetic injustice, then maybe some kind of synchronicity is balancing the scales. This whole thing is making big headlines because Bobby Bob Ferrell was a big star. Word has gotten out about Frederick's collection of blues, which everyone in Nashville, Tennessee says are bound to become American standards. And when everyone in Nashville, Tennessee talks about these soon-to-be classics, they in the same breath talk about Nashville, Oregon.

They talk about Nashville, Oregon as the birthplace of the Longtooth Blues.

I've saved the cosmic punchline for last:

Nashville, Oregon is where Jedidiah Longtooth settled after buying his freedom papers from the owner of—wait for it— Peach Haven Plantation.

GOOD FOR SALES

Eric Beetner

I wanted to write a song that would break her heart the way she broke mine.

It shouldn't have been a surprise. We'd been together for almost two years, both struggling singer/songwriters. She'd help with my melodies, I'd suggest a chord change now and then for one of her tunes. She had the better voice, the more honest lyrics. I knew all that and I rooted for her. She sang backup for me and added harmonies that would bring tears to your eyes and a flood of memories to overwhelm you. I played guitar on her demos even though she could really outplay me any day of the week.

She hit it big. I didn't.

For a little while we played together, me as the opening act. Then when the crowds got larger and the venues went from bars to clubs to auditoriums on the way to arenas, her management thought it better to book some higher profile opening acts. Me with an acoustic guitar wasn't getting the crowd pumped for her full band anymore.

Still I was happy for her, even if I saw her a lot less.

Then came the awards show in Vegas and all the photos online of her arm in arm with a one-hit-wonder guy ten years younger than her. I called to talk to her about it and she told me she'd been meaning to call me.

That was it. Broke up over the phone, a congratulations party still going in the background of the call. She didn't even duck away into a room to be alone to tell me we were through.

All the best songs come from heartbreak. The most honest and the ones everyone can relate to. Can you imagine writing a lyric like "You can't always get what you want" and knowing that every person on Earth who hears it understands what that feels like?

So I sat down with my guitar and my pain and I wrote the best song I'd ever written. I recorded it on my little 4-track. I added my own harmonies. When I was finished I couldn't even listen back to the whole thing. It was too painful.

I took the tape and drove it over to her new house. The big one with all the glass, the open staircase in the middle, the pool, the guest house, the fully equipped recording studio in the basement. I still knew the gate code so I could drive right in and drop the tape on her welcome mat, even if I didn't feel welcome there anymore.

She was out at some dinner being honored for something or another. I left it there, like a heartbreak landmine waiting for her to come home.

Three days went by and I didn't hear from her so I went back. Her new Maserati was in the driveway so I knew she was home. I hoped she was alone.

She answered the door in a silk kimono, her makeup streaky and smudged from wherever she'd been the night before.

"Did you listen to it?" I asked her.

She wasn't heartbroken. She was angry.

"Yeah, I listened to it, Tyler. And it was shit. That supposed to be about me?" She'd adopted a new fake country accent to go with how they were marketing her sound to radio. "It's trite and obvious and shallow, like all your shitty songs."

"I think it's honest."

"Because it makes me look like a bitch?"

"Because I wrote it from a place of truth."

She scoffed at me and it stung like a hornet. "People don't want truth, Tyler. They want to sing along. They don't want to be depressed and think about some poor jerk who didn't get the girl. This is why you've never written a hit."

"I think this one is a hit."

"You're wrong. And what would you know about it anyway? You still live in that one bedroom apartment above a hardware store?"

"You mean our place?"

"Fuck that." She twirled and waved her hand around the open expanse of her new modern masterpiece mansion. "This is my place. I never belonged there, and that's why I worked my ass off to get out. You belong in a place like that, with the roaches and the leaky shower head. And you'll never get out. So fuck you and your shitty song, Tyler. Leave me alone or I'll get a goddamn restraining order."

She slammed the double wide door in my face, keeping the tape of my song inside.

"Can I have my tape back?" I shouted through the glass wall. I could see her flip me the middle finger as she pounded up the steps to her bedroom suite. A place I'd only seen pictures of.

I really did think it was a hit. And I knew there was no way to replicate the hurt and the vulnerability in that original recording I'd done. All the studio tricks in the world can't recreate the raw nerve hurt I felt. I needed that tape back.

There was a decent chance she'd change the gate code after our altercation, so I knew I had to work fast. I waited until dark that night, left my car on the street outside the gate and dialed in the five-digit code that swung the gates open.

I didn't have high expectations. I knew there were cameras all over the property. I had no idea where the tape was in the house and there was a more than 50% chance she'd thrown it away or burned it. But I had to know.

I went around back to the pool. I cut myself on my arms and face wedging through some dense hedges surrounding the back yard. When I got to the stone terrace surrounding the pool I was in luck. The back wall of the house was all glass doors that folded away leaving the house open to the pool deck. I could walk right inside. She hadn't been famous long enough to learn to be worried about stalkers or over-zealous fans. I wasn't sure which category I fit into.

Lights were on so I tried to stay in the shadows and the corners, out of sight from the security cameras if I could. Then I heard it. My song. The minor chords, the double-tracked harmonies, my words of pain and heartache all playing at a turned-up-to-eleven volume from the upstairs.

I followed the sound, knowing I didn't have to try to be quiet. I crept slowly and the song ran out before I reached the stairs, open marble slabs that seemed to hover in the air. I waited. After a moment just long enough to rewind the tape, the song started over again.

I moved up the stairs. I found her bedroom, the source of the music. I stuck my back to the wall and looked through the open door. She was sitting on her bed weeping, holding a pillow to her chest and rocking back and forth slightly. I could see her lips moving to the words, but she didn't sing along. She let my voice cut her to pieces and she was crying over it, exactly the way I had wanted her to.

She did miss me. She did feel the same pain I felt. The song was a hit, for an audience of one.

I nearly broke out in tears myself. It suddenly seemed less important to get the tape away from her. Maybe she would add her voice to it and we could release it together, use her fame to make it a smash. What a story—the song that brought old lovers back together and now they're both superstars.

The song came to an end and the last chord rang out. I could finally hear her sobs clearly over the music and she was a wreck. She put her hand in a box of tissues by her side, but it was empty. She flung the pillow aside (a stand in for wanting to embrace me?) and stood. She headed for the door, off to get more tissues. I was trapped.

I backpedaled and ducked around a corner and backed into the doorway to a bathroom.

Her crying and her bare feet slapping the Italian marble floors came closer and I pushed back into the door behind me trying to look invisible. She could go right down the open staircase to the first floor, or she could turn left into the bathroom where I stood. Too late I realized if she was going for more tissues, a bathroom would be a likely place to turn.

She spun, the kimono flapping open as she turned. Her face was red and swollen from her histrionic crying, but she looked beautiful.

When she saw me she screamed.

I put my hands out, trying to assure her I was no threat.

"It's me. Just me. I came for the tape, but I heard you."

She reversed away from me, her eyes half closed from swelling. Her face was wet with tears and snot. I couldn't tell if she knew it was me or not. I stepped forward, following her as she backpedaled.

"It's okay. I don't need the tape anymore."

Her foot reached the top step, but she didn't stop reversing. I watched her tip backward as the floor gave way to the staircase. The kimono waved like the wings of a baby bird still unsure how to fly, and she fell.

The sounds as she tumbled were a mixture of breaking bones, cracking stair tiles and her tiny grunts with each impact of her body. Even her cries of pain sounded musical. Like the final drum roll of the last encore of her act, her body hit the marble floor at the bottom of the stairs and once again the house fell silent. No applause. No cheering fans. Just me with my arms out as if I might still catch her from tipping backward.

I felt blood pound in my ears and I waited for it to slow before I moved. My eyes were locked on her, hoping for the tiniest of movements, but I saw none. I slowly took the stairs down toward her. Drops of blood had smeared as she tumbled and the steps were streaked in an uneven line marking her fall.

I reached bottom and stood over her. I felt a tear roll down my nose and saw it drop and mix with the blood framing her body.

Lyrics and melody filled my head. My pain mutated into a song. It's just the way my brain works. I couldn't help it. So many songs arrive like that, uninvited but forcing their way in. Whether Paul McCartney dreaming up *Yesterday* fully formed in his sleep or *Seven Nation Army* being written by The White Stripes during a soundcheck, some of the greatest songs ever have come in a flash.

To process my own pain, I had to get it down.

I ran to the basement and into her recording studio. I grabbed a guitar off the wall, a dark Guild dreadnaught acoustic, and started playing. Within five minutes I had the chords down and the basic verse melody. Another five and I hit on a chorus that nearly brought me to tears. It would have, too, if I hadn't been so frantic not to let anything stop me getting this song out. Maybe there was some denial about what I had witnessed. My mind couldn't replay the vision of her falling away from me if I kept repeating the melody and rehearsing the chords.

Still humming, I jumped up and pressed record on the system, positioned myself in front of a single microphone, and poured my heart out into a digital file. One take. All it took.

I leaned the guitar against the chair and went to the beginning of the track. I turned the volume up high and pressed play. The sound of my own heart breaking filled the room. Words I didn't even remember saying were sung back to me in a voice I recognized but was filled with a hurt that could never be replicated. It was raw, unfiltered, like watching an open heart surgery.

I played it through again looking for any flaws but when my

voice cracked it made it even better. When I dragged my hands across the strings it made a baleful noise that fit the pain in the lyrics. Every imperfection fit perfectly.

The last note rang out and very faintly you could hear me crying even as I leaned away from the mic.

"That's a hit."

At first I thought it was my own voice. I didn't remember saying it at the end of the take, but I sure as hell felt it was true.

But the voice wasn't mine.

I spun in the studio chair and faced Mac Winstead—manager to the biggest names in music, including her.

"But first, you wanna tell me what happened here?"

Mac and I had met a few times during her rise to fame. He'd listened to my demo, but hadn't signed me up.

"She fell."

He studied me close, looking for the lie. "Fell," he confirmed.

I nodded. I knew what he thought, but I knew I was telling the truth.

"What are you doing here?" he asked.

"I came to get a tape."

He nodded toward the monitor on the studio desk. "That one?"

"No. A real tape. It's upstairs. She was listening to it."

He took that in, still studying me. I wondered if he had called the police yet. How hard it would be to convince them I hadn't killed her.

"Is it as good as this one?" Again he nodded to the song he'd just heard on the monitor. The simple two tracks filling the screen so often dominated by dozens of color-coded tracks of overdubs and fourth-fifth-sixth takes.

"Almost." I was honest to the end.

"Let's go listen," he said.

* * *

We had to step around her body and I was crying again by the time we got upstairs. He listened to the tape of the first song I'd sent her.

"You're right. Almost as good, but not quite."

"Are the police on their way?" I asked.

"No."

He drummed his fingers on his knee, thinking.

"Here's what we'll do…" He stood. He stared into the middle distance as he paced the room, occasionally looking down at the shag carpet around her bed. "She goes missing. No one knows where she is. The whole world waits. Then we drop your song. A plea for her return. You give voice to all the anxiety and the pain for people the world over. Then she's found—dead. That's when we drop the second song. A lament for what could have been. The way we all feel about her breaking our hearts by leaving us too soon. A one-two punch that'll be great for sales."

He looked up at me to see my reaction.

"Of course her catalog will go through the roof, too," he added.

The selfish, money-grubbing prick. And god damn him, he was right.

With surprising ease we moved her body into the back of his Range Rover, cleaned up the floor and soaked the tiles in bleach. We copied the file and Mac sent it to himself and then we digitized my tape and he sent that too.

Our contract was a handshake. I had to go with his plan because he could easily put me behind bars. Who would ever believe her former lover just happened to be here when she accidentally tripped and fell after listening to a song about how much she hurt me?

In the hour it had been since she died, even I started to doubt the story.

Plus, he was going to make me rich and famous. People would know my songs and they would feel genuine emotions when they sang along. Heartbroken saps would hold boom boxes over their heads and blast my song to their exes trying to win them back, or just let them know how much hurt they'd caused.

Three weeks later the media frenzy was at a high pitch. Everyone had their theories about where she'd gone. The new, younger, boyfriend had been questioned. He'd been eviscerated on social media for it all being his fault somehow. His career cratered overnight.

I signed contracts, made plans. Then Mac set my songs loose. The response was instant. Six million Spotify plays in forty-eight hours.

I got invitations to play all the late night talk shows. I got invited to the main stage at Bonnaroo. I had to find a band, rehearse the rest of the songs for a full set list, although people probably would have been fine if the only songs I played were the two I wrote about her. The before and after songs.

Mac set it up so I played both songs solo at a vigil that was being held in Central Park for her. Over ten thousand people were there and it seemed like at least that many cell phone videos of the performance flooded every platform within a half hour of me leaving the stage. It hadn't gotten any easier to sing those songs, but every new download, each stream, each invite with a higher payday behind it did blunt the pain somewhat.

I hadn't had time to move out of my old apartment. Mac hadn't cut me my first big check yet anyway. He'd given me an advance of a few thousand bucks, but it took time for the money to come through for all this stuff and he had to take his twenty percent off the top.

When the knock on the door came, I figured it was Mac maybe with one of those oversized novelty checks like a sweepstakes or something.

It was the police.

They'd found her body. She was in a shallow grave wrapped in one of my flannel shirts. She had pages from one of my notebooks of lyrics in her hands. They'd found my fingerprints on a guitar in her home.

Mac came to see me in jail. I'd pled my case, but I knew it was pointless. All I was doing now was awaiting sentencing.

"Sorry, kid," he said.

"You think I did it. That first night. You still think I killed her in the first place."

"Didn't you?"

I was done arguing it. Maybe I had. If I hadn't been there, she wouldn't have fallen. If I hadn't sent her that tape. If I hadn't tried to hurt her like she hurt me. Yeah, maybe it was my fault.

I looked at him with a mixture of admiration and disgust. "You had to get your songs though, huh?"

"You signed the agreement. A hundred percent of publishing over to me in the event of a breach of the morality clause. Murder counts as a breech, by the way."

I was beaten. I had nothing left in me.

"Missing girl?" he said. "Good for sales. Heartbroken ex? Good for sales. Dead girl? Great for sales. Jilted lover as killer? Amazing for sales, it turns out."

"I guess I'm a one hit wonder, then."

"Hey, most people never ever get one."

"What about her?" I asked.

Mac shrugged. "She had maybe one or two left in her. Then the flavor of the month changes and the fans move on. That would have killed her, so maybe you did her a favor. She would have slid into a bottle, ended up playing state fairs, gotten fat, married some backup dancer and then divorced six weeks later. Nah, she would have hated that. This way, she's immortal."

"So I killed her so she could live forever."

Mac smiled at me. "Hey, good lyric. I might give that to one of my new acts."

He stood, didn't shake my hand, and walked out.

In my head, I took that lyric and wrote it into a melody ten times better than whatever he would do with it. I'd be the only one to ever hear it, though. A guy writing songs from behind bars? Not very good for sales.

DEAL WITH THE DEVIL

Valerie (V.M.) Burns

The limo pulled up to the curb. From the back seat, I looked through its tinted glass at the fans and reporters lining the street.

"Damn! David promised this wouldn't be a media circus. He swore he'd keep the lid on this until after your recording was over." J.T. 'Moses' Carlton, my manager, reached over and squeezed my hand.

"Are you surprised he lied?" I asked.

"Nah. David Thomas would rat out his grandmother if he thought it would be good press for him or his recording empire," Moses said.

"You okay, Miss PatZi?" Seth lowered the glass that separated the back of the limo from the front.

"I'm fine," I lied. My throat was dry and my voice sounded like gravel to my own ears. My hands shook and my stomach felt like I'd swallowed a brick.

"Just say the word and I'll turn this car around and have you home so fast it'll make your head spin," Seth said.

"Thanks, but we'd just have to turn around and come back again later. If not today, then tomorrow or next week. Let's just get this over with." I forced my lips to curl upward into something resembling a smile.

Moses hopped out of the car. He raced around and yanked

my door open. He positioned his body in the gap between the pavement and the crowds and presented a human wall that blocked anyone from getting too close. He extended a hand and helped me out.

"That's her. That's PatZi Lynne," a woman with a large pink cowboy hat screamed with excitement.

A roar erupted from the crowd and lights flashed as the media snapped pictures at the speed of a flying locomotive.

I slid my sunglasses on, took Moses's hand, and climbed out of the limo.

The crowd jostled to get closer, but this wasn't Moses's first rodeo. He was a big man with broad shoulders. In college, those shoulders parted defensive linemen like Moses parting the Red Sea, which led to his nickname. If it hadn't been for a knee injury, he would have been the Tennessee Titan's first-round draft pick the year he graduated from college. Instead, those shoulders parted reporters and shielded me from any unwanted attention for the short walk inside the studio doors.

Inside, the crowd frenzy was barely audible.

A thin woman I recognized as a former beauty pageant contestant, and whom I knew was David's assistant waited. She flashed a big smile and extended her hand. "Miss PatZi, I'm so sorry about that. I have no idea how the media found out you'd be here, today."

"You must have a leak in your organization somewhere." I removed my glasses and gave her a look that said I knew exactly how the media found out.

"Yes, well. We'll have to look into that." She blushed. She was too young to have learned to lie well, but David Thomas would change that. "I'm LisaJo."

I shook her hand. No need to introduce myself. She knew who I was. Everyone knew who I was.

LisaJo escorted us to the elevator.

She pushed the button that would take us to the recording studio on the top floor of the building.

I took several deep breaths to steady my nerves. It had been two years since I'd been in a recording studio and my heart raced as memories flooded my mind.

Before the doors opened, LisaJo pulled out her cell phone and quickly sent a text. As the elevator came to the top floor, she stepped closer to the wall.

"Flee Flicker." I glanced at Moses.

I slid my sunglasses back on and turned and faced the back of the elevator. Moses stepped in front of me. The elevator doors opened and there was a flash as a photographer snapped several pictures.

Moses grabbed the camera, shoved the photographer to the side, and escorted me out of the elevator and toward the recording studio.

The photographer yelled about freedom of the press and threats of a lawsuit for taking his camera.

Moses opened the door to the studio and made sure there were no other members of the press present. When he was satisfied, he dragged the screaming photographer back into the elevator with LisaJo. Then, he removed the camera's SD Card.

"Hey, that's mine," The photographer yelled.

Moses took out his wallet, pulled out two hundred dollars, and tossed them at the photographer. He glanced at Lisa Jo. "Looks like you also have a security breach."

The color that had spread up her neck and cheeks deepened to a darker red, but she said nothing.

Moses pushed the button for the first floor sending LisaJo and the photographer back down to the ground floor.

I walked into the Control Room. It was a small room that always reminded me of the control tower for NASA. However, instead of a massive screen displaying a rocket about to be launched into space, there was a window that looked into the recording booth.

Rudy Peterson removed his headset. "PatZi Lynne." He held out both hands and looked me over. "You're looking finer than a frog's hair split four ways." He kissed my cheek.

"Rudy, you old liar, but I love you anyway." I hugged him tightly.

Rudy Peterson was a legend. He'd recorded some of the biggest names in country music. I knew David had shoved Rudy aside for younger engineers who weren't nearly as talented. David wanted engineers who were into using technology for voice enhancement. Rudy was a music purist as well as a friend. But friend or not, his talent was the main reason I demanded David use him for this recording. My other reason was that I knew it would annoy David Thomas to have him.

"It's *almost* like old home week," Rudy said.

"Almost," I whispered.

Rudy squeezed my arm. We both knew things would never be the same. Not now. Not without Bobby Lee.

The door opened. David Thomas plastered on a fake smile and waltzed over. "LisaJo told me what happened. I'm so sorry about that photographer and the crowds outside. I have no idea how the word slipped out that you'd be here today. Obviously, we have a leak, but I'll plug it. No worries. I'll take care of everything."

"I'll bet you will," Rudy mumbled.

"Look David, let's drop the games. You demanded that I come and finish my contract. I'm here. Let's just get this recording over so I can go home and we can go back to ignoring each other."

David glared at me for a few moments, shocked at my honesty. Then he laughed. "PatZi Lynn if I didn't know you better, I'd think you don't like me." He came close, too close. For a split second, I thought he was going to kiss me. Instead, he leaned over to my ear and whispered. "We both know that isn't true, don't we? In fact, we both know exactly why you're here."

His breath was warm against my neck and I could feel goosebumps rising on my arms. I shivered.

David leaned back with a smug expression on his face.

My hand itched to smack that smirk off. Instead, I balled my hand into a fist. *Not now.*

"Complete your recording. I'm going to my office. I've got work to do. When you're done, swing by and we'll finish our business." He turned and walked out.

"I would call him a snake in the grass, but I hate to insult snakes." Rudy shook his head and helped break the spell that David had cast.

"Whatever you do, don't ever make a deal with the devil."

Rudy tilted his head to the side. "Is that what happened?"

I nodded.

Rudy gave me a sympathetic look and tried to lighten the mood. "David Thomas is an evil man, but we have work to do. Let's forget about him and make some music."

I nodded.

"Good. Speaking of dealing with the Devil, why don't we start with that." Rudy grinned and pushed a button. The melodic notes of 'Deal with the Devil' floated through the room. It was one of my biggest hits. My first song to hit the top ten on the music boards and my first award, the Golden Guitar. '*Deal with the Devil*' had been the start of my career and stardom. That song garnered awards for Best Female Vocalist, Best Songwriter, Best Song, and Best Musical Arrangement.

I'd won hundreds of awards since then, but that Golden Guitar had been my favorite because I'd done it without the help of a big record company or a big-name producer. I wrote that song myself. It was from the heart and was just me singing and Bobbie Lee strumming along on his guitar. It had been simple. Raw. Real. That's what the critics said and what my fans loved. It was a song about a teenage girl in love with an older man. She didn't care what anyone thought. She just wanted to be with her man. That was me and Bobbie Lee.

I hadn't sung that song in years, and it showed. I hadn't sung much of anything in years, not professionally anyway. Not since Bobbie Lee died and I was out of shape. Like an athlete who hadn't exercised in two years, my voice had gone flat. My vocal cords had atrophied.

Rudy didn't say anything. He was too much of a gentleman to say anything, but he didn't need to. I had ears.

"This was a mistake. I shouldn't have come." I removed my headset and paced in front of the microphone.

"Nonsense. You just need to get your pipes warmed up. A runner doesn't just get off the sofa, put on their shoes, and run a marathon. They gotta stretch their muscles. Loosen up." Rudy demonstrated what he meant by squatting on one leg and stretching the other behind him. He bounced up and down in that position. After a few moments, he switched and stretched the other leg. "That's all you need. You gotta stretch those cords. Trust me."

I trusted Rudy, but when something was dead, there was no reviving it. Still, I went through the routine. We did vocal exercises. It helped somewhat. When I sang again, my voice didn't crack as much, but my range wasn't even close to where it had once been.

Rudy and I worked long and hard. We worked out ways to hide the flaws. In parts where I had hit high notes before, we took the opposite approach and went low. I riffed, slid up and down notes like a five-year-old on a slide, and when all else failed, I hummed. When we were done, I was hot, sweaty, and exhausted. If anyone ever said that singing wasn't an aerobic activity, then they've never sung for hours on end stopping only for bathroom breaks or hot tea with lemon.

It was almost midnight by the time we finished the last re-cording. Rudy had asked several times throughout the long day if I wanted to rest and come back tomorrow, but I preferred to push through. David Thomas had me over a barrel. That was the only reason I was here now. Once I did what he wanted we were done. When I completed my side of the bargain and I walked out of here, I had no intention of ever stepping foot back into this studio again.

"Whew!" Rudy wiped the sweat off his brow. He was only half-joking. We had both worked hard to get these songs recorded.

My job was done. I'd completed the vocals. Rudy still had work to do, but he didn't need me for that. He could come back tomorrow and complete his part.

Rudy stifled a yawn. "Let's get out of here."

"I need to talk to David. I'll meet you at the elevator in five minutes."

Rudy nodded and walked out.

I gave the recording studio one last glance. This was a final farewell. I grabbed all of my belongings and walked out.

The hallway was empty. Most of the rooms were offices. Dark and deserted. At the end of the hall, a light flowed under one door. It was the largest office on the floor. The largest in the building. The name on the plaque next to the door declared it to belong to David Thomas, Executive Producer.

I didn't bother to knock. He was expecting me. I twisted the knob, opened the door, and walked in.

David Thomas's office was spacious. It was a corner office with large windows that looked out over the Nashville skyline and the Cumberland River. The décor was modern, sleek, and shiny, and fitted David Thomas's personality perfectly. He too was sleek and shiny. Black leather furniture, a glass and metal desk, and contemporary artwork with various colored splotches that might have been faces decorated the room.

David saw me and leaned back in his executive chair. His grin stretched across his face and reminded me of The Joker from the Batman movies. The smile which should have been friendly with the lips curled up, wasn't. Instead, it was twisted into something sinister. "Finished?"

"I finished my part of the deal. I completed the recordings. Fulfilled my contract. Rudy will need to clean up a few things, but I'm finished." I reached into my pocket and pulled out an envelope and placed it on the desk in front of him.

He glanced at it. "What's that?"

"I want that recording."

David picked up the envelope. "You brought your own enve-lope, too. That was considerate." He turned it over. "You even addressed it." David shook his head and then looked at me long and hard without moving. "What if I changed my mind? I might not want to hand it over. Not yet anyway. I just might need it...for security."

I expected him to try to weasel out of his end of the bargain and I was prepared. "That would be unfortunate." I held up the file with the recordings we'd spent the entire day working on. I'd slipped it into my pocket when Rudy wasn't looking. As far as I was concerned. It was my voice. My songs. It belonged to me. I slipped it into my pocket and waited.

David chuckled. After several moments, he stood up and walked over to the picture that was behind his desk. He swung the picture back to reveal a safe. He unlocked the safe, opened the door, reached inside, and took out a disk with a recording.

I didn't need to listen to the recording to know what it con-tained. It was a recording of me committing murder. Two years ago, when I'd found Bobbie Lee with another woman, I snapped. I screamed, cried, and threw an epic tantrum. Then, I'd driven away and sulked. Later, I came back to the studio. I'd had time to think. I loved Bobbie Lee. I was prepared to forgive and forget, but Bobbie Lee surprised me. He didn't want to be forgiven and didn't care if I forgot or not. All he wanted was his freedom. He was dumping me and going away with his new ingenue. Carla was even younger than I'd been when Bobbie Lee discovered me. I begged him not to leave, but he laughed. Frustrated, I pulled out a gun. Bobbie Lee hadn't believed I'd shoot him, so he'd laughed again. That laughter was the last sound he made as I pulled the trigger.

The police declared Bobbie Lee's death an accident. He'd surprised a burglar.

Making it appear that the studio had been burglarized was

easy. Several nearby buildings had been burglarized over the past few weeks and equipment stolen. David Thomas had been too cheap to pay for security guards. He installed dummy cameras on the outside of the building to fool criminals into believing the building was under surveillance, but they were merely window-dressing. I grabbed a few laptops and some sound equipment and shoved them into the trunk of my car. Later, I dumped them and the gun in the river.

What I hadn't counted on was that recording. Bobbie Lee had been in the middle of a recording when I arrived and hadn't bothered to turn it off. And I hadn't checked.

"Fortunate thing, my checking that recording before I called the police after I discovered Bobbie Lee's body." David grinned. "If I hadn't, you might have gotten away scot-free with murder."

"Why didn't you turn it over to the police?" I asked.

"Because you were my goldmine. My golden ticket to the top of the record charts. Bobbie Lee was just an old, washed-up musician with a gift for spotting talent." He shook his head. "Not you. You were the real deal."

"No. You're wrong."

"Still defending him?" He sat back down at his desk. "Your voice was amazing, but you had an even greater talent for lyrics. You're a gifted poet. You could be right up there with Loretta Lynn and Dolly Parton. My God, can't you see that?"

"You're wrong. I'm just trouble. I've always been nothing but trouble. Without Bobbie Lee, I was nothing. He brought out the best in me."

"Pshaw." David snorted. "You'll see. When your new music is released, the public will fall all over you again. I'm going to promote this new release to the max. I've mortgaged everything I own. I'm throwing the whole lot behind this project. Every dime I have is going into making this successful. I believe in you. I believe you can be on top of the record charts, just like you were before. Winning awards. You were country music royalty, and you will be again."

"You're wrong. Bobbie Lee was my spark. My conscience. Without him..." I shook my head.

"Without him, nothing. I wasn't sure if I should give you this or not, but I'm going to take a chance." He went to the desk and put the disk into the envelope I'd left there. "You'll see." He licked the envelope and sealed it. He scrunched his nose at the taste of the glue, but his sour expression passed quickly. Then he handed it to me. "Once this hits, you'll see that I was right."

I glanced at the envelope that he extended toward me. "Just drop it in your outgoing mail."

David walked over to the door and slipped it through the slot that sent the envelope down to the mailroom. Then, he walked back to his desk and sat down. He extended his hand for the recording.

I dropped the disk into his hand.

He grinned, but then his face twisted. He lurched forward and then backward. He clutched his stomach and doubled over. His face contorted. He slid from his chair to the ground.

I stood over him and watched.

He convulsed and sweat broke out on his forehead. His eyes darted around the room and then they found mine. He scratched at the collar of his shirt. "What...did...you..."

"Poison."

Fear flashed across his face. "How?"

"Oh, I put it on the envelope. It mixed in well with the glue." I glanced down at him. "I was worried that you might not lick the envelope, but you were anxious to prove yourself right and went ahead and did it. Thanks. You saved me a lot of worry."

He tried to crawl to the phone but I knew he wouldn't make it. His strength gave out and he collapsed. "Why?"

"I told you that Bobbie Lee brought out the best in me. Without him, the good part was gone." I shrugged. "Evil was all that was left. Didn't you know how Bobbie Lee and I met?" I waited, but the light was going out in David's eyes. He didn't have long. "I was in juvie for murdering my boyfriend. I was a minor—barely thirteen. Bobbie Lee heard me singing and convinced the judge to give me a chance for a future. Community service. Parole. And, voila!"

David groaned.

I squatted down and removed the recording from his hand. I leaned closer to his ear as he'd done to me earlier and whispered. "Didn't anyone ever tell you not to try to make a deal with the Devil?"

David convulsed one last time and then lay still on the floor.

I stood up, stepped over his body, and walked out.

LYRE

Emily Carpenter

When October comes, I know I've got to keep a close eye on Pawpaw.

Up here in North Georgia, October is going-out weather. The air gets that snap, and leaves kick up in little ground tornados, but the mountains have trapped enough leftover summer heat to cut the cold nights. It's just cool enough to get your blood stirred up and warm enough to get you out the door to do something about it.

On the top of our mountain, there are three identical Airbnb houses that look like chalets. They were built by a Korean guy and his wife who bought the land from the Millhorns about six years ago. Every year since then, starting in October, cars drive up our gravel road, rutted from the summer rains. The people are going up there to take in the view of our mountain and our foliage and to party for the weekend with bonfires and in hot tubs. Friday and Saturday nights, those of us who live halfway up the mountain—me and Pawpaw, the Magills, and a couple other families—can hear their music and screeches of glee. All of it drifts down on us, along with the oak and sycamore leaves. The good thing is, I don't think Pawpaw's ever tried going up there. When he goes out, it's never up the mountain. It's always down.

Eleven years ago, Mama dropped me, age seven, here at Pawpaw's falling-down, old cabin and took off for Nashville for her singing career. Pawpaw's done plenty of going out in the years since, I just wasn't necessarily aware of it. I was young and didn't know shit about much. But when I turned twelve and the deacons at our church cut Pawpaw loose for getting after those college girls who were volunteering at Vacation Bible School, that's when Pawpaw started going out. And staying out, too, usually well into the next day.

Back then I spent lots of afternoons and nights over at Mandy Millhorn's trailer across the road. Nobody over there ever asked me where Pawpaw was, but I'd always get home before he did. When Pawpaw got back, he'd be all dreamy and soft. Fix me biscuits with jelly, grits and eggs and thick bacon. He'd run a hand over my hair as I ate. He never asked me what I'd done while he was gone or about school or my homework, but I took care of myself just fine so I didn't care.

The next year, though, that woman went missing from the Circle K. It was on the news, and everybody said that the GBI was going around, flashing their badges, and asking questions. I didn't think nothing about it. What did that have to do with us? Not long after that, one early morning, when I was waiting for Mandy so we could walk down the mountain together and catch the school bus, I got the surprise of my life.

Instead of Mandy, her grandfather, Magill Millhorn, came out of the trailer and started walking straight in my direction. I'd been in Mandy's house lots of times, but Magill Millhorn had never spoken directly to me. I don't think he'd ever even looked at me. Now, as his approaching form—low-slung Carhartt jeans over a big belly, suspenders over a crisp shirt—grew larger and more distinct with every second, I started to shake.

He stopped in front of me and jutted his chin in a wordless greeting, putting a huge, work-rough paw on my shoulder. It felt like the blade of a sword.

"Birdy," he said in his deep, rumbling voice. "I got a favor."

My mind was blank, nothing but pure terror as I stared up at him. His small black eyes were unknowable, set beneath bushy eyebrows and above an abundant gray beard. I was really shaking now, clenching my legs together so I wouldn't wet myself. The Millhorns own this mountain. One of the cousins was sheriff, another was sheriff of the next county over. When Magill Millhorn said *a favor,* what he really meant was *an order.* Even at thirteen I knew that.

"I'm gonna need you to keep an eye on your Pawpaw for me," Magill said, "now that your mama is gone off. Whenever he gets itchy-like, you keep him inside. In the house. You hear?"

I nodded.

"You gotta figure out a way to make him mind you and stay in the house," Magill went on, "or I'm gonna have to."

I quaked in silence.

"What d'you say, Birdy?"

"Yessir," is what I said, trembling under the weight of his massive, meaty hand, still resting on my shoulder. He would keep his word, I knew it. Magill made everybody around here mind him. So I better make Pawpaw mind me.

Magill glowered down at me, noticing my white face, I guess, or maybe the shaking. "You afraid of him, Bird? He ever come after you?"

"No, sir."

It was the truth. Pawpaw was a quiet man and generally kind to me. He kept me fed and clothed and warm. He was a grouch, and he did like to fuss about women who wore tight pants and too much eye shadow or colored and cut their hair. But I didn't do any of those things, so why would he ever get mad at me?

Magill chewed this over. I guess he could tell I didn't know what he was talking about. He eyed me. "Thing is, Bird, he's been busy down the way."

"Oh." I nodded like I understood, like I knew what *busy down the way* meant.

"I didn't mind the church keeping him on the payroll. He's done earned it after all these years. I also don't mind him cleaning up the streets either, but I can't let him be out there disruptin' the flow of my business. You understand?"

I did not.

Magill sighed. "You just figure out a way to keep him home nights, you hear, sweetie?"

He thumped me on the back. Him calling me *sweetie* made me feel safe and scared at the same time, and I knew it meant bad news. Very bad. Even just Magill Millhorn talking to you meant bad news. And anybody getting in the way of Magill Millhorn's business was in deep trouble.

"Yessir," I said in my most obedient voice, which I didn't have to fake one bit.

He gave me a push down the road, toward the base of the mountain, and I went on without Mandy.

All day at school, throughout every class, my mind raced as I tried to think of a way to do what Magill wanted. And then, during fourth period social studies, I thought of one of Pawpaw's favorite sermons. He used to preach it all the time. It was from the book of First Samuel, Chapter sixteen. In it, God sent the evil spirit to plague King Saul, and the king called for the young shepherd boy David to come play the harp to soothe the demon. Pawpaw always called the harp a lyre, and he said it looked more like a guitar than anything else and sounded like one too. Right there in Mr. Benson's class while he talked on and on about the Louisiana Purchase, I could hear Pawpaw, hollering in his preacher voice.

So Saul was refreshed and was well and the evil spirit departed from him.

When I came home, I climbed up the narrow steps to the attic and found the old guitar in the attic, an 1890 Martin that belonged to my great-great granny. The wood needed a good polish, but it had all its strings and sounded pretty damn good to me. I stayed up till three in the morning teaching myself how to pick out *Trust and Obey*.

Later, when I was over at Mandy's, I begged her to tell me

what her grandpa had been talking about. *Busy down the way.* Mandy said my Pawpaw liked preaching to girls who did blow jobs and other stuff for money at the Circle K, the Marathon, and the EZ Stop. And he mighta beat up a few, too, Mandy said. But it was when he started going after Magill's girls—that was when he'd put one foot over the line.

After she told me this, I couldn't get out of the Millhorn's trailer fast enough. I ran across the road and almost got clipped by a white Mercedes sedan that was winding its way up to the Airbnb rentals. When I burst into our house, I found Pawpaw settled in his recliner, watching the Braves. I asked him then and there to tell me the truth. Had he ever hurt a woman?

He said he would never, that it was all lies. Lies spread around town by the deacons at church. Lies Magill told because he had lost control of his junkie employees.

I asked him where Mama had gone after she dropped me off with him. Was it really Nashville? Pawpaw said it was, at least at first. But he didn't know if she had stayed there or moved on. *She mighta gone out to California,* he said. *I don't know. You see how piss-poor she is at keeping in touch. How are we supposed to know where she is? Now eat your supper. It's getting cold.*

I was surprised by the mean tone in his voice.

The October wind flings sycamore leaves at the darkening windows of the house. I can hear Pawpaw back in his bedroom, thumping around in the closet. Scrabbling through the shoe-boxes he's got stacked up in there. Going through the memen-toes he's stashed in there from all his years at the church. And from all the years since.

I looked inside those shoeboxes once. Inside were stacks of church bulletins, sermon notes, and pictures from revivals and Sunday suppers. There was also a lady's wallet. A clip-on earring in the shape of a gold shell. A lime-green scrunchie with long, brown hairs tangled in it. A driver's license with a picture of a blonde lady I didn't recognize.

I put them all back just like I found them. I didn't tell Mandy or anybody else.

Now I grab the guitar from the corner of the den and settle on the couch, plucking at the strings and twisting the pegs. I don't really know the correct way to tune it, I just follow the tutorials on YouTube. But when I pick out the first verse of *Nearer My God to Thee,* it sounds pretty close. And then Pawpaw, in his faded plaid work shirt and high-water khaki pants, appears in the doorway between the den and the hall. He looks like a ghost.

This is why I've stayed here, in Pawpaw's old cabin, even though I graduated high school back in May. This is why I never bothered to apply for University of North Georgia or Georgia Southern or Chattahoochee Tech like most of my friends did.

Because I don't want Magill Millhorn making my Pawpaw mind.

I keep on playing and singing as if I don't know I have an audience of one. I can sense the music's starting to calm him down. Pawpaw stands in the shadows of the dark hall behind him. The only part of him that moves is one of his ratty house slippers that tap, tap, taps in time with my strumming. His silky white hair, long now, is loose from its usual ponytail and falls like curtains on either side of his shiny pink-and-white moon face. His cheeks and jowls and eyelids droop, but his skin is clear and dewy. I know without looking that his blue eyes are fastened on me.

My heart beats double time, a messed-up, mixed meter that's out of rhythm with the song. It usually only takes me singing one or two hymns before Pawpaw comes into the den and sits down on his recliner to give me his full attention. That's when the music really gets to him. He'll lay his head back and close his eyes. Then I'll sing more hymns, or maybe some Hank

Williams or Merle Haggard or Lynn Anderson, whatever he wants. Eventually he'll get up, pour himself a Dr. Pepper, and settle back into the recliner. If he switches on the TV, he'll fall asleep. That's when I know the danger's past.

The danger's clearly not past.

I start into *What a Friend We Have in Jesus,* and I really cut loose with the wailing thing I do. It's my one talent, something I didn't even know I had until old Magill talked to me that day years ago. But I know it's good. I know *I'm* good. Lately, I've actually been dreaming of leaving myself, striking out to Nashville to see if I can find Mom and maybe get work playing in the honky tonks on Music Row. I might even try to get an audition at the Bluebird Café. I've got a whole notebook full of songs I've written. Not great, just so-so, but you got to start somewhere. There is one I really like, but I've only got the beginning so far. I'd set up on the sidewalk, if I had to. I just need to find a guitar case to hold the money.

But I'll wait till Pawpaw's gone. I can't leave him alone. If I do, in two shakes of a lamb's tail, another one of Magill's girls is going to turn up missing or down a well and Magill will surely bring down all manner of holy hell. So I just got to bide my time. Wait till Pawpaw's gone. Meantime, I've still got Mandy, because she didn't go to college either. None of the Millhorns do.

Halfway into the second round of the chorus of *What a Friend*, I pull my voice back, softening it, which always makes Pawpaw tear up. Instead, he disappears from the doorway, and I can hear his slippers shuffle down the hallway. A door shuts. The thumping starts up again.

I play louder, strum ferociously, and wail my guts out. My voice sounds hard and strained and scared, nothing like David the shepherd boy would ever sing. David the shepherd boy never failed his king. Finally, I give up, stop playing and sit very still on the couch. The guitar rests on my lap. I stare at the old green carpet between my sneakers.

"Pawpaw?" I call out.

No answer.

"Pawpaw!"

I hear his footsteps, and suddenly he's back in the den. Then in the kitchen, reaching in the fridge for a Dr. Pepper. I sit up straight. He's wearing his work boots now, I notice as he makes his way to the door and takes his old navy windbreaker from one of the pegs.

"I'll be back later," he says and opens the door.

For a moment, I smell the October night, the crisp leaves and swirling wind. Bonfire smoke, and a car heading up the gravel road to one of the Airbnbs where there's hot tubs bubbling and music playing. I hear the music, but I can't make out a melody—just the relentless, hollow beat. And then he's gone.

I fall asleep on the couch, still gripping the neck of the guitar like it's a lucky rabbit's foot. There's a strange green light in the sky coming in through the windows, and I can hear the low rumble of thunder. The door slamming wakes me, and I sit up, eyes a-blear and throat parched. The room is awash in the gray and green of the night sky. Pawpaw stands frozen in the living room, head tilted like he's listening for something. After a moment he makes a shuffling beeline for his room.

"You want a glass of water?" I call after him, but his door softly clicking shut says no. I'm the one who wants a glass of water, but I don't get it. Because right then, the front door bursts open again and someone else comes in.

A girl.

A girl with two yellow French braids who's wearing a pair of jeans ripped at the knees and a pink halter top. A girl with blood smeared down the side of her face and coming out of her nose and dripping down her neck. A girl I know.

Mandy Millhorn's eyes are glittering, her pupils wide and wild and depthless. "Where'd he go?" she pants. She shuts the door behind her and squints at me. A cloud of outside smells has followed her in. Fire smoke. Beer. Candy.

I say nothing. My brain is still fogged with sleep, struggling to catch up. "What time is—"

"He's stepped over the line, Birdy." Mandy's words come out in a growl. She fixes me with a glare, and I see one of her eyes is ringed in purple and is probably on its way to swelling. "I know he's your grandpa, but he's gone too far."

I swallow and swallow, but there's nothing in my throat. I shake my head.

Mandy glances down the hall then back at me. She speaks with a new voice. Softer, pleading. "Me and Darien and Anna and those guys from Fannin County were hanging out by the river, but then they had to go meet some other people. And then we left. Darien and Anna went in her car, and I was just gonna walk over to the EZ Shop and call Travis, and *he* followed me." She points toward Pawpaw's room.

I don't move. The room is electric, charged with a current that I suspect will kill me if I touch the couch or the carpet or a door. Mandy keeps talking. She is wild. She doesn't want to have to tell me this, she says, but he touched her, grabbed her, wrestled her down to the ground and she had to fight him off. She says she's doing me a favor, coming here first, telling me before she goes to her grandpa. It's because we're friends. That's why she's giving me this courtesy.

I stand, quivering.

"Can you stay just a minute?" I ask her. "Can you let me wash your face and give you a drink of something?" I need more time. Time to think or plan or do something, I don't know what. I don't know how Magill takes care of people, but I know it's bad. And I think maybe he won't stop with Pawpaw, that he'll want to take care of me, too.

"Don't go yet," I say to Mandy, and she knows exactly what I mean. I guess she's seen plenty enough living in that trailer. Seen how a king decides who's a problem and how to take care of them. She relents, sitting at the kitchen table. I get her a glass of water and a leftover biscuit. She lets me wipe her face and put Neosporin on the cuts. She won't let me take her bloody top, but I give her a sweater of mine from the pegs to wrap over it. While she picks at the crumbles of the biscuit, I go to the hallway.

"Pawpaw," I call out sternly even though my voice wavers. "Get out here."

"Go on to sleep!" he shouts back at me from behind the closed door. "I'm busy."

"Pawpaw, Mandy's here. You gotta come on out, now, and talk to me about what happened."

"To hell with you! To hell with that girl!"

Mandy's head is ducked down, but I can see her watching me with her one unswollen, glittering eye.

"Pawpaw!" I shout, but there isn't a sound from his room. I turn to Mandy. "I don't know what to do."

"You got to do something, Bird. Can't stop the sun coming up."

I go back to the couch and pick up the guitar. With trembling fingers I pick out the first verse of *The Old Rugged Cross,* then stop. Pawpaw hasn't made an appearance, and I don't know if he's going to. I need something he's never heard before. Not a hymn.

"I wrote a song," I tell Mandy.

She looks up, chewing.

I shift the Martin on my leg and think about the opening notes. "I've only got part of it."

"Well, let's hear it, I guess," she says, shrugging, like she might as well get in a concert while she's here.

I strum a couple of chords, then sing the first verse.

It's about my mother singing on a stage in Nashville, just her and a guitar. Everyone in the audience is captivated because her song reminds them of all the heartaches they have tried to forget. I finish, halfway through the second verse.

"That's all I got."

Mandy nods. "It's nice. I like it."

"It's about my mom."

Mandy folds her hands on the table and looks away. She knows all about my mom.

"You want me to help you write the rest?" she finally says.

I perk up. "You can do that?" I mean, I know Mandy's a good singer. She's been in choir at school, but I didn't know she writes songs.

"Play the second verse for me again."

I do, and for the first couple of lines she harmonizes with me from the kitchen table. At the sound of our voices blending like that, the hairs on my arm stand at attention. The electricity from the room has funneled into my body, and I'm filled with a kind of zinging sensation. Then Mandy sings a few more lines, something wistful and sad about missing what you've left behind. I hear a door creak, look up, and see Pawpaw, still in his flannel shirt and work pants but wearing his slippers. He stands in the doorway.

"And it came to pass that when the evil spirit was upon Saul…"

It's only a whisper.

Mandy ignores him. We keep going—making up more lines, harmonizing, adding little flourishes to the melody. She picks up the chorus real quick, then adds a bridge.

Pawpaw doesn't say anything or even look Mandy's way as he shuffles over to the recliner and collapses into it.

David took the lyre and played with his hand…

We keep working the song, starting over every time we hit a snag, getting it just the way we like it. When I finally look over at Pawpaw, his eyes are closed, his head thrown back. I think he's asleep because his thin, knobby hands have fallen off the arms of the chair and his mouth is open. Outside the window, the green has faded, and the light looks gray now.

…and Saul was refreshed and well…

Mandy stands up and walks past Pawpaw's recliner and down the hall. When she comes back, she's holding a pillow in a faded blue pillowcase. It's one of Pawpaw's from off his bed. She walks over to me on the couch and takes the guitar out of my hand, laying it carefully against the cushions. "Come on, Birdy. It won't take but a second."

I stand up and she nods. Together we walk over to Pawpaw in the recliner. He's snoring now, little snotty gasps, and she lays the pillow almost tenderly over his face.

"Come on, now."

I put my hands on the pillow, too. She and I hold it down together, pressing it against Pawpaw's face, hard as we can, probably for longer than we need to. We want to make sure the job is done. He only kicks and twists a little. Kicks, twists, and lets out a few muffled grunts.

And the evil spirit departed from him.

When we're finished, I go to the bathroom to pee, and Mandy returns the pillow to Pawpaw's room. I wash my hands really good. When I get back to the den, Mandy's waiting by the open door. The wild outdoor smells are gone. All I can smell now is coconut Soft Soap.

"Hey, Bird," she says, just as tenderly as she put the pillow on my Pawpaw's face. "Do you want me to show you where your Mama is buried now? I'll show you, if you want."

I think of all the stories Pawpaw told me. Stories about where my mother went, all the things he did at church. I wonder if he ever truly loved my playing and singing. I wonder if it was all a game, and he was just pretending I had the power to keep him home, to keep him out of trouble.

Because now I know he took my mother off somewhere and did something to her. Now I understand the that the Millhorns have been cleaning up his mess for me, all these years, to keep me safe. They've been my family all along, halfway up this mountain between the world at the top and the one at the bottom.

"Please," I say to her. "Show me."

We leave the house, leave Pawpaw in his chair, and I shut the door behind me.

TONE DEAF

HC Chan

Quiescent Fung was a reverse prodigy. She was color-blind, had two left feet and couldn't string two notes together without tripping over the chord.

That had to amount to something, she told herself.

When she was nine, she Googled female colorblindness and found her condition was uncommon. (*One in two hundred girls, versus one in twelve boys!*) She'd written the mutations down in a yellow hardbound notebook, *OPN1LW and OPN1MW*, and adorned the silk-finished page with glittery butterfly stickers.

The discovery made her feel special. It had taken a few years for her to understand that she saw things differently and a few more for mother to believe her. Her mother Miriam sourced high-end textiles for home design and was often jetting to places like Thailand or Indonesia or Kazakhstan and wasn't around enough to notice. Her frequent absence in fact required Quiescent's life to be scheduled and pre-ordained, down to coordinating the clothes—and colors—that she wore.

Her father had to have been colorblind too, to pass on her condition. Quiescent didn't remember her father, who died when she was four. Her mother only ever mentioned him as the person who "left me widowed," as though widowhood was an object she'd inherited, and not a loss she experienced. They never discussed if the late Eddie Fung mixed up blue shirts for green shirts.

Her mother didn't much care that Quiescent couldn't tell the color of a tomato or strawberry from a chestnut. What she did care about was wringing musical talent from her child. When Quiescent turned six, she was signed up for the Horizon International Academy of Music. Four days a week, not including performances that Horizon held to prove to paying parents that their offspring was learning something.

Not so much with Quiescent. Two years of piano. Two years of Taiko drum. Trumpet. Mandolin. Violin. Her instruments got smaller with every failure, even as her mother's donations got bigger. In the increasingly lavish musical showcases, Quiescent was inevitably exiled to the back, laboring through a cycle of discordant notes.

"Just play softly," Mrs. Yun pleaded. (*Isn't that odd coming from a Taiko drum teacher?*) "As long as you show confidence." Quiescent did develop unusually muscular biceps for a nine-year-old.

She came to see Horizon as a place she could be stowed while her mother was away and not bother Auntie Lainie too much. Quiescent knew more Horizon staff than family members, like the blue-suited, glad-handing development director Walker Lam, the plump-bottomed secretary Lucy Yu-Landesberg who gave her special treats every Chinese holiday and reassuring one-armed hugs after every poor performance, and of course the music teachers—brusque Mrs. Yun on drums, cheery Mr. Olsen on trumpet, long-suffering Ms. Chan who doubled on violin and mandolin. Not all the teachers stuck around. Not her first, the twitchy wild-eyed Mr. Tom, a former piano prodigy whose frayed cuffs gave away his frayed nerves. After he disappeared, older students whispered he'd been locked up in an institution or joined a cruise ship where he played slow jazz improvisation.

Director Lam was the only one who took to calling her Quie.

"Like a key to a treasure," he would bray, a manicured thumb stroking his groomed mustache, his other hand resting on an elaborately embroidered vest under an otherwise sober blue suit. That same hand would rest lightly on her mother's stiffening upper arm during fundraisers, when she used to attend them. "Welcome, Mrs. Fung. I am so glad you can make it to these performances in your busy schedule," Director Lam would say. "Your design business I hear continues to grow. How smart to move into healthy organic fabrics. And thank you for the fabric samples. Do you see how I waste nothing and have my tailor make beautiful vests? Mr. Fung would have so pleased how your family has helped this community grow. Everyone should benefit like Quie has."

She didn't really believe that Director Lam knew her father. Besides colorblindness, the other legacy her father had left Quiescent was her name. Her parents came from Hong Kong, where people sometimes gave their kids funny English names like Angel and Dante. Quiescent was supposed to be a translation of her Chinese name, meaning tranquility. Her name was never meant to be shortened.

When she was twelve, after beginning mandolin lessons, Quiescent Googled "tone deaf." Nadine Liu, a fellow student, kindly suggested that might be the problem. Unlike her colorblindness, though, the online definitions of tone deaf didn't seem to fit as well. Still, they were better than her mother's diagnosis.

"You don't try hard enough," rebuked the hard-driving Miriam Fung, her unflinching expression set to convey her position as a successful entrepreneur and to control her jowls. She herself didn't play an instrument. When she was home, she didn't instruct Fatima to play music (*why do all digital AI assistants given girl names ending in A?*), instead filling any silence with late-night business calls across time zones. Sometimes she told people on those calls that they weren't trying hard enough either. She'd also say how she wouldn't be cheated, and how much they would regret various actions. Quiescent realized at age fifteen, halfway through violin, that a bow scraping across untuned strings was not unlike the harsh grating of her mother's voice bouncing off the walls of their hilltop house.

Besides widowhood, her mother got their Twin Peaks home from her late husband. Quiescent though felt that the view of San Francisco from the living room plate-glass window belonged to her, a rippling carpet of white and gray buildings with downtown skyscrapers bunched up at the end before its edge disappeared into the bay's grayish-blue waters. When her Auntie Lainie would come from Sacramento to watch her, she descended to the downstairs suite. By the time she emerged to cook dinner and play games, the vista had darkened to a night sky and the buildings an electric constellation. Quiescent didn't much care for the way the freeway became a bright yellow scar, bleeding light at the edges. Or at least she thought it was yellow, as that was one of the colors she was supposed to be able to see.

Her music practice room was at the top level—soundproofed over the years. Even if she couldn't play well, she always liked the feel of the instruments. The piano keys had felt coldly yet irresistibly slick and required the eight-year-old to stretch the full length of her arms to span all eighty-eight. The thirty-six black keys reminded her of dominoes, which she'd spend hours setting up on the open-air living room floor in soldierly rows. A nudge of her plump index finger would knock down all that progress, and then she'd start again. Knocking down dominoes had been Auntie Lainie's idea, as was the trumpet and eventually telling her how her father died—a cliff hike, a daring dance on an edge, a mistimed onset of another dizzy spell, an accidental fall into cold waters.

Now, at sixteen, Quiescent was down to two strings. A new teacher, Mr. Luther Mak, joined Horizon. In an introductory session, he told the students that the name *erhu* combined the number two (er) and Hu, the family who likely invented the instruments. The Hus were at one time considered barbarians.

"So this is barbarian music," he joked, then picked up his horse-hair bow.

Quiescent had seen street vendors play this traditional Chinese fiddle, nothing more than an octagonal box with an unusually long neck.

But not like this.

Not the mournful vibrato like mountaintop echoes of other-worldly voices. Not the quivering heights that lifted Quiescent higher than her own hill of grasslands and coastal scrub, to a towering elevation closer to sky than earth, closer to heaven than man. Not the incandescent light that lit up the gray cavern within her.

Mr. Mak finished a complicated medley that transitioned ancient wailing laments to modern Canto-pop songs. He modestly waited through the students' applause before he revealed the secret. The erhu's soul came from the vibrations of the python skin that wrapped the soundbox. Snakes farm-raised, solely for the purpose of making this music. And maybe some soup.

As a teenager closing in on adulthood, Quiescent could appreciate the seduction of supple snakeskin. She imagined a fenced pasture of giant reptiles, slithering along their bellies (which Mr. Mak said was the best part for a good erhu), leaving a musical trail of weeping notes towards their doomed fate.

She would play the erhu.

Except her sad notes sounded, well, sad in a different way. Quiescent was going the direction of all her other instrumental ventures. Three months in, Mr. Mak was finding it hard to control the wincing wrinkles on his lovely pockmarked face. He was better than most teachers, but even he was being reduced to exasperated contradictions.

"Relax your fingers...No, no, press harder."

"Your bow is scratching the strings. You must glide between

the two strings. It is the space where the music comes…Why are you sawing? This is not woodworking."

"This part, these notes must cry…Your notes, they shriek like a crying child. Don't you hear them?"

No, she couldn't, despite the yearning gray cavern within her. Quiescent ended up in the corner once again, stage left by the black velvet curtains, as the class prepared for another showcase. That's why, a few days later, she saw the blood first.

On Mondays, she carpooled with Joseph (Chinese lion dancing drums) and Sophie (flute) with their mom Mrs. Han. Thursdays, Quiescent came to Horizon earlier because she took the bus, which her mother would not have liked so she didn't tell her. Sometimes Quiescent would beat Mr. Mak's arrival, and the secretary Mrs. Yu-Landesberg always let her into the room.

That Thursday, Quiescent got off the bus much earlier than usual, as her chemistry lab was undergoing an emergency cleaning. She watched the cars go by as she waited for the pedestrian light. Her mother wasn't supposed to come back from her business trip until late. She remembered her mother's dramatic gesture before leaving for her overseas flight last week, tossing a gold-embossed parchment card that announced the next fundraising showcase onto the rosewood console table. "What more do they want from me?" she'd said. "I'm not paying anymore. This is their last chance with you."

The crosswalk light began its countdown. Quiescent entered Horizon and to the muted sounds of childish halting notes. The secretary beamed at her enthusiasm and briskly waddled alongside to unlock Mr. Mak's room. It took her longer than usual to turn the key.

"Funny." Mrs. Yu-Landesberg pursed her lips, looking like a plush carnival doll. "Was this even locked?"

But the door opened to an empty room, its tidy rows of unoccupied metal chairs and music stands on a polished hardwood floor ready for the next session. As the woman continued to fuss over the doorknob, Quiescent sat down in her rear spot, ready to practice, ready to release the yearning that the erhu required.

Because she was colorblind, the liquid pool didn't look red. More like a caramel spill, its edges thinned out and soaked into the varnished wood. She'd almost put her oxford-cloth carrying case on the puddle and stopped just in time. Scooting her stool back, she cautiously poked her bow in the gap between the velvet curtains and pushed one aside.

The body was face down. The back of the head wasn't a skull anymore, just a broken depression of matted hair, bone and a little pulpy matter.

The bow started shaking. Quiescent saw it was her arm and she pulled it back. She didn't want to drop her bow on whatever that was on the ground. Even as her body quivered, an inexplicable sense of relief shot like a streak through her heart. (*It's not him.*)

Quiescent didn't remember saying to Mrs. Yu-Landesberg, "I think there's an emergency," but she must have said something for the secretary to come to the back and start screaming.

While a music school, Horizon operated like most modern American centers of education. Quiescent recognized the distant undercurrent of slamming doors, the soft patter of running feet, the metallic screech of furniture dragged across floors to barricade entries. Instead of attracting a crowd, the secretary's screams triggered lockdown mode.

Which meant nobody else was coming to see the blood-stained man emerge from behind the curtain.

Again, being colorblind, Quiescent couldn't swear the splatter on his frayed cuffs and shirtfront was blood. The hammer in his right hand seemed a giveaway.

Mrs. Yu-Landesberg's vocals hit a remarkable crescendo. She backed into a music stand and her ample bottom fell onto a metal chair. Instinctively, Quiescent stepped between her and this stranger from the shadows.

"Shut her up," he said, in a curiously calm voice, almost how a dead man might speak, except the actual dead man was lying behind him. A dark knit cap covered most of his graying hair and made his sallow sagging face appear cadaverous. Chestnut streaks covered his buttoned shirt and grimy dark canvas pants. They were almost eye to eye, a vantage point Quiescent had only recently attained in the past six months with a growth spurt.

"Excuse me? I can't hear you," she replied with trained politeness. It was hard to hear above the screaming.

"Shut her up." He gestured with the hammer. The action was less threatening than one might expect, as he waved with a surprising graceful conductor's flourish. The woman's voice however went up another piercing octave. Quiescent remembered the rumors that the secretary had once trained in Peking Opera.

"The police are coming, Mr. Tom," she said, a little louder to pierce Mrs. Yu-Landesberg's aria of hysteria. (*Would that be hystaria?*) Of course there was no way to know if anyone was coming. It seemed the reasonable thing to say.

Except it wasn't. Nor admitting that she recognized her old piano teacher. Her very first Horizon instructor, back either from an institution or a cruise ship.

"You weren't supposed to be here. I have to leave," and he raised the hammer.

Quiescent was still holding her erhu and bow. She realized this as she swung her stringed instrument up at his lunging arm and swung her bow across his face, pantomiming a big sloppy X. There was a splintering sound but it was only her delicate erhu and not his ulna.

Quiescent backhanded the bow to slash his face again, a sawing motion she'd perfected in violin. Then for no good reason, she tossed her broken erhu and bow in a three-hundred-sixty degree arc, caught them and, with a taiko drum flourish banged away at him. Downward strokes, powering with her body, thump, thump, thump.

"Get away from her!" she bellowed like a trumpet, to guard the woman who'd always been there for her at every showcase. Although, to be fair, the man seemed more intent on Quiescent. Something heavy clattered, and his bare hands went for her throat. She tucked her chin and head-butted his nose. Something crunched. Her skull stung. She dug her own fingers—every digit still strong and flexible from banging on those keys under Mr. Tom's tutelage—into his Adam's apple. For good measure, she kneed him in the groin.

That she learned from Auntie Lainie.

Quiescent probably would not have lasted long against this dead-eyed man intent on clearing the room. She was a fit hundred pounds to his withered one hundred forty, but he was a killer. It was Mrs. Yu-Lancaster who, finally voiceless, wielded a music stand like a halberd and hit the sweet spot at the back of his neck. Mr. Tom went down.

Peking Opera included training in martial acrobatics and weapons.

When Mr. Mak finally showed up, after the police arrived to take away the unconscious assailant, and asked her what happened, Quiescent could only say, "I'm so glad it wasn't you."

Her mother didn't like texts. Quiescent instead waited at the ebony-wood dining table. From there, she could see across the open expanse of understated luxury furniture to the window's darkening vista. A bruised moon dropped low over San Francisco. She thought of Director Lam's prone body, and then of her father. Auntie Lainie had said his body had taken weeks to be found. She hadn't described what that body looked like and Quiescent didn't need a search engine to imagine.

At last she heard the rolling suitcase, the clatter of keys, the silence as her mother was likely checking her face in the hallway mirror. *Mirror mirror on the wall.*

Miriam Fung came into the kitchen. The automatic lights flicked on, catching the glow of her trademark lemon-yellow leather jacket. She'd always had cat-like awareness, and caught sight of Quiescent a few steps in.

"You're still up? Don't you have school tomorrow?" She checked her wrist as she walked towards the refrigerator behind the kitchen island. "Or I should say today."

"I found a body at Horizon," Quiescent said. "Director Lam."

Her mother turned to stare. Professional maintenance and make-up were becoming less successful staving off the lines that carved borders alongside the pouches of her cheeks and under her eyes. "He's dead? How?"

"The way you wanted him to."

The stare hardened, the crevices deepened. "What are you saying?"

"Mr. Tom killed him. You remember Mr. Tom. My piano teacher from ten years ago, when you started paying Director Lam for music lessons."

Quiescent could see her mother hesitate, calculating her reactions. How to respond to the accusation behind the revelation.

"Mr. Tom? How do you know? You saw him?"

"I came to erhu class early. Mrs. Yu-Landesberg and I saw him. He tried to kill us."

Now Miriam Fung moved quickly, from behind the kitchen island. Instead of sitting by her daughter to put a hand on her shoulder, she faced Quiescent from the other side of the dining table. There was always something between them.

"What did you mean he tried to kill you?" her mother asked, barely restraining the usual condescending doubt in her voice.

"He had a hammer," she replied. No movement from across the table. A murderous attack couldn't loosen a maternal instinct that had never existed. Quiescent wasn't surprised, couldn't mourn what she'd never lost. "What did you promise him? A ticket to Indonesia? A house in Thailand?"

"You must be in shock. Why do you say such things?" And then, "Are you hurt?" she asked too late.

"Just because I'm tone deaf doesn't mean I'm blind," Quiescent said. "You give thousands of dollars to Horizon every year, on top of tuition. For what? I'm terrible. You don't even come to the showcases. But every time Director Lam brings up how much my father would want this, you give him more money. What happened? Did he see you?"

"I don't know where you get this. You must have been hit in the head."

Quiescent shook her head, which fortunately had not been hit. "Director Lam had something on you. For ten years, you've paid and you're sick of it. And you found someone who probably hated him just as much as you did. Except Mr. Tom got caught."

"The police have him?" her mother asked sharply. "I have nothing to do with this. I just got back. There's something wrong with you to think these things. Shock."

"I saw you."

The silence revealed the hidden notes in the room. The thrum of electricity. The creaking sighs of a sixty-year old home. The vibration of wind knocking at the windows. The hissing intake of breath.

"I just landed."

"How hard do you think it would be to check which flight you took? You met Mr. Tom. Maybe you dropped him off. No, you wouldn't do that," Quiescent amended. "You didn't trust him. You watched him to make sure he got inside the school. And I saw you drive by.'"

"You saw nothing. What does it matter if I catch an earlier flight?"

"Why did you kill my father?" Quiescent studied the pouched face, the play of self-righteousness and dismissive superiority in the flare of the nostrils and curl of the upper lip. "What did Director Lam have on you?"

"You're like your father. Accusing. When I do all the work and you play."

Quiescent was going to point out that she wasn't yet seventeen but decided against it. "You didn't think he worked hard enough? So you arranged an accident. And if someone searches Director Lam's home for information on how Eddie Fung died..."

She stopped. Miriam Fung's face had purpled with rage.

"Why were you at erhu so early? You're supposed to be in school. But it doesn't matter if you saw me. Nobody will believe a crazy man. Nobody will believe you."

Quiescent leaned back when she really wanted to do the opposite and put her head down on the table. She was exhausted. But the tune in her head had to be played out.

"You think nobody will take Mr. Tom seriously if he says you put him up to it? You think nobody will search Director Lam's things for evidence on how you killed my father?"

She stopped. The showcases, the director's hand on her mother's arm, the preening over his elaborate vests. From textiles that her mother gifted him from her samples. His unctuous compliments. *How smart to move into healthy organic fabrics.*

Because, too often, fabrics would be coated with dyes, fire retardant, stain repellents, anti-fungal treatment. Toxic chemicals. Forever chemicals.

"You poisoned my father with fabric dyes."

A guess. A shot in the dark. An improvised note.

Even though she'd been standing still, Miriam Fung staggered. Shock melted her face—nostrils drooping, jaw slackening, the iron control over her jowls gone. Quiescent had never seen anything like it.

"He fell. He drowned." A malignant whisper.

"You poisoned him. He had dizzy spells. Director Lam somehow found proof. You think you're going to get away with another murder?"

"I didn't get away with anything." Miriam Fung's bitter song. "You said it. I paid for ten years. Your father knew nothing about business. And then Lam deliberately made the teachers teach you poorly, so you would come home and make these awful sounds and drive me out of my own home, and embarrass me at the showcases."

For the first time, Quiescent felt encouraged by her mother's words. Had Director Lam orchestrated a plot of brilliant and punishing subtlety? Maybe she wasn't tone deaf.

Maybe she had a chance.

"Fatima," she called out. "Replay the last three minutes."

Miriam Fung finally couldn't keep silent at her own words *I paid for ten years.*

"Fatima! Fatima, delete!" she shouted but since her mother had never developed that relationship either, the AI assistant ignored her.

"What is it you want?" she turned her shouting to Quiescent. But she couldn't keep her body from shaking, her face from melting.

"I'm sure you have a house in Indonesia or wherever. Sign this house over to a trust that Auntie Lainie will manage for me. I will let you leave before the police come."

Quiescent had inherited her colorblindness and name from her father. But she wasn't Miriam Fung's daughter for nothing.

When she found out the prison hospital where Mr. Tom ended up, Quiescent had a piano delivered there. The anonymous gesture wasn't as magnanimous as it could have been. People were always giving away pianos that their children would no longer play, so she only paid delivery costs.

Quiescent bought a new erhu. The best money could buy.

She still played terribly but Mrs. Yu-Landesberg, the new director, asked Mr. Mak to move her up to the center left.

Quiescent after all was a hero. And she was going to sign up for Peking opera lessons. It seemed she had a knack.

I COULD BE THE ONE

Michael Amos Cody

In the middle of July 1983, songwriter Ezra MacRae rolled down the western slopes of southern Appalachia, picked up the fallout trail from Bristol's Big Bang of Country Music, and followed the ghosts of Maybelle Carter and Jimmie Rodgers into the heart of Music City, U.S.A. For one hundred six dollars a month, he rented a furnished one-room apartment—bath and kitchen shared with three other one-room renters—in a house on 17th Avenue South. He moved in clothes, stereo system, guitar, and a box of lyric files and cassette demos. With his room set up, he took a brief nap and then went out for a burger and a few beers too many at Brown's Diner. But he still got back to his new place and into bed before midnight, anxious for a good night's sleep followed by the first steps toward his eventual and inevitable induction into the Nashville Songwriters Hall of Fame.

Next morning, a Wednesday, he woke up with a combined summer head cold and hangover, groaned and cussed his way out of bed, and showered in cold water when the bathroom finally became available. But he didn't mind. *First day as a Music City songwriter*, he thought as he dressed, picked up his guitar, and stepped out on the streets of Nashville.

* * *

By the middle of September, the First American bank account that had held all the money he'd saved since high school dipped below three hundred dollars, so he found a part-time job in the mailroom at Triune Music, a small publisher of Christian songs and choral arrangements. The regular paycheck slowed but didn't reverse the decline of his balance. So, if on any given night he hadn't drunk enough to put himself to sleep, he tossed and turned, haunted by premonitions that he might be forced back home before the end of the coming winter, having not lasted even a year in pursuit of his dream.

He spent many of his days off from the mailroom writing in the morning and then making cold calls on song publishers up and down Music Row—16th and 17th Avenues mostly—and a few out-of-the-way offices on 18th or 19th or in some outlying area like down in Berry Hill or up in Goodlettsville. He didn't want to be one of those guys he saw looking as if they were living out of their guitar cases, so one weekend back home in the mountains for a visit, he talked his papa out of an old briefcase from seminary days. With this full of lyrics and tapes, he sometimes made it through to a low-level songplugger who would spare a few minutes to tell him what didn't work in this song or that. But far more often, rigidly polite and beautiful secretaries kept the gates to such inner sanctums firmly shut.

On the last Sunday night in October, he found himself onstage at the Songbird Café as part of the weekly songwriter's night, having auditioned for the opportunity back in August. He sang what he believed to be three of his best—"Rita's Cantina," "Angel and the Bad Man," and "Dixiana"—and received responses enthusiastic enough to give him an infusion of confidence. Afterwards, he sat with a beer and listened to two sisters sing three tunes with a very sixties folk vibe. Both women were beautiful, but he focused on the older one until he noticed the wedding band flashing on her chording hand. He shrugged to himself, turned on his stool, ordered another beer, and watched the rest of the warm-up songwriters' performances in the mirror behind the bar.

During the break before the feature writer, a hand clapped down on his left shoulder, and a gruff voice drawled close to his ear, "Hey, buddy, we really liked your songs."

Ezra turned toward the man, whose genuine smile shone from a rugged, clean-cut face. "Thanks for listening," he said, wondering if this fellow might be somebody he should know, maybe some incognito music mogul.

"Hey, no problem. You want to come over and join us?" The man tipped his head in the direction of the tables in the middle of the Songbird.

Ezra saw the folksy sisters and another man turned toward him with similar genuine smiles. "Sure," he said, picked up his beer, and shimmied through the crowd to the table, where the man introduced himself as Greg, the older sister as his wife Lynn, the younger as Cindy, and the other man as Cindy's fiancé Doug.

Greg turned out not to be an incognito music mogul but the owner of Music City Pool Management. "Your mailroom job's just part-time?" he asked.

"Yeah, at least I can say I work in the music business," Ezra said. "But I'll have to pick up another part-time gig or find something full-time if I'm gonna stay in town."

Lynn, who said she stayed home and wrote songs for fun and came out to sing whenever Cindy wanted to, nudged Greg with her elbow.

"Well, we're going into our slow time at the company," Greg said, "but I might be able to throw some pools your way if you're interested. Just had a guy quit on me."

"Ten dollars a pool," Lynn said with a smile. "If you do like three a week, that's your month's rent right there."

"I don't know," Ezra said. "I can't swim all that good."

"Then don't fall in," Greg said. "The most of it's just

mechanics and finding your way around town."

Sister Cindy worked on 16th Avenue, at the Nashville branch office of a Canadian artist management company. "We know a singer who lives over on 17th," she said. "He has a deal with Hooray Records."

"Really?" Ezra said.

"Maybe y'all could write some together."

"I've never done much cowriting," Ezra said. "Except with my guitar and a friend from home."

"He goes by Jimmy James," Lynn said. "But I don't think that's his real name."

Greg laughed. "Seems like a body could come up with something more original than what amounts to James James."

"Honey," Lynn said and rolled her eyes as Mason Queenan, owner of the Songbird, stepped onto the stage to introduce the evening's feature songwriter.

"He's written number one hits for The Bellamy Brothers and The Kendalls," Queenan said. "And a lot of other hits as well." When a tall thin man with bangs and a guitar joined him onstage, Queenan added, "Please welcome Jerry Gillespie."

Do You Love as Good as You Look" by *The Bellamy Brothers*, Ezra thought as he remembered Gillespie's two biggest hits. And *"Heaven's Just a Sin Away" by The Kendalls*.

He serviced a couple of already-winterized pools on Veterans Day Friday morning and, after cleaning himself up, decided to walk a few blocks down 17th and across the campus of Belmont College to the International Market for a late lunch. Afterwards, he would settle in for the evening with his beer and guitar and writing stuff.

As soon as he stepped down on the sidewalk and set off toward Belmont, he saw a man coming his way and, even at a distance, recognized Jimmy James from his album covers. Since that October night at the Songbird, when Cindy and Lynn first mentioned the singer, Ezra had spent some time in the bins at Cat's Records and Ernest Tubb's Record Shop and found James's first two albums for the Hooray label—the self-titled *Jimmy James* from 1978 and *A Wanted Man* from 1980. He'd also learned that the singer lived just four doors further along 17th from his own place, about halfway between it and Waylon Jennings's offices in the manor house on the corner of 17th and Edgehill. James was just passing Waylon's, so Ezra adjusted his pace in the hope that they would meet on the sidewalk before he could disappear through his front door.

When they were a dozen steps from passing each other, Ezra caught the man's eye and forced himself to speak. "You're Jimmy James," he said with a brightness he hoped wasn't creepy.

James's stride stuttered and his eyes flared wide for a moment, but then he steadied and cracked a practiced grin. "Guilty as charged."

Ezra hadn't planned past that opening line, and an awkward moment passed as their steps brought them closer together. Then Ezra stopped and partially blocked the sidewalk. "I recognize you from your album covers," he said at last as James also came to a stop.

"Well, thanks for being a fan," the singer said. "I'm glad you like the records."

Ezra hadn't bought the albums, just looked at them—judging the artwork, reading the song titles, studying the songwriting and recording credits. "Sure," he said. "Could I get you to sign one of them sometime." He aimed a thumb over his shoulder. "I just live down the street."

"Well, I'm right here," James said and nodded toward the front door numbered 1105. "I'm usually home unless I'm in the studio or on the road."

"That's cool," Ezra said. "Could I bring one by this evening?" He figured that he could hustle up to Ernest Tubb's after he ate and pick up *A Wanted Man*.

"Sorry, I'm leaving town this afternoon for a short tour. On the road until after Thanksgiving." James excused himself and started up concrete steps that rose between his front yard's low retaining walls, but he turned in the middle of his front walk. "How about stopping by sometime in December?"

"Thanks," Ezra said. "I will." His mind raced. "Hey, are you making another album?"

"Going in the studio first of February," James said and looked up at the sky. "You a songwriter like everybody else in town?"

"No, sir," Ezra said. "I mean yessir, but not like everybody else in town." He wondered if that sounded cool or arrogant. "Just moved here last summer."

"Well, I've got all the songs I need for the new album, but stop by for that autograph in early December."

"I will," Ezra said again.

It was January before he had enough disposable cash— Christmas money—to visit the record store. He walked to Cat's on West End—the Tubbs shop had deep bins but inflated prices for Music Row tourists—and bought Bob Dylan's *Infidels*, Van Halen's *1984*, and Jimmy James's *A Wanted Man*. As soon as he spied signs of life at James's house, he tucked *A Wanted Man* under an arm, tucked his chin into his winter coat, and hurried along icy walkways to the man's front door.

"Happy New Year, Mr. James," Ezra said when the door swung open.

"Goddamn, it's cold," the singer said and waved Ezra inside and quickly closed the door. He made a blowing noise like a horse and walked past Ezra toward the back of the house. "Come on in the kitchen."

Ezra laid the album jacket on the table and stood with hands in his coat pockets.

"Coffee?" James asked.

"Sure. Thanks."

"Take off your coat and have a seat." As Ezra did as he was told, the singer took down another cup from a cabinet. "And it's just Jimmy," he said.

With two coffees steaming on the table, Jimmy turned to rummage in a drawer. "Here we go," he said and held up a felt-tip pen. "Let's get this autograph business taken care of." He sat down and pulled the album in front of himself and looked a moment at the cover. "What's your name?"

"Ezra MacRae."

"E-Z-R-A?"

"Yessir, then big *m*, little *a-c*, big *r*, little *a-e*."

Jimmy looked across the table at him, pen hovering above the cover. "I'm just gonna make it to Ezra," he said.

"Sure, that's fine." Ezra listened to the squeak of the felt tip and wondered what Jimmy was writing. He knew that it was more than "To Ezra" and a signature, but he couldn't tell what else.

Jimmy finished with a flourish, picked up the signed album by a corner, and moved it from the tabletop to the kitchen counter. "Don't want to smudge it before it dries."

Ezra wasn't sure what he was supposed to do. He'd assumed he would get the autograph at the front door and shiver back to his room, but he sat with his coat off at the kitchen table and seemed not expected to leave anytime soon.

Jimmy took a sip of coffee and cleared his throat. "How's the songwriting coming?"

"Good," Ezra said. "I mean, I haven't had any luck yet, but I'm trying to get better with every song."

"Well, that's what you want." Jimmy gave his cup a half turn and then kept his hand on it. "You got tapes?"

Ezra cleared his throat. "Just what I came to town with in July. Not the recent stuff." He picked up his cup and set it down again. "I meant to record some when I was home for Christmas, but I didn't get around to it."

Jimmy stood suddenly and carried his cup to the sink. "Tell you what," he said. "I gotta run a couple of errands right now and then leave for a Gulf coast tour." He reached out for Ezra's cup, took it when Ezra handed it up, and set it in the sink as well. "If you'll run get one of your tapes and put it in my mailbox, I'll pick it up before I leave town." He emptied what remained in the cups and filled them with water and left them in the sink. "If I like what I hear, maybe we'll sit down and write one next week."

"That would be great," Ezra said. "But I thought you had all the songs you need for the next album."

"Hell, you and me both. Found out this morning that George-goddamn-Strait just stole a song I thought my people'd put on hold for me."

When Jimmy slammed his chair underneath the table, Ezra popped up from his. "I don't know what that means," he said. "But sounds like it sucks."

"Had high hopes for it," Jimmy said. "You know, it ain't every day you get your hands on a damn Sonny Throckmorton song. 'Cowboy Rides Away' was gonna be a breakout record for me."

Ezra worked his way into his coat but didn't respond—didn't know how to respond. Then, "Well, I hope you have a good tour."

Jimmy James turned away toward a different part of his house. "You can show yourself out," he said. "I just want to get out of this goddamn cold for a couple days." He disappeared down a shadowed hallway but called back, "Don't forget your album."

When Ezra returned to his apartment, he sat at his desk and looked at the autographed album cover, which read, 'To Erza' and 'Hooray for Jimmy James, January 1984.' "Right," he said. "So much for that." He went through his cassettes and found "Rita's Cantina" and "Angel and the Badman." He didn't yet have a recording of "Dixiana," so, remembering the title of the song James claimed George Strait stole from him, he picked "A Cowboy" from his batch written in 1980. These tapes he wrapped in lyric sheets secured with rubber bands, stuffed them in an envelope, and headed back out the door into the cold.

A week later, Ezra and Jimmy sat again at the singer's kitchen table, this time with guitars in their laps and sheets of notebook paper spread in front of them.

"You smoke?" Jimmy James asked.

Ezra pulled the pack of Camel Lights from his shirt pocket and laid it on the table.

"No, man," the singer said. "Not tobacco."

Ezra hung fire. "Well, yeah, I used to," he said after a moment. "But I haven't since I left home."

"Then it's high time," Jimmy said and laughed. He stood and went out the back door.

Ezra heard the man's boots on the back porch and then stood and went to the window above the sink. He watched Jimmy James unlock a blue Camaro Z28, open the driver's door, and release the driver's seat back as if he were going to climb in the back seat. Instead, he reached in, pulled hard at something, and came up with what Ezra thought must be a pound of reefer.

"Just got this for the tour starting tomorrow," Jimmy said as he reentered the kitchen.

When Ezra had smoked a bowl with the singer, he picked up his guitar and began to play while Jimmy drew another bowl to ash by himself.

"Goddamn, I like that one," the singer said when Ezra finished playing through "I Could Be the One," a new song he'd been working on since that cold day the previous week. "Play it again."

Ezra's throat almost closed with a thrill when Jimmy joined in to hum a harmony with the chorus.

I could be the lover of your dreams
I could be the stitch to bind your seams
I could be strong when your strength is gone
I could be the one
When the night is cold and you're so blue
You need somebody warm to hold on to
Girl, don't you run to no midnight sun
I could be the one

"Oh, hell yeah," Jimmy crowed after they'd repeated the chorus at the end enough times so that he took over the lead and Ezra switched to harmony. "I ain't too sure about the verses and the bridge yet, but that chorus is a killer." He stood and left the room. After a few moments he was back with a Walkman cassette player. "Let's record that like we just did it."

Ezra looked at his watch. "Man, I've got to go clean a pool before it gets dark."

"In forty-degree weather?"

"Yeah, well, some rich guy—" Ezra said and stopped.

Jimmy stood the recorder on its end in the middle of the tabletop. "Just one time straight through," he said and pressed the record button. "Damn the fuckups."

That was the last Ezra saw of Jimmy James for three quarters of a year. For a short time, he felt something of a breathless thrill whenever he thought of the way their kitchen-warmed voices had harmonized on the chorus of "I Could Be the One." He believed it was destined to replace the song George Strait was supposed to have stolen practically out of Jimmy's throat. He didn't know what the protocol was for a recording artist to lay claim to the songs he wanted for an album, so for a few weeks, he distracted himself with learning as much as he could about the song publishing business to be ready when the inevitable call came.

He spied on Jimmy James's house throughout February and

then throughout the spring, but he never could tell that the man was home. The Camaro never sat in the alley parking area behind the house. No lights ever shone from the kitchen or anywhere else inside. He didn't have a telephone number for the man, and the few times he was brave or drunk enough to knock on the door, nobody answered. He heard rumors of the new album recorded at LSI Studios with Fred Carter Jr. producing, but none of Ezra's small circle of music business acquaintances—mostly grunts and tenderfeet like himself—knew any details beyond these.

Meanwhile, he picked up more and more pools to clean. By late May, he'd quit his mailroom job with Triune and was cleaning an average of ten pools a day, writing and drinking at night but rarely getting out and about on the Row with the new songs he demoed on the Walkman cassette player—identical to Jimmy James's—bought at Circuit City with his tax refund from the previous year. In between the writing and demoing of "As Long as I Can Dream," "Dancer Stay," and "Stories from the Nightlife," co-written with hometown friend Gabriel Tanner, he paced around his room and sang "I Could Be the One," imagining how it would sound played by top-shelf Nashville studio pickers—maybe Henry Strzelecki on bass, Jim Isbell on drums, Beegie Adair on piano, and Fred Carter Jr. himself on guitars.

Late on a Friday night in October, Ezra stood somewhat unsteadily and browsed the LP bins at Cat's Records on West End, drowsily enjoying the fade of U2's "MLK" on the store's sound system. He looked up as Craig, one of the Cat's clerks he was friendly with, dropped the needle on another album.

Probably the last before closing, Ezra thought as he continued flipping through the LPs.

The first notes of a song splashed through the store—some jangling guitars over a bit of drumming that might have passed for a country cousin of Tom Petty's "The Waiting" until a twangy baritone entered and nearly drowned out the rest of the track.

Bad mix, Ezra thought, and then his attention latched on to lyric phrases that struck him as more familiar than they ought to be in an unfamiliar song. He raised his head and widened and then narrowed his eyes as he tried to focus on the album cover displayed beneath the "Now Playing" sign behind the cash register counter. From where he stood, he couldn't read the name of the album or the recording artist but easily recognized the face on the cover. He found himself singing along with the last words of the verse, and as the beat built and the track swelled into the chorus, he already knew what was coming and sang along with that, too.

I could be the lover of your dreams
I could be the stitch to bind your seams
I could be strong when your strength is gone
I could be the one

Craig and the patrons browsing the bins around the store—mostly Vandy students from the campus across West End—turned and looked at him, as did the large police officer working security by the front entrance.

"That's my song!" Ezra howled. "I wrote that!" He felt all eyes follow him to the checkout counter. "Hey, Craig, let me see that a minute." He noticed Craig glance in the direction of the officer before smiling and handing over the empty LP jacket, but he was too excited—and a little too drunk—to care. He studied Jimmy James's face for a moment and then flipped the cover over to look at the track listing.

The first song on side one of the LP was "I Could Be the One."

The thrill tightened Ezra's throat, and welling tears blurred his vision. He snuffled and had to wipe his eyes on the sleeves of his blue jean jacket before he could see the words again. He blinked and focused on the fine print below the song title.

Written by Clovis Binkley (1105 Music, SESAC)

"Who the hell is Clovis Binkley?" he growled and turned and frisbeed the jacket over the heads of ducking shoppers. "That's my goddamn song!"

"Hey, man," Craig said.

"All right, buddy," another voice said. "Let's go before you put someone's eye out."

When Ezra could finally hold something else in his mind alongside the grinning face of Jimmy James and the name Clovis Binkley, it was the realization that he was locked in the back seat of a Nashville Metro PD cruiser. Grateful he wasn't handcuffed, he watched the Vandy kids leave the store with their midnight purchases, watched them look at him and then whisper between themselves as they crossed the parking lot and then the street. At last, the policeman came out of the store, and Ezra watched Craig give a little wave as he locked the door. He waved back and mouthed, *Sorry*, as the big-bellied officer squeezed in behind the wheel and made eye contact in the rearview mirror.

"I'm Officer Calloway," he said. "Your last name?"

"Nice to meet you, sir," Ezra said. "My last name is MacRae, big *m*, little *a-c*, big *r*, little *a-e*."

"Have you got a handle on yourself now?"

"Yessir," Ezra said. "Sorry about—"

"No harm done except a bent album cover." Officer Calloway drew a loud breath through his nose and exhaled between pursed lips. "Where do you live?"

"You're taking me home?"

"Do you have a car here?"

"No, I walked."

"Where do you live?" Officer Calloway said again. When Ezra gave him the address, Calloway eased the patrol car out of Cat's parking lot and left on West End. "So, what was all that about in there?"

"That guy stole my song," Ezra said.

As Officer Calloway drove toward downtown, eventually taking a right on 17th Avenue South, crossing Broadway and rising up the hill to Music Square West, Ezra described his first meetings with Jimmy James, concluding with their January songwriting session—minus the reefer—and his inability to make contact with the singer since then.

Music Square West became 17th Avenue South again.

"What's your legal recourse?" Calloway asked with another glance in the rearview.

"My what?"

"What are you gonna do about it?"

"I've just been wondering," Ezra said. "Don't know there's anything I can do about it." He paused. "Anything legal anyway." He turned and looked out the window. "I clean pools for a living. I've got no reputation to stand on and can't afford a lawyer."

Officer Calloway drove for a block without speaking, and Ezra sat lost in thought in the back of the cruiser.

"Well, I know writing a song ain't just making up shitty ditties," Calloway said. "It's work of its own kind."

"You a songwriter?" Ezra asked.

"No, not me," Calloway chuckled. "But my girlfriend—"

"Wait, that was it," Ezra said. "We just passed my house."

"Sorry, I was thinking about what I'd do if somebody stole one of Beckie's songs."

"That's where he lives," Ezra said as they passed 1105, where, for the first time since January, a light glowed somewhere in the house. "He's home for once."

"Jimmy James lives there?" Officer Calloway rolled slowly past the house toward the light at 17th and Edgehill.

"Yeah," Ezra said.

"I'll swing right at the light and get you home by the alley," Calloway said. "You probably shouldn't be thinking what I think you're thinking." He toggled his turn signal and swung right onto Edgehill.

"That's Waylon's place right there," Ezra said.

"Yeah, Beckie points that out every time we drive by." Officer Calloway eased the patrol car right into the alley.

Ezra settled his elbow on the armrest and his chin in his palm and closed his eyes. He dreaded returning to his lonely room, where he would have to face his guitar—*my hard-working cowriter*—where it stood quiet in its corner and see the lyric sheets spread out on his desk—including the sheet for "I Could Be the One," the possession of which proved nothing. He thought about the tape he and Jimmy—*Clovis*—had made when they were stoned in the singer's kitchen ten months before but couldn't imagine how he could get his hands on it even if it still existed. He opened his eyes and saw they were passing behind Jimmy James's house, where his Camaro Z28 sat nosed up to the back porch.

"Hey, Officer Calloway," he said. "You interested in maybe making a bust for marijuana possession?"

Two hours later, Ezra lay in the darkness of his room. He hadn't been able to fall asleep with the jangling guitars, baritone twang, and perfect vocal harmonies of the stolen song looping through his slowly sobering mind. It became the soundtrack for his inevitable retreat to Runion, where he would live with his best friend Mel on MacOde Farm and eventually grow to be a fat old bachelor who went into town on Saturdays to sit whittling on a bench in front of Town Hall and airing his singular grievance against Nashville and the music business. *You ever hear that Jimmy James hit "I Could Be the One"?* he imagined himself asking anybody who would listen. *I wrote that song, and they stole it from me.* Just at the point when Deputy Boyce came out of Town Hall to tell him it was time to move along, he noticed the dance of blue light though his south-facing window and across his ceiling and the far wall of his room.

He sat up and stood up and looked outside. Then he left the house and walked down the alley toward the swirling blue lights of three patrol cars that surrounded Clovis Binkley's Camaro, both doors and the trunk of which were wide open. He stood in the shadows and saw Officer Calloway and another officer come out the back door with a handcuffed Binkley between them.

"I got a goddamn record just come out this week," Binkley whined. Then he tried to jerk away from the grip the officers had on his arms, and his voice became a roar. "You can't goddamn do this! I'm supposed to leave on tour Sunday."

The two officers made no response, only guided the outraged singer around the end of one patrol car where a third officer stood holding open the vehicle's back door.

Just as they positioned Binkley to seat him, Ezra stepped from the shadows.

"You son of a bitch!" Binkley bellowed, trying to jerk from under the hand Officer Calloway placed on top of his head. "Are you the one behind this bullshit?"

Ezra squinted in the blue light. "I could be," he said and then smiled and turned up the alley toward his house. "Yeah, I could be the one."

THE LONGEST NIGHT

Tina deBellegarde

With my guitar slung over my shoulder I walked into the Hello Dolly Jazz Club hidden in the narrow alley of Pontocho in old Kyoto. I liked to play a few sets once a month to keep myself limber, some soft jazzy ballads. The audience always quieted down to listen to the gentle chords. I preferred a later time slot once the crowd had settled in and had a few drinks.

That night the bar was in an uncharacteristic uproar.

"*Oi, Chari. Kite! Kite!* Come here!" Tengo, the bartender, waved me over. The first time I played bossa nova at the club, he called me Charlie Byrd and ever since I've been Chari.

My curiosity piqued, I wandered over.

"Sapporo, Tengo, thanks." I stuck my hand in my pocket, but Tengo stopped me.

"Drinks are on Malcolm." With a big smile he turned to the end of the bar and there he was. I should have been happy. My father. Who lives in Manhattan. Here on my doorstep, at my favorite hangout in Kyoto. The first time in ten years. I have lived here all through university and another six years setting myself up. Moving twice, falling in love and breaking up more than once, and setting up a business. In all that time, my father, Malcolm Grant, classically trained pianist, jazz master and traveler of the world, has never found the time in his itinerary to visit me. Now he was here. Most sons would have been happy.

But I never got along with my father. I wasn't the spitting image of him. We didn't like the same things. After a while we settled into a paradigm: if I said up, he said down, if I liked blue, he liked yellow. If I said something was interesting, he immediately shot it down. The older I got, the higher the stakes, the more we argued. Eventually I stopped trying, we drifted further and further apart, until finally I packed my bags and went as far away as the globe would allow.

He stood up when he saw me, walked over, a gleam in his eyes, a little watery. I could almost think he was touched to see me. I smiled in spite of myself. I have always wanted to show him my life, to share my exotic world, my accomplishments. And now I could.

"Ian." He hugged me. I allowed myself to be happy to see him. To hope for the best. This was long overdue. I hugged back. In that moment I had decided to give it a shot. What did I have to lose? I was no longer the boy he bullied and ignored. I was sure he was no longer the same either.

He looked terrific as usual, with a perfect suit tailored to his trim build. I noticed his hands, slender and strong, as he lit a cigarette. His hair never thinned, but it was graying a bit on the sides which only made him look more sophisticated. His glasses were the chicest of chic. He looked like an Italian movie star and I was as enamored as the rest of the patrons. I forgot how much charisma he had, how he filled a room. How everyone held their breath waiting for him to talk or perform or approve.

"Dad, what are you doing here? Why didn't you call? I would have picked you up from the airport."

"I finished a performance in Tokyo, and instead of running home I decided to surprise you."

"Well, I'm glad you're here." Briefly, I considered saying that it was about time. That we could have done this a dozen times if he had only bothered to come out to Kyoto or given me enough time to get to Tokyo. Many times he would call from Tokyo, say that he was off to the airport in the morning, could I come out and see him? But on short notice I was never able to drop my work, or cough up the two hundred dollars for the Shinkansen express train. He always gave me a hard time that I hadn't tried hard enough. But I had a business, I had responsibilities. He never stayed an extra day or two, no matter how many times I asked.

But he was here now.

"Where's your luggage? How long will you be staying?"

"Ah, don't worry about all that." He waved away the smoke from his eyes. "I have my stuff at the hotel up the road here."

"At the Ritz Carlton? Malcolm? Why would you come to Kyoto to stay there? Stay with me. It's not like you would be putting me out."

Too easily I slipped back into calling him Malcolm. He hated it when I called him by his first name. But I started in middle school when we were going through a rough patch and I had never stopped.

"Yes, I know, but I'm not one for quaint places. I like my amenities. Besides, I'm leaving in the morning, not even enough time to get all the way to your place in the hills."

I don't know why I was hurt, I shouldn't have been. I know the man, and yet...

That night remains a blur. We started with drinks at Hello Dolly. Tengo created a drink in Malcolm's honor: pear nectar, vodka and pomegranate seeds. Tengo is known for grilling his guests about their preferences, and not just flavors. What they do in their free time, what music they listen to, favorite colors, favorite season. He is a master of capturing the essence of a patron in a drink. And he certainly captured Malcolm. Flavorful and smooth with a splash of color.

I drank modestly. Malcolm on the other hand kept buying rounds.

"Haven't learned to hold your liquor yet?"

After a couple of drinks, it was time for my set. I hadn't performed in front of my father in years. I left New York for a reason. In fact, I didn't play at all for quite a long time. It was Japan that gave me back my love of jazz.

But I had my regular spot and I'd be damned if I'd back down. Besides, I was good. I wanted to show him I was good, that the crowd loved my music and that the crowd was mine. I grabbed my guitar and hopped up. Everyone knew me, they all clapped, but no one louder than my father. It was unsettling the way I could make out his peculiar way of clapping among all the others. Almost a tease, like he was clapping because he knew he should. But maybe I wasn't giving him any credit. He was here, right?

I played a few of my favorites. I could tell the patrons enjoyed them. Some of my regulars had seen me play my first gig in Japan in an old record shop down the street and had been following me ever since. Heads were bobbing gently, shoulders swaying, fingers tapping. Some sipped their drinks lazily.

The rule of thumb was a performer shouldn't get upset if the customers talk in a bar setting, and they rarely did here. They always listened. That night every now and then I could hear my father's voice breaking through the music. He whispered, but how quiet could he have been if I could hear him from the stage? He was taking credit for teaching me.

"He was a stubborn kid and didn't want to practice."

"Ah yes, I taught him that."

"Oh, but that there, that was a weak transition. He can do better."

I finished my set early and came down for a drink. A couple of the ex-pats were in the aisles and slapped my back or shook my hand. "Good sounds tonight, Ian."

Tengo handed me the bowl of sesame crackers he knew I loved. Before I managed to find a seat, they were calling for my father. "Malcolm, Malcolm!" They wanted him to perform. Of course they would. He hadn't been there an hour, but they were in the presence of a star. You couldn't blame them.

He feigned resistance at first. Shook his head with charm. But I knew it was unraveling exactly as he had hoped. There was nothing he desired more than to burn blue at the center of the fire. I had seen it first-hand many times.

Humbly he walked toward the piano. Then he turned as if to go back to his seat. They booed him and waved him back to the stage. Did they know he was playing them? Did they care? He wouldn't go up until they begged and they always did. He put his hands together in a practiced motion and bowed to the crowd. They cheered him on.

He finally sat at the piano, taking his time lifting the lid. He bent his head as if he were thinking, but he didn't need to think. I knew what he would play before he started. He made them wait, panting.

He lifted his head, his hand grazed the keys. He barely caressed them, like he was teasing a lover. The audience took in a breath. He knew exactly what he was doing. Then he stopped. He turned towards the audience, and in simple but gracious Japanese, a language I had not yet mastered after all these years, gave an opening soliloquy. He had them laughing before he once again touched the keys. He played a few lazy bars, then let loose with some of the most vibrant jazz piano playing ever heard at this modest club. This was a treat for everyone, even for me. We were enthralled.

When he finished, the small crowd cheered. You would have thought it was a packed theater. He glowed in the center, where he belonged, where he resided always, like the sun. He was so comfortable there, I suppose he deserved it. After all, the limelight was not for the weak.

I looked over at my empty drink and then up at Tengo. He served me a glass of seltzer with a wedge of lime.

"It's just one night, Charlie, and then we all go back to

normal. Have some *goma senbei* to munch on." He pushed more crackers my way.

"*Arigatou*, Tengo. Always got my back."

My father wandered over and took the seat next to me.

"What are you eating? Looks good."

I reluctantly passed the bowl toward him. They were my favorite and Tengo stocked them just for me. "Sesame crackers."

Malcolm retracted his hand. "Oops. Nope. I'm allergic to sesame."

Fine, more for me. Something of mine he can't take for a change.

I enjoyed that small victory for a few minutes. It was rare that my father showed a vulnerability of any kind, probably because he had so few, and I had to confess I enjoyed it for a moment. But that's not what the night was supposed to be. So I pushed the negativity away and tried again.

"Tengo, how about some wasabi nuts?"

"Coming right up, Charlie."

Then the evening took a turn. Aki and her sister Natsumi walked in. Two lovely sisters from Osaka who ran the record shop down the street. I used to date Natsumi, I dodged a bullet there. But Aki was special. She was kind, she loved jazz, she read the same things I read. She was serious and authentic. Natsumi was all flash and no substance. It was hard to believe they were sisters. Natsumi was more Malcolm's type.

Aki noticed me and I felt a twinge of redness jump to my face, she had caught me staring, but I forgot my discomfort when she opened up with a broad smile just for me.

She approached. Before I could offer her my seat, my father jumped up, grabbed her hand and kissed it. He actually kissed it. He offered her his stool with a proper, "*Dozo*." Then turned back to me. "Introduce me to your lovely friend."

They talked and talked while I played my second set. It sapped my energy. All I could see was Aki tilting her head toward his and giggling at what must have been another ridiculous story that he had practiced on every pretty face. There was a reason Mom and Dad were no longer together.

Aki was at her most attentive. I knew she was captivated once she started playing with her hair. The kicker was when he slowly lifted his hand and brushed the sweep of her hair over her shoulder. So delicately, so deliberate. He rubbed it briefly between his fingers before finishing the motion.

When my set was over, I stepped off the stage. They were both standing by the bar with their coats on. Malcolm threw me mine.

"Let's go."

We spent the night bar hopping. He had never bothered to visit this quaint city, he was a Manhattan and Tokyo kind of guy. Now he was enchanted by it.

"Why didn't you tell me how spectacular this city is?"

Bar after bar. Drink after drink. Piano after piano.

My father grew more animated, and more charming by the hour. But I could feel my legs getting wobbly. I tried to sneak a seltzer between every few drinks. I still consumed more on that one night than any month of my life. I needed a shower and a change of clothes. My father had acquired instead a crumpled appearance that somehow looked casually chic on him.

At the last bar, my friend's Irish pub, he challenged me to an arm wrestling match and then darts. I shouldn't have fallen for it. I should have remembered that I got my vulnerability to alcohol from Mom. Malcolm used it as fuel. He handily beat me at both.

To be fair to myself, the wrestling was touch and go and I even got him once. I slammed his arm down and he called me a bad winner. But after two out of three, he won, and I didn't want to keep losing in front of Aki. He made sure the entire bar knew he was my dad. He worked hard to look young, but now he wanted to gloat that he had beaten a man more than half his age, even if it was his own son.

Finally, Aki was hungry. We stopped at an all-night noodle shop first. I ordered my favorite black sesame ramen. It always warmed my soul.

My father leaned over Aki's shoulder to read the menu. "I'll have what you're having. Aki, will you order for me?"

Each sip of broth brought me relief, but I was still losing ground. Aki seemed to get her second wind and begged for ice-cream. She knew the *conbini*, the local 24-hour convenience store around the corner, carried just what she liked. We took our ice-cream and walked along the river until we found a place to sit.

Once seated and out of the limelight, Malcolm deflated. In the strong glare of the street lamp I could see the color draining from his face with each lick of the speckled ice-cream.

Then he stopped.

"Ian, I'm done for the night."

Just like that. First, he showed up out of nowhere, unannounced, upstaged me with my hard-earned friendships, my music spot, my sacred place. Even humiliated me in front of the girl of my dreams.

I desperately wanted to go home, but I wouldn't give him the satisfaction.

"Let me finish my ice-cream."

"Sorry, Ian. Now. I've got to leave now."

Then I looked over my cone and saw his face. His paleness was alarming. Not even white but pasty. His ice cream ran down the sides of the cone.

I jumped up. Aki saw what was happening and joined me on the other side of my father. He got up slowly. His legs wobbling. The sweat now making his forehead slick. He loosened his tie, a rarely seen motion for him. We each stood on one side and grabbed an arm. He started to resist and then changed his mind when he realized he needed us.

We hailed a taxi and got him to my place in no time. Despite what he said, my place was near the northern edge of the city and not far. Once in the house, we removed his jacket and made him comfortable on the sofa. Aki rushed to the kitchen. Even in the midst of all the commotion I remember stopping long enough to admire her. How lovely she looked and how much I would enjoy seeing her in there preparing a meal with me every night.

In no time, Aki appeared with a cold compress. Her brow was furrowed. "Your father is a nice man. I am worried."

"Don't be. He's as strong as an ox." She looked at me quizzically. I pulled out my arms to my sides to demonstrate something large. She still didn't understand. "*Uchi, uchi.*" I repeated. Then I made my fingers into horns on the top of my head.

"He is as strong as the horns on a big house?"

"No, no. I mean *ushi*." I stuttered. I needed to get more Japanese classes. This wasn't the first time I had mixed up my words.

"Oh, an ox, a cow?"

"Yes, it is an expression in English. Strong as an ox." She didn't seem convinced.

"Maybe I should stay?"

"No, go home, It's so late. I'm sorry I can't take you, but go. The taxi is waiting. I can handle it from here." She turned to leave, hesitated and returned. She placed a tiny kiss on my cheek and left.

I returned to the small tatami room.

"What kind of ice cream did you say that was?"

"It was *kurogoma*, Aki's favorite."

"I've never had anything like that. It was delicious. But it didn't agree with me. Can you get my pills in my jacket?"

I rummaged around. I found his business cards, a coconut

chap stick, his EpiPen, and the key card to the Ritz. "They're not here."

He withdrew two pills from his pants pocket. "Here they are. I should have taken them earlier."

"What are you taking? Are you sure? You're not looking so good."

"They're my blood pressure meds. I should have taken them hours ago. But, you know, no quicker way to look old than slugging back a few pills." He looked a little revived. Not as gaunt as just a few moments ago.

"You'd look younger taking pills than if you were dead from a heart attack."

He responded with a feeble smile. "An old leopard can't change his spots."

I brought him a glass of water and watched him take his pills.

"So kurogoma...Kuro means black but what is goma?"

"Sesame, black sesame—"

"Sesame? Sesame? What's the matter with you? I told you I'm allergic." His scolding voice was unsteady, but becoming stronger.

"Okay, okay, how allergic can you be?"

"I'm actually relieved. I was beginning to think I was having a heart attack. I might have my EpiPen at the hotel. I can't remember. But it seems to be passing I think." He finished the rest of the water in the glass.

Now it was my turn to be relieved.

"If it's not in my jacket, I guess you'll have to get me back to the hotel, just to stay on the safe side."

"I think—. Let me check."

I ran to his jacket again, my hand quickly found the EpiPen. But I didn't withdraw it. The tea kettle whistled at that moment. I grabbed the EpiPen and took it with me to the kitchen. For some sick reason I wasn't ready to give it to him.

I made tea instead. As the water rumbled, I remembered all

those times he had humiliated me in front of my middle school friends. I thought about how he didn't come to my games and how he thought my sports were not good enough. I played soccer, he wanted me to play golf. I played the guitar, he wanted me to play piano. I never measured up and he wasted no time telling me so.

I reached into the cabinet for the tea. *Matcha* or *ocha*? I picked up the *matcha* and then put it back and reached for the stronger *ocha*. Behind it was the sesame paste. I took it down and without thinking too long about it scooped a spoonful and added it to the *ocha* and warm soy milk. I frothed it up and took a sip. It was delicious.

"Here, Dad. Have some tea. It's not what you're used to, but it's my favorite and it will cure what ails you."

He sipped it. And then some more. I sat across from him. And watched.

The perspiration increased. His breathing got raspy.

"Have another sip dad. It'll soothe your throat, maybe you can sleep a little and then I'll get you to the hotel."

I watched him drink and remembered when he had to win every game. Most parents let their kids win a few games of cards or chess. But not my dad.

He took another sip.

I remembered him hitting on my fifth grade teacher in front of Mom.

Another sip. He closed his eyes. He dozed. Then started.

I remembered all those times as a kid that I wanted him to disappear and leave us alone.

I watched and remembered.

Sweat rolled down his forehead. His pristine shirt was soaked. His weak voice got weaker.

He opened his mouth in order to breathe. He unbuttoned a few more buttons. "Ian, Ian. I don't know what's going on. I think you need to get me to a hospital."

His eyes fluttered...

Then I remembered the kiss Aki gave me in the corridor.

I closed my eyes. When I opened them I no longer saw the perfect man charming a crowd. I saw an old man, slouched and unsure of himself. His hair mussed, his shirt wrinkled and drenched in sweat. A man who just hours ago commanded every room he walked into, now frail and inarticulate. I saw his pale skin for what it was, the announcement of his failing health, the end of the golden boy and the beginning of his golden years. I saw him for who he was, not who he pretended to be. I saw him vulnerable and scared.

And that was all I needed to finally see. A real person, someone with flaws, someone like the rest of us. I needed to even the playing field.

I reached into my pocket, my hand resting on the EpiPen. I felt its curves. My fist clenched around it. I pulled my hand out, the EpiPen heavy in my fist.

Then I remembered how Malcolm had played with Aki's hair by the bar during my set. How he brushed her silky strands over her shoulder but not before he slowly, provocatively, rubbed them between his fingers.

I quietly returned my closed fist to my pocket.

THE BOYZ IN THE BAND

Mary Dutta

"So," the morning show host leaned in confidentially, "any chance Charlie Drake will be joining you for your twentieth anniversary concert?"

Brandon gave his stock answer: "He's always welcome," and gave the camera an exaggerated wink.

"You heard it here first, folks," the host said. "There's a chance that country's biggest star will return to his boy band roots. A big thank you to The Boyz for joining us this morning, and now back to you, Jim."

She was out of her seat and halfway across the studio before the stagehand had removed the lapel mic from the first of the four bandmates. Sean slid off the high-backed stool where he sat slumped and started yanking out the wire inside his shirt, the mic broadcasting his slurred swearing.

The band's manager Samantha waited for them in the wings. "Great work, guys," she said. But, of course, they paid her to be enthusiastic.

"Sean, where's your jacket?" she asked, with a tight-lipped smile. "We talked about this. The band's look only works if it's cohesive."

Sean looked bemused. "The green room, maybe?"

"I'll get it," Brandon said. It would give him a chance to check his email again without Samantha commenting, and he could slip some bagels into his messenger bag while he was at it. He wound his way through the back corridors, humming the The Boyz' first hit. A couple of women seemed to recognize him, although they did not seem particularly excited about it, a depressingly common reaction. As he passed them on his way back, Sean's jacket strategically draped to hide his bulging bag, he could swear one muttered "has-been."

Samantha offered to take them to a local restaurant for a post-show recap. Brandon never turned down a free meal these days, even if it came with a lecture on using interviews to trigger viral content. Sean, who increasingly did not seem to know or care where he was, appeared to be joining them. The other two band members begged off. Again.

Sean leaned against the wall of their booth, his jacket wadded up on the seat beside him. With his trademark tousled hair pulled back to expose incipient crows' feet and graying temples, he looked a lot less like his younger self. His short sleeves exposed the tattoos acquired during his failed attempt at a solo rock career. Brandon wondered if he could afford to have them removed, or whether his bandmate's finances were as precarious as his own.

The tantalizing smell of bacon wafted from the kitchen, but as Brandon carefully folded his own jacket, which he could no longer button, he reminded himself that there was no point in the band wearing coordinating outfits if he couldn't fit into his. And he couldn't afford to buy bigger sizes.

"We need to talk about your upcoming gig in Nashville," Samantha said.

Sean raised a hip flask. "A toast," he said, "to Nashville and its platinum-selling star—our dearly departed bandmate Chazz."

"He's not dead," Samantha said, "he just changed his name from Chazz to Charlie."

"Okay, then, a toast to country music's world-class fake— Charlie Drake." Sean topped off his coffee and returned the flask to his crumpled jacket.

"Speaking of whom," Brandon said, "have you managed to set up a meeting?"

Samantha's tight-lipped smile was back. "No. I've reached out to his people several times. And I already told you I would keep you posted." She put down her menu and gave him her full attention. "There is a way to do these things, and it doesn't involve you going around me to try to contact Chazz directly. You need to focus on The Boyz."

Brandon focused on nothing but The Boyz. Promoting. Rehearsing. Dreaming up ways to keep their dwindling fan base engaged. Samantha had other clients, but Brandon had only one career. Trying to connect with Chazz was a key piece of his last-ditch plan to keep the band alive.

That night's show validated all Brandon's efforts. The venue was small but the love emanating from the crowd was tremendous, almost as ardent as the response to the Elvis impersonator headlining the event. The four of them hit every note and crushed every dance move. We've still got it, Brandon thought as he toweled off sweat backstage. Our audience is still out there. The pandemic had hit the band hard, but now people were desperate for a good time to make up for the long shut down. If Chazz would just give them one night, they could ride the nostalgia rush for at least another few years. But Chazz hadn't spoken to any of them since the band broke up. And he wasn't even Chazz anymore.

The thrill of the show wore off by the time Brandon returned home. When he was twenty-three, the view over the lights of LA from the deck of his house had been worth every exorbitant penny. Now, he was one missed mortgage payment away from foreclosure. On both of his mortgages. The once full multi-car garage contained nothing but teetering boxes of unsold The Boyz merchandise. At least the drought gave him an excuse for the dead lawn he could not afford to maintain. He had even started sweating the cost of hair gel, given his current productto-hair-strand ratio. Brandon believed in The Boyz, would always believe, but he had to face the hard truth that boy bands today belonged only to pretty Korean boys.

His phone chirped a text alert. He always hoped for Chazz, but the cracked screen showed Sean had shared a link to an article: "Ten Things Charlie Drake Can't Live Without." *I see we didn't make the list*, Sean commented, adding two rolling-on-the-floor-laughing emojis. Brandon didn't laugh. Maybe Sean's seemingly perpetual buzz gave him a different perspective. He always told Brandon not to worry about Chazz. But then, Sean was not too proud to work short-term and seasonal jobs between gigs. For Brandon, the thought of a fan recognizing him as he called their name for their latte or their rideshare kept him up at night and away from day jobs.

Brandon could not resist reading the article. What were the ten things Chazz valued more than his former bandmates? *Number 10: Waylon Jennings' autobiography.* Brandon would like to see Chazz pick the country singer out of a line up. *Number 7: His granddaddy's harmonica.* Nobody in Chazz's hometown of Anaheim called their grandparents that. *Number 4: Martin Lifespan 2.0 guitar strings.* Chazz couldn't play the guitar when he was one of The Boyz. Now he never posed without one, and had new strings delivered every week. *Number 1: The biscuits at Odette's Café in Nashville*, where he headed for breakfast every Thursday morning he was in town. That one did not annoy Brandon. It gave him an idea.

The next week, he zeroed out his frequent flyer miles and flew to Nashville. Having settled in at Odette's when it opened Thursday morning, he nursed his third cup of coffee and watched the door. The server came around periodically to ask if he wanted to order anything else. She looked doubtful, given the miniscule bites he was taking to eke out his plain biscuit, the cheapest item on the menu.

"I'm just wondering," he said, "when Charlie Drake usually comes in."

She pulled back the coffee carafe she had extended toward his cup. "Nobody bothers him here."

"Oh, I'm an old friend," Brandon said, turning on his most winning smile and cocking his head at the angle he assumed in all his head shots.

She snorted and walked away without pouring him coffee.

The conversational buzz rose around him, and Brandon looked around to see Chazz pulling out a chair at a table in a far corner. He must have slipped in the back way. He had left his prop guitar at home, but was wearing a cowboy hat which he handed to a muscular guy who surveyed the room and then planted himself between Chazz's table and the rest of the diners. The chatter died down and Brandon steeled himself to approach his former bandmate. He imagined the viral video of their reunion racing across the internet, captioned Music City Magic maybe, or Boyz and Biscuits. Should he throw an arm around Chazz's shoulders? Strike one of their poses from an album cover?

The brawny man moved into Brandon's path as he approached Chazz. "Help you?" he said.

"I just need a minute with Chazz. I mean Charlie."

"Mr. Drake is having breakfast, and I'm going to ask you to step away and let him do it in peace."

Brandon looked beyond him to where Chazz sat, absorbed in his phone.

"Hey, Chazz," he called. "It's me, Brandon. What a surprise, bro!"

The country star granted Brandon a flicker of eye contact, then gave the bodyguard a quick shake of his head.

"Alright, move along," the guard said.

Brandon gazed at Chazz. It was the closest he had been to him in years. He had aged well. Money could buy a lot of skin care and personal training.

"Move along," the beefy guy repeated, loud enough to draw attention. This wasn't the viral moment Brandon was aiming for. "I'll email you," Brandon called, waving vaguely in Chazz's direction. He headed toward the door, for once hoping no one recognized him.

That night he checked in with Samantha, who still had received no reply from Chazz's people. He did not mention he was in Nashville. She warned Brandon to leave things in her hands, but her hands held nothing he wanted. He emailed Chazz again, pouring out everything that he did not get the chance to say in person at Odette's. He reminisced about the early days of The Boyz, praised Chazz for his incredible career as Charlie Drake, and explained how transformative it would be for his former boy band, make that his former *friends*, if he could take just a moment to appear at their 20th anniversary concert. Chazz wouldn't even need to learn the choreography, just stand center stage and sing one of their old hits. Surely that wasn't too much to ask for old times' sake? Brandon recognized that his description of his own desperate circumstances bordered on unhinged, but clearly Chazz had not picked up on the hints he had dropped in all his previous communications.

Brandon was not going to leave town without one final attempt to get to Chazz in person. He maxed out his last credit card and hired an online investigator to find Chazz's carefully guarded home address. He soon realized the futility of his plan. A guard booth sat at the end of the driveway, next to two ornate scrolled gates decorated with an enormous letter D and a slew of musical notes Chazz undoubtedly couldn't identify. Even people with legitimate business did not get past the gates. Delivery trucks came and went, but the guard signed for all the packages without letting any of them beyond the booth. Brandon briefly considered sneaking in through the estate's heavily wooded side yard, but closer inspection revealed an electrified fence. He put his battered rental car in gear and rolled noisily away, keeping one eye on the rearview mirror in case Chazz emerged.

He returned to LA and tried to take Sean's advice not to

worry about Chazz, passing the time watching the band's early videos and sorting through his memorabilia. He regretted not selling a few of the backstage passes and autographed set lists while they still had some value. Stumbling across some old contact information for Chazz's family, he did not hesitate to send a barrage of messages. Maybe they could get him access to Chazz when The Boyz arrived in Nashville for their upcoming show.

When their concert date arrived, the band members trickled into Music City. Back in the day, they would have arrived together. Brandon feared the other Boyz would soon stop coming at all. Sean didn't show up until halfway through the soundcheck, then staggered around and forgot half the lyrics. Luckily, he seemed more lucid closer to showtime. He saw Brandon scanning the audience from the wings.

"He's not coming," he said.

Brandon didn't bother pretending that he did not understand. Even a zoned-out Sean could see through him.

His disappointment at Chazz's failure to appear lingered the next morning. He checked for replies from Chazz's family, a fruitless effort. But there was something better—an email from Chazz. He must have slipped into the concert like he had the restaurant, Brandon thought. He had obviously remembered the bonds they shared and decided to help them out. He would give The Boyz a jumpstart and they would live to sing another day. Brandon leaned close to his cracked screen and realized he was crossing his fingers. *Just one song*, he prayed. *Just one night*. He opened the email.

"Notice to Cease and Desist," he read. "Unwarranted harassment including but not limited to...." He did not need to read the rest. He knew what it meant. He would have to cease and desist life as he knew it if Chazz did not reconsider. No more Boyz. No more band. There had to be a way to get to his ex-bandmate and make him see that abandoning them was a mistake. Only his ringing phone stopped him from dashing out to find Chazz.

"Finally!" Samantha yelled when he answered. "Have you heard?"

"I just did."

"Thank God none of you have left town," Samantha said. "I've already been in touch with the venue and they're keeping you on for an open-ended run. People are going to be looking for any connection they can find to the star they lost."

"What are you talking about?"

"I thought you said you heard. Charlie Drake is dead."

Brandon dropped the phone.

"Are you there?" Samantha's voice was muffled by the carpet. "Listen, I'll text you the place where we'll all meeting to plan next steps. I'll see you there."

Brandon retrieved his phone and sat on the edge of his hotel bed, listing to one side on the sagging mattress. He clicked from one news site to another. The authorities had released no information on the sudden death other than to say there were no immediate signs of foul play. He scrolled through the flood of social media posts lamenting Chazz's death. The Boyz got their share of shout outs. #Chazz started trending along with the Charlie Drake mentions. But none of these internet posters had lost as much as Brandon had, whose dreams had died with Chazz.

When Brandon finally made it to the restaurant where Samantha had arranged for them to meet, the hostess gasped when she saw him. "I'm so sorry for your loss," she said, her voice breaking. He thanked her and followed her to the table where Sean already sat, jacket on and hair tousled to perfection.

Sean nodded and pushed a cup of coffee toward him. Brandon nodded back.

"I can't believe Chazz is gone," Brandon said after a long silence. "And this means the end for us too. His coming back to the band was our only hope."

"The end? I think it means a beginning."

"Are you drunk?"

"No, I've been sober for 12 years," Sean said. He pulled the flask from his jacket. "This? It's just water. Looks like vodka though, doesn't it?"

"Come on, you've been slurring and staggering every time I see you."

"I can act, not just sing and dance. Sometimes it helps to have people underestimate you. It keeps them from seeing what you're up to."

"Why would you want that?" Brandon said.

"You know," Sean said, ignoring his question, "you never would take a seasonal job. But I came to Nashville a while ago and got hired to deliver packages. Including a lot of Martin Lifespan 2.0 guitar strings to one Charlie Drake."

"So?"

"I'm just speculating here, of course, but I'd bet Chazz's cause of death turns out to be some kind of contact poison. Maybe from strumming toxic guitar strings." Sean took a sip of coffee. "I told you not to worry about him."

"But why?" Brandon said. "I'm broke. The bookings are drying up. We needed Chazz to give us a boost. Without him, we have no boy band."

"You're right," Sean said. "We have a *tribute* band. And we'll have one as long as the fans are alive and the star is dead. Just ask all those Elvis impersonators we've shared a bill with."

The conversational buzz rose in the restaurant. Brandon looked around and realized people were staring at them. A lot of people.

Sean smiled and raised his coffee up. "A toast," he said, "to our dearly departed bandmate Chazz."

Brandon smiled back, then raised his cup and toasted his fans.

MUSIC CITY ROW

Michael Ferreter

The show was over, but the crowd called out for more.

They wanted one more song, but Johnny was the opener on this tour, not the headliner, and openers don't do encores. He acknowledged the cheers with a nod and the tip of an imaginary Stetson but still walked offstage, cowboy boots clomping on wooden beams, disappearing to chants of *"John-ny Cool! John-ny Cool!"*

In the hallway behind the stage, blocking his path to the dressing room, were two men in suits. The older one was tall and rail-thin, dark close-cropped hair graying at the temples. The younger man was stocky with a blond buzzcut. They were unsmiling with rigid postures. Cops.

"Johnny Cole?" the tall one asked over the noise.

"You hear 'em shouting my name, don't you?" As Johnny said it, the house lights came up in the main room and the cheers melted to a groan and into chatter.

"Mr. Cole, Detectives Harkins and Steinkoffer, Nashville PD."

"Come on now, that might not have been my best performance, but I reckon it don't cross the line into criminal." Johnny flashed a wide smile that neither man returned.

Confusion replaced confidence on Johnny's face. "Hold on, did you say Nashville? I thought tonight is Knoxville?"

"Yes sir, we are in Knoxville, Tennessee, right now. We came over from Nashville. Did you conduct a musical performance in Nashville last night?" The lines around Harkins's humorless eyes put him at fifty, maybe mid-forties with accumulated stress.

"If you say so." The detectives glanced at each other wordlessly. "Look, I know the life of the traveling musician looks glamorous. But I'm telling you, if I didn't have a calendar, I wouldn't know where in tar hill I am on any given night. If you say tonight is Knox, then sure on buddy, I played Music City last night."

Johnny looked over his shoulder at fans gathering near the back of the music room. "Listen fellas, sorry you missed the show, but I got to go man the merch table." The cops exchanged glances again.

"Merch," Johnny repeated. "Merchandise. T-shirts, CDs...you know, the way working musicians make money in the digital age?"

"And songwriting royalties?" There was a metallic edge to Harkins's voice, an inference that Johnny couldn't quite place but didn't like.

"Yes, I suppose so."

Steinkoffer finally spoke into the silence. "Well sir, we are sorry about that, but I do believe we need to talk right now." His bulk took up most of the narrow hallway. He made no attempt to move.

As Johnny thought on how to stall the detectives, scanning from the merch table to the cops, the audio tech he had met earlier at soundcheck approached. "Hey, Keys, right?" The man stopped. "Can I ask you a big favor?" Johnny explained his situation with the police. He handed the sound tech a wad of cash and explained the pricing of items. "I'm much obliged, Keys, I'll be there right soon as I finish with these gentlemen."

Keys nodded, and the thick chain of silver at his waist jangled as he walked away.

"I guess that's why they call him Keys, don't you think?" Johnny grinned at the stone-faced cops.

"Is there a place we can talk?" Harkins's tone made clear he wanted to refocus.

"This way," Johnny said, sliding between the cops down the hallway and turning into a side room.

This dressing room was no better and no worse than others on the tour: table with a lighted makeup mirror, couch, a few chairs, enough space for instrument cases. An ice bucket filled with bottles of beer. A feeble attempt had been made to cover up years of body odor and stale alcohol with a citrusy air freshener. Johnny picked up an acoustic guitar from its stand and plopped onto the couch. He noodled riffs as the detectives took chairs across from him. Sensing their demeanor, he set the guitar back in the stand.

Johnny leaned across to the ice bucket and pulled a bottle of beer. "Y'all don't mind if I hydrate after all that wailing and emoting?" The bottle pressed against Johnny's push broom mustache.

Steinkoffer fixed him with a stern look. "Actually, we prefer to do these interviews without the influence of drugs and alcohol."

Johnny blinked and held up the bottle like a chemist's flask. "You'd deprive a working man of this? You think I'll be too gone off one beer to answer your questions?"

Harkins raised a hand before Steinkoffer could answer. "In this case, I think we can let Mr. Cole enjoy his beverage." Johnny saw Steinkoffer mouth the word 'protocol' but Harkins didn't appear to notice. Steinkoffer pouted, shaking cheeks that hadn't shed the last bit of baby fat. Just turned thirty, Johnny guessed, but could easily pass for twenty-five. A benefit in any other walk of life but probably a detriment when one wanted to present the gravitas of authority.

Harkins looked up from a worn leather notepad. "I believe we established earlier that you had a musical performance last night in Nashville. Did you have an altercation after that performance?"

"Hey, trouble finds me." Johnny took a pull from the bottle as the detectives exchanged glances again. "What? 'Trouble Finds Me,' it's the name of my first big hit, off the *American Country* record." Silence from the two cops. "Oh-kee, I guess you gentlemen aren't familiar with my earlier work." This time, Johnny didn't smile.

"Sorry mister, I know a fair bit about country music, and I never heard of you or your songs." Steinkoffer's defiant tone sharpened every word.

Johnny relaxed his shoulders and leaned back. "Yes, detectives, I had an altercation after the 'musical performance' last night in Nashville. Nothing much happened and I can't believe you'd come out to Knoxville to ask me about it. There was some shouting and shoving but nothing beyond that. I've been in worse barfights by far."

Harkins cracked the faintest hint of a smile. "That sounds like it should be a song lyric."

"Yeah?" Johnny pondered that. "I'll remember to write that down."

Steinkoffer shot a look of annoyance at his partner and held out an electronic tablet to Johnny, showing a driver's license photo. "You recognize this man?"

"Reckon it's a younger, thinner version of the guy who hassled me last night after the show."

"You never saw this man before last night?"

"Not that I can recall. What's his name?"

"Williams. Billy Ray Williams." Harkins answered this time. "He runs a fan website for an old band called The Gen-U-Wine Gentlemen."

Harkins's pause was the cue for Johnny to tell the story. "Before I went solo, I was in a band called the Gen-U-Wine Gentlemen. We all had nicknames—I was Johnny Cole aka Johnny Cool. The other main songwriter besides me was

'Fabulous' Freddie McPherson. We had a falling out over writing credits and royalties and all that bullshit. Round about that same time I fired our crooked manager—course, we didn't know he was crooked 'til the money went missing. The band broke up. I went solo and put out three records since then. About six months ago some blogger started making a stink, saying that AI and all that computer shit had proved Freddie alone wrote songs that were co-written by me or written solo by me." Johnny was suddenly aware of how long he had been talking. "But I guess y'all knew that already, didn't you. And I still don't understand the hullabaloo about a shouting match in an alley." He took another long pull of beer.

"Mr. Cole, we're homicide detectives." Harkins leaned forward in his chair ever so slightly. "Billy Ray Williams is dead. He was murdered last night."

Johnny's hand floated up to caress his stubbled chin, the lanky index finger brushing his mustache. "Goll-damn." The room fell silent. "Who killed him?"

"Well, Mr. Cole, we thought you might shed some light on that subject."

"Me?" Then it hit him. "As in, did I kill him? Sorry to disappoint you mister, but we had it out and he got his ass hauled outta there and then I left." The detectives waited for Johnny to say more, but he was silent. "How did this fella die?"

Steinkoffer scrolled through his tablet before answering. "Early indications are that he died from a direct punch to the thoracic area, causing a low energy trauma to the chest wall and ventricular fibrillation leading to sudden cardiac arrhythmia. It's called *commotio cordis.*"

"Holy hell, you lost me there. Someone hit him so hard his heart stopped?"

Steinkoffer grimaced. "That would be a layman's definition, yes."

"Well." Johnny smiled and two unsmiling faces stared back. "I might be a scrapper when the occasion calls for it, but I can't

111

punch a man mean enough to stop his damn heart from beating." No reaction.

"I mean, look at these hands." He splayed his fingers, the left wingspan broad enough to cover six frets. "These hands were made for plucking, not punching."

Harkins chuckled. "That's another good line for your next song."

Johnny nodded his appreciation. "Besides, there were half a dozen people standing around in that alley. Nobody saw anything because nothing happened. He shoved me and I shoved him back and we got separated."

"Well, you're right on that point," Steinkoffer said. "But for the fact he wasn't killed then. It happened a couple hours later after the nightclub closed. No witnesses. Can you tell us where you were around 2 a.m. this morning?"

Johnny's eyebrows crawled up his forehead. "At 2 a.m.? I was back home. Not my home of course, the house of a buddy in Nashville, up there in Buena Vista north of downtown. We met up for an early dinner before soundcheck, and he left me a key on account he didn't want to wait up that late after my show."

"What time did you arrive at your friend's place?" Harkins's eyes were down on his notebook.

"I'd reckon 1 a.m. I finished up at the club round about midnight, packed my gear, got my pay and drove to the house."

"Anyone who can vouch for your whereabouts between leaving the club at midnight and 2 a.m.?"

A cold sweat ran down Johnny's neck. "Well, as I said, my friend was in bed already. I don't suspect he heard me come in."

"Your friend have a wife, a roommate, neighbor, anyone who can attest that you were at the house or in the Buena Vista neighborhood at the time you say? Anybody out walking the dog that might have seen you in that vicinity?"

"No." He set the beer on a side table. "I don't recall seeing anyone in the neighborhood."

"What about this band?" Harkins said, pointing with his pen to where a twangy stew of Telecasters and a plaintive pedal steel guitar bled through the walls.

"The Caterpillars and me, we're on parallel paths, you might say. We're on the same tour but we ain't touring together."

Harkins leaned forward. "You know, if your van is old, maybe has a bad muffler, it might make a lot of noise, pulling up to a quiet residential area late at night. Might be the kind of thing a nosy neighbor would remember hearing at say, one in the morning." His eyes had a cool gray glint.

"I appreciate that kindly, Detective. But the thing is, my ride is fairly tuned up. She and I rolled in good and quiet. And I slipped into the house, being right respectful of the neighbors."

"Ah well." Harkins leaned back as Steinkoffer muttered under his breath. "So tell us exactly what happened last night."

"Sure thing. I played my set as the opener, same as tonight. Sold merch afterwards...which I should be doing right now." He wondered how Keys the sound guy was doing. "Stayed in the music room to sell stuff and hear the Caterpillars play their set, as I do most nights. After their set I packed and hauled the gear to my van. Was almost done when I stopped in the alley by the club's back door to chat with some lovely ladies and sign a couple autographs. And this guy, your victim, comes stomping into the alley from the street, bellowing my name."

"He approaches from your right?" Harkins asked. It was clear he knew the layout behind the club.

"That's right. The short end of the alley to the left leads to the parking lot. Only performers and club workers would have access there."

"Could you have, you know...left?" Steinkoffer piped in.

"Could I have turned left? Back to the parking lot?"

"No. Yes." Steinkoffer looked confused at his own question. "I mean, could you have just left the scene without a confrontation? Gone down the alley the other direction or ducked back inside the club?"

Johnny hunched forward as far as the sagging couch would allow. "Detective. I write and sing songs about tough men and tough times. About standing tall under hard circumstances and making life's difficult decisions. Now here I am, flirting with some ladies after singing those songs, and you're asking if I should turn tail and flee because some scrawny blogger starts squawking at me?"

Steinkoffer blushed and retracted in his chair. "You could have avoided a confrontation," he said softly.

"Well, I reckon you are right, I suppose I could have tried, but for the fact this fella was dead-set on having a confrontation." Johnny realized what he had said. "Ah, poor choice of words, my apologies."

Harkins steered the conversation back. "What did Mr. Williams say when he confronted you in the alley?"

"Oh, the general idea was I'm a thief, a fraud, I stole art from Freddie, I lied about my contributions to the Gentlemen, all that. The whole time he's waving around a stack of paper that supposedly proves the thing. To be honest, I wasn't even looking at him. You don't give hecklers any attention. It's oxygen to them. Well, he got so loud and obnoxious it was making the ladies uncomfortable. Now I don't cotton to that, so I told him he was full of shit and he could go fuck himself twelve ways to Sunday. He pushed some blonde in a white dress out of his way and shoved me with one hand, because the other hand had all that paper. So I shoved him with two hands, and he went flying. All that paper did too." Johnny smiled at the recollection.

"I was fixing to take another shot at him when Darryl the bouncer came outside and got between us. Darryl dragged him up on his feet while he was trying to pick up all his papers. Hauled him out of the alley to the sidewalk. That was the last I saw of him."

"There's one other thing," Harkins said. "Show him." Steinkoffer tapped the tablet and rotated it to Johnny.

The crime scene photograph showed a white man in his thirties, slumped in a dark alley, with a guitar smashed over his head. His eyes were visible but closed. The nose and lower face were obscured inside the body of the guitar. The instrument's neck protruded out alongside the right side of the dead man's body.

A snort of a laugh escaped from Johnny's mouth. "Sorry."

"That funny to you?" Steinkoffer's face flashed crimson.

"A guitar player leaving a guitar at a murder scene? Ain't that the dumbest calling card y'all have ever seen? I mean, y'all are the professionals."

Steinkoffer shook his tablet. "Is this your guitar?"

"Guitars aren't registered like guns, Detective. Though I'd reckon in the hands of Woody Guthrie, it's a right powerful weapon."

Steinkoffer stared blankly. "Who?"

"Woody Guthrie, he was a folk singer in the '30s and—never mind."

Harkins watched the exchange, then breathed in to speak. "I'm concerned, Mr. Cole, that perhaps you're missing a guitar."

"All my guitars are accounted for, thank you very much."

"Any way to attest how many guitars you had yesterday morning?"

"Well, no, not that I'm aware of." Johnny felt the cold sweat again.

Harkins gestured to the open instrument rack, a large wheeled case with slots for acoustic and electric guitars. "I see a few empty slots there."

"Well sure enough, I didn't bring every goll-dang guitar I own. I'm the opener on this tour. You only need a couple guitars for a solo set of forty-five minutes. Now when I travel with my full band playing headlining tours, it's different of course."

Harkins pulled a sheet from his pocket, a printout from the

internet. He read in a flat voice: "I'll smash this guitar over your head if you talk bad about my kin. Did it once I'll do it again."

"Yup, that's one of mine. 'Mountain Valley,' off the third record." Johnny got lost in a memory when he felt both men staring at him. "That song lyric you read. That's mine. The guitar? I wouldn't smash a guitar on some heckler's head. These are my instruments I use to make a living."

"And yet you bragged about it," Harkins said, folding the paper back into his pocket.

"In a song!" Johnny heard himself yell. "In a work of art. Not in real life." His pulse quickened as he saw the evidence through the detectives' eyes.

"Listen. Detective Harkins. I don't think you think I actually did this," Johnny said, ignoring the fact that the cops came from Nashville to interrogate him. "I never met this man before in my life, and while he sure had a beef with me, I got no trouble with him. I'm sorry he's dead but not in any sort of personal manner. Now I really ought to get back to my job, which is selling those T-shirts." He stood up to be dismissed.

The cops stayed seated, and Johnny knew this wasn't over.

"You claim no animosity to the dead man, who advocated a theory that threatens financial and reputational harm for you, and you were seen having a physical altercation with him mere hours before he was killed, and you have no alibi for the time of death." Harkins spoke in a clinical tone that chilled Johnny. "So where does that leave us?"

Johnny's eyes darted between the two men and landed on Steinkoffer's tablet. "Can I get another look at that photo?"

Steinkoffer shrugged and handed it to Johnny, standing over him. Johnny rotated the tablet for a better angle of the photograph.

"Does this have that expand-o-thingie?" Johnny pinched his thumb and forefinger. Steinkoffer nodded, and Johnny zoomed in to the man's face and the body of the guitar.

"All right now. We're looking at the underside of the guitar, and even though there's no label I can tell this is a Mexican Fender. See how the wood is thin with veneer? It's cheaper material, cheaper production. You could confirm if you have a photo from underneath looking up at the front side, but I'm right about the brand. Whoever did this knew about guitars and had enough respect not to destroy a good one like a Martin." He gulped and felt the detectives' fury rising. "With, ah, of course, all due respect to the deceased fellow here."

Johnny felt the heat build on his face. He had the cops thinking he cared more about the smashed guitar than a human life. He zoomed the photo out to look at the whole scene, then zoomed back into the man's head, panning along the guitar neck. His eyes got wide as he saw the end of the neck.

"A-ha!" Johnny shouted. "Capo!" He jumped, nearly dropping the tablet.

"Hey, watch it!" Steinkoffer grabbed the tablet back. "And kay-what now?"

"Capo! There's a capo on the guitar!"

Steinkoffer still looked confused.

"Mr. Cole," Harkins said with a dry laugh, "why don't you explain to my musically disinclined partner what you're talking about."

Johnny spun around the room, looking at his guitar cases. "A capo, well a capo is simply a device, a little metal tool smaller than a deck of cards, that changes the key of your guitar. So instead of learning a whole bunch of new chords that might not sound right anyway, you slap on this little doohickey and it compresses the strings to make the new key. Listen." He grabbed a Martin acoustic off the stand and strummed a big open G chord. "Without capo." He then reached into a case and clamped the tool on the guitar neck. "With capo..." The same chord sounded brighter, higher. A new key.

"Fascinating," Steinkoffer said. "Are those things very expensive?"

"Nah. About twenty bucks. Every guitar player has a couple."

"And Mr. Cole," Harkins said, "as a professional musician, do you use more than one capo?"

"I sure do. I got a Kyser and a Shubb. Not much difference really. They do the same job. Some nights, some songs, I feel like using one or the other. Tonight I used this one here," he said, jiggling the neck of the guitar he was holding. "The Kyser."

"And can you tell what kind of capo is seen in the picture here?" Steinkoffer held out the tablet but didn't let Johnny hold it.

"That sir, is a Shubb capo. See here, this one on my guitar has a curvy handle, looks like the top of a cello or a bass. The Shubb capo has a rubber sleeve and sits down snug on the guitar neck. See how they look different?"

Harkins leaned in for a better view of the tablet as both detectives looked back and forth from the crime scene photo to Johnny's acoustic.

"Okay," Harkins said, "you've convinced me. That's a Kyser on your guitar and a Shubb on the victim's guitar. But you said you use both. How do we know that's not your Shubb capo in our homicide?"

Johnny flashed his widest smile. "Because my Shubb is right here." He reached into the open case and tossed the capo in the air. Harkins caught it one-handed. He examined it and handed it to his partner, the corners of his lips turning up.

Steinkoffer held up the small tool. "You could have gone out and bought a replacement. Or borrowed one. You said they're cheap and common." But his voice was not convincing.

"I suppose you could call every music store in Nashville to see if someone like me bought a new capo this morning. Or you could look at the one right there in your hand."

Steinkoffer turned the capo in his chubby hands. The rubber sleeve was smoothed and worn. The ink was smudged and parts of the shiny metal were dulled from regular use.

Johnny removed the Kyser capo and showed it to Harkins. "I

need my capos, same as I need my guitars. They're all tools of the trade. I don't know why any musician would smash..." His voice drifted off.

Johnny spun to face Steinkoffer.

"Lemme see that picture again."

In the photo, the neck of the guitar jutted out above the dead man's right arm.

Johnny's words came out in a rush. "The guy was already dead from the punch when the killer smashed him with the guitar, right?" The cops nodded. "So you're standing in front of a dead man, no need to worry about an attack, no need to approach from the left or right."

Johnny's hands drifted up to the guitar on his chest, holding the end near the headstock with his left hand as he had so many times before. He stared at Steinkoffer, sitting in the chair across from him.

"Don't move," he said to Steinkoffer. Then to Harkins: "Back up a bit." Harkins jumped out of his chair.

Johnny slowly lifted the instrument over his head and grabbed the neck near the guitar body with his right hand. "Don't move," he repeated as he stepped closer to Steinkoffer.

"What are you—" Steinkoffer's voice was high and pinched.

Johnny planted both feet in front of Steinkoffer and lifted the guitar over his head. In half-time speed, he swung the guitar over his head down towards Steinkoffer and froze. "Look."

Steinkoffer realized he had squeezed his eyes shut. He looked around in a panic, waiting for impact. "Look at what?"

"You see it?" Johnny was talking to Harkins, who had come up behind him. "Look where the neck of the guitar is going to land if I continue on through his head."

Harkins examined the scene of assailant and potential victim. "To his left," he said.

"That's right." Johnny handed the midair guitar to Harkins and stepped away. "I'm right-handed. If I were to swing a guitar at someone's head—well, I'd never do that, 'cause that would be a crime against music. But if I did, as a right-hander, I'd lead with my stronger arm, the right side. "And therefore it would land—"

"On the victim's left side." Harkins finished the thought.

"You got it," Johnny said. "Now what you got there in Nashville is a guitar smashed by somebody swinging from the other side."

"Eddie, the pic of our vic: which is it?" Harkins said.

Steinkoffer looked up at the guitar held by his partner, still hovering above his left shoulder. The tablet trembled in his lap. He offered the tablet with shaking hands. Harkins returned the guitar to Johnny and took the tablet.

Harkins smiled and showed the picture to Johnny. "Along the right side. Our killer is a lefty."

Johnny turned to replace his guitar in the case. Facing away from the detectives, he let out a sigh of relief.

"Well, if you didn't do it…" The words came out as if Steinkoffer hadn't meant to say them aloud.

"Someone went to a lot of trouble to make us think you did," Harkins finished.

Johnny snapped his fingers. "My ex-manager lives in Nashville." Harkins raised an eyebrow. "Name is Mo Tubbs. Son of a bitch owes me money, and he's still pissed I fired him all those years ago."

"Mo Tubbs." Harkins was writing in his notepad. "Is that Mo as in Maurice?"

"Mo as in mo' trouble, mo' headaches, mo' lying, mo' everything."

"He any relation to Ernest?" Steinkoffer asked.

"Now that's a good guess, Detective, but Ernest was T-U-B-B, no 's', and Mo is Tubbs with an 's.'" Steinkoffer looked away in embarrassment, but when he looked up Johnny was smiling without enmity.

A dawning came over Johnny as he rubbed his chin. He picked up his beer bottle and started pacing. "He was there last night! At the club in Nashville! I saw him talking to the owner before the show. He probably stuck around to hear my set, purely out of spite. Wouldn't surprise me if he was out in the alley too." Harkins started scribbling furiously. "He's a vindictive bastard, short-fuse temper for sure, but murder? Gall-dang."

Harkins pinched his lips. "We're looking for a left-hand dominant. With Tubbs, do you know?"

Johnny shook his head in memory. "I'll be damned. I watched him sign enough contracts to know Tubbs is a left-hander. Don't have to take my word for it though. I'm sure you can get it through a writing test."

Harkins looked at Steinkoffer and slapped his notebook closed. "Mr. Cole, on behalf of the Nashville Police Department, we apologize for the inconvenience and appreciate your aid in our investigation."

Steinkoffer, still sitting, clambered to his feet. "Yeah, Mr. Cole, thank you. Thank you for not smashing my head with a guitar."

"Aww, now, I'd never do something like that to such a nice...guitar." He flashed a devilish grin but paused. "Oh shit."

Harkins frowned. "What?"

Johnny bit his lip. "This ain't for certain, but I think Mo Tubbs manages Freddie McPherson these days. I got nothing against Freddie, you understand. We had our spats like brothers do, but we went our separate ways peacefully. I think he's got nothing to do with this computer ruckus or your murder, but if Mo Tubbs is involved then it can't look good for Freddie from where you sit."

"What does McPherson think about this AI theory?" Harkins pulled his lips back, the skin tight against his face.

"Freddie and I haven't exactly talked recently, so I can't rightly say. But through the grapevine I hear he's not shutting it down but not talking it up neither. He hasn't taken up the cause as his own, is what I'm saying."

"And you've got an idea as to why?"

"Yeah I do. It's because he knows the truth, same as me. He knows which songs he wrote, which songs I wrote, and the ones we wrote together."

"Don't worry about it. We'll talk to McPherson," Harkins said.

The three men moved into the hallway, where the music got louder. "Safe driving back to Nashville now," Johnny said. The detectives nodded and shook his hand.

Johnny stepped into the music room where the Caterpillars were playing the same set as last night and probably the same as they would play tomorrow night.

He threaded his way through the crowd to the merchandise table. He thanked Keys for covering as two women approached the table. Both were clutching a T-shirt and a CD.

"Johnny Cool, we love you!"

"Thanks, darling. How's about I sign that for you?"

FROM BACH TO BLUEGRASS

Barry Fulton

1990

Tap. Tap. Tap. What? I pried my eyes open. Too early.

I turned over and went back to sleep.

Not for long.

The sound again rattled the window of the loft. I sat up, rubbed my eyes. A face pressed against the glass, outlined by the first rays of a crimson sunrise. I jerked back, breath in check, nerves taut, body rigid.

The face? My imagination? The doc at the VA told me to count to ten if I saw anything...weird. *One, two, three.* Eyes closed. *Four, five, six.* I exhaled. *Seven, eight, nine. Ten!*

I opened my eyes. The face, still there. Unblinking, staring, threatening. *Where was my reflection?*

I'd been warned when I bought the property. "On the market for years," the agent said, "ever since the old house burned down. A charred body found in the rubble. Murdered. Never positively identified. No dental records."

I fell silent when he revealed the owner had been a violin maker. Perhaps the reason I'd been drawn to this property, three hundred miles from my apartment in New York.

"Strange old bird. Name of Frederick Stoltz," the agent said. "Scared the daylights outta some kids at Halloween. Before long, people believed the house was haunted. And worse—dark rumors spread about him."

I closed my eyes, recalling my reaction to his Appalachian superstition and my delight that nine wooded acres at the base of West Virginia's Cacapon Mountain were selling for less than the price of a used Harley. I built on the foundation of the old house, one log at a time. Driving from New York to work on weekends, I needed five years to complete it.

Did most of the construction myself, except the plumbing.

"You're lucky you found me," the plumber told me. "Ain't many people 'round here who'd come to this place. You gonna live here? Better git yourself a gun."

I ignored his advice. Wondered if that had been a mistake as I recalled the face in the window. What to do? Pretend to be asleep? Or leap out of bed, down the ladder, and outside?

I did neither, but slowly opened my eyes. The face in the window had disappeared. Some kind of trick.

A dark rain-swollen cloud now obscured the rising sun.

I rose, walked to the bathroom, and looked in the mirror. No worse for the fright, no better, either. My deep-set black eyes gave me a distinctive look. Skeletal, some said. Unfortunately, my chalk-like pallor and balding head supported that demeaning description.

Slipped on my trousers and a fresh white shirt. Climbed down the ladder to the great room—kitchen, dining, and living all-in-one—with sliding doors that opened to a rustic deck shadowed by giant oaks. I listened to the distant rumble of thunder, typical for mid-June. I tapped the brew button on the coffeemaker, slid open the door to the deck, and walked outside.

The sky was now so dark it felt like night. More thunder. The decaying tree lying to the left of the deck had been struck by a lightning bolt years before. Had it also struck the house? Or, as rumored, had it been arson? Old Jacob, a guy down at the county tax office, warned of a *dybbuk*.

"*Dybbuk*? What's that?" I'd asked.

Jacob stood from his desk, turned to the bookcase behind him, chose a book, and opened it to a ghastly picture—a woodblock print of a shadowy figure clad in gossamer robes, its face obscured by a vaporous mist, its elongated fingers grasping a gnarled wooden staff.

"That's it," he said, "a malicious spirit ripped from the soul of a dead person."

An investigation by the county sheriff of the fire proved inconclusive. Later, I learned the case had never been closed. The coroner reported a thin steel wire had garroted the victim. Murdered!

Rain fell on the lake, pockmarking its surface. Within minutes, it drenched the deck. Before retreating inside, I looked up at the loft window, some twenty feet from the ground. No way a person could scale that wall. When a lightning bolt interrupted the darkened sky, I rushed inside, soaked, dripping a trail of water behind me.

The coffeemaker produced its pleasant gurgle. Soon provided aromatic Ethiopian coffee, the beans roasted and ground the night before. A quarter cup of grits, boiling water, and a generous dollop of butter. A perfect breakfast.

Seldom ventured out except to Vernon's General Store, where I was well and favorably known. Always greeted as Mr. Holland. Told them many times to stop the formality. "Call me Parke," I said. Still, they never do. Spent the summer on the deck in view of the lake touching my property. All quiet, except when the cabin shuddered with a calliope of eerie sounds.

Prodigy. That's what they said when I was eleven.

Julliard. That's what they said at sixteen.

Vietnam. That's what the government said at eighteen.

I should have moved to Canada, but patriotism called, and I shipped out with boys who didn't know a cello from a chain saw. Good chaps, but...I didn't fit. A musician, not a killer. I followed orders, marching through the jungle looking for

Charlie. They spotted us first. I woke up in an Army field hospital, bandaged and bruised.

"You're lucky, Private," the corpsman said. "Most of your company was wiped out."

Still alive, I agreed. Lucky, until I looked at my left hand. My luck had run out, as I confirmed several days later when the bandages were removed.

Two fingers missing.

Prematurely discharged from the Army at age 22. My papers read *Other Than Honorable.* Why? Soon after returning to duty, they ordered me to appear at an awards ceremony where the company commander pinned a Purple Heart on my uniform. I tore it off, threw it to the ground, and saluted with the remaining three fingers of my left hand.

Goodbye Saigon. Hello Julliard. If only. Nonetheless, one of the school's moonlighting faculty agreed to continue my lessons with a restrung left-handed violin. I clerked at Venus Records on West 8th Street by day and practiced by night.

Barely a year later, she urged me to upgrade the violin. "Not yet a virtuoso," she said, "but with your perfect pitch, you'll hear the difference with a better instrument." She loaned me eight thousand dollars to be repaid at fifty dollars a month. Inspired by my father, a concert violinist, I studied every week and faithfully practiced every day. Pleased by my progress and free of debt after thirteen years, I left Manhattan and moved to my rural retreat.

1985

My first year in West Virginia offered the peace I had sought. I continued my lessons, traveling back and forth to New York weekly. In the second year, my life began to fall apart. My violin instructor urged more practice, said I was regressing. Hard to concentrate with the random noises in the cabin. The incessant tapping. A low rumble late at night. Occasional fiendish whispers.

Another year passed before my instructor abandoned me, said I had forgotten everything she'd taught. No wonder I couldn't concentrate. The news of my father's tragic performance with the Philadelphia Orchestra unnerved me. A string broke minutes after he stood in front of the orchestra, playing Bach's *Violin Concerto in E Major*. With barely a pause, he continued with three strings, producing a sound, as the *Inquirer* reported, "that devolved from angelic to demonic." The conductor took my father by the arm and walked him off stage. He died the next day. Cause unknown. I wish I had attended the service.

All downhill after that. My fingers had become coarse, my bowing erratic. I hung the violin on the wall next to my student instrument, a reminder of what might have been.

1995

Ten years passed before I woke one morning to a gentle rain and complete silence. *Blessed silence.* I had stepped gingerly out of bed, climbed down the ladder, and prepared my usual—hot coffee and a bowl of grits. Nothing better to start the day. Unless it's a Bach concerto. I fired up the audio and selected Bach's *Cello Suite No. 3 In C Major*, BMV 1009. For the first time, I didn't have to turn up the volume to drown out the haunting sounds.

The breathless movements and dramatic silences of this magnificent recording exhausted me. But I was not merely listening. Baton in hand, I stood and conducted the entire suite. I felt compelled to ensure the recording reflected Bach's every intention, my passion plain in the window's reflection of my energetic movements. Exhausted as the last note faded, I bowed. Bach's genius deserved my respect.

The rain slowed, the clouds parted, and the sun reappeared. I walked to the deck and sat at the table I'd made with timbers rescued from a nearby barn. The sun, now overhead, did not cast a shadow. The music resonated in my head. I closed my eyes and smiled at the last movement, picturing the Scotch-Irish jig Bach had so beautifully captured.

Suddenly, the music came alive again. My ears perked, my eyes opened. Immediately before me sat a cellist repeating the suite with such loving care that I wept. She perched on a tiny chair holding a beautiful miniature instrument. And she...no more than a foot tall.

I had heard them all: Rostropovich, Casals, Yo-Yo Ma. But this! Never had I experienced such a profound interpretation, precisely as Bach had intended.

As I savored the vibrato of the last note, she rose and bowed.

"Who are you?" I asked, my eyes wide.

She tilted her head and smiled. "Happy Birthday, Parke."

I had forgotten. My forty-fifth birthday and alone with what...a musical apparition?

She sat and began again. *Suite 3 in C Major*, but...too fast, far too fast. Sixteenth notes tumbling over each other.

"No," I cried. "You're destroying Bach's music."

She nodded, but continued even faster.

"Stop!" I shouted.

And at that instant, she disappeared.

Stunned, I leaned back and closed my eyes. A dream? A mirage? A trick? She seemed so real, but...I knew better.

2003

Exactly eight years since the tiny cellist had played for me. Another birthday. Fifty-three. Astonished to discover a telegram on my kitchen table, I tore open the envelope—an invitation to perform at the Vienna *Konzerhaus*. The next evening, I boarded

Austrian Air at BWI in such a rush I'd forgotten my violin. Confident they would loan me a fine instrument, I didn't worry.

Memory fades…except for the applause from my Viennese triumph. The magic in the hall was so powerful that Austria's most distinguished music critics were rendered speechless.

Skipping the reception planned in my honor, I took an overnight train to Paris. I lay awake all night, guarding the priceless Guarneri, delighted with my performance. *Not bad for a left-handed fiddler with two missing fingers.*

But…not a word in the papers the following morning. *Why not?*

2011

Day after day. Year after year. A monotony of visions and sounds. Suspense gave way to boredom. Coffee and grits every morning followed by Bach. At the foot of the ladder from the loft, I stood before my trophy wall. Three violins that rekindled precious memories. I had resolved that Bach would not be silenced.

After breakfast, I poured a second mug of coffee and stepped outside to listen to the rustling of leaves and a chorus of birds. I sat at the table, eyes closed. The cooing of the doves mixed with the sweet tweeting of a family of bluebirds hardly rivaled a Bach concerto, but nonetheless lifted my mood.

Thunk. My half-full mug lay on its side. What startled me out of my stupor? Bach's *Violin Partita No. 2 in D Minor*, BWV 1004, one of the greatest pieces of music ever composed, filled the air.

A violinist, a miniature young man with tousled blond hair, appeared in the very place I had listened to the cellist years before. He played with such beauty that even the birds stopped to listen. The sound from that tiny violin was sublime. I basked in its magnificence.

I held my breath until he raised the bow and nodded in my direction.

"Who are you?" I asked, pleading with my eyes.

He smirked, wagged a teeny finger, and disappeared.

I rushed inside, removed the Guarneri from its display on the wall, and began the first movement of *Partita No. 2*.

I hadn't dared to play it for years. Age and arthritis had compromised my talent. Still, on the Viennese stage, when the violin rose to its legendary sound, I acted as the mere agent of its mastery. At the instant I concluded the fifth movement of the *Partita*, my TV spontaneously came to life with an ear-splitting advertisement for Powerball.

The BWV catalog number of the cello and violin performances on my deck pulsated in my head: 1009 and 1004. And they instantly rearranged themselves: 10 09 41 19 14 followed by 04.

"The drawing will be held tonight," the TV screamed. "Twenty million dollars."

An hour later, I arrived at the General Store and greeted Vern. He wore the same faded flannel shirt I'd seen for years. Of course, I wore my black gabardine trousers and a starched white shirt.

"Afternoon, Mr. Holland," he said. "What can I do for you today? We have a new batch of peppery scrapple that'll knock your socks off. And just got some fresh brown eggs from Merle over the old Stutzman farm."

"I'll take a dozen eggs," I said, "but I've come over today to play Powerball." I asked for one ticket, selected the numbers, and gave him a five for the eggs and the lottery.

"Only one ticket?" Vern asked.

I nodded, took my change. "I have a feeling about it."

I slept poorly, dreading the morning, fearing another illusion or the incessant creepy sounds. A foolish fear. No tapping, no face at the window. Not a cloud in the sky. I bounded out of bed, thrilled to spend the day in the company of Bach, listening to a new recording of the six Bach suites for solo cello, transcribed for solo violin. I couldn't wait to hear the sixth suite—the one performed on a five-string violin to honor Bach's instructions. Imagine, five strings! *Does this virtuoso violinist have an extra finger?*

Mesmerized by the interpretation, I wanted to sing, to dance, to celebrate life. But after the first five suites, I took a break and walked outside. A beautiful summer day with a slight breeze and the sun high in a cloudless sky. No tricks, no illusions.

My stomach rumbled, and I went back inside. The sixth suite cued, ready for my enjoyment after lunch, when a tap, a rap, and then a heavier knock on the door of my cabin interrupted the silence. The first in months. Maybe years. I hesitated. The knocking became more persistent. I peered through a side window at a white truck with an imposing array of satellite dish antennas. What the hell? Why were they here?

I opened the door.

"Mr. Holland?" asked a woman in the doorway. Young brunette, short hair, wearing an A-line skirt with a vibrant, colorful blouse. Behind her stood a man in a T-shirt and cargo shorts balancing a TV camera on his shoulder. "Mr. Parke Holland?"

Slightly confused, I nodded.

She smiled broadly and said, "Congratulations!"

Still confused, I pointed to the distinctive butterflies on her blouse. "Ceraunus Blue," I mumbled. "Not native to West Virginia."

"Uh-huh. May we come in?" she asked. Before I could answer, Ms. Butterfly and camera guy had pushed by me into the great room.

Then Bach's Sixth Suite filled the room. It had begun without my intervention.

She spoke as I backed away. I heard only a few disconnected

words. "...surprised?"

I turned, walked to the amp, and lowered the volume. "Why are you here?" I asked.

"You haven't been told? Announced last night." She paused, her eyes wider. "You have won—twenty million dollars!"

"Twenty million? Just me?" She nodded. "So, I don't have to share. Good."

Powerball, of course. I wasn't surprised. Bach never disappoints.

As camera guy aimed his lens at me, I resolved not to show my annoyance with these intruders. I spoke softly. "How did you know it was me?"

Ms. Butterfly answered, directly addressing the camera. "We learned the winning ticket had been sold at Vernon's General Store. Vern was already celebrating when we arrived. Two empty cans of Bud Light on the counter and a fresh one in his hand. 'Guy lives way down in the hollow,' Vern said. 'Mr. Holland, a quiet gentleman, always asked me to call him Parke. Never did, out of respect. Bought one ticket. Two bucks. Only one I sold yesterday.' Cut."

As soon as camera guy stopped, she motioned him to follow her, stood behind the sofa, and pointed to the fireplace. "Too dark," she said, and then turned to me. "Would you mind if we moved the sofa over to the wall facing the window? Better light."

"What?"

"To shoot the interview. It'll be on Channel 7 tonight, maybe picked up by ABC."

"No thanks, I'd—"

"Mr. Holland, please. My producer'll kill me if I don't get the interview." She and camera guy were already moving the sofa. "You and I can sit right here below the violins displayed on the wall."

I should have objected, but she wouldn't stop talking.

"This'll be great color," she said, as camera guy unfolded a tripod. "You must be a violinist. And apparently ready for a concert."

I raised an eyebrow. *Ready for a concert?*

"The way you're dressed. Tuxedo trousers, formal shirt with cufflinks and studs. Add a jacket and bowtie, and you're ready for the stage."

I couldn't explain why I dressed formally—not unlike Johann Sebastian Bach at his first public performance in Leipzig. Seven days of the week, I dressed to perform, driven by a force I couldn't control.

The six o'clock local news opened with an exterior shot of my cabin and the newscaster's breathless introduction. "A Vietnam vet living alone in a rustic cabin in Hawthorn Valley learned from our TV crew he had won the Powerball lottery—twenty million dollars."

I watched myself struggling to answer her questions. Sitting next to her on the sofa, I kept scrunching up my nose from the scent of her cloying perfume: tropical orchids that complemented her blue butterfly blouse.

I stumbled when she asked about the three violins and smiled awkwardly when she joked they must have been made by Stradivarius. I blurted out that one was a Guarneri. She had no idea what I meant, but before the interview aired, someone at the station must have done a little research.

I gasped when I saw a closeup of the violin and heard the announcer's voice. "We were surprised to learn this humble man owns a rare violin made by Giuseppe Guarneri in the 18th century, worth millions of dollars."

To say I was warmly received at Vernon's General Store a week later would be an understatement. Vern received a hundred-thousand-dollar Powerball payout for selling me the winning ticket. When I walked through the door, he rushed from behind the counter and hugged me. "Mr. Holland, I can't believe it. The wife and I are flying to Orlando, gonna visit Disneyland, and..."

I suggested he and the missus might also enjoy visiting Nashville to visit the Grand Ole Opry. I bought a pound of bacon, a gallon of milk, and two Hershey bars. Wished him well and returned home.

When I pulled in, I found a late-model Ford in my driveway. The driver stepped out and asked if I was Parke Holland. Probably there to help me manage my money or offer to share it with a good cause. I stared, silent.

"I'm an FBI investigator," he said, as he opened his wallet and showed identification: Agent Lawrence Sommerdahl.

I froze.

He was a slight man, far from imposing, with gentle eyes, crewcut, pinched mouth, and a determined look.

Finally, I spoke. "Okay, yes, I'm Parke Holland."

"I have a few questions," he said. "May I come in?"

I nodded, fumbled for the key, opened the door, and entered. He followed, but stopped in front of the three violins. "Which one's the Guarneri?"

He didn't know anything or he wouldn't have asked.

"A little joke," I said, "to amuse my interviewer." I suggested he sit on the sofa, now back in front of the fireplace. I sat on a hickory rocker to the side.

"The one on the right," he pointed. "If it's not a Guarneri, I'll eat my hat."

Shit! He recognized it. Or faking? Hard to tell.

He opened a slim leather folder, removed a glossy photo, and handed it to me. "Does this look familiar?"

I pretended to study it. "Hmm. No...well, yes. Looks similar to mine, maybe even an original. Mine's a 20th century reproduction, also made in Italy. You can buy them on eBay for a thousand, two thousand dollars."

I stood and handed back the photograph, offered an iced tea.

He got up and followed me to the kitchen. "Mr. Holland, the FBI received this photograph from Interpol. It shows a genuine Guarneri protected by the 1970 UNESCO Convention on Cultural Properties. It's been missing from Vienna's *Kunsthistorisches* Museum since 2003."

Busy pouring a glass of iced tea, I didn't respond.

"My German's a little rusty," he said. "Did I pronounce the name of the museum correctly?"

He stepped so close I could feel his breath.

"In case you've forgotten, my Austrian counterpart assures me you visited Vienna in 2003 and dropped by the museum. I'm sure you can recall its name."

I engaged a prominent Manhattan attorney specializing in the arts. Cost me a fortune, but I could afford the best. She spent a full day with me in West Virginia, inquiring about my tour in Vietnam, the face in the window, the musicians on my deck, and the concert in Vienna. "Would you agree to an evaluation by a psychiatrist?" she asked.

"Didn't do your homework, honey," I said, and dismissed her then and there. If she had inquired, I'd have told her the VA had declared me completely sane. The following day, I mailed her a copy of a letter from their shrink with this phrase highlighted: "Your issues are neither neurological nor psychological in nature."

Left to defend myself, I insisted the statute of limitations protected me. "Not in West Virginia," the judge said. "Not for felony theft." He unfairly upheld Austria's request for extradition. From there, the Austrians controlled my fate.

2013

Most of the trial remains a blur. My lawyer presenting, pleading, objecting. The state accusing, insisting, condemning. Two so-called experts swore the violin belonged to the museum. I swore my innocence before a judge so deaf I had to shout. *What could he know about music?*

"Your Honor, I am the beneficiary of an 18th century royal decree wherein it was ordered that Bach's genius must never be tarnished by musicians playing inferior instruments."

The judge scowled.

"The concert master presented the violin to me as a state gift in recognition of my performance that, in his words, 'pleased even God Almighty and a host of heavenly angels.'"

I spoke of the musicians who gathered on my deck. "Violinists, cellists, even a string quartet. Not a one of 'em over a foot tall, but what magnificent music."

The judge shook his head. "A foot? Thirty centimeters?" His voice betrayed his disbelief. "I've heard enough," he roared. "There is no record of your so-called Viennese concert, nothing more than the documented evidence that the violin was stolen on the day you took the train to Paris."

"Your Honor," I pleaded, "Bach would be offended if—"

"Hearsay! Enough. Miniature musicians, dead composers. Not in this courtroom. Because of your age and...uh, your current state of mind, I will *not* sentence you to prison. However, you will forfeit the value of the violin ten times over—fifteen million Euros—to create scholarships for young Austrian musicians. Furthermore, the Guarneri will be returned to the *Kunsthistorisches* Museum to be displayed in the exact location from which you stole it."

"No, never!" I shouted. The courtroom began to spin.

My lawyer snarled at me and furiously bowed a five-string violin while shouting obscenities in German. The face of the judge began to melt, his features distorted, a waxen memory. A string quartet suddenly appeared in the courtroom and settled before me. They played, louder and louder, with such spirit that their instruments burst into flames.

I didn't recognize the composition until a stout soprano with floor-length golden braids joined them. "You Ain't Nothin' but a Hound Dog. Cryin' all the Time."

I stood, waved my fist at the sacrilege. My body convulsed. I writhed in pain. Then a blinding light followed by a throbbing release from...from something that escaped with burning laughter. An evil force. *Whoosh. Whoosh.* A terrifying sound in E flat filled the courtroom as I collapsed.

"Where am I?" I asked.

"*Mittagessen*," a middle-aged woman replied, smiling as she cranked the bed to a sitting position and sat a tray before me.

"Lunch? But, why..."

When an older man entered the room and introduced himself as Dr. Schneider, I understood.

"You suffered a seizure," he said, "yesterday in the court-room."

"Yesterday?"

"Yes, July the twenty-eighth, to be precise."

I gasped. "The anniversary of Bach's death!"

Dead: two hundred and sixty-three years. As the doctor checked my vitals, I closed my eyes and saw Bach's face, a death mask, so like the face I had seen in my cabin window.

"Your blood pressure reveals a surprising calm," Dr. Schneider said. "And your pulse registers as that of a young athlete. I'm surprised to find you so peaceful."

"The first time in thirty years," I replied.

Dr. Schneider then confirmed what the VA told me years earlier. "Your condition—neither neurological nor psychotic." He failed to mention demonic.

2015

Following my release from this Austrian sanatorium, I returned home to West Virginia. First stop: Vernon's Country Store.

"Mr. Holland," he said, "where've you been? Sheriff's been looking for you?"

Before I could respond, Vern continued. "Remember the charred body they found on your property some forty years ago?"

"Yeah," I said, "happened before I moved here."

"They finally made a positive I.D. of the victim—Frederick Stoltz, the violin-maker himself, as everyone had assumed. Then some reporter started pokin' round and found a list of names, all musicians who'd owned one of his violins, including your father—"

"My father?" I exclaimed.

"Yep. Read it in the *Gazette*. And every one on this list tragically died after performing with one of Stoltz's hand-crafted violins."

"What?"

"Yes sir, Mr. Holland. Pure evil. Possessed, they say, by some kinda spirit."

I shuddered. I understood.

"Thanks, Vern," I said. "I'll talk to the sheriff."

Eager to hear more, I hurried to his office.

"Here's the story from the *Gazette*," the sheriff said. "Tells you practically everything. The victim was garroted by a violin E string. With a steel core, it survived the fire."

"Surely Stoltz didn't die by his own hand," I said.

"Hard to say. I don't necessarily believe it, but some blame his death on an evil spirit that then escaped to seek another host."

I felt my heart racing. *Possessed by a dybbuk.*

"Mr. Holland, there's one name we didn't share with the *Gazette.*"

He shuffled through papers, found the list, and pointed to my name. I sucked in my breath.

"Stoltz sold his last violin to a Julliard instructor who

bought it for you."

"So, if I'd performed with that violin…I might have followed my father to the grave," I said, trembling.

The sheriff shrugged. "We'll never know."

I hurried home, found my bow on the fireplace mantle, grabbed the New York violin, tucked it under my chin, and drew the bow across the E string. *Screech. Screech.* I joyfully smashed the instrument against the stone fireplace. Then I burned what was left.

2023

Within a few weeks, I'd begun lessons again, this time with a high school music teacher who coached me for several years. On my seventy-third birthday, I was invited to perform with a local trio, Vinegar in the Barrel, at a concert in Shepherdstown. Billed as Pappy Parke, I could barely keep up with a young banjo player killing "Foggy Mountain Breakdown" or the guitarist featured on "Worried Man Blues."

When the time arrived to feature me, I stepped forward, caught my breath, and began. My first time on stage. First time in well pressed Levi's and a brand-new plaid shirt. And the first time I performed a few bars of Bach's *Toccata and Fugue in D Minor* at a Bluegrass concert. Then I segued to "In the Jailhouse Now." Even with my hesitant beginning and a few sour notes, the crowd shouted its approval. "Go, Pappy, go."

Freed at long last from the spirit that haunted me…that accompanied me on the night train to Paris with the purloined Guarneri. Good night, Bach. Hello, Flatt and Scruggs.

MUSIC LIVES FOREVER
Heather Graham

Kari Hastings felt the circle of cold pressure against her back. And she instantly knew what it was.

The cold steel of a gun.

What she didn't know was, *why?*

She had been standing in the wings, smiling, and watching a group called the Hedgehogs perform their last rehearsal. The doors were due to open soon; and the event, labeled as Music Lives Forever, was scheduled to start in about thirty-five minutes. Major country headliners would be performing along with many "garage-band" groups that had once been popular in Nashville and environs.

"Just stay still and don't say a word, and you just might live," a whispered voice warned so close to her she could feel the whisperer's hot breath against her ear.

"Listen to them!" the voice snapped angrily, probably something not meant to be said. "And they don't even have you!"

Once upon a time she'd performed with the Hedgehogs, and she would have been happy to jump in with them for this occasion; but the timing was tight, and she had agreed to come in that evening with her own old "garage" band, the Creepers. And since their time slots were short—people were coming for the major players, naturally—she hadn't wanted to steal any thunder from the Hedgehogs' current vocalist, Randy Trait. It had all sounded like so much fun—a trip down memory lane, a long way from where she stood and what she did today.

Except that...

She'd never thought she'd be standing in the wings with the metallic-cold nose of a gun stuck into her back.

"Now, you're going to turn around. You're going to walk straight back to the dressing room assigned to you. You move, you twist, you try to look at me, and you're dead and...maybe whoever else might be around at the time. Do you understand? I will kill not just you, but another person. Maybe I'll kill them and leave you to bleed out, knowing it's your fault another person is dead. Got it?" the voice demanded. "Don't speak. Just nod. Slightly!"

She nodded slightly.

He gave a hoarse, low, guttural laugh. "Behave, and you just might wind up being the only one to live!"

It was a whisper. A strange whisper. And there was something about it...

"Move!"

She did so. She knew people; she'd studied the human psyche with the best. And she knew one thing for sure.

He meant every word he was saying.

"Hey, Flynn!"

Flynn Sherman turned as Oscar Magnus called his name. Oscar was staring at his computer screen.

Oscar was barely out of college, but he was one of the best techs Flynn had ever met. A true computer "geek," Oscar had found his calling, and he was simply amazing at what he did.

He was now frowning as he stared at the keyboard.

"What is it? Something on the bank robbers?"

They had been working with the local police on taking down a pair of bank robbers; luckily no one had been killed, but the pair had escaped with nearly a million dollars. They had identified the robbers; now they had to find them.

"No...I don't know. But something about this..."

"What? What is it?" Flynn demanded.

"'Sometimes the music is offkey, out of beat,'" Oscar read. "And sometimes it's stolen, pure and simple, and when the music is taken...then even music has to die.'"

"Sour grapes?" Flynn murmured. "I know you're tracking social media sites, but—"

"No, Flynn, nothing to do with bank robbers—I don't think. But...there's something about this threat—"

"Oscar, you know better than anyone else that the internet is filled with angry people lashing out and that threats are out there all the time. Except—"

He broke off himself.

Tonight was an occasion that had been heralded in the city for months. Famous acts were coming together with old friends, with Nashville musicians they'd known before, with garage groups who had contributed to the music of the area—and, in some cases, to friends who made it big.

"The show is tonight," Flynn said. "The big music show, but..."

"Flynn, there's been more before this. Written by some guy who calls himself Clef Note. Here, let me go back...same writer on the same site. 'Grist for the mill. The best songs aren't about love, they're about pain. Death and loss, betrayal. Why not contribute more to the music?'"

Flynn stared at the screen over Oscar's shoulder.

The night crew had come in and would continue following up on any leads they had. They'd all been on high alert, ready to move. But it had been past time for him to head out because Special Agent in Charge Mallory considered exhausted agents to be worthless. He did intend to get out, though he wasn't going straight home. He had a ticket for the night's event. Music! The thing with the power to soothe the savage beast. He could shake off some of the day, then get a good night's sleep, and be ready to start again in the morning. But Oscar was seriously worried.

"He sounds angry. But Oscar, it seems that since the pandemic, people latch onto things to be hateful about. Maybe they were shut in too long, or they see hateful things and need to write hateful things themselves—"

"Flynn!" Oscar said, his voice tense with worry, his face knitted into a mask of concern. "Flynn, Kari Hastings is at that event. She sang through college with a group called the Creepers. Special Agent in Charge Watkins gave her the time off months ago when it all came up. Watkins said, yeah, Nashville is music and that means us, too! Flynn—"

Flynn had his phone out.

"I'm just going to call her and ask her if anything is going on. And—"

"Flynn, please, I don't know if anyone else would worry, and I know they must have security there, but—"

Flynn had already dialed Kari's number. But she wasn't answering.

"There's another one!" Oscar exclaimed, shaking his head. "'Those who listen to the fruits of evil will hear the music of the damned!'"

"All right, Oscar, stay on this, will you? I was going to see the show anyway, so I'm going to get over there and..."

This wouldn't be official. And Flynn was afraid if he brought it to his Special Agent in Charge, Mallory might not agree it was a threat worth investigating. But...

Flynn had a friend with the local police, a friend he'd known since they were both kids back in grade school.

"Flynn!" Oscar exclaimed. "I think this guy has a bomb."

"I'm on it, Oscar. Just keep communication open!"

Flynn quickly headed for the door. But even as he did so, Brent Mallory came out of his office.

"Flynn, great, get home, get some sleep. Tomorrow is going to be one hell of a day for us all."

Flynn was a good agent, he knew. He was good at interrogation, at easing down a situation that threatened to be lethal.

But he wasn't a good liar.

And Oscar spoke before Flynn could say anything.

"Sir! There's a credible threat at the concert hall. Disgruntled musician maybe, and I think he has a bomb!"

Mallory was a good man. He walked over to Oscar and wanted to know what he was talking about. But as he read over the man's shoulder, he shook his head. "Do you know how many garage bands out there never made it? How many disgruntled musicians there are? This is just someone spouting off. There's nothing to indicate this man plans to do anything tonight at the concert venue. He's just being hateful and bitter. Oscar, there's nothing about tonight or the venue."

"I know, but—" Oscar began.

"I was heading over there tonight anyway," Flynn said. "Kari is going to be performing with her old group. You know that."

"Yes, and I know…never mind. Flynn, you are going to need to be at your best in the morning. I'm sending you as point to the bank we believe they're hitting next—"

"Sir, I will be at my peak, I promise!" Flynn said. "Hey, I'm just going to listen to a friend—"

"Friend, yeah," Mallory said dryly. "Right. As long as you two work on different teams, I'm all right with your friendship."

"I'm just going to hear some great music and go home," he said.

To his relief, Mallory grinned. "It is Nashville. Music City. But no celebrating—get some sleep."

"Right."

Flynn was out the door at last, pulling out his phone, hitting speed dial.

Why the hell wasn't Kari answering?

Again, it could be nothing. She was going to be part of the fun. She might just be on stage, or backstage with her phone off, laughing with the old group, getting ready…

Kari could have been anything she wanted to be. She was beautiful, she was talented; but when she'd had a friend killed by a known predator when she'd been in college, she'd switched her major to criminology. She was determined to be able to stop such predators and to keep them from doing to others what had been done to her friend.

"Kari, answer, answer!" he whispered.

What if there was a bomb at the venue? Did he get someone to go in now and destroy the evening for the performers, for the audience, for everyone?

And if he didn't, would it be worse because they might all die?

He dialed his phone again. No Kari. Once again, as he drove with his siren and lights on, he hit a speed dial number. Hank Wilson answered him quickly.

"Hey, my friend, what's up?" Hank asked.

"Trouble. Oscar found what he sees as a credible threat against the show tonight. Can you meet me there? You know any bomb techs?"

"What?"

Flynn explained that Oscar had called him over. The internet buzzed with threats constantly, and he understood how Mallory might believe someone was just spouting off. And the pressure on them constantly trying to second-guess the bank robbers had been fierce.

But...

"I'll meet you there. I have a heck of a lot of friends from the force who have had tickets to the event forever. I'll get in touch with them."

"Thank you! Meet you there."

He cut his lights and siren as he drove the last few blocks. When he arrived, he showed his credentials to hurry through to the back and raced into the wings.

There was almost as much chaos backstage as there was out front where the last of the audience members were filing in.

Two Nashville—and world—famous groups were playing along with five opening acts, locals who had once reigned in the area clubs and gone on to different lives. There had to be about twenty-five musicians, all segueing into their places or hanging out to talk to one another, along with another twenty-five or so roadies, two stage managers, video techs...

But he saw Sean Harper, lead guitarist for Kari's old "Creepers" band.

"Sean! Where's Kari?"

Sean was evidently aggravated. "You tell me, man! Hedgehogs are due to start, and we're supposed to follow them. I can't find her!"

He felt a flurry of fear. Flynn knew. He knew in his heart. Kari was in danger.

And yes, there might well be a bomb at the venue.

Kari was tied and a blindfold had been wrapped around her eyes, but her attacker was not a criminal genius; he had never searched her for the Glock stuck into its holster at the rear of her Gothic-style jacket, nor had he checked her pockets for her phone.

Not a genius...

But he was off the deep end. She had walked obediently with him to the tiny dressing room that had been assigned to her. And while not a genius, he wasn't stupid. So as soon as they were away from others, he'd blindfolded her and tied her hands behind her back. He'd never allowed her to see his face.

Did that mean she might recognize him?

Yes. This was someone from her past. She was certain. But...

"So good, so good," he murmured.

He hadn't left her yet; and now that he had her under his control, he seemed happy to wait.

"What's so good?"

"Music, of course."

"Are you playing tonight?" Kari asked.

She'd thought about screaming, but he did have a gun. And that might well mean he was crazy enough to kill anyone who might try to save her. The venue had security, and the Nashville police were watching everything. But...

There was something else.

And she needed to know what.

Then again...

Things would shake up soon enough. Flynn was coming tonight. Despite the pressure they'd been under, he'd been determined he would come. Just as Special Agent in Charge Watkins had pushed her to agree to be part of it. They were no good as agents if they didn't remember how to be human beings as well.

There was a tap at the door.

"Gun is aimed straight at your face, but I might just shoot whoever comes in. I'm going to cover you with a curtain in that corner. Keep your mouth shut—or someone dies. I promise. I plan on dying tonight, so...I'll just take whoever with me."

"I won't speak!" Kari promised.

She was trying, the best she could, to work at the ropes he'd bound her wrists with. Not easy, when she was trying to appear as if she wasn't doing anything. But again, her attacker was no tactical genius. She could do her best to break them thread by thread, and she could feel the ropes were loosening.

"Kari! It's Leslie, your drummer, remember me?"

Leslie Canton, father of two, a man who had taken his talent with percussion and turned it into teaching. A man with a wife and two little kids...

Her attacker, she sensed, was against the wardrobe hidden from the doorway. And as he had promised, there was a wall of fabric over her head and covering her body.

The door opened. She didn't dare breathe.

"Damn! I don't know where the hell she is!" he said.

The door closed in Leslie's wake.

But while the fabric was covering her...

She worked furiously at the ropes.

The fabric was suddenly lifted from her. "We can't talk much longer though I always did enjoy being around you, Kari. I don't think you ever judged anyone. What the hell happened to you? Did you wind up selling cologne at a chain store? What a waste. But you worked with some real jerks, too. Guys who were never serious."

"Some people just love music!" she whispered. "It doesn't have to be—"

"Recognized!" he snapped. "Yes, it must be recognized. Songs, songs, songs. They are everything! Music is a person's youth. It's there when someone leaves someone else, when something is good, when something is bad. Come on, a man's music is his music!"

"I'm sure your music is your music," Kari said. "I mean think about it. Even here, we have different music. We're great for our country music stars, and country music that combines with other music, country rock and so much more."

"You—of all people—making fun of country music?"

"Making fun—no! I love country music. I'm a Nashville girl, born and bred—"

"And a traitor!"

Okay, beyond a doubt, she had to know who this was. But she'd been gone from her old music

scene since she'd graduated from college and gone into the academy, almost ten years ago now, so...

"We all have our loves and our favorites...music, books, movies...we're all different, we all love different things. There will be country music tonight, the evening is based on country music!" she reminded him.

"And tonight, the music will die!" he promised.

She sensed he was moving. That he was going to head out and...

And what? Someone would die.

She could feel her phone vibrating in her pocket, and she was grateful to the powers that be she had remembered to put it on silent.

Flynn. Of course. Flynn was trying to reach her. And if he walked in...

This man would shoot him before he realized there was any danger.

He was moving about the dressing room, humming. Humming a tune she'd heard earlier during the day when the Hedgehogs had been rehearsing.

And then she knew.

She knew exactly who had seized her, and she knew why, but...

She didn't know just how far his bitterness might take him.

She listened intently.

And when she knew he had left her dressing room, she began to move.

Flynn didn't know local musicians the way that Kari did, but then his feeble efforts at the xylophone hadn't gone all that well in grade school.

Still, Flynn knew the members of her old group. And when Hank approached him, trying to figure out whether to be angry or worried, Flynn warned him that he was afraid something had happened.

"She's not in her dressing room," Leslie told him. "I just looked. She didn't answer so I opened the door—it wasn't locked. But she's not there."

"I'll find her," Flynn promised. "How much time do I have before this thing starts?"

"Doors are open; canned music is playing, and it will be another ten to fifteen minutes before the Hedgehogs open and then—"

"Ten minutes. I've got to find her."

As Flynn turned, he almost crashed straight into Hank.

"The words that were written that Oscar found...he thinks there's a bomb here. I'm afraid if we start an exodus, whoever is doing this will set it off before as planned. I'm trying to find Kari; she may know who the writer is and what he's planning or..."

His voice faded.

He couldn't think about the "or."

"She's all right; Kari is resourceful. She'll be all right. We both know her. She'll manage."

Hank frowned suddenly.

"What is it?" Flynn asked him.

"I know that guy. It's Austin Brooks."

Flynn looked at the man who appeared to be setting one of the mics that belonged to the Hedgehogs group; one that would shortly be moved on stage.

He looked to be early to mid-thirties, but a rough version of that age. Flynn had seen it before.

What drug abuse could do to the human body. Brooks was tall with shaggy blond hair, but clean-shaven. And his face showed rough years.

"A roadie?" Flynn asked Hank.

Hank shook his head. "Yeah, I guess. I arrested him about five years ago. He was selling meth. Then again, maybe being a roadie is what you do when you're not selling meth."

"Stay here. I'll go say hi and ask him something about the Hedgehogs," Flynn said.

Smiling, he walked toward the man. But as he did so, the man spun around. "What? Leave me the hell alone. Can't you see? I'm busy."

"Um, yeah, I can see that. But I was curious about the music. Don't the Hedgehogs do that great song they wrote themselves. I mean, I think they sold it to a big name, but if I'm right, they still do it themselves when they get together. What was the name of that song? Oh, yes, I remember! It was 'Yeah, I've Got a Pit Bull!'"

Two things happened at once. He felt his phone vibrating; and the man, identified by Hank as Austin Brooks, stared at him as if he'd just burst into fire.

"Hang on!" he said casually, reaching into his pocket for his phone.

To his relief, it was Kari. And she spoke quickly.

"It's a guy named Austin Brook but don't—*don't*—try to shoot him or accost him. He's got a bomb out there somewhere. I think he plans on igniting it with remote detonation through his phone. I'm coming out there…let me try to deal with him!"

"Um, yeah, I'm just talking to the guy!" Flynn said.

"I'm there!"

He turned around. Kari was hurrying toward the two of them.

"It's time!" Austin roared.

"No, no, no!" Kari told him. She wasn't placating him, she was speaking determinedly. "Austin, I know what you're upset about. I do. That was your song. 'Yeah, I've Got a Pit Bull.' I remember, because I was there, I was in Terry's garage the day you were working on it. I remember us all laughing about the typical perception of people in the outer regions, that we all had pick-up trucks, rifles, and pit bulls. And we were laughing and talking about the fact your mom had a Volvo, and my dad drove a little Toyota, and my dad had a Skye terrier! You had most of the words—"

"And I had the damned melody, too!" Austin snapped. "It's my song, and they kicked me out of the band—"

"Wait up, Austin, please!" Kari said. "Come on, please! They gave you a choice. You were getting into drugs. You were getting into drugs so heavily you were missing gigs. They had no choice when you wouldn't stop!"

"They sold the song!" Austin raged. He looked at her and then at Flynn.

"He's a cop, huh? What? Did you become a cop, too?" Austin asked.

Kari shook her head. "I'm not a cop—"

"But you think you are so cool cause you think you beat me because you were hiding a gun somehow. Oh, and this dude has a gun, too. But you don't get it. I figured someone would have a gun. Well, too bad, because I'm holding my phone. And there's no way either of you could shoot me fast enough to keep me from pressing the button, and the whole place goes up in flames! Well, we might live back here."

The bomb was in the audience.

"We might live back here?" Kari said. "Austin—"

"Well, okay, I wanted to set it off when Hedgehogs was playing; but...if you force my hand, well, whatever. I told you, I planned on dying today."

Kari was doing great with the man, but maybe...

"Well, that would just be crazy," Flynn said, stepping in. "Kari knew it was your song—I didn't. If you die, who is ever going to know it was your song? I mean, shouldn't the world know you wrote the song; and you were the one who created both the words and the music?"

"When the bomb explodes—"

"Everyone will just think a sick drug-pusher who was a wanna-be musician blew up a bunch of people and killed himself," Flynn said.

"You need to do the song," Kari said.

"What?" Austin demanded.

"I can make it happen," Kari said. "Please. I won't do any-thing—trust me! I don't want you to blow anyone up, Austin. I understand your pain. It wasn't your fault. Drugs can take over and...you were a brilliant musician. You can still be a great musician. You can play—"

"Oh, hell, no! There is no way I am letting go of my phone. Someone is going to pay, and they're going to pay today!"

"Austin, fine, you don't need to play. Oh, wait—you don't remember the lyrics?" she asked.

"Of course, I remember the lyrics!" he snapped. "They were mostly *my* lyrics!"

"Then let's do it—you and me. I'll tell the guys, and you and I will sing the song. Austin! Think of it—you'll open to a massive audience!"

"All right. But I won't let go of the phone. I will have it in my hand if anyone tries anything!" Austin told her.

"Fine. Should I go tell the Hedgehogs?" Flynn asked. "They'll accept what I'm telling them."

"Why? Cause you're a cop, right?"

"Something like that," Flynn told him. "Is it all right—the announcer is going to come on. The curtain is going to go up."

"Yeah, yeah, go. But remember, any funny stuff, we all go boom!" Austin said.

Flynn glanced at Kari and she nodded to him. She had a plan. He had one, too. He knew Hank had been discreetly watching them. He got to his old friend to warn him the bomb was somewhere in front—that it was to take out the front of the audience along with the group playing on stage.

"Get Hedgehogs. Get those guys playing and announcing they're opening with 'Yeah, I've Got a Pit Bull' and that the writer, Austin Brooks, will be on vocals along with Kari Hastings."

"We have a dog that can smell explosives a mile away. We'll put him in a support dog uniform."

"Right. Everything must be fast!"

Flynn hurried back to Kari and Austin.

"It's all set! They'll be announcing you in just a few minutes. You ready?" he asked Austin.

"To sing my own song? You bet!" Austin said. "You bet." He lifted his hand. "I just want to remind you that I can push this button any time. Hey, the Hedgehogs are the assholes I want to take out the most. Though, honestly, I wasn't planning on doing anything but making sure I got Kari out of the way. Still...happy to share with you, let's get moving!"

"Wait!" Flynn said.

"Wait for what?"

"We...uh...can I say goodbye?" Flynn whispered.

"What?" Austin said, confused. "Oh!" he said then, after studying them. "I got it! This is the guy you're seeing these days, huh? Yeah, sure, say goodbye, since we have no idea how this is going to play out!"

Flynn pulled Kari into his arms, kissed her, and held her close for a minute, and whispered, "Hank has a bomb dog out there. Give him all the time you can!"

"Got it," she whispered against his cheek.

And it all happened. Hedgehogs was announced, and then their lead guitarist talked about the incredible wonder of having one of their lead singers back along with Creepers' vocalist, Kari Hastings.

But Kari, as charming as one could hope, also got on the microphone, laying it on. She was so grateful to have the chance to sing with the Hedgehogs—and Austin Brooks.

She could only talk so long. But even as she stepped back to join Austin, she glanced at Flynn. He could see Hank in the audience and his friend made a motion.

They'd found the bomb. They had to disarm it.

Flynn looked at Kari, making a face he hoped alerted her to the fact that she needed to keep Austin Brooks looking at her. And so...

The song began.

The thing was "Yeah, I've Got a Pit Bull" was a good song. It was akin to John Rich's and Gretchen Wilson's "Redneck Woman," a song that made fun of itself. The country twang and beat of it were nearly perfect. And Austin Brooks could sing it well, enhanced by Kari's backup vocals.

And she kept Austin looking at her, looking at him, performing, singing a song to one another, and keeping it...

Alive. With the audience singing, clapping...

But like all things, the song was coming to an end.

Flynn couldn't be sure Hank's people had disarmed the bomb. He hoped he could catch Kari's eye again.

He did. And he moved backstage. It was a risky move. But it seemed there was little choice. As the last notes sounded, he pitched himself through the back curtain just as Kari jumped for Austin's arm.

The phone flew up into the air as Flynn brought Austin Brooks down. For a moment, he watched the phone fly...

Moments that seemed like eons.

Kari caught the phone just as Hank shouted, "Disarmed!"

Beneath him, Austin Brooks sobbed. Police rushed in to take him; but as they did, Kari still made things better. "You're alive, Austin. We're all alive. And now, people will know it's your song. You can have a great band."

"A prison band!" Austin moaned.

"But you'll be doing what you love!" Kari said.

Of course, the entire venue was in pure mayhem. Hank and his officers tried to assure people the danger was over. True. The danger was over, but so was the night.

Well, for some.

For Flynn and Kari, there was an incident interview with Mallory who was incredibly apologetic, saying he'd never doubt Oscar's feelings about potential threats again. Then there was paperwork with the NPD. Then there was just...confusion. And finally...

Finally, the night was over. But it was almost day, and they were both reminded they didn't work alone. Other agents would be working on the bank robberies. They were to take the day off.

"It ended incredibly!" Kari told Flynn. "No one died— Austin didn't even have to die!"

"And even better," he told her. "I've already read a story the Hedgehogs have put out. They're crediting Austin with having written a large portion of the song, which is legally property of the band; but they're going to use proceeds from it for his defense and for instruments so he really can have a prison band."

"Best of all!" she told him. "Hm. I kind of 'die in your arms.' But you know what's way better?"

"What's that?"

She laughed as she crawled atop him and looked down into his eyes.

"Living in your arms!" she said.

He smiled, reached to draw her closer, and whispered, "Then let's live! Like music! Let's live on and on forever!"

ALL TOO WELL

A Short Story
inspired by
Taylor Swift of Tennessee
Rachel Howzell Hall & M.G. Hall

I'm standing here, watching him feed her parmesan truffle fries.

Today, June 22, should be our anniversary.

She's blonde. Long coltish legs. Can't walk in heels—she entered Café LaLAW, knock-kneed in her mini-skirt and thirty-dollar Forever 21 shoes, sighing with relief as she toppled into the chair. And he held her elbow. Chestnut hair brushed away from his face, his eyes, shiny and bright and that one dimple in his cheek...

My phone vibrates in my hand.

The order for Angelica is ready for pick-up.

Two dry-aged beef burgers. Grilled peach salad.

Even in the restaurant's commotion, his laugh bounces across the tiled floor.

He fascinates me...

My phone vibrates again.

The order for—

Fuck off, Angelica's food.

I approach the hostess at the podium.

"Over there." She points to cubbies filled with paper bags.

Jeremy will regret not loving me anymore and he will come

back to me, and I will laugh and then, who knows what I'll do next.

2.

Angelica lives a block away from Café LaLAW.

I drop off the order, rush back to the restaurant and make it in time to see The Girl tromp to the women's bathroom. I weave through the crowd and slip into the restroom.

There she is! Red eyes. Shaking out her hands.

I approach the empty sink next to hers and thrust my hands beneath the spigot.

"It's okay," she's whispering. "You got it, don't freak." A teardrop wobbles on the lower eyelashes. Her blue eyes match...

"Scarf," I say. Faded steel blue and soft pink stenciled with flower petals and butterflies, the scarf is draped around her neck.

"Excuse me?" Her voice soft, twangy.

"Your scarf," I say. "It's gorgeous."

The Girl holds my gaze. "Thank you. A gift from my fiancé."

An almost-anagram of "fiancé" is "finance."

"You're engaged!" I say. "When's the big day?"

"Two months, but I'd be okay if it was tomorrow. Less stress to just...*do it*. But he wants the whole..." Tears pop into her eyes. "Ohmigod, I just stopped and now I'm..."

"I'm sorry you're stressed," I say. "Just be firm with him. He'll understand."

"You're sweet. You have kind eyes. As for the love of my life..." She smirks. "He drives me crazy. He has a very strong viewpoint, and he knows that my parents...They passed a few months ago. Covid. And my caterer just canceled and..." A teardrop tumbles down her cheek. "I'm lost, and alone, and I think he's still talking to one of his exes. And here I am, failing at life in a public bathroom."

I make a sad face. "I know we just met, but...I'm a caterer."

She cocks an eyebrow.

"Ask my best friend—Laura's the executive chef here. Here's my..." I fish around my bag and find a business card.

The Girl takes it. "Do you do tastings?"

"Of course."

"Could you schedule one, like, soon?"

"Soon as in...?"

She stares at my reflection like she's looking for something. "Friday. If I don't kill him before then, ha."

Two days away Friday?

"Well?" Her eyes flick down to my FLIP of Hollywood t-shirt. "Vintage. I like your style. So?"

"Umm...Sure."

"I hate avocado," she says, "and he's allergic to shellfish."

Yes, I know. "He's Jeremy, and you're...?"

"Taylor. And you are...?"

"Ruby."

Sure.

"Could you come to our house?" Taylor asks, pulling out her sparkly-cased cellphone. "We live in the Hollywood Hills."

"Sure," I say, eyes on that scarf. "Will the ceremony be there or off-site?"

"At the house. It's gorgeous. Robert Pattinson used to live there after he broke up with what's-her-face."

I used to live there with what's-his-face.

She's ready to text me.

I pat my jacket pockets, then lie. "Damn. I left my phone somewhere. Just...tell me the address. I'll remember. You have my card—send me a confirmation text."

Taylor recites the address on Woodrow Wilson Drive with a skeptical eyebrow.

I parrot it back.

"How about eleven o'clock?"

Guess *Paw Patrol* ends then.

"Perfect," I say. "No avocado, no shellfish, Friday at eleven." I recite the address again. "And that's such a lovely scarf. It complements your eyes."

Jeremy gets older.

We get younger.

Taylor's mouth is moving.

I say, "Sorry. Missed that."

More women have crowded into the bathroom.

"I *said*," she shouts, "that I'm glad that I had a mini-breakdown in the bathroom."

If she stays with Jeremy, this won't be her last panic attack.

She waggles her fingers. "See you Friday, Rue."

I like that name.

Rue

3.

I just want to be my old self again.

Would the old me be driving two cars behind Jeremy's convertible Beemer, following him and Taylor up La Brea Avenue in my hand-me-down Sunbird?

There they are, golden, even beneath harsh streetlights. The car's top is dropped and that blue scarf—*my scarf*—billows in the wind like she's Stevie Nicks and he's Mick Jagger and they're on their way to the Whiskey to see Guns N Roses play.

She's laughing and he's singing and this route he's taking is bonkers since there's something at the Bowl and there's stop-and-go traffic and he kisses her, and he weaves, and they need to get home in time for her to finish that AP Bio test before 11 pm.

At Franklin, he slams the brakes as tourists cross the street and because there's a traffic cop right there.

Do you know why I stopped you, sir?

Cuz I blew the red. You see, officer, I'm in love with this beautiful woman right here. Wouldn't you break laws, too?

I need to be my old self again.

I'm letting him run my life again.

"Run" is an almost-anagram of "ruin."

We're on Mulholland Drive now, and it's all up and curves, twist and up, and here we are, at Robert Pattinson's old house.

The automatic gate slides to the left, and the BMW slips through.

The gate doesn't slide back to close.

He was supposed to get that fixed.

But he lies.

And I believed every lie he told me.

Like "I can't live without you."

Like "I'm yours."

The gate remains open, like it knows I'm here.

I follow the long brick driveway, car headlamps off, and park as soon as the hacienda sits before me. Red tile roof. Brown doors and window. Pomegranate trees.

The living room light pops on. Then, the kitchen.

My legs wobble as I leave the Pontiac and sneak across the driveway. I reach out to ring the doorbell—

"I can't fucking believe you!" Jeremy's shouting.

I've heard those words before…

"Stop! Please!" That's Taylor, and her words are high-pitched, filled with fear.

Glass breaks against those terra cotta floors.

Pieces of me still stain the grout on those cold floors.

Jeremy hasn't changed.

She now has.

I did.

Poor Taylor.

I can't leave her now.

I reach for the doorknob and—

4.

I see bright green leaves through the French doors.

There are no bright green leaves outside my bedroom window—just a dying jacaranda with gnarled limbs.

Above me, a wood beam ceiling. Beneath me, a hardwood floor...

A sticky, strange dark red something has dried on my wrists. I'm sore. Sweaty. My body is many adjectives right now.

Those pomegranates on the fireplace...

That acoustic guitar in its stand...

These things aren't my things.

My head rests against the floor and my mind rewinds last night's tape.

Café LaLAW...Angelica's burgers...La Brea...The Girl.

Jeremy.

That guitar is his. He can't play, he confessed back then. "But it impresses girls," he said.

I wince as fragments of last night fall into place.

There'd been shouting and glass breaking.

I didn't run back to my car; I didn't leave Taylor to fight alone.

I stare at my hands and wrists, so much of me stained red...

Jeremy is still in bed behind me. Blood on the pillows and comforter...

His eyes are closed but his chest isn't moving.

The whites of his eyes are red.

Where is Taylor?

I crawl to the French door.

There she is, at the garage, setting bags of garden soil on the cobblestones. There's a hole on the hilly side of the backyard. Pots of lavender line the lawn. She moves like a housewife ready to get in a little gardening before a workout and a twenty-dollar smoothie at Erewhon.

I remember now!

He was attacking her (he's been violent in the past, it's in the record) and I tore him off her, and he must've come for me (he has in the past, it's in the record) and she hit him on the head with…

My eyes scan the floor.

A five-pound weight sits beneath the bed.

I saved her life. A Good Samaritan: that's who I am.

I peek out the French doors again.

She's now carrying an ax and saw from the garage.

Since when does lavender require a saw?

5.

I careen around Jeremy's bedroom in search of a better weapon than a five-pound barbell.

Footsteps tap against the terra cotta floor.

Taylor has left the backyard—she must be in the house.

Jeremy drives me crazy—that's what she told me in the restaurant bathroom last night.

I think he's still talking to one of his exes, she confided.

I'd totally kill him if he cheated on me. She said that, too…I think.

I'd said something like that once. Jeremy—was it Jeremy?—you're gonna push me and I'm gonna freaking explode.

Last year, I think, it's a blur, what is time, after all.

A weapon…Nothing in the closet. The dresser drawer…*Ooh!* A clean t-shirt.

I slip out of my FLIP t-shirt and pull on the clean Henley. I crumple the shirt into a ball, then hurry over to the room's fireplace. I reach up and find the small ledge in the chimney, then set the t-shirt on that lip.

I creep out of the bedroom.

Where are the police?

Did I dial 9-1-1?

No one's standing in the living room. There's another guitar on its stand that Jeremy can't play, will never play. There's broken glass and spilled red wine on the floor. There are birds chirping as though nothing has happened. And there's crying.

I wander...

There is Taylor, weeping and hunched in the bathtub.

"You okay?" I ask.

"Is he gone?"

To heaven or...?

"I don't know how I messed up my life so much," she cries. "I didn't recognize you at first last night, but then, on the drive home, I swiped around his phone, and I found you there and you were wearing my scarf...

"You kept complimenting me on that fucking scarf and I asked him about you and he went off on me and...and..."

Taylor dries her face with a towel. "And then, when I saw you on the front porch..." She gazes at me with wounded eyes. "He couldn't explain you. He kept saying, 'Babe, you're imagining things,' and 'She isn't anyone to me,' and he's such a liar..."

She grasps her neck with a skinny hand. "I just...*blacked out*. You must've grabbed something and hit him in the head."

I must've hit him on the head?

There are many times I pondered ways to kill Jeremy.

A delicious bisque made from crustacean shells.

Radiator fluid in his smoothie.

Cutting the brake-lines on his BMW.

But!

I threw out that bisque.

I dumped that smoothie.

I didn't Google, 'where are the brake lines on a BMW.'

"He tried to hurt you," I say now.

She nods like a bobblehead. "He did—"

"Your fight was so loud, I heard it outside. And I tried to pull him off you and—"

Someone knocks on the door.

Cops knock with all knuckles.

I'm not scared. I've done nothing wrong...right?

Lights on police cars and an ambulance shine up and down the driveway.

A short bald guy wearing a badge escorts Taylor to the patio outside the kitchen. I'm sitting with Detective Reynolds, a sleek woman with a sleek chignon. She's asking me questions and I don't know the answers.

"Jeremy was a cheater," I say. "A predator. He likes younger women. Feels he can dominate them. He hurt her."

The detective cocks an eyebrow. "You keep saying that, but I'm not asking about him nor am I asking about Taylor. I'm asking about your relationship with the deceased."

I pull a string on my Henley shirt sleeve. "We were together—"

"For how long?"

"Months. A year. Almost two. He betrayed me and I couldn't function, and it feels like it was just yesterday."

"Before last night," Detective Reynolds says, "when was the last time you saw Jeremy?"

"About three days ago. He acted like I was nothing to him. He treated me like a tossed-away shopping list, and I remember how he treated me and—"

I blink. "He treated her just like crumpled paper."

6.

I watch a police car roll away from the house with a weeping Taylor in the back seat.

Men who arrived in a white and blue van are now rolling out a gurney with Jeremy tucked inside a black bag. A group of detectives wearing latex gloves and paper shoe booties huddle on the front porch.

I'm sweating right now in the back seat of this patrol car, moments away from tearing out this blurping police radio—

"Thanks for waiting," the lady-detective says.

I blink.

The sun has dipped behind the hills.

How long have I been sitting in this back seat?

"May I go now?" My mouth hurts from not drinking or eating anything since…since…

I hate Jeremy—for what he did to me, for what he's done to Taylor. A month ago, she didn't even know that she was doomed—with Jeremy dead *or* alive.

She hit him on the head. She went through his phone and found…

A picture of me.

My heart buoys in my chest—he still loved me!—but then, my heart sinks again. *She's nothing to me,* he'd told Taylor who then told me.

I don't believe her—she hit Jeremy. Who gardens with a dead body just a few feet away?

She's a liar.

He's a predator.

And I'm…

Both—that's what Jeremy used to say. *Your name's not Kendra,* he said once. *Do you even know who you are?*

I am who I need to be to survive. That's what I told him.

A liar.

"A predator," he'd said.

The moving box labeled "JEREMY" sits unopened in the middle of my living room. He shipped it to me days after our ending. It hurts my heart to look at it, especially now that he's gone. Opening this box will destroy me—inside, I'll find our matching plaid shirts, a stuffed owl, a picture, and other stuff. I want to burn it just like I've burned the other "JEREMY" boxes. But I won't burn it now that he's gone.

I cry as I stand over this box until the moon shines milky light through my living room window. I am a widow without the benefit of marriage. A no one in the eyes of California.

I cry and remember how Jeremy would grab my neck, then rub his nose against my face and tell me how he loved the way I smelled when I was scared.

I text Taylor.

Just checking in again.

We should really talk.

Let's connect as soon as possible.

I want to add "or else," but I don't want to sound menacing.

The phone vibrates with her response.

Message undelivered. This account no longer exists.

7.

My former best friend answers the front door of her beachside house wearing a striped sweater and skinny jeans. Her bun looks like it's been fixed into position with pencils and glue.

I'm a total mess in a Vans hoodie, two-dollar flip-flops and turquoise leggings.

Michelle's eyes peck at my bare toes and the hideous turquoise leggings. Her thin lips twist into a smile. Lipstick bleeds into the wrinkles around her mouth.

"Look what's happened to me without you in my life," I say, trying to smile.

"I thought you were gone for good," she says. "But you're just like herpes. Going away, coming back, going away..."

Michelle has always been jealous of me. She'd been friend-zoned since Jeremy didn't date women who'd watched *Laverne & Shirley* on their black and white televisions.

I say, "I still think of you as my friend."

"I don't think of you at all."

"Can you pretend for a moment that we're cool? Something bad has happened, and we're gonna need each other. For real."

She squints at me. "What did you do?"

"Not me. Taylor."

"Taylor Greenridge, Jeremy's whatever? Or Taylor Thompkins, the stripper?"

"Jeremy's fiancé."

"What about her?"

My eyes swell with tears. "Jeremy's dead."

Michelle sits still as a stone in the deck chair overlooking the Pacific Ocean. Her gray cat Lady weaves in between her ankles, but Michelle doesn't reach to stroke Lady's back.

"I'm sure she needed to protect herself," I say. "He brought out the worst in her. I know this because he brought out the worst in me. He forces your hand."

Michelle stares at me like I'm a stranger. "Why are you here?"

I scratch Lady's ear. "Something's off with Taylor. She disconnected her number, and yesterday, she had an ax—"

Michelle lifts her hand. "No. I don't want to hear anything else from you. Jeremy didn't want you in his life, and I'm sure he'd want you to stay away from him in his death."

"Don't say that." A sob breaks from my chest, and the cat darts back into the house.

"You should go."

I rise from the loveseat. "Did he ever regret ending us?"

Michelle rolls her eyes. "You are so fucking delusional. Shoo. Go home."

A minute later, she leads me down the walkway toward my car. "I always told Jeremy to be careful who he slept with."

"I *loved* him."

She laughs. "Oh, for fuck's sake, you don't know Taylor. You didn't even really know Jeremy. *You* don't even know you. I don't remember the last time I've seen you, but your hair is a mess, your makeup is crazy...And those leggings...*Turquoise?*"

Light dances in Michelle's eyes as she berates me.

My heart flutters in my chest because she *does* care about me. "Hate" is an almost-anagram of "heart."

"Jeremy was my friend," Michelle says now, "but I'm not gonna pretend that he was a good guy. I'm just amazed it took this long for someone to finally kill him."

8.

At home, I open my laptop and log onto RADAR. Anyone can subscribe and gain access to names, aliases, addresses, anything in public records. I type TAYLOR GREENRIDGE into the search field.

Graduated four years ago from the high school just around the corner from my apartment. Arrested last year for shoplifting. Also arrested for identity fraud. Pleaded "no contest," was fined and required to complete community service.

Taylor Greenridge is no angel but then again neither am I. Really: If anyone poked around my RADAR records, they'd gasp and say, "Rue did *that?* Sweet little *Rue?*"

Except they wouldn't say "Rue?"

I click the "RELATED RESULTS" link.

The woman in the picture is Kylie Becker, 27 years old. She's brunette, a little heavy, and her blue eyes are set close together...

Arrested for shoplifting. Drug-dealing. Simple assault...

Alias include Selena Green and...

Taylor Greenridge.

9.

I've sat here on Woodrow Wilson Drive forever, but my tenacity has now paid off.

Taylor, driving Jeremy's BMW, turns left out of the driveway.

I follow her.

To McDonald's. To Sally Beauty. To Whole Foods. The Sunbird's gas needle hovers slightly above "E." I need to refuel but if I stop, then I've wasted a day.

Taylor-Kylie—zooms onto Fuji Way. She makes a left and now, the harbor is right there, and the houses are tall and crammed together. She pulls into the driveway of a Mediterranean house in the middle of the block.

Michelle's house!

Wearing those cheap heels, Taylor-Kylie clomps up the walkway. She reaches beneath the welcome mat, grabs an envelope, then clomps back to the BMW.

Does Michelle know she's here?

What is in that envelope?

10.

Standing over the unopened box of things, I text Michelle.

We need to talk about Taylor!!

That's not even her name!!

I found out some things!!

No ellipses. No response.

I don't move.

On the box, there's a tiny piece of packing tape that I can peel back...

My phone rings.

I blink.

The clock says it's ten-fifty but there's no way I've been

standing here, unmoving, for three hours. I'm losing time.
Again.

11.

Detective Reynolds smiles and lipstick stains her front tooth.

"Are you thinking about something more important?" Detective Reynolds asks.

I shake my head and stare at the mailboxes. "How can I help you?"

Detective Stumpy nods up toward my apartment. "I asked to talk inside."

I force myself to smile. "I'm house-sitting a very anxious pit bull. Not a good idea."

"How are you holding up?" Detective Chignon asks.

I sigh. "He meant so much to me."

Detective Stumpy pulls out a photograph from his leather binder. "You recognize this?"

I blink at the picture. "Umm…"

"That's a scarf," he says. "And that red there? Forensics says it's blood."

I say, "Whose blood?"

"We're waiting on those results right now," the lady detective says. "In the meantime, maybe you could shed some light."

"On?" I ask.

She says, "Like why your scarf—?"

"*My* scarf?" I say, eyes bugged.

"We've seen pictures of you wearing this scarf. And we found *your* scarf shoved down Jeremy's throat. There are also marks around his neck that were made by this very scarf. So again: how did your scarf—?"

I shake my head. "It's not mine anymore. He gave it to Taylor—"

"Who's Taylor?" Detective Stumpy asks.

"His fiancée," I say.

"He isn't engaged," Detective Reynolds says.

"That's not true," I say, shaking my head. "I was gonna cater their wedding."

"You're a caterer?" he asks.

"Not yet."

"You lied to this Taylor?" she asks.

"Whose blood will we find on this scarf?" Detective Stumpy asks.

"Not mine," I say.

She nods. "We've been told that you stole a few of Jeremy's things. A few plaid shirts, a pocketknife, some briefs…"

"I don't remember those things as 'stolen,'" I say.

"So, if I got a warrant," Detective Stumpy says, "to search your apartment, I wouldn't find that knife, those briefs or plaid shirts?"

I just wanna be my old self again…

But who was that?

"We're gonna continue this conversation at the station," Detective Stumpy says.

"Am I under arrest?" I ask.

Detective Reynolds guides me toward the blue sedan parked at the curb.

"What about my dog?" I ask.

"You don't have a dog," Detective Stumpy says. "We've already talked to the landlord and a few of the tenants in the building. And your name isn't Ruby."

12.

This room is cold. There's nothing in here except a scarred table with metal loops in it, hard chairs, carpet that stinks of feet, and this sweating can of Mountain Dew.

I don't drink Mountain Dew. Unless maybe I do.

"I didn't kill him," I repeat to Detective Reynolds. "He was beating up Taylor-Kylie-Serena, and I stopped him. He must've hit me because I fell to the ground, and when I opened my eyes…He was dead. Have you talked to Taylor yet?"

"We have," Detective Chignon says.

I exhale. "I didn't make her up."

Detective Stumpy chuckles. "You do that, right?"

"What did Taylor say?" I ask.

"She's not doing well," Detective Reynolds says. "She's under a doctor's care and staying with her parents in Sherman Oaks."

Doctor's care?

Sherman Oaks?

Her parents are dead.

13.

I *do* know the owner of Café LaLAW. We are best friends. We *were* best friends.

Until Jeremy.

Then I kinda lost the string of the story and lost my way.

"And I apologize again for that," I say to Laura, my former best friend.

Laura tends to the burgers on the grill. "You must need something because it's been how many months since you told me this?"

"He's dead, you know."

"Yeah."

"But I didn't do it."

She cracks a lopsided grin. "That is the first truth you've told in ages."

My cheeks burn. "The cops are circling cuz they think I did. His fiancée did—her name's not Taylor and she has a record—"

She slaps a slice of cheese on top of the burger. "Sounds

familiar. What do you want?"

Proof.

Laura sits in front of the bank of TV monitors. "What night am I looking for?"

"Wednesday, June 22, like around ten that night."

Laura double-clicks on a video.

Five minutes after ten—a group of eight arrives at the reception desk.

Ten fifteen—Jeremy enters with Taylor on his arm.

She's wearing the scarf!

Four minutes later, I walk in to pick up Angelica's dinner order.

Laura then finds the video clip of the happy couple leaving the restaurant. Taylor's wearing the scarf and as she lifts her left hand to adjust that scarf, that big diamond engagement ring catches the light.

I pace the living room, ignoring Sal the Landlord's latest barrage of text messages.

I have a mortgage to pay!

Please Stacey! Just leave

Leave and go where?

Pay with what?

And my name's not Stacey...anymore.

My phone rings.

"The blood on the scarf," Detective Reynolds says.

"Yes?"

"Does not match your DNA profile," she says.

"Whose blood is it?"

"Can't share that," the detective says. "Something you mentioned to me yesterday."

I collapse on the couch, all adrenalin gone. "About...?"

"Taylor. You said that her parents are dead."

"Yes, she told me that the night we met."

The detective grunts, then says, "Have a good night, Stacey."

14.

The woman on the other end of the phone sounds old.

"Who?" she says again.

"Kylie Greenidge," I say.

"How did you get my number?"

"She's a college friend," I say, "and she told me she was staying with her parents—"

"I have no idea who you're talking about."

"Oh, wait," I say, cheeks warm. "I meant Taylor Greenidge. Got mixed up."

"Young lady," the woman says, "I had one son, and he came back home from the Vietnam War in several pieces. He had no children. I have no grandchildren. Taylor Greenidge isn't my daughter. She's my day caretaker. Her and Michelle D'Antoni."

Michelle and Taylor *work* together?

I dump ice cubes into the kitchen sink filled with cold water. Then, I dunk my head to quiet the voices, to follow the string, to—

A hand pushes my head.

My eyes pop open, and I bat at the body behind me. I keep my mouth closed and try to stay calm, but the hand forces me to stay under.

I grab the paring knife on the counter, and I swing.

And I miss.

I swing again.

The knife catches.

The grip on my head relaxes.

177

A gasp.

I spin around.

Michelle is gaping at the slash on her stomach.

"What are you doing?" I blubber, breath burning in my throat.

"You've fucked me up again," she snarls. "Kylie and me, we were so fucking close to pulling it off."

"She...was your partner?" *I* was Michelle's partner once upon a time.

But I was thrown aside for a younger woman.

"You fell in love with that asshole," she says. "You lost sight of the mission. I told you that I'd fuck your shit up if you fucked up again. And you fucked up again."

"I...I..."

Don't know what's happening.

"You haven't been yourself in a long time," Michelle says.

"He made me fall in love," I say, my tears mixing with sink water.

She laughs. "You went out with him *one time*, Trina, then he ghosted you after you stole his shit, and he caught you and threatened to call the cops if you ever came near him again."

I shake my head. "That's not...We were...in love."

Michelle looks at me like I've grown a third ear. Then, she waves a hand at the walls. "What the hell is all of this? I move out and you just...What the actual fuck?"

There's a picture of Jeremy skydiving and Jeremy eating an ice-cream cone. There's Jeremy hugging a poodle, chopsticks up his nose, napping in a hammock and staring at a sunset.

"You just printed them off social media?"

I bite my lip.

"Sal *will* have you evicted," she says. "Squatters ultimately lose."

"Just because you decided to give up—"

I lunge at Michelle with the paring knife.

She ducks and dodges.

Something cold sinks into my gut. Then I feel hot, and I'm on the ground.

Michelle kneels over me. "I'm going away. Kylie's already there. I just needed to handle loose strings. You're the loose string."

Her words sound fuzzy. Her skin looks furry.

"You had a good run," she says, moving away, "but you let him change you, and in our business, that can be deadly."

I smile—but it's not for Michelle. My smile is for Jeremy, now waving at me from the bluffs high above the Pacific Ocean. The sun makes the sky sherbet and wind tousles my hair. Jeremy's beckoning me to follow him to the tidepools.

The scarf tickles my neck. The wind catches it, and the scarf dances in the air. I watch it dance in the tangerine sky until it floats away…away…and I smile at Jeremy and…

Content warnings: mention/implication of sexual assault; on-page violence.

GOODBYE PEARL

Sarah Zachrich Jeng

We're scattered across the country now. Aimee moved to Boulder in '99; Michelle ran even farther, to the Bay Area. Jenn spent some time in New York, though she and her wife bought a house in the suburbs after they had their second kid. I'm the only one still here in Gainesville.

We're not great at staying in touch day-to-day. Still, we're lifers. Every July, the four of us—the former members of The Simones—go on a girls' trip. Last year it was Nantucket. Up there it's the same Atlantic Ocean as in Florida, but somehow it feels different. Like it isn't full of other people's washed-off sunblock.

So we get together in some lovely place. We eat and drink, not as much as we used to. We catch up on one another's lives and gossip about people we used to know, most of whom we haven't seen in years. We never talk about what happened in the summer of '97.

The Suffer, we called it, because it never got below eighty even at three a.m. At three in the afternoon, the sun blazed like a black metal guitar solo. I was working as a banquet server at a hotel that has since been torn down to build "luxury" student housing. My uniform was a white dress shirt and black pants. I walked to work. By the time I got there, that cheap polyester-blend shirt would be plastered to my back with sweat. I'd feel like I had already worked ten hours, but I still had a whole shift to go. Didn't help that I was usually hung over.

When I got out, the temperature would only have dropped by a few degrees. Yet the heat was softer in darkness. I'd slip through the back streets, a floating ghost in my white shirt and dark pants. Not invisible, though. A girl in public is always being looked at, if only by the made-up people inside her head.

I knew walking alone at night wasn't the best idea, especially in the neighborhood where I lived, but I didn't have a car and my bike had been stolen. I made myself as unobtrusive as I could. If the men I passed told me to smile, I smiled and kept walking.

Downtown, though, I felt safe. We had our usual haunts: Durty Nelly's, The Down Lo. Sometimes The Simones had a show. Other nights we'd just be seeing our friends' bands play. I was in my element, surrounded by friends.

Oh, there were rumors of danger, but mostly outside of our little bubble. It was assumed that the people *we* hung around with would be cool. Of course, you heard things about certain guys. There was this one kid who always had weed, but you didn't go out back to smoke with him unless you wanted him to try and stick his tongue down your throat. Still, our scene was utopia. It would never throw anything at us we couldn't handle.

The Covered Dish always had a show going on, whether it was some shitty college band or a national act like Yo La Tengo. For the last year we'd played the Dish regularly, building our audience from a scattering of barflies (and when a space that big is empty, boy does it look empty) to a respectably-sized local crowd. People liked us. I actually used to feel flattered when they said things like "You guys rock pretty hard for girls!" (They never could bring themselves to leave off the "for girls.") They said other stuff too, comments that had nothing to do with our musical ability, and I didn't have the sense to get pissed off about it.

I wasn't in it for adulation. Nor, precisely, for art. My favorite thing about being in the Simones was the way we became a unit when we played, how we could communicate without words. I lost myself in it.

We weren't playing the night Pretty Pete and the Models played their last show, but all four of us were there.

People talked about that show like it was transcendent. Part of it was the aura of mystery that hung around Pete's disappearance, but even I can admit they were a fucking great band. They had that garage-rock thing going on, the sound that blew up a few years later with The Strokes, but most of the Models' appeal came down to their frontman, who was also their principal songwriter. If they'd ever made it out of Gainesville, Pete's talent and charisma would've made Julian Casablancas look like even more of a pretentious clown in comparison.

Just goes to show you how the people who create the greatest art can be the biggest assholes.

Last year the four of us vacationed on Nantucket, but this summer we've chosen Jekyll Island for our girls' getaway. It's closer to home, at least for me, and peaceful. The kind of resort where guests and staff alike mind their own business.

On the back side of the old hotel where Gilded Age robber barons used to bring their families, there's a pub with an inner room where we can have a quiet drink. I bide my time, waiting for the alcohol to loosen us up. Figuring out how to put my news into words.

Paynes Prairie, a broad wetland to the south of Gainesville, drains into the aquifer via the Alachua Sink. When the sinkhole becomes blocked with logs and debris, as it periodically does, the result is a vast lake. There was no lake in 1997. But the water level around the sinkhole was deep enough for our purposes.

Now, however, we're in a drought that's lasted long enough to uncover ground that hasn't been seen in decades. In the emerging sea of sticky, anaerobic mud, people have found a lot of stuff. Prehistoric dugout canoes. Dead alligators. Bones of deer, horses, and bison that frequent the prairie.

And most of the 1978 Pearl W-5 Deluxe kit I used to play as the drummer of The Simones.

When I tell the band, silence falls over our table. Aimee covers her mouth with her hand. Jenn goes still, but her eyes dart toward the door as if she's thinking of making a break for it.

Finally, Michelle clears her throat. This does nothing to temper the hoarseness in her voice when she speaks.

"Did they find anything else?"

"Pretty Pete" was one of those ironic nicknames that wasn't really ironic. In our little scene people went by whatever names the others saw fit to bestow on them. Gutterpunk Joe, Danarchy, Aimee the Virgin. (Because she was such a slut—get it?) She wore it as a badge of honor, since it was either that or be scorned as a humorless harpy. It was all sarcasm anyway. We didn't know any other way to be; I guess we'd all watched too many John Hughes movies growing up.

Pretty Pete, though. Clean him up a bit and he could have graced a cologne ad. Six-two and razor thin, with dark hair and high cheekbones, his performing voice ranged from a rasping bark to a blood-curdling bellow. He played guitar on a few songs, but he was at his most magnetic when he left his Strat leaned up against the amp and freed himself to strut around the stage with the mic like a handsome Mick Jagger.

He could have had practically any girl he wanted.

I'd hooked up with him the previous winter. I'd been more wasted than usual, and I could never remember the series of events that had led me into his sheetless bed, or much of what had happened there. But I told myself it gave me a certain power, a certain cachet, that he'd chosen me.

The problem was that afterward he basically acted like I didn't exist, and *that* made me feel about two inches tall.

I couldn't stop trying to catch his eye again. Like if I could recreate the specific alchemy that had made him take me home that February night, I would prove my worth.

The night of their last show, Pretty Pete and the Models had just returned from a mini-tour along the East Coast, so they were tour-tight and could practically read one another's minds onstage. After they finished, I went to the side of the stage, dragging Jenn as backup, to let Pete know what an amazing set they'd played.

He was shirtless, slick with sweat. It dripped off the ends of his hair in shining beads under the stage lights.

"Pete!" I had a specific comment all teed up: something about a new pedal he'd gotten, as if my technical knowledge would impress him.

At the sound of my voice he turned, grinning. His eyes, brilliant against black eyeliner, slid across me and landed on Jenn.

Two things about Jenn. One: she's a knockout. In 1997 she looked a little like Milla Jovovich with dyed-black hair. Two: she's a hard six on the Kinsey scale. The whole idea of being attracted to men is absurd to her.

If Pete had looked at me the way he was looking at her, I would have melted into a puddle on the beer-slicked floor. She just shifted her weight and caught my eye as if to say *Do your thing, if you must.*

"Great show!" I yelled up at him.

He gave me a single, dismissive nod, then hopped off the stage and spoke to Jenn as if I wasn't there. "*Heyyyy.* Do you wanna come out to the van for a minute? We've got some…" He leaned in and murmured to her. I didn't need to hear what he said to get the gist, especially once I saw the way it made Jenn perk up.

A third thing about Jenn: she liked drugs. Not in a way we

considered self-destructive at the time, though in retrospect maybe it was. But we trusted her to keep it in check and not be too fucked-up to play. And she wasn't above using a man's attraction to her to have a little fun.

I was clearly not included in Pete's invitation.

Jenn glanced at me, a question in her eyes. The night was pretty much done, at least from the perspective of the club, which was playing Limp Bizkit over the speakers in an attempt to clear the place out. Michelle and Aimee had left earlier to go see some friends of ours play at a smaller club. They'd wanted us to come, but I'd had my whole Pete agenda and Jenn hadn't wanted to leave me on my own.

I knew I shouldn't leave her on her own, either. Back then, women weren't as conscientious about watching out for each other, or ourselves. We didn't take our drinks with us to the bathroom. But we knew what could happen. We were told, in many ways, that risk was the toll we had to pay for being out in the world.

Yet I couldn't stem the wave of bitterness that rose up because Pete had made his offer to my friend and not me. Anyway, Jenn would be fine. The rest of Pete's band would be there. She would accept the drugs and reject the hookup Pete clearly had in mind.

The idea of Pretty Pete, king of the scene, taking his swing and striking out—it created a vicious symmetry in my brain.

I looked at Jenn, then away. "Do whatever you want," I said.

Then I stumbled home and passed out.

The front door slammed hard enough to shake the walls of my room, vibrating me out of a fitful sleep. The sun roared through my window. I'd forgotten to close the blinds.

Jenn was home.

She, Aimee, and I lived together. I heard her pause outside

my door; then a hesitant, scratching knock. She said my name. "Are you awake?"

I told her to come in. She looked like she'd spent the night with her head over a toilet. Fear unfurled inside me as soon as I saw her face: I knew what shame looked like.

I sat up in bed, my cobwebbed brain struggling to find words. In that moment I was terrified she'd done something she regretted, something she knew would hurt me.

It was much worse than that.

Her delicate features distorted and she burst into tears. "Why the fuck did you leave me last night?" She was crying so hard I could barely understand her.

She collapsed on my bed, at my feet. I stroked her hair, my confusion turning to horror as the story came out.

Pete's bandmates had been in the van, but they hadn't gone to his house afterward. Jenn's last clear memory was of sitting next to him on his couch as he cut lines for them. She'd woken up alone, on the floor wedged between the couch and the filthy glass coffee table they'd snorted coke off of. Or whatever it was he'd given her. She'd had to search for her pants. She told me how her hands trembled, how she'd strained to hear any sound, afraid he'd come out of his room before she left.

"That piece of shit."

We looked up. Aimee leaned in my open doorway, listening.

Shame flickered across Jenn's face again, and it made me furious that she felt that way.

"We should kill him," I said. It was a joke. A bad one, the kind you make when you've spent most of your life not being able to take anything seriously. I was trying to make Jenn feel better.

"I never told you guys this," Aimee said, "but in April I was at a party at the Hippie House and I'd passed out in the hammock, and I woke up with my pants down and him on top of me. I had to flip the hammock to get him off."

"Why didn't you say anything?" I asked. I was almost mad

at her. She'd let me keep mooning over that dickhead for months. And if Jenn had known Pete was sketchy...

"I should have. I'm sorry. But you know how guys are. They do dumb shit all the time when they're drunk."

Aimee was right. Even some of the ones we considered harmless said and did things that would never fly in these post-#MeToo days. At least, I hope not.

So I redirected my rage where it belonged, sharpening it with thoughts of all the energy I'd put into lusting after Pete. And now that I thought about it—what *had* happened in February? What had he done to me? None of us had heard of enthusiastic consent. The lines were as unclear as my memories of that night. But I couldn't deny he'd treated me like garbage ever since then.

Things were looking dispiritingly consistent.

"Everyone knows you're gay," I said to Jenn. "Even if you didn't say no, he would have known you wouldn't be into it."

We had the discussion where we weighed our options and concluded that we had no good ones. There was no realistic scenario in which Pretty Pete went to prison for this.

"I just want him to say sorry," Jenn said. "And if he's not sorry, I want to *make* him sorry."

Those words—*make him sorry*—dropped an idea into my mind. Despite my aching head, I smiled.

We got Michelle involved for two reasons. One: she owned the van that was our only way of getting out to the warehouse. Two: when we called her to ask if we could borrow the van, it turned out that Pete had already tried his luck with her. Apparently The Simones were a matched set and he wanted to collect us all. She'd thought nothing of it at the time; she hadn't been drunk enough to go off alone with him. But she'd had her share of weird experiences with men—encounters in which you didn't think you'd said no, but couldn't remember saying yes.

When she heard what he'd done to Jenn, she was keen to help.

The plan was simple. Lure him out to our practice space, lock him in with us, and beat the ever-loving shit out of him. He was one of those rangy guys who was probably stronger than he looked, but we figured we could take him four against one, especially if Michelle gave him a Xanax first.

Our object: convince him he was about to have his dick severed from his body with a garrotte made out of a guitar string, then drag him outside and leave him. The four-mile walk home would give him plenty of time to think about his choices.

We weren't planning anything permanent. We just wanted him to know on a visceral level that we were not defenseless. Maybe he'd think twice before he fucked with another woman.

Our practice space was a storage unit in an industrial park off Highway 441. Bands rented out several of the other units too, and occasionally we'd throw keg parties with a different band playing in each warehouse. But that night—a Sunday—the area was deserted.

Our space had a sliding garage door, behind which a previous tenant had built a plywood wall with a regular door that locked with a dead bolt. The concrete room was as soundproof as we could make it, to cut down on noise complaints.

Earlier in the day, Michelle had called Pete up asking if he wanted to come out and jam, just the two of them. He knew what that meant. Our concern was that he'd turn her down because it was too easy, but all he'd said was that he would bring the beer.

Michelle dropped Jenn, Aimee, and me off at the warehouse before going back into town for Pete. She padlocked us in. With the lights and fans off it was airless, oven-hot, and so dark I could hardly tell whether my eyes were closed or open. I kept feeling my skin twitch, as though the palmetto bugs that lived in there were crawling on me. Nervous, I picked up my sticks and tapped them together.

"We should be quiet," Aimee said, her voice small. "We

don't want to tip him off when they get here."

After a while we heard the van pull up. The padlock clanked open, and the garage door ground up on its track with a metallic shriek.

Carefully, I stood and came out from behind my drums. Pete was talking, his voice muffled by the soundproofing. Slurring a little. He must've washed down the Xanax with a beer or three.

The inner door opened, showing two figures silhouetted in the pallid glow of the lone security light outside. "After you," Michelle said, her voice hoarse with tension Pete never heard.

He stepped through the door. Michelle followed, closing it behind her.

"Man, it's dark as fuck in—" Pete began, as Michelle turned the key in the deadbolt and Jenn flicked on the light switch.

An unshaded bulb glared down from the ceiling. Pete took in the four of us: one anchoring each pole, each quadrant of the clock. His forehead wrinkled in confusion.

Eventually, he came to the conclusion that this was not where he wanted to be.

He whirled around in slow motion, giving Michelle plenty of time to step out of his way. The doorknob turned ineffectually in his hand. And now his back was to us.

Jenn was the first to hit him. I hadn't noticed she had a guitar in her hands, and I cried out in dismay as she struck him a glancing blow with it. I was worried it would break. However, it wasn't the hollowbody Gretsch she played on our more rockabilly-ish songs but her second favorite, an Ibanez Stratocaster copy, basically a solid slab of wood.

He turned so she caught him in the ribs rather than the spine. He stumbled sideways but stayed on his feet as his hand went to his battered side.

"What the fuck, Jenn?" He had the nerve to sound outraged. He staggered toward her. She backed away, looking petrified.

"Aimee!" I yelled. She stood in his blind spot, holding a delay pedal in her hand like a brick she was preparing to throw through a window. But she seemed rooted to the floor.

Michelle sprang into action. She grabbed the torchiere lamp that stood in the corner and swung it, connecting with Pete's shoulder. She should have turned it upside down and used the heavier base. The top part of the lamp shattered, along with the bulb, sending a glittering rain of glass into his hair. He lurched toward me—was pushed toward me—but I danced out of his way.

Aimee's bass cabinet was on wheels, an Ampeg that was three-quarters as tall as she was. I launched it as hard as I could into Pete's body, sending him falling backward into my drums.

He landed faceup on top of them, almost knocking them over. His arms and legs flopped back toward the floor. He looked dazed, and more than a little like a flipped turtle as he struggled to rise.

Adrenaline pumped through me, filling my limbs with strength. I moved the speaker cabinet aside, then snatched up my crash cymbal, stand and all. I positioned the edge at his throat so he couldn't get up.

I leaned over him. "Do you know why you're here?"

He blinked and swiveled his head until his gaze found mine. His mouth worked; he seemed to be struggling to focus on me.

Does he even remember my name?

Incredibly, he started to laugh. "I don't even...I have no idea what's happening here."

He wasn't afraid. The goddamned Xanax had done its work too well.

Rage boiled inside me. Had he forgotten what he'd done to us?

I clutched the cymbal so hard it cut into my palm. Letting go, I drew the stand back to hit him with it. But then he reached up and seized the front of my T-shirt, jerking me off balance.

The cymbal stand dropped to the floor with a crash. I pushed against him while he pulled on me, each of us fighting for leverage. He was on his back, but his guitarist's hands were stronger than mine.

Then I felt a punch, but it was like a second-hand punch. Pete's grip on my shirt relaxed. He roared in pain and grabbed a handful of my hair.

I screamed. I felt another punch. This time when his hand opened, I was free.

I stepped back, legs shaking. Jenn stood beside me with a long, bloody screwdriver in her hand. She'd driven it between Pete's ribs. Twice.

He was bleeding all over my drums, both from his side and from a scalp wound he'd gotten at some point. I could hear the amplified *drip-drip-drip* of fluid falling through the porthole of my kick drum and landing on the batter head. It wasn't just the heads; blood pooled around the rims, staining the wood on the inside of the shells, smearing the snow-white wrap on the outside. I'd never get it out of the small holes around the lugs.

Why was I worrying about my drums? We'd fucking killed Pretty Pete.

Well, not killed him. But his normally vampire-pale skin had turned an alarming bluish gray. His breaths were quick and desperate but didn't seem to be getting enough air into his lungs. His eyelids flickered; he barely seemed aware anymore that we were there.

But then his eyes opened, their brilliance dulled. He raised his head a fraction and looked straight at me. "Help me," he rasped.

It felt like lightning had struck me. I took a step toward him before I thought better of it. It's not easy to refuse someone who's helpless and in pain, no matter how much of a shit they are.

"We could take him to the hospital," I said, though he didn't look like he'd make it that far. "We could drop him off. Maybe he won't remember it was us."

"I want him to remember," Jenn snapped. "That was the whole point."

"What if he dies?" Aimee's voice was thick, tears streaking

her cheeks. She crouched behind her bass cabinet, making it into a rampart between her and the rest of us. She was the only one of us who hadn't touched him. If she decided to go to the police, she might get off clean. Comparatively.

Jenn walked over and crouched down to Aimee's level, the long black veil of her hair obscuring her face.

"If he dies," she said, "he won't be able to do to anyone else what he did to us."

She placed a bloodstained hand on Aimee's arm. "Do you think we deserve to go to prison for this asshole?"

Aimee's gaze went inward, as though she was remembering that night in the hammock. She shook her head.

Pete had lost consciousness. We moved him off my drums— he was shockingly heavy—and laid him out flat on the floor. I fished the sound-dampening pillow out of my bass drum and stood clutching it, unable to make my feet move.

I felt the pillow taken gently from my hands. Aimee's face was still tear-streaked but resolute. "Help me," she said.

She pushed the pillow onto Pete's face while I held his shoulders down, just in case. When it had been ten minutes by the battery-powered clock on the wall, she sat back.

"He had it coming," Michelle said, and we all looked at each other and agreed it was true.

The screwdriver and the lamp went into a storm drain and a dumpster, respectively, after we'd wiped them down. We'd always joked that the toilet down the way hadn't been cleaned since Darby Crash was alive, but we found a couple gallons of bleach under the sink.

We rolled Pete up in the rug that had sat under my kick drum to keep it from sliding as I played. His feet stuck out from one end. I couldn't stop looking at his battered Converse.

Had I helped kill him because he'd hurt my friend, or because he'd hurt my pride? I didn't know.

I still don't know.

But Jenn was right: he wasn't worth ruining our lives over.

"We could try to clean them," Michelle said doubtfully as she surveyed the bloodstained shells of my drums. The kick drum and rack toms were completely covered, though the floor tom had only been splashed.

It was four in the morning by then. A couple of the storage units were rented out as workshops by people who would be in bright and early on a Monday morning. And we still had plenty to do; we didn't have time to save my drums. Into the back of the van they went with Pete.

Aimee had been dating a park ranger, a sweet himbo named Liam, for a few months. He'd given her a key to his place. On our way through town, she slipped into his apartment and came out with the key to the Camp Ranch Road gate. I still don't know if Liam woke up, or what she told him if he did. But he was the guy she ended up moving to Colorado with.

We saw no other rangers in the park. No early-morning hikers. We drove right onto the Hawthorne Trail, branches scraping the sides of the van, and as close to the Alachua Sink as we could get. The water was black with a film of algae around the edges. As we splashed in, wetting our shoes, I tried not to think about the eyes I saw glowing in the dark. About alligators dragging me off my feet and into the depths.

We wrestled Pete as far out as we could, hoping he'd be sucked into the sinkhole. No body, no crime.

The drums were easier, being light enough to throw. They filled with water, sinking at different rates. Watching them disappear was like watching my child drown.

Killing Pete was The Simones' last performance together. People felt bad for me that someone had broken into the warehouse and stolen my drums, but there was no such thing as Go-FundMe back then. Besides, everyone we knew was broke.

A couple of times, I practiced on friends' drum sets. But every time I picked up my sticks, it was as if I could feel the beating of Pretty Pete's heart through his shoulders while I held him down for Aimee. I hadn't felt his heartbeat while we were actually killing him, but the mind does strange things.

Other than that, I've been relatively untroubled by guilt for the past twenty-seven years. As long as I stay away from the drums.

Now, making the drive home from Jekyll Island, I catch a report on the radio of human remains found in Paynes Prairie. At first I listen with detached interest, as if it has nothing to do with me. Then the full implication hits and I have to pull over.

The steering wheel seems to throb under my hands. Like a heartbeat.

I could turn west. Keep driving until I get to Aimee's, or Michelle's. I could make a U-turn and go north. Jenn would shelter me, and the Canadian border's not far.

But in the end, I get back on the road and keep driving south. If I run now, I'll always be running, and I don't know how to call any other place but Gainesville home. My drums are the only thing tying Pete's body to any of us. I don't want to lead suspicion to my friends.

No matter what happens, I want to protect them. Once a band, always a band.

THE FAVOR

D.P. Lyle

It was the flip of blonde hair in the middle of the raucous crowd that caught his eye. A peripheral flash. But that wasn't what revealed that she was the one. The tell came from the bass player.

Broadway, Nashville's answer to Bourbon Street, embraced a half a dozen blocks of music, alcohol, and chaos. Once the sun gave up the day, music lovers and pub crawlers flocked there to party, decompress, and make new friends. Crawdaddy's Lounge, one of the playground's more popular venues, anchored the eastward end. Riverfront Park and the Cumberland River prevented further expansion in that direction.

Based on the energetic crowd, country rock band Jake and the Highlighters possessed a devoted following. This week's gig? The opening act for an even more popular group. Bassist Billy Langston worked the right side of the stage, playing to the crowd as much as did the front man. Long hair framed his face, his long fingers thumped a steady beat from his low-slung guitar. A cluster of young women stared up at him and gyrated to the music. Billy had a devoted following too, it seemed.

Which is why Jason was there.

Not that he wanted to be. Not tonight, and not last night, when his efforts produced nothing. No sign of Billy's secret lover. He should be home, working on the paper, due in three days, for his comparative literature class. Far behind schedule, he still faced cross checking his footnotes and citations, polishing his writing, and whipping it into an acceptable finished manuscript. Completing his master's degree depended on it.

Instead, he stood among the frenzied crowd as a favor for someone he hadn't seen in years. How did he get talked into this? He knew the answer. That deep burning flame for her that had followed him since high school. Morgan was the one he could never forget. Never shake the hook. Never possess. The one he still dreamed, even daydreamed, and fantasized about. But he never had a chance. Not really. A couple of dates during their junior year, but nothing more. There was Scotty, the football quarterback, Matt, the star baseball centerfielder, and Will, from the richest family in the neighborhood, who drove a bright red BMW convertible. To her, Jason had been little more than an afterthought. Sure, she was friendly, smiled, even flirted, but none of it meant anything. Not to her.

Last week when he ran into her, out of the blue, at a coffee shop, he struggled to corral his enthusiasm, not wanting to seem overly eager. Even as his heart banged in his chest and pulsed in his ears, and moisture gathered along his back and scalp. They ordered coffee and sat at a corner table. The world melted away as if they were in a protective bubble. Small talk followed. She seemed relaxed, comfortable, delighted to see him. Her fingers occasionally brushed his arm as she laughed. The warmth of her touch flowed upward and expanded in his chest. He forgot to breathe.

Had her feelings for him changed?

The tone of their reunion changed when she spilled her troubles with her current boyfriend. Not an unusual issue for her, but now that they were older, more mature, did her current strife crack open a door for him? The hope that he had worked for years to smother rekindled. When she asked for his help, he rolled over like a puppy. Again. He could never refuse those blue eyes.

The favor brought him to Crawdaddy's. Its weathered wooden walls and industrial overhead gave it a juke-joint vibe. The music and free-flowing alcohol fed the party atmosphere. He leaned against the crowded bar, near the back, where he possessed a view over the nearby tables, and the dance floor that fronted the elevated stage.

Too crowded for anything that resembled dancing, the floor became a writhing mass of inebriated twenty-somethings. Was Billy's new distraction among them? Or was she at the bar where Jason stood, or at one of the tables he continually scanned? The problem? He didn't know who he was looking for. Morgan had given no description or name. She didn't know. Only that she believed Billy had someone new. Why else would he be out of touch so often, and pay less attention to her? Quickly end conversations and pocket his phone when she approached. Secretive about where he had been. Band practice his typical answer. Morgan believed he hooked up with his new bitch—her word—after his gigs.

As the band delivered its final encore, Jason, tired and frustrated, finished his drink and placed the empty on the bar. Another bust, a waste. Like last night, there was nothing to see here. He had a paper demanding he get his ass home and get to work. He dreaded calling Morgan, telling her he had again failed, and that he couldn't do this anymore. With the crush of grad school, he had no time to play private detective. He could already hear the disappointment in her voice. Worse, if he bailed, he might never see her again. Could he pull that plug?

That's when Billy revealed his secret. Still playing the crowd as the band rolled through the final strains of their most popular song, he moved forward, locked his gaze on someone near the stage, smiled, jerked his head toward the back.

That's when Jason saw the flip of the blonde ponytail.

Knowing he was too far away, but desperate for something, anything, to show Morgan, he tugged his phone from his pocket and snapped a quick picture. Checking it, he saw she had turned away before he could get the shot. He caught only her blonde hair. Proof of nothing. He needed a picture that allowed Morgan to identify her. Even better, one of her and Billy together.

He felt like a tabloid journalist. He hated those guys.

Pushing through the crowd, he angled toward the right wall, hoping to catch up to her. Thinking he would smile, all friendly like, and say hello, or maybe something about what a great show it was. Engage her, ask her name. Two guys in plaid shirts, beers in hand, blocked his way. He excused himself and they turned to let him pass. No sign of the girl. He stopped and did a three-sixty. Where did she go?

The band hit its last note, holding it to the crowd's delight. Billy waved toward the audience, unplugged his bass, and disappeared into the darkness behind the speakers and drums. The house music rose, blasting from the ceiling-mounted speakers.

To his right, Jason saw a dim passageway that led behind the stage. Two roadies, changing out equipment for the headliners, lugged a drum set up the stairs. He nodded to them as he walked by.

Backstage, pandemonium ruled. Roadies dragged speakers off the stage, packed up guitars, and rolled cords into knotted loops. Two guys dismantled a complex drum kit, the large round bass displaying Jake and the Highlighters in black script. No sign of Billy Langston, or the blonde.

A guy zipping a stack of cymbals into a round case glanced at him. "Can I help you?"

"I'm looking for Billy Langston, but I don't see him."

The guy jerked his head. "Probably out back smoking a cigarette."

Jason saw a door, cracked open a couple of inches. "Thanks," he said.

* * *

Jason stopped near the door. The couple must have exited this way. No other choice. He leaned toward the opening, his ears tuned to conversation, but heard nothing over the thumping of the house music.

He flattened his palm against the door, hesitated. What would he say if they were just outside? What if they were kissing and touching each other? Maybe that he needed some air? Maybe that he needed to make a call? He liked that better. With luck, he could snap an image of them while pretending to talk. He pushed the door open. It scraped against the asphalt. He stepped through.

No couple, no activity of any kind. Only a dark alley. He moved forward and scanned up and down the narrow passageway. Where did they go? He spun back toward the door. That's when he saw the boot. It protruded from behind an over-stuffed dumpster. Another forward step. A jeans-covered leg. Three more steps and he recoiled.

Two bodies. Billy Langston and the blonde. They lay on their backs, glassy eyes staring into the night sky. Each with blood on one side of their head, and a surrounding halo, as if their heads floated on a black mirror. Was it blood? It had to be. His heart pounded, fluttered, and a pulse of dizziness took hold.

A gun, a revolver, lay ten feet away, against the brick wall of the building across the alleyway. He walked over and looked down. It seemed so small. Shiny metal, white handles.

He had to call someone.

Then, to his left, movement. Halfway between him and the end of the alley. He searched the darkness but saw nothing.

The killer? Was he escaping, or was he coming for him? The witness? Did he have another weapon? Panic set in. Jason scooped up the revolver and pointed it that way.

"Who's there?"

A silhouette darted across the alley.

"I'm armed," Jason shouted. "Stop."

A shadow slinked along the brick wall and disappeared

around the corner.

His first instinct was to pursue the killer. But that seemed silly and dangerous. He turned back to the couple. Could they still be alive? He needed to call 911.

"Freeze. Show me your hands."

He jumped, startled. Two police officers came from the darkness, weapons drawn.

"Hands," one of them said again. "Show me your hands."

"Wait a minute," Jason said. "I just…"

"Drop the gun." Their weapons leading the way, the two cops moved apart, but closer. "Now."

Jason released the revolver. It clattered against the pavement.

Then they were on him. One twisted his arm behind his back and they took him to the ground. Face down, rough asphalt against his cheek. A knee in the middle of his back.

"Listen," Jason said.

"Don't move."

He felt cuffs snap into place. Hard, cold metal.

"He's getting away," Jason said.

"Who?"

"The guy that did this."

One cop grabbed his arms and lifted him to his feet.

Jason jerked his head toward the end of the alley. "He ran that way."

The officer looked that way while he maintained his grip on Jason's arm.

The other officer squatted near the bodies. He checked each neck for a pulse. When he stood, he shook his head. He glared at Jason. "And here you are with two dead people and a gun in your hand. Want to tell me what happened?"

"I didn't do anything. I just found them."

Jason couldn't remember a single situation in his entire life as frightening as the interrogation room. Sickly green paint, no windows. A camera near the ceiling aimed at him. The uncomfortable hard-backed chair. One wrist cuffed to the metal table. Worst of all, no one listened to him. He tried to explain what had happened to the two cops in the alley, then the one that drove him here in the backseat cage of a patrol car, and finally, the female cop who escorted him into this room.

For over an hour, he waited. A cop handed him a bottle of water as soon as he sat, but since then no one had entered the room. He knew they were watching. He felt it.

The door swung open. A mid-forties man in a gray suit, white shirt, and blue tie. He sat across from Jason and opened a folder on the table before him. "I'm Detective Walt Fuller. Before we get started, I need to read you your rights."

"Why? I didn't do anything."

"I still have to read them." And so he did.

Jason sat there, only half listening. He knew this dance. Everyone did. If you watch anything on TV, particularly crime shows, this ritual is routine. It was the fact that they felt the need to go through it that made him uncomfortable. They seemed to believe he was guilty. Without hearing what happened. Were they uninterested in the truth?

"Okay. Tell me what happened?" Fuller said.

Finally.

Jason laid it out. How he had stumbled on the dead couple. He had seen the killer. Not fully. Only a shadow. How he feared the killer was coming for him, so he picked up the gun. How he knew that wasn't smart, but in that alley, at night, with a murderer, it seemed his only choice.

Fuller listened, took a few notes. "Why were you in the alley?"

Oh. This wouldn't sound good. "I was looking for Billy Langston."

"Why?"

"I needed some information from him." As soon as the words escaped, Jason knew that answer would only generate more uncomfortable questions.

Fuller clicked his pen. "What sort of information?"

"It's personal."

Fuller placed the pen on the table. "So is murder." He leaned forward. "Don't you think?"

"I do. But I didn't do it."

"Let me tell you what I have. You were in the bar, looking for Mr. Langston. In fact, you were there last night, too. The bartender remembered you and we have you on video, so don't bother denying it."

"I don't deny it."

"You entered a restricted backstage area. You asked a roadie where you might find Mr. Langston. You followed him and Ms. Cindy Sanders into the alley. You shot them. Probably thought you could get away. Dump the weapon. No one the wiser. But a pair of officers showed up faster than you thought. Someone heard the shots. They were right around the corner when the call came in." He shrugged. "Best laid plans never work out. You panicked, had to make up some bullshit story on the fly. About some mysterious killer running away in the dark. No description. Only a, what did you say, shadowy figure. Convenient. Yet there you were with the murder weapon in your hand."

"I didn't shoot anyone," Jason said.

"The gunshot residue test we just did on you? The preliminary result was positive."

"It's not what it looks like," Jason said. "I was only doing a favor for a friend."

"Is that right? Did this favor include murder?"

"Listen to me. Please." Jason went over Morgan asking him to find out who Billy, her boyfriend, was seeing. That was why he was in Crawdaddy's. Otherwise, he wouldn't have been. Not his kind of place. How he saw the girl, someone he didn't know, and merely wanted to prove they were together. For Morgan.

"This Morgan person. She a friend of yours?"

"Morgan Hunter. We went to high school together."

"Close friend then," Fuller said.

Jason sighed. "No. In fact, until I ran into her last week, I hadn't seen her in years."

"Yet she asked you to take on this sensitive mission for her? To spy on her boyfriend?" He raised an eyebrow. "Does that sound reasonable to you?"

It didn't. Not now. Not put that way. At the time she asked, it did. Or was he still so infatuated with her that all he wanted was to make her notice him? Why didn't he tell Morgan no? Because he wanted to prove Billy was cheating. Be the knight in shining armor. Ride off into the sunset with the damsel. All that fairytale stuff. How stupid. Didn't most people resent the bearer of bad news? Even Sophocles knew that. In *Antigone*, hadn't the guard who brought proof of treason to King Creon said, "Nobody likes the bringer of bad news?" The paper he should be home writing was on Sophocles. Why hadn't he paid attention to what he was reading and not pine after some lost love he would never possess?

Detective Fuller pulled him back to reality. "Tell you what, partner. You better find a talented attorney."

The trial didn't take place for two months. With his bail set at a cool million, despite heated arguments from his public defender, he passed that time in a claustrophobic cell. The inmates were scary and aggressive, the food inedible, the bed thin and hard, and the constant noise maddening. Didn't anyone in jail sleep? Why did they feel the need to shout and bang on the bars day and night? The only silver lining was that his cellmate wasn't some gangbanger, or worse. He was older, in his fifties, awaiting trial for an armed robbery. He was smart and well-read. They had some interesting discussions, which made the mind-numbing monotony almost bearable.

His grad school? No dismissal, but a suspension, pending the outcome of his trial. That amazed him. From the moment the cell door slammed, he assumed his academic career had collapsed. So close to the finish line. Not only was his master's degree only weeks away, he had a doctorate program waiting for him.

Unless he went away for life, as the prosecution planned.

The humiliating trial was arguably worse than jail. He sat next to his attorney on full display in the packed courtroom. The case had generated the usual over-amped news stories and public interest skyrocketed. Everyone wanted to see the mad grad student who gunned down two people in cold blood.

The prosecution didn't disappoint them.

The Assistant DA, Marcia Lombardo, a woman who wanted, maybe needed, a high-profile victory, was sharp, efficient, and aggressive. More scary than most of the guys in the jail recreation yard. In a tailored gray suit and white blouse, long black hair pulled into a broad ponytail, a hawkish face, and dark flashing eyes, she seemed like a character from a horror story.

As she laid out her case, the evidence piled up. According to her, the defendant, Jason Hammond, admitted that he had stalked the couple and followed them into the alley. Of course he denied killing them. Didn't everyone deny their crimes? Yet the police apprehended him as he stood over them with the murder weapon in his hand. She called several witnesses to support that story. The bartender, the roadie, the arresting officers, Detective Fuller, the crime scene techs that analyzed the weapon, the bullets, and the gunshot residue evidence. The medical examiner stated the victims died from close-range gunshots.

But the worse part? Morgan on the stand. She had been called by the prosecution. Jason knew this would happen. His attorney warned him. Apparently, she was reluctant, but she really had no choice. Yes, she had asked Jason to find out if her boyfriend was seeing someone. Something she couldn't do herself without being seen. Why Jason? Billy didn't know him. Jason was smart and reliable. She trusted him. She believed he was a good person and would do nothing wrong. That she couldn't imagine Jason killing anyone.

The DA wanted more. She wanted a motive. Jason knew that even with a mountain of physical evidence, juries wanted to know why. The thing, the defect, that drove a criminal to kill. He felt they already believed he was guilty, and now wanted the twisted reason he had left two bodies in a dark alley.

"Did you ever date Mr. Hammond?" Lombardo asked.

"Not really. We went out twice during high school. One of those to the junior prom."

"Why not more dates?"

"He wasn't my type. Not for anything serious. A little too studious for me." She smiled at that.

"Did you tell him that? That he wasn't for you?"

"I did."

"More than once?"

"Yes."

"Did he accept that?"

Morgan hesitated, as if reluctant to answer. Then she said, "No. He called a lot and kept asking me out. After we graduated, I went off to the University of Mississippi. Jason to Vanderbilt."

"Was that the end of his contact with you?"

"No. He called several times that first year and when we were both home for summer break between our freshman and sophomore academic years, we met for coffee. Once anyway. I had hoped he was over everything. But that wasn't the case. He still wanted to go out. On an actual date. I reiterated we were only friends. Nothing more."

"So you told him no?" Lombardo asked.

Morgan nodded. "Yes. Maybe a little too harshly. But I wanted him to understand it would never happen. That he should move on." She looked down, toward her lap, then back up. "I wanted what was best for him. And for me."

"Did that end his advances?"

She took a deep breath and shook her head. "No. He called from time to time over the next few years."

"An attempt to kindle some flame?" Lombardo asked.

"Yes." She glanced at him, then quickly away.

Jason felt a sharp pain in his chest when she looked his way. Her eyes sad for revealing his secrets. He wanted to hug her. Tell her it was okay. That he wanted her to tell the truth. And so far, everything she had said was true. Over the years, how often had he resisted the desire to call her? If only to hear her voice. How often had he failed to ward off that need and dialed her number? Each time, hoping she had changed and now felt the same way he did. Disappointment always followed.

He could feel the probing gazes of those in the gallery behind him. Hot and angry. They wanted the killer's blood.

His attorney had only a few cross-examination questions. What could he possibly ask that would change things? The mass of evidence pointed in only one direction. He ended with, "Yet despite your reluctance to see Mr. Hammond romantically, you asked him to follow your boyfriend? To dig up dirt for you? Why him?"

"I told you. Jason is smart, clever, and reliable. I knew he would do it."

"Because he was in love with you?"

She nodded.

"Is that a yes?"

"Yes."

Six months later, Jason entered the compact lecture room, a series of long tables welcoming him. He settled in a chair in the next to the last row. He pulled an empty notebook and a pen from his briefcase, placing them on the tabletop, then rested his briefcase on the floor next to his feet. Other students filed in.

First day of his comparative literature doctoral program. He looked around, taking everything in. The old-school smell, the subdued lighting, the chatter of his classmates.

It was a miracle that he was here. After serving only two months of his twenty-five to life sentence, the judge threw out his conviction. With prejudice. Jason's attorney informed him that meant no chance of a retrial. Ever. He completed his master's degree and the doctorate program welcomed him back. So here he sat, embarking on his life's next stage.

Without Detective Fuller, there would have been no miracle. He apparently never felt comfortable with Jason being the shooter. As he told Jason after the dismissal, "You didn't look like a killer to me."

Fuller kept digging. Mainly into the forensic evidence. The shell casings inside the revolver yielded no fingerprints, so he asked the crime lab to swab them for DNA. They located some on two of the unspent shells and the cylinder. Jason's DNA did not match. The profile suggested female DNA. Who? To Fuller, only one person made sense. Morgan Hunter. Knowing he couldn't simply ask her for a sample without revealing to her she was a suspect, he followed her and grabbed a discarded paper cup at a local coffee shop. A match followed. Morgan now served Jason's twenty-five to life.

Best of all, this ordeal allowed him to put her behind him. Being framed for a murder will do that. The anger toward her that followed killed the infatuation. Only then did he realize what a burden she had been. Her memory, his need for her, his refusal to accept her rejection, a weight he no longer felt. He could breathe again.

A girl shuffled behind him, nodded toward the seat next to him. "Is this one open?"

He looked up. Beautiful, a welcoming smile. She actually resembled Morgan. Somewhat. "Sure."

She sat, stuck out a hand. "I'm Tracy."

"Jason."

They shook.

"What brings you to comparative lit?" Tracy asked.

"I wish I knew." He smiled. "I guess it was the only thing left after I discarded everything else."

She laughed. Musical. "Me, too."

RUBY'S RODEO TAILORS AND WESTERN WEAR EMPORIUM

Jenny Ramaley

On a warm May afternoon, singers and musicians trooped in and out of the dressing rooms at Ruby's Rodeo Tailors and Western Wear Emporium. After their stage outfits were tried on and fine-tuned, the clothing was hung on a garment rack that would be wheeled into an equipment truck for Cory Conway's Summer Tour. Ruby stood at a worktable piled with stacks of colorful fabric, keeping one eye on the embroidery pattern she was drawing and one eye on the action swirling throughout the room. At 57, she still spent as much time hunched over a sewing machine as her talented staff of nine, but these days she left most of the fittings to LuAnn.

Once they finished today, everyone in Cory Conway's band could hit the road next week in style. Everyone except for Cory. She whipped out her phone and sent him a text, "Get your sorry butt in here tomorrow or you'll be playing your guitar in the buff."

He couldn't wear any of his prior suits. Ruby knew for a fact he'd put on weight since last year's tour. She cussed under her breath thinking about Cory. His thoughtlessness meant she and her staff would need to work around the clock to cut, embroider, and assemble a new suit.

That son of a bitch.

A box of pain-relieving stick-on patches flew through the air and landed in front of her.

"I see you rubbing your back, Miss Ruby," LuAnn said. "Time for a patch. They always help."

"You're right." She grimaced. "I just wish they didn't feel so wet and clammy."

"Ah, but that moisture helps your skin soak up the medicine."

Ruby glanced around the room. "Any word from Marnie? It's not like her to be late." LuAnn's niece wasn't with the other backup singers, who had already finished their fittings.

"No. She's not returning my texts. I'm going to give that girl a talking to. If she wants to stay the lead backup singer, she needs to be on time."

The singers left with the keyboard player. As the drummer and bass guitarist strolled out, Marnie rushed in.

"I'm so sorry," she said. "I've been sick all day. At first I thought it was the flu, but it's let up some so it must've been that dicey sandwich I got at a food truck last night." She hurried into a changing room and kicked off her boots. LuAnn handed a two-piece, shimmery white outfit behind the curtain. "I shoulda known better, but I played till two a.m. on the Honky Tonk Highway and I was starving."

"LuAnn, you look exhausted." Ruby worked the moist patch under her shirt and onto her lower back. Ick. "Thanks for working late last night. Go home. I'll finish up with Marnie."

"I won't argue with you," LuAnn said. "Love you, Marnie. If you show up late again, I'll tan your hide," she called as she left the room.

Still zipping her skirt, the young woman traipsed from behind the curtain and climbed on the twelve-inch raised platform used for fittings. "I'm ready to be poked and pinned, Miss Ruby."

"Shake your hips like you're on stage." The flippy skirt swayed just the way Ruby wanted. Perfect. But when she tugged the low-cut, shimmery crop top into place, Marnie winced. Odd. Ruby murmured an apology, noting how Marnie's breasts strained the fabric. Instead of showing a bit of sexy cleavage, the top threatened a nip slip every time the singer moved. Ruby wrapped a measuring tape around the garment and double-checked her notes. While the fabric measured spot on, the singer's chest did not.

Ruby had worked with performers for decades and knew the chaotic lifestyle could pack on pounds. But a quick glance at the young woman's midriff showed taut muscles, without any hint of a recent carb binge. Although she'd written off Marnie's green-around-the-gills-look to working late last night, now she wasn't so sure.

LuAnn's niece impressed Ruby in a way few did. At nineteen, she sang with the maturity of a seasoned performer, like a Lucinda Williams 2.0. Her voice wavered between a husky rage and vulnerable quiver. Marnie possessed all the makings of a country star with crossover potential. Unless someone derailed her before she got started.

The fitting room sat at the rear of the building, quiet and private. Beyond its walls, Ruby's staff buzzed about their tasks—sewing pricey custom jackets, punching holes in tooled leather belts, and helping tourists in the front store—but the backroom held only the two of them.

Ruby pushed a strand of graying hair behind her ear. "How far along are you?"

The singer's eyes grew wide. "I only took the test today. How did you know?"

"Your bustline's changed. That's usually the first sign."

"Please don't tell my aunt. She'll put me on the next bus home."

Ruby's heart broke for the young woman, barely six months off her family's farm in Obion County. "Let me guess. Cory, the charming devil?"

Marnie sunk to the edge of the platform. "I wish he'd never

seen me sing at Puckett's. He sweet-talked me, told me I'd get more experience being his lead backup singer than sitting in on gigs all over town." Her voice grew tearful. "He said he'd take me 'round town after the tour. Help me get a recording contract."

Marnie wasn't the first girl to sit in Ruby's backroom and sob about Cory. She was the *thirteenth,* and those were only the ones Ruby knew about. "He's not a liar. He will help you. It's just, a lot of these guys expect a payback. Whether you agree to it or not."

"I didn't agree to nothing. It happened so fast, I froze." She drew in a ragged breath. "I don't know what to do now."

"Oh, sweetie. Go change." Ruby unrolled a bolt of shimmery white fabric on the worktable. "If I make you a very short dress with a drapey neckline, no one will notice how your body's changing. At least for a while. Come back tomorrow at two o'clock sharp."

Painful memories rushed back while Ruby laid out a pattern for an A-line dress. All those poor girls, their lives and dreams ruined in one way or another by Cory Conway.

He'd gone from being a nobody to having a top-twenty hit in 1991. That's when he ordered his first custom embroidered jacket from Ruby. He offered to help her get a small business loan from his banker, so she could rent space and quit bringing clients to her apartment's dining room for fittings.

Cory tried to collect his payback from Ruby too. He caught her off-guard and shoved her down on a table. Like with Marnie, it happened in a flash. Only by the grace of God was she able to grab her work shears and jab the point into his right hand, swearing he'd never play guitar again if he didn't get the hell off her. The man shrugged off what happened like it was nothing and strolled out, calling over his shoulder that he'd be back in a month for his order.

That son of a bitch.

Ruby glanced at the wide leather belt around her hips, sewn with trembling hands that night thirty years ago, complete with an embroidered holster for her shears. Since then, she never met a client alone without wearing her belt. No one ever threatened her again.

Cory kept his promise about the banker and gave her steady work over the years outfitting him and his band in classic western wear. She gave him price breaks as he inched his way up the chart to a solid 'B-level' stardom and, by wearing her clothes, he helped establish her reputation as a reasonably priced option to the Nudie Cohn's and Manuel's of the industry.

But she'd never forgotten the feel of his weight as he pressed against her. She never forgot the gagging scent of his Polo Sport cologne or the sight of his stained teeth where he tucked his Skoal, years before his dental veneers.

Ruby kept quiet about what happened. Her shop hummed with business, but the burden of her silence weighed on her, more and more as the years passed. If she had done something to stop him years ago, she could've saved all those young women from their traumas. But those regrets felt miniscule to today's guilt. She should've protected Marnie.

She needed to stop Cory from hurting anyone else.

As Ruby finished cutting the dress pieces, a bell tinkled at the workroom's entrance and a lanky man in a pink and black western shirt loped into the room. She flashed a guarded smile at her visitor. "Hello, Danny."

The man settled on a stool and glanced around. "Looks like everyone's left for the day. Good, we can talk. I need a favor."

Her eyes narrowed. "What?"

"We're taking the kids and leaving tonight for Vermont. I'm moving my dad into assisted living." Danny pulled two fat, sealed envelopes from his backpack and set one on the worktable. "Can you give this to Cory when he comes in?"

Ruby's nostrils flared. "I'm not holding onto an envelope stuffed with cocaine. How much is that? Enough for an entire tour?"

"No. This is enough for *half* the tour." He set down the

second envelope. "I'm not giving him the other half until he pays what he owes me. I'll be out of town when the tour starts next week. I need you to hold onto this one until he transfers me the money."

"You're doing bank transfers now for illegal drugs?"

"No, we do bank transfers for my massage therapy business."

"Yeah, right."

"Hey, I'm licensed in the state of Tennessee."

She stretched. "Could you help me with my back?"

"Uh, I can offer you some oxy."

She snorted. "So why hasn't he paid you?"

"I don't know. He used to be an occasional customer. Now he's one of my regulars."

"Cory always pays his bills."

Danny pointed toward the garment rack labelled 'Cory Conway Summer Tour.' "Has he paid you for all this work? Because he's stiffing people left and right."

Years ago, when Danny realized his limited talent meant he'd never make it as a songwriter, he transitioned from selling a few joints to becoming the drug dealer of choice for Nashville's elite. He knew everyone, even played in the chief of police's weekly poker game.

"Stop over at Cathy's Country Catering. She did a huge party for Cory this summer, spent all this money on food and waitstaff, and he never paid her. He even threatened to sue her over some contract crap. And then his bank called in her loan. She's closing shop and moving back to Pigeon Forge."

"Poor Cathy."

"He screwed the guitar store too. That's why I need your help. I can't afford to go out of business. I've got kids to feed." Danny tapped the envelopes.

"No."

"Come on, Ruby. You owe me."

"That was ten years ago."

"Yes, and it was my good word that got you off a cocaine possession charge and back to your sewing machine. I've never asked you for anything before."

"I've kept you in fancy shirts since then." Before she'd expanded her staff, Ruby sometimes needed a drug-fueled energy bump to meet a client's deadline. Who knew that the police would pull her over that night? Or that local law enforcement would listen to Danny when he vouched for her upstanding character.

On one hand, she understood that no one in the city wanted to see a country music star get busted buying drugs in the shady part of town. But on the other hand, Nashville police treated Danny like a respected businessman, but wanted to lock up a tax-paying businesswoman over a tiny bit of coke.

"All right. I'll find a way to slip it to him."

"I've known you a long time, Ruby. You always find a way to get things done." He handed her the envelopes. "Give Cory one tomorrow. Tuck the other one away until I text you to hand it over. I appreciate your help."

"After this, we're even." She watched him lope out of the room, then dug out her phone and dialed her accountant. Cory's account, as Danny predicted, loomed in the red.

That son of a bitch.

After she locked the shop that night, Ruby went home to her small, neat house, feeling a mixture of pride and relief that she'd mailed the final mortgage check last February. She poured a healthy shot of Jim Beam Select over ice, pulled a small red notebook from a rolltop desk, and settled into her favorite chair.

She flipped through the pages where she'd catalogued stories about Cory, going back three decades. Her long simmering anger heated to a rolling boil. Sipping her drink, she thought about Marnie and the other young women. About the caterer and Danny. About her hip holster.

Careful business practices meant she possessed something the other businesses didn't. Ruby had a little money tucked away. Which meant one thing. If she could find the courage after all these years, she could afford to stop a monster, even one who wore her clothes.

Ruby pulled the pain patch off her back. She studied the soft damp surface and kept thinking.

Designing one-of-a-kind suits required creativity. Measuring clients for a perfect fit required precision. Using her precise, creative, and patient approach, Ruby channeled her guilt-ridden fury into a plan. She examined every angle, considered what might go wrong, and developed contingency options. She took another sip of bourbon whiskey and nodded. Her idea was doable.

The real challenge lay in not getting caught.

Marnie arrived on time the next day. She slipped into the new dress and stepped through a few dance moves without complaint, despite the dark rings under her eyes. The drapey neckline showed a hint of cleavage while the bottom twirled loosely around the hips. The garment would look picture-perfect onstage while hiding the young woman's secret.

The singer crooned one of Cory's heartbreak songs while she changed, then came and leaned against the worktable. "Thanks for helping me, Miss Ruby. Got any words of advice? I sure could use some."

"For now, tell no one. If he finds out, he'll throw you off the tour and smear your name." She hung the white dress on the rack with the other tour outfits. "Remember that song by the rapper Eminem, the one that says you only get one shot, don't miss your chance?" She looked Marnie in the eye. "Always be prepared. Keep your old flat-top guitar close by. Because you never know when that once-in-a-lifetime shot will come along."

* * *

Cory strode into the workroom later that afternoon like he owned the place. At 62, silver hair showed at his temples. A taste for craft beer added a tire around his midriff. Decades of red meat clogged his arteries, now kept open by two stents. "Let's get to it!"

Ruby stood waiting, wearing the blue latex gloves she wore when handling stage wear. In Cory's case, that meant a custom suit with piping details, worth more than six-thousand-dollars. She held the jacket up and helped him slip it on. The shoulders pulled tight. So did the stomach.

"For heaven's sake, Cory. How much weight have you gained?"

"Maybe five pounds."

"Liar."

He stared into the three-panel-mirror, turning to study his reflection from both sides. "Hmm. Looks like you might have to let out the seams again."

"I can't. We let out the seams last year when you promised to lay off the pecan pie." She wrapped her measuring tape around his chest and jotted notes on an order form. "Since you need a new suit, how about something old school? I could make you a get-up Porter Wagoner would be proud to wear."

Cory let out a whoop. "Well, all right, Ruby! Make me whatever you want, as long as you make me look handsome, young, and thin."

Ruby's snort morphed to a sly smile. "You were so skinny when you were young. You couldn't bear the weight of a long, embellished coat. We had to put you in short jackets. But now you're big and strong, so we can use all the rhinestones we want."

Before Cory left, she used a gloved hand to slide an envelope toward him. "Danny left this for you."

Alone that night, Ruby unrolled a bolt of thick satin on a long table. The dark gray fabric glowed under the work light. She worked fast, drawing a pattern and cutting the pieces for Cory's new jacket. Then she used the pieces as a pattern and cut a second set.

Ruby worked without stopping the next day, refusing LuAnn's help with the jacket but asking her to cut, embellish, and sew the matching pants.

For two more days, Ruby focused on the individual pieces, pushing sleeves and lapels under the needle of her old chain-stitching embroidery machine. She worked with perfect hand-eye coordination as her left hand turned the handle from below and her right guided the fabric from above. She stitched a horseshoe on the jacket back, whiskey bottles on the upper arms, and record labels on the lapels.

Rhinestones came next. Heat fused tiny crystals onto the fabric in curved lines, sunbursts, and arrows. Pieces grew heavy with her labor. Next, her deft hands assembled the pieces on a Dritz Mr. Tailor male dress-form adjusted to Cory's bulky frame. She added padding along the shoulders and interfacing inside the lapels. The jacket took shape during the light of day.

The lining took shape during the dark of night.

Alone in the small staff kitchen, Ruby snapped on a fresh pair of latex gloves. She spread out the cotton fabric she would use to line the back of Cory's jacket and filled a plastic basin with water.

Next, she took a deep breath and pulled Danny's second envelope from her office safe.

"Can we finish the interview about your experience in the industry, Miss Ruby? My paper's due on Friday," said the new intern. "You were telling me how the 1970s and early '80s were a great time for western-wear tailors around the country."

Ruby paused to refill a bobbin with thread. "When I was a

kid, everyone—from George Jones to Hollywood stars to Japanese tourists—wanted custom embroidered western-style suits. For a while, every store in town offered shirts covered in rhinestones. But styles changed. Business slowed down over time.

"But, lucky for all of us, Dwight Yoakam liked the short coats Buck Owens used to wear. In 1989, he went looking for stage wear and found Manuel Cuevas, who used to work in Hollywood before he set up shop in Nashville. After Dwight wore an embroidered turquoise jacket with a bolo tie on an album cover, the demand for rodeo wear surged again. I started my business right after that."

"And you've rode the ups and downs of rodeo-inspired fashion ever since?"

"Yes. Lately, I'm grateful for newer stars like Brandi Carlile and Jack White. They've reignited interest in the type of clothing I design and sell."

"Like this suit you're making for Mr. Conway?"

She turned back to her sewing machine. "Cory's always loved this look."

Cory Conway arrived the next afternoon to try on his new outfit. He walked around the male-dress-form admiring the elaborate design of the long coat. "Look at that. You worked in references from my hit songs. Here's the whisky and the picket fence." When he reached for the jacket, she smacked his hand with her latex-covered palm.

"Wait. Put this shirt on first. The thin fabric will keep you cooler."

"You're gonna be there tomorrow, right?"

"I'm always there opening night, for any last-minute tweaks."

Cory slipped on the jacket with her help. "Whew, this thing weighs a ton."

"Don't whine. It's only fifteen pounds. One of Elvis's outfits weighed seventy-five." She tucked her hands in her pockets so he wouldn't see them shake.

"If I didn't know you better, I'd swear you were trying to kill me." But when the aging, husky man looked at himself in the mirror, a charismatic, broad-shouldered star grinned back. "You're a freaking miracle worker, Ruby."

The crowd cheered and stamped their feet on the other side of the closed stage curtain. The tour manager had chosen a small theater an hour outside Nashville for the show's first night. Better to work out any last-minute kinks here, before the tour buses rolled down the road to larger venues.

Backstage, Ruby glanced around the red velvet curtain at the packed seats, filled mostly with heavy-set older gals and grey-haired men whose bellies hung over their belt buckles.

She wore her blue gloves, as always. The garment rack stood beside her, half-filled with extra stage outfits—and the dark gray jacket. Her heart pounded while her mind raced. Could she, should she, go through with her plan?

While an announcer bantered with the crowd, the band musicians and singers filed onto the stage. Marnie gave Ruby a thumbs up as she hurried with the other singers to their mike stands. Her white dress sparkled and swayed when she moved.

Cory strode over, sniffling and wiping his nose. Ruby's hands trembled as she slid the new garment up his arms and adjusted it on his shoulders.

"Wow. This jacket feels heavier than it did yesterday." He strapped on his famous blue Gibson guitar.

"I forgot to congratulate you." Her voice turned cold. "Marnie told me the happy news. Fatherhood will be a big step for you."

"What the—?" His eyes grew wide with panic. "No way. It's not mine."

"No? Then you'll want a DNA test." She smoothed the front of the jacket. "You do know she's LuAnn's niece, don't you?" Her eyes bore into his. "That girl is like family to me."

A red flush crept up Cory's throat as the announcer's voice boomed from the speakers. "And now, let me introduce Nashville's own, Cory Conway." The crowd cheered as he shoved past her. He strode onto the stage and ripped into a hit song from his 2011 album. Marnie's voice melded with Cory's in perfect harmony.

Twenty minutes into the set, bright stage lights, stressful news, and a heavy jacket made Cory sweat. A lot. He used a white handkerchief to mop his face.

As he continued to perform, perspiration leached through his thin shirt and made contact with lining fabric that had been soaked in a cocaine slurry. The newly wettened material then transferred chemical compounds through the thin fabric and onto Cory's sweaty back. Like LuAnn said, moisture helped skin suck up a drug.

Combined with the bump of coke Cory did before he hit the stage, the extra dosage wouldn't be enough to kill a man but could knock a monster out of commission for a while.

At least, that's what the seamstress thought.

Thirty-seven minutes later, the singer, weighed down by the extra ten pounds Ruby had sewed into the coat's hem, swung the guitar to his side. A tuning peg snapped, and the jagged stem ripped the sleeve of the jacket. Perspiration poured down the star's flushed face as he clutched his chest. He managed to thrust the fancy Gibson out of the way before his legs crumpled and he collapsed.

Ruby rushed to his side along with two crew members and a doctor who'd been snacking at the craft table backstage. She found Corey's sweaty handkerchief, wiped his face, then slipped it in her pocket. Gasping, he watched her with wild eyes.

"He can't breathe," Ruby yelled over the commotion. "Hold him up. Get that heavy jacket off him so he can catch his breath." The crew guys knew better than to argue with Ruby. Together they wiggled off the jacket while the doctor pressed a stethoscope against Cory's chest.

Ruby lugged the hefty coat backstage and carefully zipped it into a garment bag while chaos swirled around her. She unzipped a second bag, pulled out an identical but ten-pounds-lighter gray jacket, and hung it in plain sight on the rack. She wiped the handkerchief inside the new coat, leaving streaks of perspiration across the back and under the arms. Her pounding heart rate slowed as she used a seam-ripper to tear a hole in the sleeve to match the original, damaged jacket.

Marnie rushed to her side. "Oh, Miss Ruby. Everything's ruined on the tour's first night. What should we do?" They watched two emergency medical technicians wheel an unresponsive Cory offstage.

Maybe she'd used too much coke in the slurry. Even so, she couldn't summon any pangs of remorse. She brushed a piece of lint from the dark satin. "Is that your flat top on the equipment cart?"

"What?"

"Wouldn't it be nice if someone spoke to the crowd, maybe played a few songs while we wait to hear about your boss? All those good folks came tonight to be entertained."

Marnie's eyes opened wide with hope. "One shot," she whispered, then turned to the bass player who stood nearby. "Jerry, get everybody back onstage!"

Ruby's focus turned to the last phase of her plan—taking the embellished, bedazzled evidence home so she could rip it apart and destroy it piece by piece. Although her shoulders slumped with fatigue and the garment bag weighed her down, she wound her way through the backstage area feeling a lightness as decades of regret flew off her shoulders.

Behind her, the band blasted into a beloved hit from 2005. Ruby looked back as she reached the exit door. Now that Cory and his dark-colored suit were gone, the musicians and singers looked youthful and fresh in the stage wear she'd designed. As Marnie's unique voice brought new life to an old song, her shimmery dress shone under the stage lights, tailor-made for a once-in-a-lifetime opportunity.

THE GUADAGNINI CELLO

Merrilee Robson

Her cello wasn't a Stradivarius, but it was a beautiful instrument. Celine had chosen it carefully, testing the tone, how it felt when she held it. Discussing her choice endlessly with her teacher, and watching her parents weigh parental pride against the considerable cost.

It had been with her through music school, early concerts, and the beginning of her orchestra career. She could close her eyes and recall every inch of the grain in the glossy brown wood. She knew what it could do. She could pick out the sound of her cello in a room full of instruments. With a total stranger playing it. Not that she would ever let that happen. She loved her cello.

So she was speechless when they returned home from rehearsal to find a strange cello case with a festive red ribbon wrapped around it.

"Open it," Stephen urged her.

This wasn't a Stradivarius either.

But it was a 300-year-old instrument made by Giovanni Battista Guadagnini.

"How did this get here?" she said in astonishment.

Stephen gave her an odd smile, almost like the oily villain in a silent movie. "It's yours."

"But I can't afford…"

Stephen waved his hand, as if whatever this stranger of a cello cost was of no consequence. Celine knew that Stephen's family had money. Their nights at the theatre, the restaurant meals, the places they vacationed were all far beyond what he earned, even as concertmaster. But an instrument of this calibre couldn't be bought for less than a million dollars. Likely much more.

"You're ready to be a soloist. You need an instrument that's worthy of a solo career," Stephen said.

"But I've only just joined this orchestra. And no one is offering me solo gigs."

"Trust me. The world will be beating down my door with offers, once they hear you play this cello."

The white walls of the enormous apartment seemed to close in on her, despite the sweeping views from the floor to ceiling windows. His door? As if she hadn't been living there for six months, thinking of it as *their* home. And as if he had somehow changed from her lover to her manager without her noticing.

And shouldn't a woman who's ready for a solo career also be ready to pick her own damn cello?

She shivered but Stephen didn't seem to notice.

"I think you'll find it's perfect for you. You're so tiny." He stood too close to her, as he always did. Stephen wasn't huge but he was much taller than her, with long limbs that made him seem bigger than he actually was. His shoulders were wide from hours swimming in the building's pool and even more hours in the adjoining gym.

He reached for Celine's small hand and kissed it.

Her skin crawled a little at the memory of Stephen at this evening's performance. The young soprano had reached out her hand to offer a businesslike shake to thank Stephen at the end. But he had held on to her hand and then kissed it, as if he alone—not the conductor, not the dozens of trained musicians—had been responsible for the perfection of the music. As if it had been him and not the soprano's spectacular voice that had brought the audience to their feet.

Stephen ran his hand over the smooth varnish. "It's mid-1700s, from his Milan period. It's a smaller size and designed to be wider at the front and narrower at the back," Stephen went on. "It should be more comfortable for you and let you focus on your playing."

"I can't…"

"My dear, trust me. You're ready for this. And with a cello like this one, you will be ready for concert stages around the world."

Celine picked up the luminous red instrument and settled in her practice chair. Stephen was right; it was shorter than her cello. And the front was wider, with a narrower back, allowing the cello to nestle comfortably between her legs.

She tried a few notes from the prelude to Bach's first cello suite, thrilling at the rich tone as she drew her bow across the strings.

She had heard similar instruments in concert, never expecting to be able to touch one, let alone play it. She had been expecting the pure notes. But what she wasn't expecting was how the sound wrapped itself around her, at first in a comforting, pleasant way, and then, as she fingered the strings, drawing her bow more confidently, in a way that was almost sensual.

She knew that Guadagnini has worked closely with musicians. There was no indication that he had played himself but she thought he must have, at least well enough to know if the instrument was built right.

It was almost as if the spirit of the luthier had encircled her with the sound, guiding her arm with his rough carpenter's hands, touching her shoulder to suggest a gentler touch with her bow.

She gasped and moved the cello away from her, thankful that the heavy clothing she had worn in the cold rehearsal space hid the flush spreading over her body.

She placed the cello back in its case and turned to Stephen, making an effort to slow her breathing. "Oh, Stephen, it's magnificent. But I'm not sure I'm ready for such an instrument."

Stephen kissed her cheek in the restrained way he preferred, even in bed. "You will be ready, I'm sure. Now are you going to start dinner? You know I'm always starving after rehearsal."

Stephen ate the dinner she'd prepared in a perfunctory manner, not noticing the perfection of the cheese souffle, the heights it had risen to, the freshness of the asparagus she had rushed out to buy from the greengrocer during a break in rehearsal.

His lovemaking had always been mechanical, but Celine had always thought it didn't matter too much, as they had so much else in common. But tonight she had to force herself not to shrink away from his hard, dry kisses.

He seemed to pay her less attention than he had given the asparagus, going through his lovemaking in the same perfunctory way, like a programmed machine, and ending without noticing, or caring, that she hadn't climaxed.

She surreptitiously looked up Guadagnini the next morning. She knew the basics—an Italian luthier, not as famous of Stradavari, but certainly one of the greatest makers of cellos and violins, known by musicians around the world.

Music magazines had raved about the bold, deep richness of sound at the low end and the brilliance and clarity of the higher notes. Not much was known about him personally. One patron had referred to him as coarse, and he must have been virile, almost as enthusiastic in producing children as he was with his instruments.

But, of course, no had one mentioned feeling the touch of the luthier while playing one of his instruments, being swept away by what seemed like a shared passion.

She waited until Stephen was in the shower before trying the cello again. And, as before, she was caressed by the sound, the music swirling around her, vibrating on her skin. Her breath grew faster and she pressed the cello closer to her as the sound caressed her. directing her playing like the phantom touch of its maker.

She was in her own shower by the time Stephen was out of his, running the water slightly cool to reduce the flush on her skin.

He asked if she was going to take the Guadagnini to rehearsal and she made excuses, saying she wasn't used to it yet, that surely their insurance wouldn't cover taking it on the subway, when, really, she was afraid of being swept away by passion, wanting to keep this musical revelation to herself for a while.

But she played it every moment she could, running through some exercises while Stephen was home but waiting until he had left the apartment to play properly.

The cello made her feel passion; it almost made her feel loved.

And she came to realize that it wasn't the ghost of some 18th century luthier that possessed her, but the cello itself, surrounding her with sound, giving her a sense of power.

And she began to feel that she did deserve the Guadagnini, that she could use it to bring music to the world, that she was good enough to play this cello on the world stage.

Stephen arrived home early one day while she was playing the Guadagnini. The notes flowed around the apartment with joy and heartbreak, with anger and love, bringing the music to life in a way she had never been able to.

She hadn't heard him come in but she saw him now in the entrance way, his face white, his jaw hanging open.

"That's amazing," he said finally.

She smiled at him, glad that he had seen the potential in her, when she hadn't realized she had it. "You said it would be. Thank you, Stephen."

But he brushed past her, going into the bedroom to change. And when he came back he only asked what she was planning to cook for dinner.

And things started to change.

"Are you cheating on me?" he asked. "You're different."

He didn't hit her. That might have been better. She would have left then.

Instead he was beating her self-confidence. Hitting her over and over again. Her table manners (so middle-class,) her clothes (too tight, too loose, too revealing, too cheap.) She ate too much; she was getting fat.

His lovemaking was fast, almost angry, driving himself into her when she wasn't ready and finishing before she was even close to aroused. She started to avoid him touching her, making up excuses that she was tired or feeling ill.

But, most of all, he criticized her playing. She had the tempo wrong; she didn't understand that passage, she came in too soon, too late.

He still told people about buying her the cello, bragging about giving his girlfriend a famous instrument. And he still talked about getting her solo work. Celine thought either he wasn't trying or his influence wasn't what he thought it was.

He seemed to imply that she wasn't as good as he'd thought, that maybe she didn't even belong in this orchestra.

But Celine was doing her own work, making contacts, setting up auditions.

And she found she could be almost as good on her own little cello. It wasn't as easy to hold as the Guadagnini, and it didn't have the tonal quality of the famous instrument.

But she found that the passion for the music was in her, not in her cello. And she believed with all her heart that one day she would be able to buy her own Guadagnini, or even a Stradivarius.

Because she was going to have to leave the Guadagnini behind. Because Stephen owned that cello. And she was going to leave Stephen.

But she didn't worry about parting with the Guadagnini. It had taught her well. She was that good.

Celine hurried back to the apartment, anxious to get packed and ready to leave as soon as she had made the break with Stephen.

She hurried inside, glad that she had made it back before him.

And stopped.

The Guadagnini's case lay on its side, the red ribbon it had worn when he first presented it to her wrapped ironically around it.

The cello itself was smashed into splinters of glorious red, silenced forever.

Celine waited by the door, her back pressed against the wall.

How fortunate that Stephen had left behind the...she thought of it as the murder weapon, for all the cello was an inanimate object.

Stephen had bought the Guadagnini cello. She supposed that gave him the right to destroy it.

Although, how could anyone destroy something capable of producing such beauty? A magical instrument that had survived over 300 years, built by a man who must surely have had great pride in his work, beyond the need to feed his family. Treasured by the musicians who owned the cello in turn.

But she could understand his feelings, the anger and jealousy he had felt. Knowing that he had fostered the talent that was going to take her away from him, out of this home and then around the world, on to stages he was never going to reach.

She held the sledgehammer Stephen had used to create the shards that were all that remained of the Guadagnini cello.

She could understand that anger, his feeling that the cello was what had caused all their problems.

It was the other thing that she could never forgive. That made her glad she had no trouble hefting the hammer. The years of carrying the heavy instrument—to her classes, to busk in the street when she was a student, to rehearsals and on tour—had given her the strength she needed for this.

She planned it now. Knowing he would come striding into the room, looking straight ahead, probably expecting to find her in tears, needing his comfort.

She would start with one blow to the back of his head, a second, if needed, to knock him to the ground. Then as many blows as he had used to reduce the Guadagnini to rubble.

And then many more.

Because that she could not understand, not forgive.

That he had taken the hammer to her own sweet little brown cello. An instrument that had stood by her, never hurt anyone.

That it was lying in broken brown pieces was why Stephen was going to die.

THE SAME OLD SONG

Peggy Rothschild

I shivered as I waited for Ricky near the bus stop, making sure to stand clear of the amber cone cast by the streetlamp. That was one of his rules: Always wait beyond the pocket of light, never under it where someone could drive past and remember my face—while zipping by at thirty-five miles an hour. Minimum.

Ricky had a lot of rules. Some worthwhile, others ridiculous. Like wearing only soft fabrics on a job; no noisy clothes. Which was why I wore my black hoodie, rather than my leather coat. And why I was cold. It was late December and in the low thirties—of course, I was cold. Since we only entered empty houses, Ricky's caution on this topic struck me as weird and unnecessary. But I did it. I followed all his rules. Which meant I wasn't allowed to bring a cell phone or wallet along on our jobs. Not even one of the burners he regularly provided.

Early on I asked how could I get in touch if I was running late? Ricky said if I wasn't at the pick-up point at the appointed time, the job was off. Which was why I'd always been on time. These jobs were more important to me than he realized.

Except for his neurotic rules, working with Ricky was fun. Plus, a nice bonus: He was easy on the eyes. But from the start, sex wasn't part of our equation. What he offered was danger. Something I'd been missing since the move. I assumed Ricky viewed me as a project. His chance to shape someone. Maybe he saw me as his criminal Pygmalion—though I doubted he knew who Pygmalion was.

Because of his rules, the only calls Ricky and I exchanged were via the burners. Which didn't happen often, making life simpler for me. I had no idea whether Ricky followed his own rules. But I hoped he was. Especially tonight.

A black muscle car with gleaming chrome pulled to the curb. Leave it to Ricky to eschew stealing the usual nondescript vehicle in favor of something striking and powerful. The man was peacocking. Tonight marked a huge change in our dynamic and I expected him to act like a control freak throughout the job. This was the first heist I'd brought to him. If the promised take hadn't been so good, he never would've agreed to loosening the reins. This whole night threatened the upper hand he'd held in our relationship.

He'd seemed shocked when I told him I'd found a viable high value target. After I ran him through the jewelry, guns, and cash stored in the safe he couldn't say no. It was usually Ricky who researched targets, alarm systems, homeowners' habits and schedules. Though he'd agreed to this job, he'd made it clear he wasn't comfortable with the change.

I climbed into the passenger seat. That was another of Ricky's rules: He always drove. Normally that rankled, but tonight it served my purpose. "Hi."

The latest Eddie Bang song blasted through the speakers. Ricky turned to me and said, "What's the address?"

I recited it.

"Huh. The way you talked about the take, I expected the house to be in Belle Meade."

"Are you turning up your nose at Green Hills?"

"Nah. They got serious money there. Why you think they call it Green Hills?" He rubbed his thumb and forefinger together, grinning at his play on words. "Give me the address again. But this time with the street first, then the house number."

I did as ordered, giving him time to punch the information into his GPS. Ricky wasn't nearly as savvy as he thought. He'd told me repeatedly to memorize the address and not write it down—like he was giving me some sort of impossible assignment. And here he was making a record of our destination in his GPS.

He pulled away from the curb, heading toward the interstate.

"Can you turn the music down?"

"I've told you Lucy, you live in Nashville now. You gotta learn to let country music fill your veins."

"Filling my veins is fine. Just don't make my eardrums bleed."

He lowered the volume. "Did I tell you how I was a fan of this guy long before he made it big?"

"You did."

"Got to see him at the Bluebird. Place only seats ninety. Awesome show. Now he's playing Wildhorse and the Grand Ole Opry. Dude's finally getting his due." He sped up and changed lanes again. "So, tonight. You sure about all the details?"

"I am. The house will be empty until at least midnight. There's an alarm system, but it's not usually on unless the owners are in for the night."

"What if—"

For a change, I cut him off. "If the alarm is on, I've got the code."

"How? You working with a maid or cleaning lady? Someone who can be pressured into ratting us out?"

"No."

"Then how?"

I gave him a Cheshire Cat grin. "That's my secret. You're going to have to trust me on this. The take is worth it."

My partner's baseline motivation was greed, so he shut up, moving like a shark as he cut between cars. After five more minutes of Eddie Bang serenading us, Ricky spoke. "Just because you found this gig doesn't mean I'm changing the cut."

Since he did all the research and prep, Ricky always got sixty-five percent to my thirty-five. I knew he'd expect me to object so I said, "That doesn't sound right."

"I may not have scoped out the house, but I got us a clean ride. And I'm the one with the fence. Besides, until the job's done, I'm not ready to trust your work. If tonight goes well, we'll talk about a percentage change for any future jobs you bring in."

"Okay." Ricky didn't know I wasn't in this for the money. That would shock him almost as much as learning this was our last job.

We approached our exit. The dusting of snow along Highland Rim sparkled like the promise of better days. As the estates in Green Hills grew larger, the streetlights became sparse. A sprawling mansion marked our turn. Lights shone from all the downstairs windows and cars lined both sides of the street. Looked like they were having a party. Good thing they didn't live next to our target.

A mile later we reached the address: A large gabled home with a brick façade, located on over an acre of land on a quiet cul-de-sac. Ricky cut the music and I directed him to park in the shadowy area next to a section of privacy hedge. I climbed out and softly closed the car door—another part of Ricky's no unnecessary noise rule.

I waited for him to join me on the sidewalk before slipping through a gap in the hedge. He shadowed me down the slate path running alongside the house. Soft light came from the backyard where the sugar maples nearest the patio were spotlighted, and the wide back porch glowed with faux flickering lanterns.

At the backdoor, I pulled a key from my pocket and waggled it at Ricky. He snatched it from my hand, then unlocked the door.

Such a Rick move.

I followed him inside. Except for the hum of the refrigerator, the house was silent. "Told you the alarm would be off," I whispered.

"Yeah, right. So, where's this safe?"

"Come on." I crossed the pristine kitchen. The wood floor squeaked when I stepped near the central island. I froze, silently cursing my carelessness. After a deep breath, I continued into the dining room then took a right at the central hall, crossing the tile to the office. Once Ricky joined me, the smell of sweat mixed with the leather scent of the sofa. I clicked on my penlight, illuminating the abstract pattern of an area rug between the desk and the built-in bookcases, moving the beam until it landed on the bronze-toned Liberty Magnum.

"Shit. That's a mother of a safe."

"Yeah." I pulled a scrap of paper from my pocket and approached the six-foot tall behemoth.

"You wrote down the combination?" Outrage laced his voice.

I smiled. "Don't worry; I'll eat it after the safe is open."

Predictably, he snatched the small piece of paper from my fingers and nudged me aside. He aimed my penlight at the dial. "Hold the light there." He bent forward and spun the dial twice before finding the first number of the combination.

Thirty seconds later, the safe silently swung open. Designed to hold long guns as well as valuables, the right side held a Mossberg 30-06, Remingston .270, and a Springfield bolt action rifle. On the left were shelves of ammo, valuables, and cash. Ricky pulled bound stacks of bills off the second shelf, then grabbed the wooden jewelry box from the top shelf and lifted the lid. "Score." He glanced over his shoulder at me. "You weren't lying about the take, Luc."

"Nope."

While Ricky dropped the cash and jewelry into a black cloth bag, I eased my way to the wide cherry wood desk. Making sure he was still focused on securing the wads of cash and jewelry, I slid the top drawer open and grabbed the Glock 19 nestled at the back. By the time I aimed it, Ricky had turned to face me. His mouth dropped open.

"What the—"

I pulled the trigger, hitting him center mass.

His eyes widened and he let out an "Ooof" before tumbling backward against the open safe. Slowly he crumpled onto the Oriental carpet, blood already seeping through his dark coat.

When my ears stopped ringing I said, "Sorry Ricky. This is the only way to end things between us safely. At least for me." I blinked back tears and crouched by his side. I'd never shot anyone before. Avoiding his bloody chest, I patted him down. No cell phone, no wallet. Good.

I walked around him to the drinks cabinet and poured myself two fingers of whisky. The burn settled me as I drank. Planning was a different world than executing.

Ugh. Bad choice of words. I refilled my glass and downed it.

I grabbed the receiver of the cordless phone on the desk. I glanced at Ricky; his chest barely rose. I opened the French doors and stepped onto the back porch, then punched 9-1-1.

"What's your emergency?"

I let the sobs break free. "A man broke into my home. I went out for a drive and...I guess I didn't set the alarm. I heard someone walking around and thought it was my husband. I went into his study and...Oh God...I shot him."

"Is the intruder still there?"

"Yes. I think he's dead. Or dying. I told him to get out, but he kept coming closer and I...I took my husband's gun from his desk and..."

"Are you somewhere safe now?"

"Yes. I'm outside. He's inside...bleeding."

"A car is near your neighborhood and on its way. Stay on the line."

I hung up and went back inside. My cell phone was charging in the kitchen. I scrolled to Dougie's name and hit dial.

"Annabelle, baby. I've got maybe another thirty minutes here. Can I call you back?"

I breathed in and out rapidly. "Dougie. Oh God. It's awful. I just shot a man."

"What?"

I knew he was picturing the possible headlines, already figuring how to spin them to his advantage.

I threw him some helpful tidbits. "I went for a drive. When I came back a man was inside the house. I thought it was you. That your thing ended early but…"

"You shot an intruder?"

"Yes. I think he's dead. I already called the cops."

"Okay. You did fine. We live in a stand your ground state now, babe. You were within your rights. And the cops on their way?"

"Yes."

"Okay. I'm going to wrap things up and come straight home. Bob's already here. I'll explain the situation. We're maybe twenty minutes away and I'll bring him along."

"You think I need a lawyer?"

"No, it's just a precaution."

I gave him a weepy sounding "Okay."

"Keep cool, babe. I'm on my way."

Back in L. A., Dougie had repped a lot of pretty people who could dance and sing, but not play their instruments. Yet they still managed to hit big—with his help. When he moved us to Nashville, he'd stopped in a nearby café and met a whole new world of performers who were actual musicians. To sell them on his skills, he changed the way he dressed. Changed the way he talked. Changed the way he did business. That's when I began fearing I'd have to change as well.

I walked back to the office and stared down at Ricky. "Sorry. I'm sure you heard Eddie Bang is up for a Grammy. My husband's his agent. There are going to be awards shows. Lots of press. There's no way to guarantee my picture won't wind up in some of the publicity. With a big fan like you, the risk of you figuring out my real name...It was just too great. I can't have regular people knowing about my little...habit. I owe my husband that much."

By the time the cops arrived, sirens wailing and lights flashing, I was standing on the front porch clutching a third glass of whisky. I cried as I told them what happened. I was genuinely sorry about killing Ricky. He'd made life here bearable. The cops seemed sympathetic to my fictional version of events. When the detectives arrived, I retold my story.

As usual, Dougie underestimated his travel time, showing up forty-five minutes after the police. He and Bob separated me from the investigators, then the lawyer had me run through my story again. After that, he okayed me answering another round of questions from the detectives before telling them it was enough.

Ricky's body had been removed, but techs still milled about the study. I got the okay to head upstairs. Leaving Bob to keep an eye on the police, Dougie followed. After closing our bedroom door, he sat on the bed and gave me his "spine of iron" look.

"Sit down, Annabelle and tell me what really happened." Dougie wasn't good at his job just because he was charming; he was smart and a pro at reading people. "Who's the guy?"

"I called him Ricky."

"Called him?"

"I don't know his real name."

"How'd you meet?"

"He spotted me shoplifting at Hill Center and followed me from the store."

Dougie's sigh washed across me. "Again? I thought we'd left all that nonsense behind in L.A."

I shrugged. "If you wanted that, you should've left me behind too."

"You know that's not happening." He knotted his hands in his lap. "Go on."

"I thought he was undercover security and jammed the bracelet I'd lifted into the front pocket of my jeans. I figured I could bluff my way out of it. But instead of busting me, Ricky made me an offer."

For the first time, genuine concern crossed Dougie's face. "What kind of offer?"

"He asked if I wanted to make some real money."

"Real—Why would you need money? We're set."

"He didn't know that. He never knew anything about me. Not even my name. He called me Lucy."

"Then why is he dead on the study floor?"

I stood and paced the length of the bedroom. "Since moving us here, you're always off checking out music, scouting new clients. Then working with those new clients. And I'm here in this huge house in a neighborhood where I don't know anyone. I was going crazy from boredom. Ricky was like a sparking wire. In a good way, you know?"

"Can't you find something less criminal to meet your adrenaline needs?"

"You used to help me manage my craving for risk."

"Babe. My work…It means socializing with my clients. And prospective clients. I've got an image to maintain. I can't be going to high-end open houses with you anymore so you can pocket valuables."

"I get it. I do. But you knew who I was—what I needed—before we got married. Since the move, I've tried to keep it to a minimum, but I need the thrill. Otherwise, what's the point?"

"So, Ricky thrilled you?"

"Not like that. He taught me a new skill set."

"Meaning?"

"He showed me how to pick locks. How to jimmy doors and windows. Showed me where most people hide their jewels and cash."

"How many places did you rob with him?"

"We burgled. We didn't rob."

Dougie quirked an eyebrow.

"Just nine. No ten. But no one saw us. I don't think we're even on the cops' radar."

"Until today."

"Dougie, if you think about it, this is really your fault."

"What the—"

"The Eddie Bang Grammy nomination? You said some life-style magazine wanted to do an interview here at the house. Meet me. See how you live. Do a story about your keen eye for talent. I couldn't risk getting caught in a publicity shot. Ricky's a huge fan. He could learn my identity." I moved to Dougie's side and took his hand. "I didn't want to do...what I did. Really. I just couldn't see another way out."

"I thought this move would be a fresh start for us."

"It was a fresh start. For you. You had your work. Me...since moving here, my life has turned into a blurry watercolor. No sharp lines. All blah. No excitement. No friends. No risk. No nothing. Working with Ricky was my something."

"Jesus." Dougie rubbed the back of his head, mussing his hair. "What—I don't even know what to ask..."

"Look, Ricky dealt with the fence, unloading the take. No one but him knew I was involved in any of the thefts." All of Ricky's rules were paying off—at least for me. "And we never called or texted each other—except on burners. Nothing we did together can come back on me."

"Except for tonight."

"Yeah but, I'm the victim here. At least as far as the cops know."

Dougie looked at me, eyes damp. Then he squeezed my hand, and I knew everything would be okay.

"Sure, babe. And maybe we can check out an open house in Belle Meade next weekend."

A PIPER HAS FALLEN

H.K. Slade

For some people, music is the wail of a guitar or the twang of a banjo. For others, it is a beat to dance to. For Ambrose Broyhill, music was the swelling rumble of a snare drum and the skirl of massed bagpipes.

The venue for this year's Winston County Pipe and Drum Corps Christmas Celebration was an old converted church. Ambrose hovered at the edge of the packed chapel, contentedly sipping on his whiskey and enjoying the exceptional hors d'oeuvres. This was his eighteenth consecutive year attending the party, his fifth since retiring, and he was well past the point of feeling obligated to mingle.

"Look at all these peacocks," Hector Fuentes said as he emerged from the press of partygoers in tuxedos, kilts, and evening dresses. The stocky man's knack for slipping through crowds had made him one of the best undercover detectives Ambrose had ever worked with, and his ready smile and generous nature made him one of the most well-liked.

Ambrose gestured with his glass to a kilted young man holding court over a cluster of admiring women. "I assume you're talking about Aiden?"

Hector popped a mini-quiche into his mouth and nodded without having to look back. "One among many," he said around a mouthful of egg and puff-pastry. "But he's the belle of the ball."

While most of the pipers were of an age with Ambrose and Hector, Aiden was the exception. Handsome, with neck tattoos and heavy gauge piercings, the young man was the pipe band's bad boy. Instead of an anti-social personality, though, Aiden was the life of every party. The band would play bars on St. Patrick's Day, and Aiden would hop on a table and belt out a raucous rendition of "Shipping Up to Boston" to the cheers of everyone in attendance.

"A guy can't help it if people like him," Ambrose observed.

Hector snorted. "Not everyone. Marc would shave his beard off if it meant he could kick Aiden out of the band. He pops a blood vessel every time the little turd shows up missing a piece of his uniform."

Ambrose could see that. As the pipe band's oldest member, Marc was a somber traditionalist and Aiden was most definitely not. For that matter, a lot of the old guard didn't seem to care for Aiden and his little idiosyncrasies. Ambrose's old boss, retired Deputy Chief Georgia Tucker, was working the crowded room like she was running for mayor, but she conspicuously avoided Aiden. When the Brownian motion of the crowd brought the two together, she found a reason to divert course. It wasn't blatant, but Ambrose had been a professional investigator for twenty years; it was hard to break the habit of looking for suspicious activity.

Ambrose's eyes went to Marc, who was clinking his glass with a knife. Initially, the sound was lost in the general cacophony of the party, but as people joined in, the clinking drowned out everything else. Soon, the chapel was as silent as it could be with eighty people standing on an old wood plank floor.

"Pipers and drummers," Marc said, "It's that time. Make your way downstairs. The rest of you, enjoy the quiet. It's about to get loud."

Hector ate another quiche and downed it with the rest of his beer. "That's my cue. We'll catch up more after the performance? I haven't heard from you since Jerry's thing."

That was the way it was with retired cops. It was too easy to only see each other at funerals.

"I'd like that," Ambrose said and gave his old friend a smile.

As the band members filed out of the room, some of the pressure began to bleed off and Ambrose felt more comfortable leaving his perch by the buffet table. It was good timing, as his whiskey glass was in need of just a touch more whiskey.

"You're looking fit, Ambrose," someone said as he stood waiting for the bartender's attention. Ambrose brushed his thick grey mustache to rid it of any crumbs and turned to find Judy Heckner watching him and holding her own empty glass.

Judy and her husband Bart had been making the rounds all evening, and Ambrose had been glad they hadn't made their way to him. Old Bart was downright irascible, one of the most no-nonsense K9 officers Ambrose had ever worked with. His wife Judy, on the other hand, was what they used to call a free spirit. The Christmas party was an excuse for everyone to dust off their best dress or rent a tuxedo, but Judy wore a colorful macramé blouse rife with so many holes that it was immediately apparent she'd left her bra at home. While that didn't bother Ambrose, Bart hobbled around on his bad knee throwing dark looks at anyone taking too much notice of his wife's wardrobe choices. Ironically the two had met when Bart arrested her for shoplifting lingerie from a boutique in the mall fifteen years earlier.

"Judy," he said as neutrally as he could. "How's Bart doing?"

She smirked, her mouth puckering like she was thinking of a joke she couldn't share. "He went downstairs with the rest of the band to get ready. Did you lose weight? Or is it just the tuxedo?"

Ambrose looked down. Back when he'd been on the homicide squad, he'd been known for his bulk almost as much as for his exceptional clearance rate. Retirement had been good to him, and he'd lost fifty pounds through the simple process of sleeping enough, eating regular meals, and walking his pit bull, Lilo, every day. "It's probably a little of both. My mother always said I cleaned up nicely. When I did clean up."

Patting his forearm, Judy said, "She's not wrong."

A goose-like honking started at the back of the room, and then the drone of three dozen bagpipes roared into existence. Ambrose's chest swelled as the pipe major, Battalion Chief Zack Balzac, led the long procession of marching pipers into the chapel.

Ambrose couldn't fully articulate why pipe music affected him so. He'd stood, dry-eyed, as slain officers were laid in the ground, only to break down in tears at the first wail of the pipes. In the confines of the chapel, the raw volume of thirty-some-odd pipers playing in unison pressed down on Ambrose from all sides like a physical force. It wasn't music he heard so much as felt.

The band circled as they began the third refrain of Amazing Grace, and the volume somehow grew even louder. Hector was smiling around his mouthpiece. Georgia's ears were bright red from the effort. Zack was pulsing his mace up and down, the steady center of the group.

And then a strident note appeared like a tiny crack in the wall of sound. Most people wouldn't have heard it, but Ambrose had been listening to pipe music his entire adult life. Marc noticed it too, and although Ambrose didn't have the ear to pinpoint the culprit, all he had to do was follow the line of Marc's glare.

Aiden didn't look good. In fact, he looked half-dead. His skin was so pale it was almost translucent. His eyelids drooped and sweat poured down his face. The tassel on his drones swung back and forth as the young man swayed on his feet.

Another mistake and Marc's glare turned to daggers. Aiden tried to wipe his face, but his arms appeared to be too heavy to lift. Ambrose was already pushing forward when the young man collapsed, falling face-first on the church floor. The music ground to a halt.

The thing about having a medical emergency among a group of first responders was that there wasn't much for someone like Ambrose to do but watch. Georgia was on her phone instantly, updating the dispatcher on the situation in real time. Marc backed the rest of the band away to give Zack and the medical personnel room to work. Bart tried to collect Aiden's pipes so they wouldn't get trampled, but Hector convinced him to leave them.

The atmosphere of the room changed instantly when Zack ripped open the young man's shirt and started CPR. Hector called for an AED. Twenty minutes later, the paramedics terminated resuscitation efforts, declaring Aiden Fogel deceased at 2108 hours.

Most of the death Ambrose had seen had been during the course of his work as a detective. He rarely saw the last few moments of someone's life first hand, and the new experience was uncomfortable. Instinctually, he shifted to a professional mindset and looked around the room filled with former law enforcement officers and high-ranking firefighters, men and women used to being in charge in these types of situations. Ambrose was glad to be retired. He did not envy the poor detective that had to sort this mess out.

Detective Friday Hampton sat in her car outside of the crime scene taking deep, mindful breaths. Ostensibly, she was gathering her gear to respond to the dead body call, but in reality, she was gathering her courage. Only having been in the investigative division for two months, this was her first shift as the on-call detective. She had a good reputation as a street cop, but that only meant the call was hers to mess up.

The problem with raising everyone's expectations is that all you can do is disappoint people.

Sucking in one final breath, Friday grabbed her portfolio, hung her badge from the pocket of her jacket, and stepped out from the shelter of her unmarked car.

Strobing police lights lit the old church in blue. It had been an entertainment venue for as long as Friday had been a cop, but her dad had told her stories of chasing criminals through the downtown streets only to have them seek sanctuary in the little church. As she ducked under the yellow crime scene tape and flashed her ID at the officer holding the perimeter, she felt the memory of her dad like an angel on her shoulder.

"Do you know who I am?" a bearded old man in a kilt was shouting at the sergeant trying to manage the crowd that had been moved to the hall in the basement of the church. The young sergeant, Terry Greene, looked to be drowning in his new position. Friday went to his rescue.

"Detective Hampton, sir," she said to the man in the kilt. Friday stuck out her hand to shake, and the man couldn't help but return the gesture. "If you'll give me a few minutes to get a handle on the situation, I'll be happy to see what I can do for you."

It was such a reasonable statement, the bearded man sputtered, unable to do anything but agree. Friday hooked Terry's arm and pulled him upstairs into the relative quiet of the vestibule. "Sarge, what do we got?" she asked.

Terry looked ready to spit. "It's a shit show. Guy fell over dead while playing pipes."

"And?" Friday asked, knowing there had to be more to it than that.

He lowered his voice. "Everyone down there is connected. My phone's been blowing up with calls from captains to city councilmen and everyone in-between. I've had my career threatened more times in the last half-hour than I've had hot showers."

Friday looked at the crowd gathered in the hall below them. She could almost see the collar brass. Eighty people, mostly old men, and none of them looked happy.

"Ladies and gentlemen," she said, descending the stairs and raising her voice to address the group. "Thank you for your patience. We'll be as efficient as we can, but there are certain protocols we have to follow."

"Don't tell me about protocols, missy," a bald man with thick salt-and-pepper eyebrows barked. "I was humping calls when you were knee-high to a June bug. You're not keeping me here all night like I'm some street thug."

Georgia Tucker, the old deputy chief, smacked a table. "When did they start sending children to do police work? I want to talk to Danny Morgan right now, or I'm walking out and you can try to stop me."

Frowning, Friday was about to wade into the fray when she recognized a friendly face in the crowd: the great Ambrose Broyhill.

"Don't blow out your catheter, Georgia," he said as he made his way to Friday's side. "That's Tony Hampton's daughter. Her blood's as blue as anyone's in this room. Young as she is, she's taken more calls than you did in your whole career. Everybody just calm down and let her work. We've all been on the other side and there's nothing worse than a bunch of old farts trying to tell a working detective how to do her job."

It was a testament to the respect everyone held for the former detective that all the objections suddenly went quiet. Friday could almost hear the thought in the minds of everyone in the room: *If Ambrose Broyhill's working the case, it's as good as solved.*

"Good to see you, detective," she said as she ushered him upstairs. "Wish it was better circumstances."

He gave her a wink only she could see. "You're the detective now. How about we go by first names?"

She'd known the man her whole life. He'd been her father's partner, best friend, and, later, her mentor. "All right, Ambrose." It sounded weird coming out of her mouth. "I've got a dead body. Walk me through the crime scene?"

The area in the center of the chapel had been taped off. The EMTs had draped the body in a blanket and left the detritus of their life-saving efforts on the floor like discarded party favors. A set of bagpipes lay on their side arranged in a pose not entirely dissimilar to the dead body's.

Ambrose dug his hands in his pockets. "That's Aiden Fogel. Twenty-six-year-old white male. During the performance, he appeared to become disoriented and collapsed. It's possible that he had an underlying condition that no one knew about. It's stuffy in here and in all that wool, blowing into his bagpipe...there is no telling how much strain it put on his system."

Friday peeled back the sheet. Though it was her first death investigation as a detective, she'd seen plenty of bodies on patrol. She didn't recognize the young man with the tattoos and piercings, but she instantly recognized what killed him. She went for her gloves, careful not to touch anything until she had a layer of nitrile between her and the decedent.

"No obvious signs of injury," Ambrose said from over her shoulder. "No petechiae. Nails look normal, maybe a little bluing at the cuticles."

All true, but to her, the answer was obvious. Friday was a little surprised Ambrose hadn't spotted it, but most of the overdoses in his day were from cocaine. He'd retired before the opioid crisis.

Friday searched the body for pills. She rolled back the decedent's sleeves. *Clean forearms. Muscular, too.* His pupils were slammed shut, practically pinpoints.

"Ocean David," she said, standing up and peeling off her gloves. "Probably opioids."

Ambrose lifted an eyebrow, clearly skeptical. "Heroin? Are you sure?"

"It's not heroin these days. It's pills and powders."

And that was a problem for Friday. Policy said that all opioid deaths were to be treated as homicides, and that meant she was going to have to find a way to keep all those witnesses downstairs until the homicide unit could come in. That could take hours. She'd have to call in more officers, officers patrol couldn't spare. It was a no-win scenario. If the political fallout didn't get her, the irreparable damage to her professional reputation would.

Next to her, Ambrose squinted and rubbed his mustache. It was a gesture Friday knew all too well. The old detective was onto something. A few seconds later, he asked, "How long does it take for something like that to onset? Hours?"

"Minutes, usually."

"Hmmm."

"What are you thinking?"

He pointed to the body. "Aiden wasn't the type to slip away without anyone noticing. He was shoulder to shoulder with other pipers up to the minute he keeled over, and before that, he was in the middle of a crowd. Someone would have noticed if he was popping pills or snorting powder. The last time he had a chance to take something was two hours ago."

Friday didn't waste time asking Ambrose if he was sure. The man's mind was a steel trap.

"Someone slipped it to him," she thought aloud. "He was poisoned."

Ambrose suggested that Friday start with Marc since he was the event's organizer. She had the young sergeant bring the piper up from the hall. Marc was huffing into his beard even before he got into the chapel.

"Marc Brannigan?" She shook his hand. "Detective Hampton. I've been told that you know more about what's going on in the band than anyone else. Can you help me get to the bottom of this so we can get everyone home?"

The man's chest inflated, and his expression became serious. He even changed the angle of his stance to stand shoulder to shoulder with the two of them, as if he were joining the investigation. Ambrose smiled behind his mustache at how easily Friday defused Marc's complaints before he could even make them.

"When was the last time you saw Aiden Fogel leave the party?" she asked.

Marc checked his watch. "Let's see…just around 7:20. The caterer was setting the food out and Aiden and Hector slipped away for maybe five minutes."

"And then they came back into the party?"

He shook his head. "Hector did. He and Bart started arguing about the Packers' game. I didn't see Aiden for another twenty minutes."

Friday made a note on her pad and asked, "Did you notice anything different about him when he came back?"

"No, he was still the same insufferable ass he always was."

Friday's pen stopped. "What do you mean?"

After the bare minimum of hesitation, Marc said, "He was a nice enough kid, but he was a showboat. All eyes had to be on him, and if they weren't, he'd do whatever it took to make sure they were."

"Did you see him take anything tonight?"

That got the old patrolman's ears twitching. "What do you mean, 'Take anything?'"

"Pills," she said, "anything like that?"

"Nope. Someone would have noticed. Half the people in the room were cops. You think he overdosed?"

Friday realized her mistake; Ambrose could see it on her face. She'd been hoping to keep that suspicion to herself for a little while longer, but Marc had been on the job for thirty years. Friday was good, but it was obvious she wasn't used to questioning other cops.

Ambrose tried to buy her some time to recover. "Marc, you know better than that. It's for the medical examiner to determine."

Marc turned to face Ambrose, putting his back to Friday. "How many murders did you solve before the ME's report came back, eh, Ambrose? If he didn't take something, that means someone slipped him something, and that means we're here until dawn waiting for the suits."

Friday waved for the sergeant to escort Marc back to the fellowship hall with the others. In Ambrose's opinion, she made the correct call cutting the interview short instead of trying to recover from her mistake. Marc was a dog with a bone. Better to move on.

Hector was next. Ambrose's old buddy would be easier to deal with. He'd known and respected Friday's father, plus he was just drunk enough to be helpful.

"Oh, yeah," he said, "we went outside about 7:15. Judy got a big cake for Bart's birthday. We were going bring it out after we got done playing. She wanted me to distract Bart while she and Aiden snuck it into the fridge downstairs. As far as I know, everything went smooth as pudding. Bart and I argued about football for a half-hour, and wham-bam, Bob's your uncle."

"How about the rest of the night?" Friday asked. "Did Aiden have any unusual interactions with anyone?"

Ambrose saw that Friday restructured her question so as not to give away her suspicions. Unfortunately, Hector was a lot smarter than he looked.

"Are you asking if I saw who poisoned him?" he asked casually. "No, but I didn't exactly hang around him all night. A little Aiden goes a long way. Went a long way? Anyway, it's going to be the food or the drink. Aiden drinks—drank—like a fish."

When Hector was safely downstairs and they were alone with the body, Ambrose put a hand on Friday's shoulder. It wasn't a gesture he would have been comfortable making with most people, but they had history together. He'd helped her through several cases during the start of her career and the end of his. Even if Friday's father hadn't been his old partner,

Ambrose felt like he'd made enough deposits in the trust bank that his words meant something to her.

"It's okay to punt," he advised. "Hold the scene until homicide gets here. I'll go down and help keep everyone calm."

Friday shook her head resolutely. "I've got this. I didn't go through all that work to make detective just to stand around at a murder scene. I've got witnesses and suspects to interview. Can you bring me up Our Lady Judy of the Perpetual Cake? Is she the one with all the holes in her shirt?"

Stubborn, but that's not always a bad thing. Over the long course of his career, Ambrose had seen more cases solved by dogged determination than feats of brilliance. He fully believed Friday would be a good investigator one day, maybe even great. He just wished she'd gotten more of a ground ball for her first one.

"Why haven't you arrested the bartender so we can go home?" Judy asked as Ambrose led her up the stairs. Behind them, the crowd was growing restless. "Are you thinking it's the caterer? He does have that look to him, doesn't he?"

"Judy," Friday asked, cutting to the chase before they'd even made it into the chapel, "when was the last time you saw Aiden Fogel?"

Judy's eyes went hard. She refused to look at the shrouded body behind Friday. Instead, she waved at the rafters, indicating the entire church. "Right here, just before he fell over and died. Surely someone has described it to you?"

Friday continued to take notes, outwardly unperturbed. "Before that. Did you step outside with him earlier in the evening?"

"Oh," Judy said. "Yes, we went to get the cake for my husband's birthday. Nothing nefarious."

Friday scribbled a few lines. "Why Aiden?"

"Because Hector is the only person Bart will talk to for more than a minute," Judy explained and threw a look at Ambrose that said she expected him to corroborate her statement. "I needed time to get the cake into the building without him seeing."

Friday forced a polite smile, but her tone went brittle. "That doesn't answer the question."

With her hands on her hips and a heavy, contrived sigh, Judy became the picture of indignation. "Aiden was a peach, one of the few people kind enough to do something nice for Bart. I asked him to help me because I knew he'd say yes. If someone poisoned him, you need to figure out who did and put them *under* the jail."

Judy rested her hand on Ambrose's arm again, her voice softening. "You'll do that, right Ambrose? For Aiden?"

Ambrose found Judy cloying, like a perfume that was nice but too damn strong by half. Friday saved him by having the sergeant escort Judy back to the hall.

"In a room surrounded by people, how does a guy go about getting poisoned?" Friday asked once they were alone again. "It's not the food. There's nowhere to set a plate down. Impossible for someone to tamper with just one person's food."

Ambrose had been out of the game too long and didn't have the knowledge to understand all the factors involved with this type of murder. But he had his brain, and he had Friday, and what he didn't know, she could tell him. *The drug would need to be targeted,* Ambrose thought as the wheels in his mind started turning.

"Friday, how big a dose are we talking about here?"

She didn't have to think about it. "Fentanyl is about fifty times stronger than morphine. We're talking grams. Or less. Ingested, injected, snorted...even skin contact."

Skin contact. A solution fell into place. "What sort of protection do you use to handle this stuff?"

"Gloves. An N95 mask. And a buttload of caution."

"Do you have all of that on you?"

The growing racket from downstairs was getting louder. Friday pulled another pair of gloves from her pocket and had the sergeant bring her a mask. When she was ready, Ambrose told her what he was thinking.

"Those are his pipes on the floor there. Very carefully, grip the chanter by the neck and pull it out of the bag. Don't worry, it's designed to detach."

"That's the flute thing?"

"Yes," he said patiently, "it's the flute thing. The air from the bag blows through it. The piper covers the holes with his fingers to change the sound. Remind me one of these days to take you out to the Highland Games. We've got to get you cultured."

Friday did as he asked, and the chanter came away from the bag. "Well, damn," she said, looking inside the chanter stock. "I'll need a TruNarc unit to field test it, but in my considered opinion, those are crushed Fentanyl tablets." She looked up at Ambrose. "You just found the murder weapon."

Setting the pipes down, careful not to put any of the white powder into the air, Friday stood and unhooked her mask. Ambrose could read her thoughts by her expression: *Once again, the legendary Detective Ambrose Broyhill has managed to pull the answer from wisps of smoke.*

Ambrose wasn't satisfied. "Unfortunately, that doesn't give you a suspect. The instruments were laying out in the hall downstairs all evening." He'd given her the how, but in police work, that was usually the least important of the questions that needed to be answered. They still had no clue as to the who or the why.

Then Friday surprised him.

"Terry," she said to the sergeant, "Bring me that lady's husband."

The sergeant coughed meaningfully. "Sure, detective. I don't know how much longer I can keep a lid on that crew, though."

Friday glared at him, and the young sergeant scampered off. Ambrose had no idea what her plan was, but she had a head of steam now.

Limping up the stairs, Bart Heckner looked to be in an even worse temper than usual. His attitude failed to improve when Friday put him in handcuffs.

"What the hell is this?" he thundered as the cuffs clicked shut. "I'll have you walking a beat for the rest of your short career, missy!"

Friday spun Bart around and met his glare with one of her own. "I'm going to search you now, Bert. That's going to happen. Period. If I run across anything that sticks me, cuts me, or makes me sick, you and I are going to have serious issues. Now, is there anything you need to let me know about besides that fancy little dagger in your sock?"

She didn't know it—she *couldn't* know it—but in that moment, Friday was the ghost of ol' Tony Hampton come to life. The resemblance in tone and phrasing sent a shiver up Ambrose's spine and put a lump in his throat.

Bart looked to Ambrose for help.

Ambrose crossed his arms. "I'd take her seriously, Bart."

Bart scowled, his big bushy eyebrows coming to a point above his nose. "I've got some prescription medication in my sporran."

"That's this little purse thingy, right?" Friday asked. With her gloved hand, she reached into his sporran and drew out a prescription pill bottle. She shook it and the pills inside rattled.

"Fentanyl. I suppose you have a prescription?"

"Knee surgery," Bart said quietly.

Waving the sergeant forward to come take charge of her suspect, Friday said, "We can talk all about that down at the station. Terry, can you make sure Mr. Heckner gets there safely? I'm sure he's going to want to call his lawyer."

Bart didn't say another word as he was led out. Ambrose didn't understand what had just happened, but he knew what a guilty suspect looked like, and if Bart wasn't guilty of something, he was doing a heck of an impression.

Friday showed Ambrose the bottle of heavy-duty painkillers.

"I doubt we'll have any problems matching this up to the crushed pills in Mr. Fogel's pipes."

Ambrose was concerned. "I know you're feeling pressure to get this solved quickly, but how are you going to explain your PC for the search?"

"Means, motive, and opportunity," she said, beaming with pride.

Ambrose shook his head, genuinely at a loss.

Friday's eyes widened in mock surprise. "Man, it's weird having to explain something to you for once. He's been here all night with access to everyone's pipes. The scars on his knee told me he'd had surgery. Knee surgery means painkillers. It's a good thing Scots wear kilts. If he'd been in pants, he might have gotten away with it. Motivation?" She pointed at the body. "The victim was sleeping with the man's wife."

Ambrose raised an eyebrow. "Because they went out for cake?"

Friday pointed down the stairs to where Judy and the rest of the party guests were waiting. "Didn't you see her blouse?"

"I noticed it," he admitted ruefully.

"Then you should have noticed the seams," Detective Friday Hampton said. "It's on inside out."

A SHORT GARSH

Clay Stafford

Mandy Dylan stared in the mirror, mascara brush poised, transforming herself into something near beautiful, but not quite.

She'd jogged this morning to Manhattan Nite to check out the parking spot Toby had reserved for her.

The phone rang. She didn't recognize the number.

"Mandy," she said.

"Oren Etovin. Manhattan Nite. Rehearsals are running faster. Wondered if you could be here earlier…"

"How earlier?"

"Thirty minutes…"

"Sure." Mandy clicked off.

The phone rang again. Caller ID: her husband.

"Garsh, Mandy." The voice was Goofy. From Disney.

"Robert, I'm late. They called…Stop with the Goofy." Robert had computerized his voice to sound like Goofy to match his iPhone case. As a comedy writer and technophile for *The Branson Comedy Hour* his AI voice-cloning parodies of country celebrities had become a hit. He loved the app so much he'd put it on everything. He could make his voice sound like anybody.

"Break a leg."

"Turn off Goofy."

"I like Goofy." Then in Robert's voice: "Better?"

She didn't answer.

"I'd like to be there."

Mandy wanted to tell him she felt terrified. Her regular band couldn't make it. With Robert hanging, she checked her social media where she had posted the time she would perform, that everyone should tune in.

"I'll watch you on TV," Robert said. "Tonight, we'll drink champagne. Pop the cork."

"Don't you have that backwards?"

"Nope."

Robert hung up the phone. It was New Year's Eve. He should be front row for his wife's performance, yet he had to work. His marriage had tanked. Mandy had someone.

His cell rang: Diageo and Suntory. The law firm he had hired.

"Robert, I called Toby Dean yesterday and…"

"I thought we weren't going to tell him until after all this…"

"Your email said 'as soon as possible'."

"But we talked…" Robert had not discussed this with Mandy. At least Toby had traveled with Sarah to Michigan.

"He said we could set up a meeting on the tenth to discuss."

"I know the music business," Robert said, "and I don't want to see my wife hurt by not getting what she wants, but bluegrass and…"

"I'll set it up. Mr. Dean seemed agreeable. Said he understood. His words: 'open and shut'."

Robert had just had lunch with Toby yesterday, planning. He and Toby Dean had a relationship through Sarah. He'd worked with Sarah long before he'd known Mandy. If he had known, he would have said something to Toby yesterday.

Robert didn't have the money, but he called the Kroger flower shop.

* * *

In the kitchen of their third-floor two-level apartment, Mandy cored an apple and hurried out the door. She had a run-through with the house band, then make-up, hair, and wardrobe, and a 7:20 appearance on *New Year's Eve Live: Nashville's Big Bash*. A projected eight million people would tune in. She longed for when she didn't have to moonlight as a shoe salesperson at Off Broadway. Everyone thought having a song on the charts meant success. Her manager, Toby Dean, told her this appearance would propel her career.

Mandy was so glad she wouldn't see Toby tonight. Married, six kids, loving wife, and he hit on Mandy continuously. Robert said he'd call Toby and make his voice sound like Toby's wife with his voice app, but Mandy told him a flat 'no'. Toby changed after Mandy broke from the pack. She tried to get the terms of her contract revised a couple of times, but Toby wouldn't hear of it. She'd signed with him when she first came to Nashville. She hadn't had a lawyer look it over. Robert had set it up. It locked her in for the rest of her career.

Oren Etovin sat on the toilet. His stomach killed him. Rehearsal times had run ahead of schedule, so his boss, the producer, also his professor, had him reach out to all the lesser acts to let them know to come in earlier. Now the professor blamed him because the performers weren't showing up. He'd be making Cajun Ranch Chicken Wraps at Cook Out for the rest of his life.

Traffic and blockages had gotten worse than when Mandy had jogged down to Manhattan Nite. Two-hundred-thousand people would surround the area around the Bicentennial Capitol Mall State Park. A mob of people blocked the road. She honked her horn to move them. Some shifted kindly. Others blew her off.

Robert pushed for Mandy to be on his Mayberry-TV show, but Mandy never considered it. She'd be small-time. Mandy needed to play stadiums like Taylor Swift, not casinos in Branson. Mandy was embarrassed now to be with Robert, her first love. She detested him because he felt needy, accused her of having an affair. Mandy didn't need another man.

"Not again!"

Her car's warning light glowed red. It had turned on and off for a month now.

She parked her white Corolla and jaywalked across 3rd Avenue. Her face grew white as she saw her manager Toby looking out the lobby window. He was supposed to be in Michigan.

Robert thought about what he should do. This was his fault. He didn't want Toby ruining this night for Mandy. Toby hadn't called Mandy yet, otherwise Mandy would have said something. Toby had taken his family to Michigan. Robert decided to call Toby directly. Toby answered immediately.

Toby didn't sound angry. "I understand Mandy's dreams, so there's several ways we can address this. This is Mandy's night. I haven't said anything to her."

"I appreciate that, Toby. You have a Happy New Year. Give my regards to the family. Be careful driving back from Ann Arbor."

As Mandy entered, Toby put his phone into his pocket.

"Mandy, my girl," he said, hugging her tightly. Toby wore his sunglasses and smelled of whiskey and pot. "You'll knock 'em dead."

A red-headed young man approached carrying a brown leather portfolio organizer. "Oren Etovin."

Mandy recognized Oren but couldn't place him.

"The band..." Oren said.

Toby snapped his fingers to get Oren to look at him. "Ms. Dylan needs some water."

Toby wanted to be a big player, but he wanted to do it by pushing people around. Toby had worn his rhinestone jacket and slacks making him look like Porter Wagoner. When Mandy started to break out, he'd contacted Manuel Cuevas who wouldn't return his call, so he got some seamstress in Smyrna.

Oren returned and Toby snapped his fingers at him and pointed at Mandy. Toby reached his free hand into his jacket and pulled out a ten-dollar-bill. Toby kept a wad in his jacket or pants. He could always speedily peel off a single ten.

"The dress?" Mandy asked.

"Got it. You'll love it. You. Boy." Toby addressed Oren. "I don't like the timing of where Mandy is playing. She needs to be closer to when that gaudy note-thingy drops..."

"I don't have anything to do with..."

Toby dramatically held his hands to the sides of his head and turned to Mandy. "Robert..."

Mandy's phone rang. Robert. "Speaking of the devil." She answered.

"Yes," Toby said. "The devil."

"Making sure you made it." Robert had programmed in the voice of Reba McEntire.

"Thanks, Reba," Mandy said. "I'm here. Need to go. Love you." She hung up, embarrassed, not waiting for a reply.

"Overheard," Toby said. "Loves his little sound machines. His little *Hee-Haw* job. Loves you. Nice to be loved."

Oren cleared his throat. "Your band is rehearsing, if..."

"What the..." Toby said. "They're rehearsing without her? I'm flip-shocked." Toby put his arm around Mandy, following Oren towards the theater. Mandy felt she was being engulfed by a glorified rhinestone maggot.

***

Mandy took her place onstage, with Toby Dean and Oren Etovin in the audience. The opening bars began. Oren was in the audience, but Toby had gone. Mandy began to sing, going over the top in charisma to counter her feelings of fragility.

Oren stared raptly at her performance. The more she sang, the more familiar he looked, then, in the middle of the second song, it hit her. She recognized him. She'd seen him at her performances. She had even talked with him on several occasions during autograph signings and selfie sessions. She remembered him saying that he followed her around on her tours when he could, that he had all of her merchandise, that—and she heard this all the time—he was her number one fan. Why hadn't Oren mentioned it?

Mandy was near the end of the third song when Toby came back into the auditorium. He hurried towards the front and then he started yelling, "Stop! Stop! Stop!" He shouted the band was awful, the levels of the instruments were too high, the lights on Mandy were all wrong.

An older woman, saying she was the producer, told Toby it was time to rehearse the next act. Toby protested and the woman said she would call security. Mandy took Toby by his rhinestone-covered arm and led Toby out of the theater with Toby yelling "I ought to pull Mandy from this show. Mandy Dylan. You'll remember her name!" Mandy glanced back. Muffled laughter filled the stage.

In the lobby, Toby took Mandy's bag from Oren, peeled off a ten-dollar bill and gave to Oren, and told him, "Dismissed." Toby led Mandy away. Toby handed Mandy her bag; Mandy saw black marks, like oil marks, on her new bag she'd purchased just for tonight. Toby had black smudges on his hand. Mandy didn't think the black would come out.

Toby led Mandy down several corridors to a dressing room hallway. Toby talked the whole way, fast talk, high-as-a-kite talk. "While you were rehearsing. They put you in a dressing room with three *backup* singers and that was not going to work. You're a headliner. I told some squirrely little jerk that if they didn't move the singers, my singer, you, would not perform."

"I'm really fine with..."

"I'm not. My job. Take care of you."

Mandy followed Toby down a hallway to a dressing room that had her name in a little printed plaque holder next to the door. It looked like there had been other names there, but someone had pulled them off—probably Toby—leaving the double-sided sticky tape behind.

"My wife took the kids to visit her parents in Saline...right outside of Ann Arbor. They'll watch the show from there tonight."

"I've got to take a picture." Mandy pulled out her phone, took a shot of her name, and texted it to Robert.

"Let me get the door."

"I can take it from here," Mandy didn't need Toby watching her get dressed.

"Okay, then," Toby said with a wry smile that Mandy did not understand. "Dress. Then I'll see you. If you need help, let me know." She watched him as he walked leisurely down the hall, weaving slightly. At the end of the hall where it teed left and right, Oren Etovin stood watching them both.

Mandy entered and walked into her dream-come-true. She thought about Toby. As odd, annoying, and embarrassing as he was, he had made all of this happen.

She saw a single dress. Unlike Toby's Porter Wagoner-gaudy, her dress was a beautiful blue-sequined.

She noticed the huge vase overflowing with white roses. She touched the petals. This close, the smell engulfed her. Someone had pinned a note to a clear, plastic stick stuck into the arrangement. In a penmanship she recognized as her husband Robert's, he had handwritten "Mandy". Maybe, like she had been with Toby, maybe she had been too hard on Robert. He was there for her. Robert had stuck the top flap into the hand-written envelope, not sealing it. She pulled out the single-sided white clipped piece of typing paper, cut at jagged angles, like a kid might do with scissors. The penmanship did not match.

> White roses for the Bright Light you are.
> —Love, Toby

Mandy stared at the note before throwing it onto the dressing table. She grabbed the paper note and the vase of roses and looked around the room. A trashcan. She threw everything into the trashcan. A knock came at the door.

"Wardrobe." The man was thin with black straight hair, flawless hazelnut and unblemished skin, and dressed in a flowing gown, highly colorful, something one might see in a stereotyped African chieftain.

Mandy looked at the trashcan. She picked it up and put the trashcan inside the closet and closed the door. The man didn't question, didn't even raise an eyebrow.

"I'm Nevaeh."

Nevaeh scanned Mandy. Mandy doubted Nevaeh was his real name, and—frankly, though it didn't matter—was not sure that Nevaeh was not a woman.

"I shall have you as a beauty you have never seen," Nevaeh said.

"Are you from here?"

"I'm from Nowhere. I'm in Nashville journeying to New York." He waved his arm theatrically. "A journey-person. Makeup and wardrobe on Broadway: The Broadway. I work here, elsewhere. Saving money. Building credits. Working my way up. That's been the goal, anyway, since leaving Browns-ville."

"Brownsville?"

"Tennessee. Tina Turner-fame."

"So why here? Why not straight to New York?"

"I do anything but straight." He laughed. "Nashville seemed the next step. I have a few friends here."

Nevaeh began to work and, as he worked, he sang softly. His voice was beautiful, better than what one normally hears from professional performers. He sang without the least degree of self-consciousness. Yet there was a look of sadness, of something hollow.

"You should be a singer," Mandy said.

"No. No. Some of us were not made for the stage."

Nevaeh transformed Mandy to the point that Mandy didn't recognize herself. "Makeup and costumes. On Broadway. You will do well."

As he slipped the dress on her, Mandy thanked him for knowing his way around the fabric because the dress seemed to have strings going everywhere. Mandy couldn't believe what she saw in the mirror. She felt transformed. The dress showed a lot of her back.

Mandy adjusted the straps to show more of her breasts, but Nevaeh said, "No, no, no," and readjusted. Mandy let it be. "Remember an orange peel."

"An orange peel?"

"It conceals the juicy fruit beneath. Remove it…"

"The peel…"

"And it's only an orange. You never ever want to be only an orange."

The dressing room door flew open. "Amorcita!" Toby said. "Finished?"

"Ready," Nevaeh said, collecting his makeup case. "All yours."

"All mine!"

"Nevaeh, thank you," Mandy said as she took both of Nevaeh's tender hands in hers. "More hair to do?"

"No. You are my last."

"You should watch tonight."

"I can't watch." The sadness came again in his eyes. "I never watch."

Toby followed Nevaeh to the door, smirking at Nevaeh's feminine ways, then closed it and locked the door. "Mandy, my Mandy," His eyes were dilated. "If I had champagne, we'd toast."

"The dress is beautiful."

"And you're even more so. In it."

"Why'd you lock the door?"

"I didn't realize I did." He crossed to her and clasped both of her nervous hands. His eyes went to the dressing table. He looked around the room. He's looking for the roses, she thought. "I thought New Year's Eve would be our night."

"For what?"

Toby kissed her on the cheek. When she didn't resist, he reached his arms around her.

Mandy pushed him away. "Toby, stop it."

"I hear you and Robert have troubles. Robert, he's like a partner with me in your career. That's how he thinks. He told me he thought you guys were splitting. You're moving on. Leaving him behind."

"Robert told you that?"

"Over lunch. Yesterday."

"I think you need to leave."

"Celebration night, Mandy. A new year. Five years we've worked for this. About to break out. Both of us. Celebration. After the show? You could come over to my place. Robert working and all."

"Robert is waiting at home," she lied.

"Is he? Or is he working his little country show?" He reached out and fixed her dress over her left breast. "We need a picture." He crossed to her and put his arm around her, his cold hand on her bare ribs. He took several selfies. He stepped back. In the makeup mirror behind him, she saw him click on a picture and then with his two fingers zoom in on her breasts. "I'll post these. You know you want me."

"What?"

"You think I really believe all this you and Robert have cooked up?"

"I don't know what you're talking about."

"Oh, don't tell me you don't know. Your attorney you and Robert hired to get you out of your contract with me. 'You can make it as difficult as you want,' the attorney said. 'But there are loopholes all over it.' My contract is as solid as any contract can be…I stayed behind and let my family go to Michigan to try to save this."

"I don't know what Robert has done."

"Robert knows the feelings that you and I have. He's trying to stop the inevitable. That you and I will be together. I've already told my wife I'm leaving her. That's why she's taken the kids to Michigan."

"No."

"I'm your ride. I built your career. I took you when you were nothing. This garbage that you were seventeen. You told me you were eighteen. A verbal contract counts in Tennessee. You signed it, telling me you were eighteen!"

"I was almost eighteen. What does seventeen have to do with it?"

"You said you were eighteen. And that's binding."

The realization of all this went off in Mandy's head. "That means I was a minor? That the contract isn't valid?" A knock came at the door. "Come in."

Someone tried to turn the door handle. Toby had locked it. Mandy hurried to it. So did Toby. "You stay back."

Toby stopped. "I'm in love with you. You're in love with me."

Mandy opened the door. The red-headed stage manager stood outside. "Places," he said.

Toby watched the door close. He would fight it, but the truth was she was only seventeen when she signed the contract. This was supposed to have been their night. He couldn't watch her perform. He had all his dreams tied up in Mandy's career. And she and Robert were leaving him. He knew the music business. He knew how it turned out for people like him, little guys who found talent, and then lost it to managers and attorneys who already had everything. He should be in Michigan right now. He should be with his wife and kids. A resolve spilled over him. He would go ahead with his plans. This was a new year. He would stick to the vow he made for this night. Mandy would either appreciate it, they would stay together, or they wouldn't.

Mandy followed Oren Etovin.

"Ms. Dylan. I was wondering. If you might have a job available. An assistant? I'm graduating."

"Oren, what are you doing?"

Oren looked up and saw his professor, the show's stage manager, staring at him. "Dr. Jefferson…"

"Oren," Dr. Jefferson said, "The bands are running behind. I've looked everywhere for you. You've tried to get a job from every person here and…Get your things and leave."

"You can't do that," Oren said. Mandy looked at Oren. His voice had changed. It was almost a Dr. Jekyll and Mr. Hyde moment. "You can't do that!" Oren shouted. "You can't make me leave."

"Oren, I'm calling security."

"I'm leaving," Oren said. He hurried down the hallway leaving Mandy and Dr. Jefferson behind.

"You need to be onstage," Dr. Jefferson said. "We're already running behind."

"Is this airing live?" Mandy asked.

"What do you mean?"

"Have they already started the note drop, the show?"

"No," Dr. Jefferson said. "You won't be on TV tonight."

"What?"

"You're *only* one of the warmup acts."

The band sensed Mandy's uncomfortableness, but when the lights hit her, and the crowd started cheering, whatever wronged Mandy vaporized.

In the middle of the second song, she saw Nevaeh. In his African robe, he didn't fit in. She waved, but he did not wave back. She finished the second song, the crowd roared rowdily, but Nevaeh was gone, lost in the sea of cowboy hats and jeans.

Mandy played her set as if she owned the night. When the three songs concluded, Mandy thanked the band, shook hands with a few of the attendees on the front row, took a selfie from the stage, until Dr. Jefferson called, "Clear the stage." Mandy saw the next band waiting. The vacuum always filled.

Mandy didn't want to go back to her dressing room. Toby and Oren terrified her. But she needed her things.

Her name plate had been removed by the dressing room door. Her phone rang. She grabbed it.

"Garsh! How'd it go?" Robert asked in the modulated voice of Goofy.

"Stop it, Robert." She opened the closet door. She saw the trashcan, but the flowers, note, and envelope disappeared. "Did you send flowers?"

"Didn't you get my note?" Robert asked in his own voice.

"Thank you. Coming home."

She traded her heels for her tennis shoes, threw the heels in the bag with her other clothes, threw the bag over her bare sequined shoulder, opened the door to leave, and screamed when she saw Oren Etovin standing in the doorway holding her bouquet of white roses.

Mandy threw her bag into the passenger seat, slammed the door, and tried to lock it. The button didn't work. The phone rang. She saw Toby's caller I.D. She threw the phone in the passenger seat. She inserted the key. Nothing. She turned the key again. No dash lights. No sounds of a motor turning. She found the latch that opened the hood, and clicked it. She got her phone and turned on its light feature. Robert had jiggled some wires around the battery before when she had trouble starting it.

Mandy went around to the front of the car and looked under the hood. "Oh, my god." Two wires connected to the battery, a red one and a black one. Both cut. Both literally cut!

Mandy remembered she had left her keys in her bag in the dressing room while she performed. She dialed Robert.

"Robert, can you come get me? Car won't start." She told him where she had parked.

Oren Etovin, Mandy's self-proclaimed number one fan, watched her from the sidewalk.

Mandy got cold and pulled her sweatshirt out of her bag and slipped it on. Twenty minutes passed. The phone rang. Robert. "You here?"

"I can't get through," Robert said in his own voice. "All roads are blocked. Letting people out, not letting anyone in."

"How far away?"

"Broadway."

"Go back home."

"How will you…"

"I'll catch a ride."

They hung up. If she walked, she could get the two miles to their apartment in about forty-minutes. She cherished her tennis shoes.

Mandy walked down 3rd Avenue. She heard someone running behind her. It was Oren Etovin.

Oren held up both hands. "We got off to a bad start."

"Get away from me," Mandy said.

"I really, seriously, am your number one fan."

"I don't need a number one fan. I've seen that movie."

"I need a job, Ms. Dylan."

"I'm not hiring."

"I need connections. I'm just about to graduate. I've been producing and making music for a long time. I need to connect myself with someone big, someone like you..."

"Oren, I'm not big..."

"You're big. You're important. You're powerful. People look up to you. I just want to help you in your career. Can't you see that? And I know you're the kind of person who cares."

"I'm covered, Oren. I'm really fine. I'm sorry."

"I have no prospects. You don't understand that. I have no support from my parents or anyone else. Right now, I'm living on campus supporting myself with student loans and my part-time job at Cook Out. People don't realize how clever I am. They don't understand my loyalty. I can take care of you."

"I don't need anyone to take care of me."

"Like right now, I want to make sure you get home safely."

Mandy stopped and stared at him. "I'm. Not. Going. Home. Right. Now. Oren." Fear washed over Mandy. She realized that Oren had her bag when she performed, her bag had her keys, Oren knew where she had parked, he had cut her wires. "Oren, stay away from me."

Oren stopped. His face looked as though he had been slapped.

* * *

When Mandy unlocked the door of her third-floor apartment, she smelled fried rice and orange chicken. Her favorite. "Robert!" She locked the door behind her. "Robert!" He didn't answer.

Mandy looked out the window from the kitchen towards Broadway. She couldn't believe it. Oren Etovin was standing at the corner of 12th Avenue looking straight into their apartment. He crossed to the front of her building. Mandy jumped when the intercom bell rang. With trembling hands, she pressed the button.

"Hello."

"Ms. Dylan..."

"Oren, I'm calling the police..."

"I just want to talk to you. I think we got off to a bad start. If you'll let me in..." He looked directly at the black-and-white camera as though he were talking on a TV show.

"I'm not letting you in."

Mandy saw the front door of the building open and a burly man walk out. She saw Oren grab the door and disappear. Oren was in the building.

Mandy ran to her front door and made sure it was locked. She kept yelling for Robert, but he didn't answer.

Mandy pulled out her phone and dialed 911, but then hung up, and speed dialed Robert.

"Mandy?" Robert answered.

"Are you home?" she asked.

"Yes?"

"I'm home."

"Just got out of the shower," Robert said. "Give me a second. Coming down."

"Upstairs?"

"Bedroom."

She didn't wait. She bounded the stairs and rushed into the

bedroom. The first thing she saw was Oren Etovin's leather organizer laying on the bed.

"Robert?"

The bedroom door squeaked as it closed behind her. Her manager Toby Dean leaned his back against the door.

"Where's Robert?"

"He let me in," Toby said. "He's drying off. The shower."

"What are you doing?"

"You remember the song, *Hole in the Bottom of the Sea*? Robert agrees. There are two *nots* on this log. You're *not* leaving me, Mandy. And I'm *not* Barry Manilow."

"I don't understand."

"I gave Oren Etovin sixty-dollars to follow you home and make sure you got here safely."

"Toby, he cut the wires on my car."

"I told him you were interested in hiring him."

"What?"

"He's obsessed with you. I told him I saw you leave your car, that it wouldn't start, that your husband wanted you to drive around in a piece of junk..."

"Robert!"

"...and I assumed you'd try to walk home, that you didn't live that far away, and he'd just been fired, and he'd get to see where you lived, he'd have your address."

"Toby, I don't...Robert!" She made a move towards the bathroom, but Toby stepped between her and the bathroom door. He wore latex gloves. They were dirty. Covered in blood?

"I had him follow you so people on the street would see him. I told him to stay a safe distance from you, don't talk to you, just make sure you got home safely. He's going to kill himself, you know. Tonight. Because you turned him away. He was your number one fan."

"Robert!"

"Stand back, Mandy."

"You'll never get away with this. It was you..."

"Oh, I will. I parked my car in the parking lot of my office on McGavock and went inside to work. I entered the front door where there's a security camera. I left via the stairs and the side door. If anybody needs to corroborate my story, they need only look at the surveillance."

"You're crazy."

"In love, Mandy. Crazy in love. Robert was killed by a love-obsessed fan, a loner, a loser. Oren Etovin has one more thing he's discretely doing for me tonight and then, unfortunately, he's going to look like he killed himself. Once he's gone, there'll be nobody to question."

"Out of my way!" She rushed at Toby and he stepped aside as she ran into the bathroom and saw Robert dead on the floor. Blood everywhere. She saw the knife she'd used to core the apple. Toby quickly picked up the knife. "I just talked to Robert!"

"No. You haven't been talking to Robert tonight. You've been talking to me. And his little gadget."

Toby had a phone in one hand, and he brought it up to his mouth. He held the chef's knife in the other.

"Robert's phone?" She saw Robert's iPhone case in Toby's hand: Goofy. Toby spoke into the iPhone. Mandy heard it out of her phone she still had on, holding in her hand, hanging from her side. "If I can't have you, no one else can either." She heard Robert's voice. Toby pressed a button with his thumb and Dolly Parton spoke, "But I will have you once. At least." He pressed again, Glenn Campbell: "We can be happy together. Or we can both die." Toby pressed again for Reba McEntire: "Welcome home, dear." Toby smiled. Toby lowered Robert's phone, the phone with the voice modulator, the one that sounded like all the country stars...including Robert himself.

Blood covered Toby's shirt. Mandy looked at Robert, splayed on the floor. Toby's thumb moved again on Robert's phone. Like in slow motion, she saw Toby's mouth moving, saying the words, but the last words she heard before she screamed replicated that countrified voice that Robert loved so much.

"Garsh, Mandy. I didn't expect you to take it so hard."

FOLK SONG

Kelli Stanley

Stanza I

It was in the month of May
When the flower buds were swellin'
And a gay young man from Tennessee
Went courtin' Barbr'y Ellen

Her finger tapped on the small insert under "Local Interest". The old lady looked up, gazing out over the porch railing and the well-tended patch of purslane and wishbone flower, goldenrod and Black-Eyed Susan, and stared into the brushy shrubs and bronze-gold trees. They'd be red soon, blood red, like the eclipse that was coming tonight.

A patch of green glinted through the orange, the heavier scent of wild grass and flowers, pasture land and creek.

She took a breath. It was time.

Clay drove her into Williamson. It was earlier than she'd wanted; there was more ginseng to be gathered and the cushaws were ripening late this year, but maybe he could take her in again before Hallowe'en.

The old lady looked at the thin, taciturn man behind the

wheel of the '38 Ford truck. Clay was a good neighbor and a good man, not too much drink, didn't backhand Lydie, stayed out of fights, minded his own. The thin man coughed and bent over the wheel, almost stopping the truck.

Ten years in the Cinderella Mine. Lydie would be lucky to keep him for another five.

The Huff store in South Williamson was full of the usual late afternoon customers and complaints, pale sunbeams slanting through the windows, dust motes floating like tiny faeries over the canned goods and pickled vegetables in glass jars.

The old woman carefully counted out her money while Phil wrapped the parcels. Hiram Smith, Rhoda Lycans, Edith Maynard and another woman she didn't know chewed over the day's news about the attack on Seoul, how the Norfolk and Western got derailed ("Plunged right into the river"), the Shirley Marcum shooting, the UMW meeting, another mine closing down in Logan.

Phil Huff shook his head. "And them Commies. Says in the paper they're everywhere, but I ain't seen one yet." He shook his head again. "We was fightin' beside 'em just five years ago. I ain't forgotten."

The old lady cleared her throat. "Saw in the paper Donald Cline's come back. He's a preacher now. Pentecostal. He weren't in the war, I don't think…"

Edith Maynard stopped folding the pretty flowered cotton cloth she was holding and leaned forward. "Where was that? I didn't see it—"

This morning's *Williamson Daily News* lay open on the broad wooden table with the fabrics and notions, and the old lady stretched a finger to the insert, framed between the "Personals" and an article on the Bevins family reunion. Edith took off her glasses and bent over it.

She spoke slowly. "That's him, right enough. Never expected

to see him again. And you're right, Nancy Jane, he didn't fight. His cousin Frank always said he had an ailment, but Frank was always a liar. Heard he went up to Ohio in '38, but never heard much about what he did after—"

A young woman with a baby carriage, two toddlers and two older children rang the door chime and Phil eagerly exited the counter to help her. The old lady nodded to Edith and walked slowly out of the store, carrying a large box with paper-covered packages of tea, flour, butter and sugar.

A middle-aged woman with more gray than black in her wiry hair stared after her and spoke in an undertone to Edith. "Isn't that ol' Nannie Shockey? The one who lives up by Caney Cemetery and folks says is a witch?"

Edith snorted. "You ain't been here very long, Lurene, and a lot's changed in Pike and Martin and Mingo, but gossip sure ain't. Nannie Shockey's family's been here for a couple hundred years and there ain't nothin' 'bout this land she don't know. She buried her husband and children...last of her family, she is. People movin' down from the cities are the ignorant ones, not knowin' what to plant, what to pick, what to pull up. Whatever folks you been talkin' to ain't worth listenin' to."

Stanza II

He courted her for six long months
But she refused to marry
And Willie went away and was taken sick
For the love of Barbr'y Ellen

The old woman fingered the possum berries. Too hard. Leaves were still pliable, though. Good enough for tea.

She looked back toward the sloping hillside, the grass and greenbrier still green among the gravestones thanks to the earlier rain. She stooped, ignoring the sharp pains in her lower back and left leg, and brushed off some dirt on a small bronze marker.

The Old Regular Baptists hadn't had a cemetery cleaning meeting for Caney and Wolf Creek in a long, long time.

She sighed. Never was much good at writing—only had a little schooling before she went to work in the fields, and then she married Tom and then there were the children...at least the few that lived.

She turned toward the wood and headed back to her home.

With the Lord's help, she'd remember.

She watched the eclipse, how it hung in the black sky, copper-red like a ruby pendant surrounded by diamonds. Then she went back inside to work on the letter.

The kerosene flame burned steadily, but the shadows it threw danced on the wooden walls, distorted figures baying at the red moon outside.

Writing meant remembering. Not just letters and spellings, no—that was the easy part. It meant remembering Ella and Billy, and after remembering, with all the emotions that suffused her like the copper blood of the lunar eclipse, composing, planning, as careful as when she delivered babies for the Maynard girls in the dark barn on their father's land.

Billy Howell from Tennessee. Billy Howell, the boy who wanted to learn, to write, to work on a newspaper, and who had saved enough money, through work and inheritance and sacrifice and luck, to start his own.

Billy Howell, whom folks said was a Melungeon and other folks said was colored and still others said was an Indian. Hardly any folks said he was just a boy, a smart, good, handsome boy, pure-hearted as so many weren't, not even in those days, not even during the Depression when you couldn't get enough to eat to get up to no good.

Billy Howell and Ella King, her niece, a girl with shining hair and a shining face, a girl who stood out like the moon among stars, eight brothers and sisters, no, a sun, not a moon, a yellow-haired girl who outshone them all.

Late in the night she read it again, the final time. She licked the envelope and sealed the letter. Clay would get it to the church for her, and the church would do the rest.

Stanza III

He sent his servant to the town
To the place where she was dwellin'
Said Willie's sick, on his death bed lies
And he sends for you, Barbr'y Ellen

She read the letter out back of the house. The Redbud pods were ripe and ready, a little late this season because of the rains. She lowered the hand holding the letter, remembering the lavender profusion of the flowering tree in the spring.

Most people loved the Redbud because of the purple flowers, but she loved it for the heart-shaped flowers—beautiful and delicate and sometimes as red as a rose. A stand of greenbrier had grown up clinging to the base of the tree, deep green, shiny and strong.

She stood and read the letter again.

"Of course I remember you and Ella and Billy. Billy was my best friend in those days—he gave me my first chance to really make something of myself, working for him on the *Herald*. He was taken from us far too early, as was your Ella, but the Good Lord gathers the choicest flowers to Himself to adorn the Heavens. I am only in town for a short preaching tour but may be coming back to stay, as we are opening another church in Kermit. I would be delighted to pay you a visit after the service on October 1st. Yours truly, Donald Cline."

Stanza IV

Then she looked up and she looked down
And she saw the cold corpse comin'
The more she looked, the more she wept
Said "Young man I believe you're dyin'."

Donald Cline, dressed in black with a red tie and black hat, looked around the small room and smiled. He sniffed. "Corn bread baking?"

Such a tall man, she thought, taller than she'd remembered, with a tendency toward a paunch and some saggy, yellowish skin around his large-pored face.

"Yes. With ham hock and greens."

He smiled again. "You're spoiling me, Mrs. Shockey."

She wiped her hands on her apron and opened the front door wider. A light breeze blew through the house, ruffling the faded blue calico curtains on the small, high windows.

"It's good to have a young man to feed again. Helps me remember. Not all that many folks left in Williamson who remember what it was like before the war, and even fewer who remember when I was young. I'm the last of the Shockeys in these parts."

He laughed. "I'm glad to still count as a young man. That was...let me see. Twelve years ago? The war made it seem double that. I'd left for Ohio already—right after Billy died—and I recall hearing about your niece just after. So sad. 'Course, they weren't engaged no more..."

The old lady stooped over the wood stove and shoved in a piece of split black locust.

"Bought a gas oven in '47 but I still like to keep a hand in on my old stove. Got an apple honey cake in the oven here—we can have tea before supper, if that's not too countrified for you, Pastor Cline, now that you've been away so long."

The tall man loosened his tie. He laid his hat down on the

small oak kitchen table.

"Oh, I ain't forgot everything, Mrs. Shockey. Spent time in Ironton 'til I grabbed a chance to head up to Cincinnati. Big city, hustle and bustle. Learned some things, got more education. And proud to say I found the Lord. You ever go to a Pentecostal service?"

She shook her head. "Born and raised an Old Regular Baptist. But that said, I believe the Lord feeds all of us, whichever flavor we choose. Billy was a Methodist and my niece and him were to marry down at the Enon Baptist church near Road Fork."

The kettle gave a shrill whistle and the black-clad man jumped, then laughed again. "They don't even make tea whistles the same in Cincinnati."

She gestured toward the open door. "Why don't you go sit outside and I'll fetch your tea. It's pleasant today. The most comfortable chairs are on the porch."

Cline stood up. He stepped out of the old house and looked around, at the trees and wild green shrubbery, the cracked dish filled with bird seed on the gray wood fence and the wildflowers that bunched and ran along it.

Quiet—had it always been this quiet? No trains, no cars, no juke box, no sound of life...

He lowered himself into a wooden rocker and looked around uneasily. Same old one- room house, same old, hard land, same old, stupid hicks.

Nothing changed in Martin County. He'd just been away too long.

He stretched his long legs in front of him. The old lady was right. It was fine outside, sunshine, a light breeze. Almost like summer.

He closed his eyes and relaxed some more, a slow smile spreading across his face. There was a soft hum above him and he looked up. He raised his voice.

"You got a mud dauber nest up here. Want me to knock it down?"

She emerged from the close wooden darkness of the interior carrying a tarnished silver tray. On top was a brown tea pot with two old blue and white china tea cups.

"They don't trouble me, Pastor Cline. I don't bother them and they don't bother me. Let that tea sit a spell. I'll be back with your cake."

She returned a few seconds later with a blue and white china plate, mottled and crazed and of ancient vintage. On top was a large piece of yellow cake, dripping with honey and full of bits of brown-white apple.

"You ain't joining me, Mrs. Shockey?"

She shook her head. "Baking is as good as eating. Can't eat as much as I used to. It'll be all I can do to eat the ham and greens." She picked up the tea pot, poured, and handed him a cup. "Here you are."

His large yellowed teeth bit into the moist cake shining with syrup and he chased the bite with a swallow of tea. "Not too hot", he nodded approvingly. "I don't like sippin'—takes too long." His loud laugh seemed to grate against the softness of the afternoon.

The old lady adjusted a woven woolen cushion and lowered herself into the other rocking chair, an old brown-stained one made of hickory. She took a sip from her own tea cup and watched him while he ate and drank. "Eat your fill, Pastor Cline. Greens and cornbread are done but we'll need to sit and talk some before the meat's ready."

He set the empty dishes on a small wrought iron table between the two rockers.

"That was delicious. Thank you, Mrs. Shockey. So—did you have something particular in mind you wanted to talk about or see me for? I thought maybe you was considering a change in your church—"

"No, I'd never do that."

"Then this is all just—reminiscing? I can understand that. It's healthy to remember, even when it pains us. Billy and Ella—

losing both so close together, so sad and tragic—like, like Romeo and Juliet. He loved her and she didn't know if she loved him back until it was too late—blamed herself, poor girl—"

Nancy Jane Shockey rocked the hickory chair slowly, staring into the bronze trees and the patch of green in the distance.

"That's how folks took it, Pastor Cline. How the story came down. Ella couldn't give him her heart full enough to marry."

She glanced over at him. "You would know all about that. You worked as his apprentice. You were his best friend. You carried the messages between them when they had that big argument. I remember. Billy was printing the *Herald* up in Pilgrim and Ella came to me weeping and said the wedding was off. Something to do with Billy being Melungeon…"

Cline sighed and shifted his weight in the chair. "I think his sickness was the reason they had that fight. He thought he was going to die and then he did. The Lord had sent him a sign. Though him bein'—what he was—was a sound objection. Still is. Billy was dark enough to be considered colored. All them— all those people up by the Clinch River, where he came from. A lot of colored up there. I told him there might be trouble. I told him from the very beginning. Weren't fair on Ella."

The old lady's eyes glinted blue in the afternoon sun. "You never went down a mine, did you, Pastor Cline? Every man who comes out is black. Don't make no difference what he was when he went in. As I remember, neither Billy nor Ella were full of worry over his complexion. Lots of folks here 'bout got Melungeon in 'em. Your own folk on your father's side came from Tennessee, too, didn't they, up by the Cumberland Gap?"

"A long time ago, Mrs. Shockey." His tone was short, sharp, before he softened it again. "As I said—I think the real reason they broke it off was because he knew—he knew he was dying, that the Lord was taking him away. And he didn't want to make your Ella a widow, so he told her they couldn't marry."

She nodded. "And folk blamed Ella for it because he died

before they could reconcile. 'Hard-hearted', some called her. Until her heart broke, seein' him there, seein' him go like that. And then it was her turn."

The old woman sighed, her gnarled hands tightening on the handles of her rocking chair. Then she leaned forward and poured more tea. "I'll fetch another slice of cake."

She picked up the used plate and returned with another slice, thick, syrupy apple chunks poking out from the pores of the yellow crumb.

"You're tryin' to make me fat, Mrs. Shockey. Too much of this and I won't be able to eat your ham hock and corn bread and greens."

She shook her head. "Don't deny me my little pleasures, Pastor. They come fewer in life, especially when you're old and living alone."

Cline ate again, forgetting the cloth napkin she'd handed him and wiping his fingers on his pants. He drank down the second cup of tea, smacking his lips.

"Best cake I've had in a long while, Mrs. Shockey. Thank you. Will the ham and greens take much longer? I only ask because I promised Esther Varney—you remember, Alex Varney's daughter—she's a widow now, and has joined the church—anyway, I promised her a Bible lesson tonight for her young'uns." He smiled, showing his teeth.

"I'll just go and check, Pastor Cline. I don't think it'll be more than a couple of minutes."

She stood up and went back inside. He closed his eyes again and tried to take a full breath and made a face.

Must be heartburn. Too much goddamn tea and cake. What the hell was he doing, sitting here jawin' with this old woman? Just to prove he could? Esther was ripe and ready and rarin' to go...

He raised his voice. "Mrs. Shockey? Could I have some water? I'm, uh, perspiring some. Must be the tea."

The old woman returned in a few moments with some water

in an amber-colored glass tumbler and a small unmarked bottle of brown liquid. She handed him the glass.

"I put in a little homemade whiskey for you, Pastor. That'll help settle you. I'll just keep the bottle handy if you need more. The ham's cooling now. It'll just be a minute or two."

He swallowed the whiskey and water in two gulps. Tapped his chest and finally managed a full breath. He leaned forward, smiling at her.

"Can't say I'm as hungry as I was, but I'm ready for it. Now, then," he added genially, "Let's finish up our talk before we eat. We were reminiscing about Ella. Such a pretty girl. I remember the whole King family—Ella's brothers and sisters. Terrible how many were took—taken—by that fire, then old John King perishin' in that accident. Only had a couple of brothers left when I knew her. I guess she relied on you, didn't she, Mrs. Shockey?"

The old lady rocked once, twice, three times. She was looking off into the distance at the flash of green.

"She relied on me, Mr. Cline. Particularly the night she came back from Pilgrim. The night you came to fetch her to see Billy, when he lay dyin'. The night you killed her."

Stanza V

"Oh father go, and dig my grave
And dig it deep and narrow
Sweet William died for me today
I'll die for him tomorrow."

The tall man tried to stand up, mouth open, eyes wide. He fell unsteadily back into the chair, almost tipping backwards.

"What—what the hell are you prattlin' about—crazy old woman—"

"Your stomach should start to pain you right about now, Mr. Cline. You might bring it all up eventually but by then it'll be too late." She poured more whiskey into the empty glass. "Drink this—it will help retard the effects."

He struggled to stand again, arm muscles straining, knuckles on his hands white. Sweat was beading on his forehead and he wiped it with the back of a shaking hand.

"You—you old bitch—what the hell are you doing? You tryin' to kill me?"

"You took in some Destroying Angel mushroom, Mr. Cline. And some other things. Things of this earth that God gave us. Something to keep you weak and something to keep you from discharging what you ate. The cornbread helped mask the odor of the Angel and the tea and honey and apple helped mask the taste."

His eyes were wide, whites all around. He strained to stand up again but this time only rose a couple of inches from the chair and fell back again, panting and wincing.

Jesus Christ Almighty...

"God—Goddamn it! Help! Help! Somebody—help me!"

His voice, trained to shout and exhort and exhilarate, was as loud as he could make it, but it wasn't loud enough. An afternoon cuckoo call, late in migration, was the only response.

The old woman turned her head toward the sound. "Must be rain comin'. No one is near enough to hear you, Mr. Cline. Hardly anyone goes to the cemetery these days. Afternoons are always still and calm, this time of year."

His voice was raspy now, and his breath was coming in gasps. Sweat ran in rivulets down his neck and face. "You—you said—I—I'm innocent—I didn't kill her—"

The old lady shook her head. "You should confess for the good of your eternal soul. You were always jealous of Billy. You coveted everything he had—his money, his gifts, his way with people. And especially—Ella."

He doubled over, clenching his stomach. Red eyes peered up at her.

"Whiskey", he croaked. "More whiskey."

She calmly poured another shot. "I'm old, Mr. Cline, but I won't lose count." She pushed the glass toward him on the table. He clutched it, claw-like, and held it close and sipped it, whiskey and saliva dribbling down the front of his red tie.

Her blue eyes, clear and sharp for a woman her age, watched him.

"Ella came to me as I told you. Her and Billy argued; he figured he was dying—dying from something nobody could cure. You planted that seed along with the arsenic in his stomach, little by little, the summer they fell in love. Oh, I recognized his symptoms—too late. I spoke with neighbors, with salesmen who travel through a few times every year. I know what you fed him. I blame myself for not acting to prevent it, but you were convincing, Mr. Cline. Convincing as his apprentice, his best friend."

"Please—don't do this—"

"At first, you kept them apart and quarreling by passing false messages between them, and then you spread lies about Ella rebuking him because he was Melungeon. Then, when it was too late to save Billy, you came to her and told her he was dying and that he wanted to see her before he went."

A shrill cry of a red-tailed hawk pierced the air. The old lady's voice seemed to grow heavier, as if it had weight and substance and was crushing the man bent over in the rocking chair next to her.

"And then, Mr. Cline, you claimed he died of love for her. You tried to damn even her memory. The Good Lord may forgive you for that. I won't."

He gave a sudden, desperate lurch and managed to stand at last, wavering, before again falling backward, this time tipping the chair over and rolling out of it onto the planked wooden floor of the porch.

"I wish you'd be still, Mr. Cline. There's not much time."

Face contorted, he struggled enough to sit up and braced himself against the railing, panting.

"Help me—help me up."

"I will not. You would try to murder me even now, dying. And you have not confessed. I fear you will not see our Savior in Heaven."

"All right—I—I confess. I—I'll sign a paper. I killed Billy. Just...give me something. Fix me. I didn't—didn't kill her. Ella..."

"Martin County was even poorer in those days. What government we have can't help the living, let alone avenge the dead. You murdered Billy. Cold and deliberate."

"Please—more whiskey—didn't—didn't kill her..."

The old lady's voice continued, smooth, final, imperturbable, amid the yellow sun and drowsy buzz of insects, neither rising nor falling in the flat, humid air.

"When you came to tell Ella and took her to him and watched them together, watched your best friend die at your hand, you offered yourself to her, which had been your plan all along. She was horrified and shocked and she rightly spurned you. And then...then you raped her, Mr. Cline."

The old woman started to rock again, looking away from the man slumped over at the waist and propped against the porch railing. Another cuckoo sang past the bronze trees. A mud dauber buzzed by and flew into the nest above carrying a large brown spider.

"As I say, my niece came to me. Broken, bleeding and dying. She crept into a wagon headed south past Pigeon Roost and stumbled and crawled to my house, still blaming herself, swearing me not to tell because she was fearful her remaining brothers would wind up dead or in prison after killing you."

Stanza VI

They buried her in the old church yard
They buried him beside her

And from his grave sprang a red, red rose
And from her grave sprang a briar.

She rose slowly from the rocking chair. She could still smell the ham hock and corn bread and greens, though now there was no breeze blowing through the house. She looked down at the man in black, his tie raw and red like a welt around his throat.

"I am the last of the Shockeys, Mr. Cline. I am an old woman and no one would believe me if I told them the truth. I let them sing their songs and tell their tales. I tend the graves and I've waited. Waited for you to come back."

She tilted the whiskey bottle into the empty glass, still perched on the small wrought iron table.

"This is your last drink. For the sake of your immortal soul, I wanted you to know I know the truth."

There was no answer from the man slumped against the railing.

Nancy Jane Shockey stood for a few seconds before walking inside the house. She turned off the stove and put on her field dress and some gloves and went out to the back. Her leg was hurting again, but she paid no attention. She picked up the wheel barrow and drove it to the shed and hoisted three twenty pound bags of lime into the bottom, and slowly, carefully, rolled it down a leaf-covered trail toward the old lime pit her grandfather had dug a century earlier.

Stanza VII

They grew as high as the old church tower
They never grew no higher
And there they stood, in true lovers' hearts
With the rose wrapped around the briar.

Edith Maynard was asked the following spring to help clear out the old Shockey house. Nancy Jane had died after a short illness and was buried in back of her homestead. The congregation at the church was full; everyone knew she was the last of her line. Jeremiah Justice, the Old Regular Baptist preacher for the occasion, remarked how lovingly she'd tended the graves at Caney. She left her property to the cemetery, in fact, for the poor and the isolated who didn't have family cemeteries to reside in.

Edith organized ancient newspaper clippings of recipes, found old, paper-wrapped bundles of herbs and greens, even a few faded family photos, some of Nancy Jane and the Shockeys and Kings and more than one of a pretty, smiling girl with blond hair standing next to a handsome, dark-complected young man.

They looked familiar somehow.

She walked outside to the back of the house for some fresh air, and stopped in her tracks.

The Redbud tree was the most profuse she'd ever seen—full, succulent purple and lavender and white flowers—and strangely, it seemed to grow from a deep green well of leafery, a magnificent vine of greenbrier that climbed up the trunk like foliate armor.

Edith stood and marveled at the site, remembering Nancy Jane's talents with plants and herbs and wild things.

No wonder she chose to be buried under that tree, she thought.

No wonder.

Author's Note

"Barbara Allen" was already a folk song in seventeenth century Britain and Ireland and soon after arrived on the shores of what would become the United States. There are many, many verse variations. The above stanzas are what I grew up hearing my father sing and what he'd grown up hearing in the hills of mid-century Eastern Kentucky.

CROSSROADS

J.D. Trafford

As the last surviving member of the band, I figure this story needs to be told before I'm six feet under like the others. I ain't never told nobody. The reasons why shall soon become apparent. You see, it doesn't cast me and the famous Jackson Tall in the most favorable light. There is, however, a lesson in this story somewhere. It's just buried mighty deep. I've been trying to figure out that teachin' for a long time, but I'm still not sure what the lesson is, exactly.

It certainly ain't that ol' chestnut, "crime don't pay." Crime pays mighty well. In fact, this particular crime has paid me handsomely for over fifty years. So, like I said, it ain't about that. Maybe it's about how guilt can both eat you alive and also be the fuel to push you forward to greater things, or, maybe, it's about desperation and dreams, or selling your soul to the devil, just like ol' Robert Johnson at the crossroads.

Promise me, you'll think about it when I'm gone. I'm now too tired to figure out the morality of my actions, or, perhaps, I just want to rationalize what we did, transforming a wrong into something heroic. Ain't that the American way? Winners get to write the history and the losers are forgotten?

I don't know. You tell me.

So, I guess the best place to start is at the beginning, and I suppose that's sort of a trick. It might be an attempt to curry some sympathy with you, but it also might provide context for what we were thinkin' and why we did what we did. It's not an excuse, exactly, but sometimes people don't act proper when they come from next to nothin' and that's where me and Jackson both started in life.

As you know, Jackson Tall wasn't his real name, but that's what most everybody called him after his growth spurt. You see, there were a lot of boys named Jackson in the bootheel of Missouri and it was hard to keep them all straight. So, for example, there was Jackson Tall, of course, along with Jackson Short. There was Jackson Red, on account of his red hair, and then Jackson Finger, on account of him havin' only four fingers cuz' his momma smoked bad weed with Chet Nexlar behind the Piggly-Wiggly while the boy was in her belly.

That's the rumor, anyway.

Jackson Tall was known for many things, even back then. He was smart, good lookin', and a natural athlete, but the boy was unlucky. Everybody knew it, and when I say "unlucky," what I really mean to say was that my best friend was jinxed. I don't know who did it or why, but somebody cursed him.

Jackson Tall's dog got hit by a car when he was five. At nine, his family's trailer burned to the ground along with all the money he'd earned cuttin' grass and weedin' gardens. His daddy took off around the age of eleven, leavin' his momma and Jackson to fend for themselves. Then, there was the election for student-body president, which he lost by one vote to Carla Duggins.

Finally, there was the big Homecoming football game. That was the one that was truly tragic. Jackson Tall was the star quarterback and team captain. He was having an amazing year, and college scouts were in the stands watchin' every game. He already had offers from a handful of Big Ten schools along with Mizzou, of course, but also some of the even bigger schools like Tennessee and Ol' Miss were sniffin' around.

The game was tied going into the final minutes when Jackson

Tall dropped back to pass. He fired a zinger out wide to Jiggy Winthrop. It was a beautiful throw, but Jackson Tall never saw it completed. There was a late hit by a kid who must've been close to 280 pounds, maybe 300. Jackson Tall's leg twisted all wrong. His knee popped. Then, his head hit the ground. Rain had been scarce that year, and the field was packed, hard as concrete. As Jackson Tall disappeared into the looker-room on a stretcher, all those scholarships disappeared as well.

Unlike me, Jackson Tall wanted to get out of our little town, but school wasn't the same after that game. He had a hard time readin' for any length of time, and then there were the migraines. He got his diploma, but college wasn't gonna happen. He tried to sign up for the military but couldn't pass the medical.

As I worked in my daddy's back forty, Jackson Tall spent a lot of time alone in his room, thinking about what coulda' been. His hair grew out long, and he stopped shaving. He didn't eat much, and contemplated death on the regular. More than a year down the line, that was how things stood. It was also how things would've remained, 'cept his momma couldn't stand it.

He told me, she knocked on the door to his room one day and said, "I got something for you."

Jackson Tall seen the guitar in his momma's hand and had shook his head. "I can't play no guitar, ma."

And she had said, "You can learn."

That's how it all got started. Pretty soon, we was practicin' every day in my daddy's pole barn. There was Jackson Tall on lead guitar and vocals, Danny Christ on bass guitar, and me on the drums. Pretty soon Jackson Tall nicknamed me the Dinger, on account of me lovin' to bang that top hat. We practiced for hours in the barn, and pretty soon we started gettin' booked for gigs and the crowds got bigger. Now don't go misunderstandin' me, The Bootheel Gang wasn't the Beatles or nothing. When I say the crowds were getting bigger, I mean they went from a half dozen to maybe three dozen on a Friday night.

That was the way it was for some time, but Jackson Tall wasn't content with just playing for beer money at Woody's. He was ambitious, despite all his disappointments. He wanted to play bigger rooms, and that meant we needed a bigger sound. Three guys on a stage wasn't gonna cut it, so Jackson Tall recruited a fiddle player named Clay Martini along with Aiden Harris for the electric guitar and the slide. If the timing worked and the stage was large enough, Jackson Tall would also get some backup singers from the local A.M.E. church who brought a nice touch of gospel to the Johnny Cash covers.

People loved it, and soon there was enough money to buy a reliable, used cargo van and a trailer to tour the Ozarks, up to Colombia, and over to Memphis. The name of the band also changed a little. Instead of being "The Bootheel Gang," it was now "Jackson Tall and the Bootheel Gang." Nobody could quite say how or when this occurred, but it coincided about the time that the band started playing more songs that Jackson Tall wrote all by himself.

I 'member one Saturday night before everything really blew up. We were at the Tin Roof. Jackson was backstage, staring out at all these people waiting to hear us play. I stood right next to him, taking in the scene. We both knew they weren't all there for us. It was Beale Street in downtown Memphis. So, there'd be plenty of tourists just lookin' for live music to drink and dance to, but we also knew that there were others who'd come just to listen to our songs.

They'd come early to be close to the stage, seen 'em before. These were a growing army of Jackson Tall's fans, and I could tell that he both loved and he also feared it. I said, "You don't look too good."

"That's because I don't feel very good." Jackson Tall's hand trembled, just a little. "I'm right on the edge, Dinger" he said, "and I got that feeling that somebody's gonna come and snatch all this away, just like every time before."

"Nah, don't you worry about that. It'll be okay." I patted

him on the back. "We'll go on out, get warmed up, and then you can follow." And that's what we did. Me and the rest of The Bootheel Gang came out to thunderous applause. From my seat behind the drum set, I looked over at Jackson Tall, still backstage. I seen him shove a couple pills into his mouth and that was the moment. I remember doubt creeping into my head, thinkin' maybe things wouldn't be okay. Jackson Tall was jinxed, no doubt about that. Maybe his time was just about up.

We soon had a solid manager. His name was Hank Getty, and he kept us on the road for almost eight months as an opening act for some of the big ones. After playing a gig in Austin, Texas with David Allen Coe, Getty told us we were on the verge of landing a big record deal. He had lined up a bunch of producers and other record company executives to hear us play at different spots around Nashville at the end of the month.

Getty's plan was simple. He'd reserved a bunch of rooms at a little motel outside Ashland City, which was about 45 minutes northwest of Nashville. It was a beautiful spot not far from the Cumberland River and surrounded by poplars, Sugar Maple, and pine. He told us that we'd have a week to relax and recharge our batteries before the shows. Everybody was excited about this little break. Much to the delight of the Bootheel Gang, Getty had promised to provide plenty of BBQ, beer, and weed.

Jackson Tall, however, was not excited. He wouldn't be getting any break. He'd be working. Getty had told him that we still needed a breakthrough song, and the pressure was on him to write it. As soon as we arrived, Jackson Tall got off the bus and locked himself in his room. He was up there for days, trying to find his muse, but he never found her.

Instead, it went the other way. She found him.

Her name was Heather Bristow. Getty had been commuting back and forth to Nashville every day to promote our upcoming shows. He heard her singing and playing guitar at the Station Inn, and then, at the end of her set, he'd invited her up to meet the band. I don't know what Getty intended, whether he was thinking of her as a new backup singer for the band or maybe he wanted to sign her up as a new client. Regardless, she was the kind of girl that Jackson Tall liked to get friendly with.

Heather Bristow was a confident woman with a blue sense of humor. She was easy to like, and she hung around the bonfire drinkin' and talkin' with us until midnight. Then, she clapped her hands and stood up. "Well, I better go meet the star of the show since he obviously isn't coming down here to greet me like a gentleman."

We all watched as she grabbed a couple bottles of beer from the cooler, walked up to Jackson Tall's room, and knocked on his door. Collectively, we held our breath. We knew better than to interrupt Jackson Tall when he was writing, but there were no fireworks. The door opened, and Heather Bristow went right inside.

Nobody saw or heard much from either one of them for a couple days. The temperature just kept going up. It felt like we were living in the middle of a swamp, but Getty kept the coolers filled with alcohol and our minifridges full of food.

Around two in the afternoon on Friday, we were all outside. A couple people were throwin' a frisbee. The rest of us were just sitting around when Jackson Tall and Heather Bristow emerged from his room. Jackson Tall had his guitar case and Heather Bristow was holding a blanket. They told us that the window air conditioning unit had started blowing nothin' but hot air. So, they decided to wander.

As they walked toward the road, I shouted. "Wander to where?"

Jackson Tall shrugged. "Anywhere we want."

Heather Bristow laughed, and said, "Come with us."

I thought long and hard about that. The polite thing to do would have been to leave the new couple alone, but I was not polite. I was also very bored. So, I trailed behind them like Jackson Tall's dumbass little brother.

We walked down the side of the road, as the cicadas did their thing, and we kept walkin' until we came upon a creek a couple miles further north. It was neither deep nor wide, but the water was swift and clear. We all climbed down the slope. Then we took off all of our clothes and waded into it, naked as the day we was born. That might surprise you, but this was the era of peace and love and all that shit.

The temperature was a shock, at first, but that tapered as we submerged our bodies fully into the cool water. We floated in that creek, listening to all the sounds. "When was the last time you did something like this?"

Jackson Tall was the one who responded to my question. "Probably high school, right before the start of our senior year. It was hot back then, just like now. Me and Mindy gone skinny dippin' down by Hog Island, and that night everybody gathered for a kegger at an old, abandoned barn. Remember that?"

I smiled at the memory. "I hooked up with Candy...and man o' man was she ever sweet."

We both laughed, and then heard some music, a simple chord progression. The sound surprised us, and we looked over to see Heather Bristow sitting on a blanket with Jackson Tall's guitar. The chords repeated, and then changed as a melody developed. Then she began to sing. It was a riff based on our memories, coming out easy.

Party in the barn
On a Saturday night
Dancin' with my girl
Feelin' all right.

Doin' what we love,
Fire in the fields,
Gazing at the stars

Feeling all the feels.

Come on kids,
Let's gather all around
Live for today
Cuz' we're nowhere bound.

I say,
live for today
Cuz' we're no-where bound.

Heather Bristow played it again, and then Jackson Tall and I got out of the water. We both knew that this was it. She had done what we couldn't do. Heather Bristow had written our band's breakthrough song. We knew that this was going to be the song that changed our lives. Unfortunately, Heather Bristow wasn't going to live long enough to see that happen.

We all walked back to the motel, singin' it over and over. Sometimes we sang it fast, and sometimes slow. We could sing it happy or sad or a little bit angry. It didn't really matter. The song was magical. It worked regardless of the version.

Jackson Tall called Getty from the lobby of the motel. I held the phone out as Jackson Tall sang and Heather Bristow played the guitar. The rest of the yahoos gathered behind us, listening as well. When Jackson Tall and Heather Bristow were done, everybody cheered and soon there was a party going on.

I don't know where all those people came from, but there were a lot. Somebody found a rusty grill and started cookin' up burgers and hot dogs. Another person brought potato salad and bags of chips. A chocolate cake materialized from out of nowhere. It was like a church potluck, but with lots of drugs.

I must admit that what happened after dinner is a little fuzzy on account of me being stoned out of my mind, but I will never forget waking up later to the sound of Jackson Tall pounding on my door. He said, "Dinger, let me in, man. Let me in."

Bang, bang, bang. "Let me in, man. Come on, Dinger, open the damn door." Bang, bang, bang. "Dinger, wake up. Let me in."

This continued as I emerged from my fog, but I eventually pulled myself out of bed, stumbled over, and opened the door. Even though it was the middle of the night, the air was still hot and humid. It rushed into my cool room. The blast of heat felt like it'd came out of an oven, causin' my eyes to burn and water.

Jackson Tall stood before me in the doorway. His hair was wild, and his hands were covered in blood. "You gotta help me, Dinger. You gotta help me, please."

Jackson Tall had told me she overdosed, but it didn't look like no overdose. Heather Bristow was naked on the bathroom floor of his motel room. There was a gash on the side of her head, split open wide. Blood was everywhere. It was pooled on the floor and splattered on the wall. She looked as if she had showered in it.

I stepped away as I started to gag, trying my best to keep from throwing up. Bent over my knees, I said, "You gotta call an ambulance, right now."

Jackson Tall held out his hands, still covered in Heather Bristow's blood. "No way, man. I can't do that."

"We *have* to do that."

"Why?" It was obvious that Jackson Tall had been thinking about this. He lowered his voice to a whisper. "She's already dead, brother. There ain't nothing anybody can do for her. She's gone, Dinger, but we're still here."

"What the hell is that supposed to mean?"

"It means we gotta take care of ourselves." Jackson Tall ran his hand through his hair, which did nothing to tame it, then stepped even closer to me. "If we call an ambulance, then the cops are gonna come, and what do you think is going to happen to me?"

My eyes narrowed as I thought about his question. "Did you kill her?"

"No, of course not," he said. "She overdosed or passed out or slipped on something. I was asleep, and I just heard a big crash. I think she hit her head on the side of the sink."

"So just tell the cops that—"

"They ain't gonna believe me," he said. "And even if they do, what about the band? We're so close, but we ain't there, yet. This is gonna be in the news, Dinger. What record label is gonna sign a guy who might've murdered somebody? What kind of gigs are we gonna get when everybody knows?"

I looked over at the nightstand. Next to the lamp, there was this huge mustard colored phone with a tangled cord. I took a step toward it but stopped. I'd known Jackson Tall since we were kids, and I'd also seen the many misfortunes that always seemed to follow him. If it were me, the cops might believe the story and write it all down as some tragic accident. This, however, was Jackson Tall and, like I said before, the boy was jinxed.

He whispered. "Dinger, you gotta believe me. It was an accident." He took a step toward me. "And it ain't just about me. It's also about us. You been working just as hard as me, and you deserve this just as much as me. We can't throw it all away. We just can't. We are so close."

I turned away from the phone, put my hands on my hips, and took a deep breath. Then, I said, "Okay, what's the plan?"

"I'm gonna take down the shower curtain," Jackson Tall said. "Then, we're gonna wrap her up in it and take her back down to the creek. When people ask in the morning, I'll say she was hot and told me she wanted to cool off. Then, I'll tell the cops that I told her not to go because she was totally wasted. I reckon when her body is found, they'll just think she slipped and knocked her head on a rock or something."

"What about all that?" I looked past Jackson Tall toward the bathroom covered in blood. "How we gonna deal with that?"

"We'll take the towels, clean it up, and burn them in a bonfire when we get back?" Jackson Tall looked at his watch. "We ain't got much time."

"Wait," I said. "How we gonna walk down the road with a dead woman wrapped in a shower curtain without getting caught?"

"Dinger, it's the middle of the night. Everybody is asleep. Nobody is going to see us, but we gotta go. We gotta do it now."

And so we did.

We wrapped Heather Bristow up in the shower curtain. I found some duct tape in my gear bag. We sealed her up tight, and then carried her out the door and down the road. Neither one of us had a flashlight, but the sky was clear and the moon was full. That was enough.

The whole time I expected somebody to stop us or, maybe, for a police cruiser to appear with flashing lights. The road, however, was abandoned, just like Jackson Tall had told me it would be. Nobody was out. Nobody saw us.

We arrived at the creek, wired with adrenaline and sweaty as hell. We both waded into the cool water with the body of Heather Bristow. We paused to catch our breath as she floated between us. It was like some sort of ancient death ritual. Neither one of us said a word.

Jackson Tall, then, took out a little pocketknife and cut the tape. We unwrapped her like she was a piece of candy, and then stepped back as she floated away. After she disappeared, I pointed at the shower curtain. "What do you want to do with this?"

"Wash all the blood off, fold it up, and we'll burn it with the towels when we get back. I'm also going to burn my clothes, and you should too."

"Right," I said. "I'll do that, too."

Then, Jackson Tall put his arm around me. "We're going to be okay, Dinger. You just have to trust me. Everything is gonna work out."

* * *

A hunter found Heather Bristow's body or what was left of it about two months later. There was never a real investigation. This was rural Tennessee, and it happened long before the existence of all the fancy forensic analysis that we see on television every night. Nobody really cared. She was not a local girl or famous. Heather Bristow may not have even been her real name. She was just a young woman who got wasted and fell in a creek while skinny-dippin' in the middle of the night.

Around the time the Cheatham County Sheriff's Department closed the case, Jackson Tall and the rest of the Bootheel Gang were recording our first album at the legendary Omnisound Studios on Music Row in downtown Nashville. It was entitled, "Party in the Barn," but you already know that. Everybody knows that album. We had other hit records after that one, but "Party in the Barn" was special.

The whole thing was built around Heather Bristow's song, and it was everything we thought it would be and become. If there's a list of the best country music tunes of all time, "Party in the Barn" is always near the top. It's what the people wanted to hear at every concert and still gets played on the radio after all these years.

But, this is something you don't know, because I never talked about it. After we'd recorded everything, there was a meeting with the lawyers, our manager, Jackson Tall, and me. We all sat around this table and the lawyer passed out these forms from ASCAP. At the time, I didn't know who the hell they were, but I learned pretty quick after that meeting.

The acronym stood for The American Society of Composers, Authors and Publishers. They were the ones who distribute royalties to the people who write the songs that are performed. Every knowledgeable musician will tell you that this is how we make money in the music business, not from a record company deal.

Anyway, I looked down at the form. It had a list of all the songs that were on the album. Then, next to the names, there was a space to identify who wrote the song. It wasn't surprising to see Jackson Tall's name on the form, but it surprised me to see that my name was also listed. I looked across the table at him, and Jackson Tall nodded, confirming that it wasn't a mistake.

Then I looked at the list, again, and noticed that Heather Bristow's name wasn't given any credit for writing "Party in the Barn." It was her song, but her role in its creation disappeared with her down that creek. I paused. Then, I looked up and across the table at Jackson Tall, again. There was something there, something in his eyes, but I pushed it away as I signed the piece of paper.

Later that night, it came to me. I realized what I saw. It was guilt. Hopefully, it was just guilt for stealing credit for Heather Bristow's song, but I can't help but thinkin' Jackson Tall was guilty of something much more than that.

THE CAR HANK DIED IN

Mark Troy

Delaney pushed Richard's hand from under her blouse. "No," she said. She took a slug from a bottle of fortified wine.

Richard pulled a long drag on his cigarette and reached for her again.

"Didn't you hear me? No!'"

"C'mon. A minute ago you wanted to." His hand closed over her breast. "You know you do. I can feel it."

She pushed him away, more forcefully. "Not here. Someone could see us."

"Not in the dark."

"They might come along here."

Richard ground his cigarette against the bench. "Where then?"

"Follow me." Delaney stood and smoothed her denim mini. "Bring the bottle." She headed down the path that would take them out of the park. Richard hurried to catch up.

"There," she said. "See it?" They had reached a quiet avenue that bordered the park on one side and a prosperous neighborhood on the other. Some of the residences housed law offices and music publishers. "I saw it earlier. Second one down."

"The house?" Richard said. "The one with the sign in the yard? You want to break into a house?"

"Not the house. In the driveway. Back by the garage."

The car was a convertible. Big. Larger than most cars on the road in 1974. The car's sleek curves glimmered in the moonlight on the clear summer night.

"You want to break into someone's car? They might hear us."

"They won't. The house is air-conditioned. What's the matter? You chicken?"

Preston entered the kitchen through the back door and went immediately to the sink to wash his hands. "All done, Mr. Terrell," he said to the man at the table.

"Everything good for the run tomorrow?" the older man asked.

"Yessir." Preston pulled two chairs out and arranged them facing each other. He sat in one and raised a booted foot to the other one. "Long day, sir."

"Longer tomorrow," Terrell said. The sign in his yard billed him as a music promoter.

Preston nodded. "The car's ready. Washed. Waxed. Finished with a coat of baby oil."

Terrell snorted. "Baby oil. You treat that car like your own baby."

"Nothing but the best for your car. One of the white walls got scuffed up, so I changed the tire. Will get that fixed before the next time. So what's the run?"

Terrell leaned forward and spread a road map across the table. "Red, White, and Blue Parade in Goodlettsville." He x'd a spot on the map with a ballpoint. "North of here, about fifteen, twenty miles. The parade kicks off at nine from the VFW, so you need to be there about seven-thirty because they'll want to afix a banner and streamers."

"Who'm I carrying?"

"I don't know. The city manager and his wife, maybe. They'll tell you when you get there. Does it matter?"

Preston rolled his shoulders. "Just curious. I drove the STP Oil Treatment Queen down at the speedway today. I swear whenever I checked the mirror she was flashing her coochie at me."

"You won't have that kind of luck in Goodlettsville. They'll want pictures after, so stick around."

"They can pose with the car, but they're not gettin' in. Can't have kids messing the upholstery."

"Good call," Terrell said. "From there you go to Galatin for an auto show. Same thing. Hang around, let folks get their pictures, then move on. Here's your longest ride. Carthage." He marked another spot in the Eastern part of the state. "A patriotic celebration with bands and fireworks. You'll be ferrying the Senator."

"He better not mess the upholstery,"

"Keep the schedule. That's the important thing."

"Count on me." Preston folded the map. He leaned forward and massaged his leg. "Gonna be a long day, like you said."

"Leg's gonna hold out?"

"The leg'll be fine. Car's an automatic. What I'm thinkin', though, is a lotta places will be closed tomorrow, the fourth and all. I should gas her up tonight."

Terrell looked at his watch. "You should hurry then. Not many places are open this late."

"Right. Also, since I'm heading out early in the morning, maybe you could expense me now."

"Yeah, okay." Terrell left the kitchen, He returned a couple of minutes later with a wad of bills clipped together. The outside bill was a hundred. "Bring back what you don't spend and make sure you get receipts."

"Will do, sir." Preston lifted his leg off the chair and stuffed the clip in his pocket. He let himself out the back door.

* * *

Delaney ran her hand over the shiny metal hood. The baby blue paint gleamed brightly. The massive chrome bumper with its twin torpedo heads seemed to create its own light.

"What kind is it?" Richard asked.

"A Caddy. Can't you tell?" She traced the V-shaped emblem beneath the shield that adorned the nose. "I always dreamed riding in a Caddy. Let's go."

"You mean get in it?

"Of course."

"We might get caught."

"C'mon."

Richard held back. "It's probably locked anyway. Nobody would leave this kind of car out unlocked."

Delaney opened the rear door. The interior lights came on.

"Shut the door. Someone will see the lights," Richard whispered.

"Cluck, cluck, cluck." Delaney dropped onto the rear seat and slid across. Richard scampered after her. He pulled the door closed behind him with a solid thunk. Delaney giggled. "They might hear us."

"I can't believe I'm doing this."

"Shh." She opened her blouse. Richard stared at the shadowy contours. Delaney placed his hand on her breast. Richard let out a groan and pawed at her body. He mashed his lips against hers. Delaney urged him on. She opened his belt and unbuttoned his pants. "Did you bring something?"

"Like what?"

"Like, you know, protection, stupid."

"Oh, yeah, that." He dug into his pockets.

Delaney used the respite to down more wine. She reached under her skirt and skimmed her panties off. Richard produced a condom and tore at the foil.

"Did you ever use one? Do you know how to put one on?"

Delaney asked.

"Sure. Of course I do."

"No you don't." She took it from him and pushed the wine bottle into his hand. "Let me."

Richard drank deeply from the bottle while Delaney took charge. "How do you know how to do this?"

"Health class. We used a cucumber."

It was Richard's turn to giggle. "Do I look like a cucumber?"

"No way. Principle's the same, though." Delaney raised her skirt and slid down onto the upholstery. Richard crawled on top of her. His movements were crude and frantic. Suddenly he raised himself up.

"What?" Delaney said. "Done?" she wailed.

Richard dropped back on top of her. He covered her mouth with his hand. "Someone's coming," he whispered into her ear.

Earl's Amoco Station had two islands, with two pumps each. One of the islands was dark when Preston arrived. Both islands were empty except for a mechanic coiling an air hose. Preston pulled the Caddy up to the island closest to the street whose pumps were still lit. Each had a gold crown on top. He killed the engine.

"Supreme's all I got, son," the mechanic said. His blue overalls bore a patchwork of old and new grease stains. Both overalls and cap said, "Earl," in embroidered script.

"Supreme's what I want, Earl."

"Lucky for you, then. I'm just shuttin' down the pumps. Five minutes later, you'd be shit out of luck. How much you want?"

"Fill it," Preston said. "I'll need a receipt."

"Check oil and wash the windshield for you?"

Preston looked at the bucket sitting on the island. Two squeegee handles protruded from oily black water. He'd spent a good twenty minutes on the windshield getting rid of the streaks. No way was he putting dirty water on it. "Skip the windshield." He withdrew a pack of Winston's from his jacket pocket and shook out the last one. "You sell smokes?"

"Yep," Earl said. He appraised the car. "Some kinda beauty, ain't she? 1952 62S model. Was a great car back in the day. Better than the junk Detroit's rollin' out nowadays."

"Got that right," Preston said.

"Looks like you're takin' good care of her, mister. You headin' somewhere?"

"Parade tomorrow." He waited for what he knew was coming next. It was the part that always thrilled him. He never tired of it. He didn't have long to wait.

"You know who owned a car just like this?"

"Tell me, Earl."

"Hank Williams, that's who." Earl nodded like he'd delivered the world's most treasured secret.

"Naw," Preston said. "He didn't own a car like this."

Earl jerked his head back like he'd been challenged. "Sure did. Just like this one. Took his last ride in it. Don't believe me?"

"He didn't own a car LIKE this," Preston said. He paused a beat before the punch line. "He owned THIS one."

Earl's jaw dropped. "No shit? You ain't be shittin' me, now."

"Wouldn't shit you, Earl. This is it. This is the car Hank died in. So take care of her. For Hank." He headed over to the station where he leaned back against the wall to take weight off his bad leg. He lit the cigarette.

Delaney lay pinned beneath Richard. Her thighs were beginning to cramp up from holding position the entire ride. Richard's breath filled her ear and the smell of cheap wine and cigarettes filled her nostrils. She tried pushing him off her but he wouldn't take the hint.

"Did you hear that?" he whispered.

"Get off me," she hissed.

"This car belonged to Hank Williams."

"I don't care. Get off me."

"I can't. He'll see us. He'll hear us."

From outside came the shush of fuel being pumped, accompanied by the sound of a bell with each gallon of gas.

"Wait till he's done," Richard whispered.

"Uh, hurry," Delaney said.

Earl spent a couple of minutes examining the engine. Every part looked original and new as though just from the factory. He checked the oil and the other fluids. All were as they should be. He closed the hood and wiped every surface he had touched. Then he shut off the two gold crown pumps and headed to where Preston was finishing his cigarette. "Come inside. I'll write you a receipt."

Preston followed Earl through the door. The station was small but tidy. A rack of batteries lined one wall. A rack of oil and anti-freeze lined the opposite wall. Preston put thirty cents into a cigarette machine and pressed a button. A pack of Winstons dropped into the tray. He turned to find Earl behind a glass showcase displaying Buck knives and Zippo lighters.

"Twelve and three quarter gallons. Fifty-nine cents a gallon," Earl said.

"Fifty-nine," Preston said. "Goddamn Arabs're gonna destroy us."

"Got that right. Seven dollars and fifty-two cents total."

Preston peeled a ten from his clip of bills. Earl wrote a receipt. A chime caused both men to look up as a boxy car with faded paint rolled across the bell cord. Preston recognized the vehicle as a Datsun B10.

"That's the other thing that's gonna destroy us," Preston said. "These foreign rice wagons."

"Yep. World's goin' to hell in a hand basket. Won't be long

you cain't buy ethyl, either, and that Caddy'll be knockin' like a zombie in a coffin."

Earl counted out Preston's change. The door opened and a man in a rolled brim cowboy hat entered. "Pumps shut down, mister. You best come back in the morning," he said without looking up.

"I ain't needin' gas," the cowboy said. "Just hand over what you got there."

Preston saw the gun in the man's hand. He threw up his hands and stepped back. "Hey, I want no trouble."

"Me neither, pardner. Won't be none if you don't cause none. Just leave that fat money clip on the counter. You got a watch on you and a wallet in them fancy pockets, put 'em there, too."

Preston did as he was told.

The cowboy turned to Earl. "Everything in your register. No tricks, now." He pulled a folded paper sack from his jacket pocket. "Put it all in here."

Earl opened the sack and scooped in the cash.

"You, fancy suit, grab me two cans of that Penzoil there."

Preston sidled around him to the shelves holding the oil.

The cowboy had to swing his head back and forth to watch both men. As he swung back to Earl, the knives in the case caught his eye. He bent to look at them. "You know what," he said to Earl. "Toss in that pretty bone handle Buck knife."

Preston seized that moment to escape. He crashed through the door.

"Godammit," the cowboy shouted. He raised his gun, but Preston was already outside and heading to the pumps. He turned around for the money sack as Earl brought a shotgun up from behind the counter.

Richard rocked back on his knees while Delaney repositioned herself. "He's gone inside. The driver, too."

"What are we waiting for?"

"I just want to be sure it's safe."

"Just go," she said.

Headlights from a car turning into the station flooded the interior. "Oh crap," Richard said. He watched a cowboy emerge from the new vehicle and enter the station. "Now, I think." He swung his legs to the car floor, but his pants, which were tangled around his ankles, impeded his movement. He struggled to pull them up while Delaney cursed at him.

"What is taking you so long? Just go, damn it."

"All right. All right." Before he could free himself, Richard saw the door to the station fly open. The Caddy's driver hurried out, limping. "He's coming back."

"Then go. Now," Delaney said.

A bright flash lit the store followed by a loud boom. The glass door shattered and the cowboy ran through. The driver stumbled and went down as Earl emerged with a long gun. He raised it and fired. Delaney screamed at the noise. The cowboy staggered and turned around. Two cracks from a gun followed in rapid succession.

Richard saw Earl fall as he threw himself back on top of Delaney.

Preston ducked between the pumps and around to the driver-side door of the Cadillac. He wrenched it open and jumped inside. He cranked the engine to life and dropped it into drive. The car started forward as the passenger door was flung open and the cowboy leaned in. He shoved the gun in Preston's face.

"Stop the car," Cowboy said.

Preston jammed the brake. The car lurched to a stop. The passenger door swung back against the cowboy, who yelled in pain, but he managed to stay on his feet. He tossed the sack onto the floorboard and climbed in.

"Get out of my car," Preston said.

The cowboy shoved the gun against Preston's face. "Drive," Cowboy said.

Preston stepped on the accelerator and the car shot forward.

"Take it easy," Cowboy said. "Speed limit. Attract cops and you're a dead man. I already kilt one. Another won't make no difference."

Preston dropped the Caddy to the speed limit. "Where to?"

"Ain't none of your business. You just drive. Keep off the main roads."

"How about moving that gun out of my face? Point it somewhere else. If we hit a bump, I don't want it going off."

"Then don't hit a bump." Cowboy said, but he lowered the gun to his lap and pointed it straight ahead.

Preston took some turns, getting off the broader, lighted streets, until he found a road heading away from the city. "You shouldn't have shot Earl. Old fellow like that, what harm was he gonna bring you?"

"Had to shoot him. That old bastard pulled a gun on me. What was I supposed to do?"

"I don't know. But kill him? For what? A couple hundred in the register?"

"He shot up my car. Radiator like to blow. Hell, he shot me."

Preston glanced over. Despite the dark, he could see the cowboy holding one arm tight against his side. "How bad?"

"Never mind how bad."

"I don't want you bleeding on the upholstery."

"This your car?"

"No. I'm just the driver."

"Then what do you care?"

"The owners will be pissed if I bring it all bloody."

"Bring it where?"

"Goodlettsville. There's a parade tomorrow."

"What time you gotta be there?" Cowboy asked.

"Seven thirty."

Cowboy sank back in the seat. "Well then, we got all night 'cause nobody'll be lookin' for you till then."

Preston realized he'd made a mistake. "Think you'll last the night? We should get you to a hospital. Get you patched up."

"And get sent to jail? No thank you. You just drive."

"They're gonna catch you, you know. Turn yourself in, it will be better for you."

"You're startin' to get on my nerves, you know that Mister Fancy Suit?"

"It's Preston."

"What is?"

"My name. Preston. As long as we're ridin' together we might as well get our names out there. What's yours?"

"You no never mind what my name is. You ask too many questions."

"Just trying to be friendly."

"Hell with friendly. I don't need friendly and I don't need talkin'."

They were out in the country now. On one side, dark fields stretched into the distance where now and then a light could be seen on a lone house or barn. On the other side, tall pine trees formed a dark, impenetrable wall. The road was narrow and crowned. The Caddy's powerful engine cut through the night.

"This your first robbery?" Preston asked.

"Told you, I'm tired of talkin'."

Preston ignored him. "Figure it for your first. You didn't think things through. Left too much evidence behind. The car for example. Fingerprints, registration, all kinds of trace evidence."

Cowboy inhaled deeply through his nose and exhaled through pursed lips.

"Pain getting to you? Maybe we could find a vet out here."

"What do you know about fingerprints and trace evidence? You a cop?" Getting no reply from Preston, Cowboy said, "Know what? I got your wallet in my bag here. I'll just look. I better not find no cop ID."

"I'm not a cop," Preston said.

Cowboy bent forward for the bag. Preston jammed on the brakes. The Caddy skidded with a squeal of rubber. Cowboy flew forward. His head hit the metal glove compartment with a loud bang. Richard flew off Delaney. He slammed into the seat back. Delaney screamed.

"What the hell!" Preston yelled. He wrestled with the wheel and finally brought the fishtailing car to a stop. He jumped from the car and yanked open the rear passenger door. The interior lights revealed Delaney sprawled on the back seat. Her blouse was open and her skirt was hiked up to her waist. Her eyes were wide.

Richard lay on his side between the seats. His pants were bunched around his knees. Preston grabbed Richard's feet and pulled. "Get the hell out of my car."

"Don't hurt me," Richard said.

"Thank God," Delaney said. "Thought I would suffocate,"

"What are you doing in my car?" Even as he said it, he was struck by the absurdity of the question. He knew what they'd been doing.

Delaney straightened her skirt. "We wanted to, you know, try out the car."

Preston had no response to that. He seized Richard's legs and yanked. Richard clawed at the carpet to keep from being pulled out. Preston stumbled backwards, taking Richard's pants with him.

Cowboy exited the car. He came up behind Preston. "That was real stupid." He whipped his pistol at Preston's head. Preston fell to his hands and knees in the road. "You wanted kill me, didn't you?"

Preston shook his head, as much in answer as to clear the pain and darkness that clouded his vision.

"Hell you didn't." Cowboy's face streamed blood from a gash on his forehead. He clutched one hand tightly to his side while he steadied the gun in his other hand. Blood leaked between his fingers.

Cowboy turned to Richard who was pulling himself from the car. "Who the hell are you?"

"Please," Richard said. "We didn't mean anything. We didn't see anything." He raised his hands above his head.

"His name's Richard. I'm Delaney," she said, getting out of the car. She knotted her blouse closed. "We're unarmed."

"What are you doing here?" Cowboy said.

"Nothing. Well, maybe something. Just some fooling around. But really nothing." She glanced at Richard. "He hadn't got there yet."

Cowboy pointed his gun at Preston and said, "So how do you know this guy?"

Delaney said, "I don't. I never saw him before. Richard was on top me all the time."

Cowboy smirked. "Damn. How did I miss all that in the back seat?" He turned to Preston. "Did you know there was ruttin' goin' on in your pretty car?"

"No," Preston said. "So what now?"

"Well for starters," Cowboy said, "you get over here next to Goober and the Hee Haw Honey so I can see all y'all. And you, Goober, get your pants on. I don't like lookin' at your shrunken pecker."

Preston levered himself to his feet and stood beside Delaney. A gash had opened on his cheek. He covered it with his hand.

Richard struggled into his pants, hopping on one foot while he tried to get his pants leg over his shoe. Cowboy lost patience. "Fuck it. Just pull up the tightey whities. You won't be needin' no trousers anyway."

"What are you going to do with us?" Richard said.

"What do you think?" Delaney said. "We're in the wrong place at the wrong time. He can't leave us around to identify him. So don't get all crybaby. Be a man."

"No, no, please," Richard said. His lips trembled. Tears

rolled from his eyes. "We didn't do anything. We didn't see anything. Please don't hurt me. It was her. She wanted to mess around in the car. I didn't want to. I told her we shouldn't, but she insisted."

Delaney rolled her eyes.

Preston sneered. "Well aren't you the gallant fucker. You thought you'd get a choice piece and then you go and throw her under the bus."

Snot ran from Richard's nose. He said, "Listen, my daddy's got money. Lots of money. More than you could ever want. He owns two savings and loans in Nashville. He'll pay you a lot for me. I can talk to him."

"How much?" Cowboy asked.

"As much as you want. He carries insurance. He told me so."

"For both of you?"

"No. Not her. He can't know about her. He'd kill me if he knew about her."

"What's daddy's name?" Preston asked.

"MacCloud Emerson the second."

"Heard of him. Big shot all right," Preston said. "So that makes you Richard Emerson?"

Richard wiped his nose and shook his head. "MacCloud Emerson the third. Mac."

"Mac?" Delaney screamed. "You lied to me. You didn't respect me enough to tell me your real name??"

Richard shrugged sheepishly.

"Respect. Was that so much to ask? Well you're no Richard. You're no Mac. To me, you're Dick. Dickhead."

Preston looked at Cowboy, whose face still streamed blood and whose gun hand appeared unsteady. "Got yourself into some mess now. You might reconsider turning yourself in. I know some people could help you."

"I knew you're a cop. Can always tell."

"Was," Preston said. "Before this leg. So what now? You

need me to drive. What's your plan for these bickering love-birds?"

"Please," Richard said. "Believe me, I can get you money. A lot of money."

Delaney gave him a shove that sent him to the ground. "Only if I'm out of the picture. Dickhead!"

Cowboy said, "Shut up, all you."

Preston said, "Don't add to your trouble. You already killed one man who tried to kill you. But killing these kids is going too far."

"Ain't killin' nobody," Cowboy said. "You're drivin'."

"And them? You gonna let them fight in the backseat?"

"Puttin' 'em in the trunk."

"In the trunk with me? He'll be screaming to get out," Delaney said. "He won't last five miles."

Richard began to plead, but Cowboy cut him off. "Shut up, Goober. You might need to start makin' nice with her."

"Nobody's riding in the trunk," Preston said. "No room."

"Shit," Cowboy said. "Caddies got more trunk than a circus fat lady."

"Trunk's full," Preston said.

"Open it," Cowboy said. When Preston made no move, Cowboy said, "Dickhead, get the key from the ignition."

Richard scooted around Cowboy and returned with the keys. He opened the trunk and stood back. Delaney peered in. She saw a guitar case with the name "Martin" in gold letters.

"Is that...is that his?" She asked.

"One of them," Preston said.

She lifted it out carefully and stood it against the rear bumper.

"What else?" Cowboy asked. He steadied himself against one of the car's airplane-like tail fins.

"Some bags," she said.

"Get 'em out," he said in a weak voice.

Delaney and Richard brought out three duffels and set them on the pavement. "Heavy," she said. With the bags gone, the only item remaining in the trunk was a cross-shaped tire wrench.

Cowboy made a hacking cough. "Open 'em."

Delaney unzipped a duffel revealing brick-shaped packages wrapped in plastic and sealed with tape. "What is this?" she asked.

"Heroin," Preston said.

"All yours?" She could see a row of packages on top and more underneath.

Preston shook his head. "Not mine. I'm just the delivery man. But you, all of you, are in some deep shit. The dope belongs to some very bad men who will do some very bad things to anybody who tries to take it."

Cowboy hacked up some blood. "Delivery man. Heroin delivery." He coughed again.

"Oh my God," Delaney said. "It's genius."

"What?" Richard said. "What's genius?"

"Don't you see? He travels around the state using Hank Williams's car as a cover for distributing dope. Is that right?"

"Smart honey," Preston said. "Maybe too smart."

"Drugs," Richard said. "Bad people."

"With money," Cowboy said.

"What about the police?" Richard said.

"That's the genius," Delaney said. "Nobody suspects what's inside this famous car, not even the police."

"The law gives me escorts," Preston said.

Cowboy coughed up more blood. He wiped his mouth on his sleeve. "Load that shit back up. We're takin' it."

"Taking it where?" Preston said.

"Them boys in Goodlettsville. They'll pay to get their dope back."

Another coughing fit took Cowboy, which was what Preston was waiting for. He reached into the nearest duffel and brought out a gun. Cowboy had barely straightened up when Preston shot him.

Delaney gasped.

"Whoo whoo," Richard cried. He turned and ran into the ditch between the road and the trees. The slope was slick and he lost his balance and slid down. "No, no." He scrambled up the other bank on hands and knees. He reached the top and took a step forward. Preston fired twice. Richard windmilled his arms, pitched forward and lay still.

Preston stepped over to Cowboy's body. He kicked him with his boot and then rolled him into the ditch. He threw Cowboy's gun after him.

When Preston returned to Delaney, she was sitting on the edge of the open trunk with her legs stretched out in front of her and her thighs parted.

"You going to kill me, too?"

"Do I have a choice?"

"Maybe."

He stood over her. "How did you ever connect with some-body like him? What did you ever see in him?"

"His daddy's money."

"You knew all along?"

"I ain't saying."

"He didn't make any move to save you."

"Like I expected him to. Don't expect much from men any-way."

"I'd have saved you."

Delaney looked up him. "You still could."

"How would that work?" he asked.

"We could be partners. Like Bonnie and Clyde."

"The men I work for wouldn't like me taking a partner." Preston's leg threatened to give out. He steadied himself on the trunk lid.

"We could do the fairs together." She looked up at him. "I play a little guitar and sing. It would add to the cover." She glanced at his leg. "Does that hurt?"

"Sometimes."

"Well, I could drive while you rest. And another thing..." She smiled. "...that backseat is big and comfortable. Two can fit nicely."

Preston straightened. "I'm not expected at Goodlettsville until morning."

"We have plenty of time then. But not here."

Preston backed away. Delaney grabbed the tire iron behind her as she raised up. She swung it low at Preston's weakened knee. He went down with a cry of pain, grabbing his knee and dropping the gun. Delaney swung again, connecting with his other knee.

Preston bellowed again. He rolled on the ground, unable to rise. "You busted my knees."

"You shouldn't have killed him. Dickhead didn't deserve to die." Delaney threw Preston's gun into the woods. She put one of the heroin-filled duffels in the car and dragged the other two to the side of the road.

"Men in Goodlettsville are gonna kill you," Preston said.

"I'm staying away from Goodlettsville."

"You can't leave me here. I can't walk."

"I'll put out breadcrumbs so the police can find you."

"If I ever see your again..."

"You won't." She hefted the guitar case. "Unless the prison library gets Rolling Stone."

Delaney lowered the Caddy's top and sped into the night. She tossed out packets of heroin at intervals until all were gone. From the first pay phone, she made an anonymous call to the highway patrol about heroin on the highway and then pointed the car Hank died in toward Memphis.

SATAN'S SPIT

Gabriel Valjan

An old song says that no matter what happened the night before, a new day will come tomorrow, and with it, a new chance for all of us. Not that day in May, not that Sunday morning, and not that year for the town of Trinity, Tennessee that year.

In the morning hours, Sheriff Presser and Deputy Garland were driving down to the crossroads in their Ford Model A Police Car. A mysterious voice over the candlestick phone at the station summoned them to Satan's Spit, where they'd find 'an abomination before God.'

While Presser drove, Garland read from a days' old copy of *The Tennessean.*

"Seems like the family of Sergeant Henry Johnson are at it again. His people in Nor' Carolina feel he is a credit to his race, and he ought to receive the Medal of Honor like Sergeant York."

"No Negro can hold a candle to a God-fearin' patriot. I'm surprised the army allowed Johnson to become a sergeant."

"Relax, he was a sergeant for coloreds only. No self-respectin' white man would take orders from a former Pullman porter."

"Was? Is he dead?"

"Yep," Garland said. "Family claims he'd succumbed to

complications from some twenty-odd combat injuries. They say he couldn't work his last few years."

"I had a cousin gassed during the Great War, and he didn't complain none, and he worked whatever jobs he could find until he dropped," the sheriff said. "Posthumous medal. What will they think of next? What else does the paper say?"

"Rangers killed the Texas Rattlesnake and Suicide Sal."

"They killed Bonnie and Clyde?" Presser whistled, surprised. "How old was she?"

Garland rustled the page. "Twenty-three, and the gal didn't go easy."

Presser looked. "Put up a fight?"

"Women will always put up a fight. Paper states he died first, and she went in a blaze of lead, so I'm inclined she gave them Texas Rangers hell's fire on her way out." Garland paused, "Speaking of a spitfire, isn't your little girl's birthday next weekend?"

"Don't remind me," Presser said. "Hard to believe she'll be sixteen."

The deputy put down the paper when he saw what was ahead of them. "What the hell is he doing here?" Campion, the town's physician, had his car parked on the shoulder of the road. "I didn't call him. You?"

"You know I didn't."

Doctor Campion, known for wearing tailored linen suits during the high swelter of summer, bucked convention in his choice of color for handkerchief. That day, he wore workman's shoes and dungarees, a black shirt, and a fedora on his head. He waved to them, dark handkerchief in hand. The Ford came to a halt, and the sheriff cut the engine. The deputy folded his paper and said, "Hear that, Sheriff?"

"I don't hear a thing."

"That's my point."

On a normal day, broods of cicadas produced a sound to rival a symphony. There was nothing but ominous silence in

Satan's Spit now.

Presser greeted the physician and asked what had brought him out to the Spit.

"Received an anonymous call. I was told I'd find something."

Presser looked fast to Garland before he asked the question. "And did you?"

"I did, unfortunately." The doctor wiped his brow with his handkerchief. He pointed toward the thicket of trees. "Body is about thirty yards in. My gladstone bag is next to it."

"Whose body?" the sheriff asked.

"See for yourself, Sheriff."

Garland came forward. "What time did you get the call?" The doctor answered, and the sheriff added, "We got a call like that an hour later. Care to tell us who we'll find on yonder."

"Charlie Taylor. Know him?"

"Know of the child," the sheriff answered. "His people live in the holler, along with all the other colored folks. Quiet family, the Taylors." He looked to Garland for verification. "Anything you'd like to add?"

"Nothing, Sheriff, just curious as to who called us and Doc."

The three men discussed the call, the wording the caller used. They agreed that their anonymous Samaritan was female; the voice, vague but familiar to their ears.

"Charlie murdered?" the sheriff asked.

"And more."

"Lynched?"

"Raped, and that's where the mystery begins, Sheriff. Have a looksee, the both of you. Twenty-five, thirty yards in, and don't disturb the body too much for the Examiner's men."

"Will do, Doc," the sheriff sighed. "Nothing worse than the murder of a child. Colored or not, it's the Devil's work, especially on the Lord's day of rest."

* * *

Crossroads were always places of superstition and legends, and Satan's Spit was no exception. It was so named because nothing is said to grow where the Devil spits. There was a large yew tree behind Mama Raye's juke joint and not much else. On each side of the bald spot of earth, trees, and that was where the body lay.

Like the Witches' Sabbath, people journeyed into the woods once the sun set on Friday. What made Mama Raye's and the Spit notorious was that Blacks and Whites mingled, and they used the acre of hell as their private playground for all kinds of deviant behavior. There'd been rumors of miscegenation and morphine, of orgies and other obscenities, such as abortions, and adulterous rendezvous. A secret in plain sight, the festivities ran from Friday to the wee hours of Sunday morning before the guilty attended services at their house of God and prayed for forgiveness, left absolved and refreshed, only to renew the cycle of sin the next week.

Mama Raye's was a stop on the circuit for itinerant blues-men, such as Robert Johnson and Son House. Drinks were aplenty inside, and they ranged from legitimate standards to rotgut from moonshiners in the hills. People came from all three corners of Tennessee to hear bluesmen stomp all night long.

The lawmen returned from the scene. Doctor Campion was waiting for them. Sheriff Presser asked him, "Doc, how do you know for certain that Charlie had been violated?"

"Didn't you see how the body was positioned?"

"Indeed, but I'd like to hear your professional opinion."

"Before I do that, Sheriff, I'll ask you, what else did you notice?"

"He was a she, but as a healer in these parts, did you know her true sex?"

"Don't assume that because I'm a doctor everyone sees me, Sheriff. One half of Trinity can't afford me, and the other half is scared of what I might tell them. I'd like to make two things clear. One, I never had Charlie Taylor as a patient. Members of her family, yes, and I hadn't a clue as to her sex in all the time I was in the presence of her kin."

Campion stopped to remove his hat and wipe the band inside the fedora.

"You said two things, Doctor. What's the second item?"

"Whoever took her into the woods for the jump must've been disappointed."

"Disappointed how?"

"Take your pick, Sheriff. Disappointed on how little money was on her, angry at the price she cited for you know what, or her killer discovered that he was a she. It's one thing to expect meat and potatoes, another thing to find the garden of Eden."

Presser said, "Few people in Trinity have money for a prostitute, Doc, and the lavender kind of thing doesn't remain a secret for long."

"Perhaps a stranger killed her."

"Perhaps, but robbery and rape don't go together, in our experience." Presser looked to Garland. "Ain't that right?"

"Yep," Garland said, "and I have question for Doc. Victim was on all fours and you said raped, correct?"

Campion answered, "You saw the body, Deputy."

"I did, but what was the cause of death?"

"Strangulation from behind. Small hemorrhages were visible in the whites of her eyes."

"Is it possible that her death was an accident? You know, ecstasy turned lethal."

"Enthusiastic intercourse notwithstanding, other marks on his body indicated a struggle."

"Her body, Doctor. Hers."

Sheriff Presser said that would be all for now. Campion brushed past them and said he'd call for a Weegee from his office to document the scene, and then summon the Examiner to collect the body for the autopsy.

Presser said to Garland, "This won't play well, once the news hits. The Taylors and their kind will be anxious for justice. Life could turn from mean to ugly."

"No disagreement with you there, but none of this will stop folks from comin' out to the Spit."

They watched Campion's Ford drive off. Gravel bristled and dust kicked up.

"Doc was here before us," the sheriff mused. "Ain't it odd that someone called him before the police?"

"Guilty person may have thought the good doctor could do something for his victim."

"Or maybe, the killer had an accomplice." Garland sensed that the sheriff had calculated another angle to their case. "What is it?"

"His clothes?"

"Charlie's?"

The sheriff shook his head. "Not Charlie's." The sheriff looked down the road towards the vanishing car. "Doc came here in Levi's."

"You'd ruin linen out there."

"But blue dungarees would hide any stain of violence, wouldn't they?"

Garland said, "As in on the ground, and behind the victim?"

"The question isn't why he wore denims, but how did he know to wear them when the caller didn't tell either of us what we'd find out here?"

After Charlie was taken away, they decided they'd visit Mama Raye. In the ride over, Presser discussed how he and the wife had saved up for their daughter's sweet sixteen party. Money was tight for them, for everyone, but he had set aside a sum each week, so he could buy the pinafore dress she's seen in a fashion magazine.

As for Mama Raye, she kept her juke joint locked up during

the day, and used the daylight hours like most people used evenings for rest and recovery. On this Sunday or any other Sunday, she wouldn't be found inside a church, even if Christ himself had opened the first four of the seven seals and the Horsemen of the Apocalypse galloped forth.

She owned her own home on the edge of town, and she tithed a percentage from her various enterprises to grease the democratic machinery to keep her homestead and businesses safe from the Klan. Before she became a businesswoman, she'd worked all the trades common to poor women, from housework to minding children. It was rumored that she'd worked in the flesh trade when she toured as a torch singer. After she achieved financial success, like Madam C.J. Walker, Mama donated vast sums of money to the Tuskegee Institute, the NAACP, and the Black YMCA.

Her butler answered the door. If the two lawmen were surprised that a man in a formal black suit with a white shirt and black tie answered the door, they were shocked that he was white and that they knew him. With white gloves on, he parted the door wide and used a tone of voice they expected from a mortician. "Gentlemen, this way, please. Mama has been expecting you."

He offered them refreshments and to take their hats, but they said they didn't expect to stay long. He escorted them through the foyer of dark wood and portraits of Benjamin Banneker, Phyllis Wheatley, Frederick Douglas, and Harriet Tubman. In the parlor, they spied the Victor in one corner, a handsome handmade bookcase in mahogany next to it for the pressed discs of Mama's music library. Framed photographs of musicians, most of them inscribed to Mama, dotted the wall. Garland nudged the sheriff. "There's Josephine Baker," but the sheriff was interested in the Winchester rifle next to the andirons.

Mama entered the room. "Welcome, gentlemen; and yes, the rifle is loaded."

"Is it licensed and registered?" the sheriff asked.

"Ask me that question after I shoot someone with it."

She lit one of her Ashton cigarillos, and returned the lit match to the lucifer. Her butler returned and asked whether she needed anything. The sheriff's eyes tracked the servant's exit, as the sweet-smelling Cameroon wrappers and Dominican tobacco filled the air. Mama noticed and said, "I won him in a game of cards."

The sheriff and deputy stood there speechless.

"I'm teasing. I know you know Grady, and he pretends this is the first time he's laid eyes on you. Ain't it the devil's delight knowing a grandson of the Klan waits on me?"

"It was a surprise, yes," Presser answered.

"Want of money is the greater equalizer. Black and White alike are desperate for scratch during this depression. Grady swallowed his pride to work for Mama. Now, let's discuss why you are here."

Sheriff Presser summarized what had been found at Satan's Spit. They did not exclude Dr. Campion's presence, nor did they spare her any details, while Mama enjoyed her hand-rolled smoke. He asked her, "Did you know Charlie Taylor was a girl?"

"You want to know if she was turning tricks at my establishment?"

"It's not the first question I would've asked, but since you've come straight to the point."

"Charlie wasn't whoring, Sheriff. I wouldn't be surprised if the Coroner said she was a virgin, despite what the doctor said. In an effort to save you time, I'll answer the two questions that are plaguing you. Why was she there, and why did she disguise her sex?"

Presser looked to Garland and then to Mama. "Those questions do come to the forefront."

"Think about it, Sheriff. A young Negro girl has fewer opportunities than her White counterpart, so why not pass as a boy? Girls of either race are predestined for work that pays them low wages. Come what may, be it depression or prosperity, it's wife, schoolmarm, or nightingale for White women. Us Black folks might receive your people's largesse, if that."

The sheriff seemed at a loss, so he fixed his eyes on the Winchester. Mama asked whether he knew who Ida B. Wells was, and he said he did not.

"There's a photo of her on the wall behind you. Miss Wells covered the People's Grocery Massacre in Memphis. She said, and I quote, 'A Winchester rifle should have a place of honor in every Black home.'" Her eyes visited the weapon. "Hence, the rifle. Now, back to Miss Taylor."

"You established she needed money. What did Charlie do at your juke joint?"

"She worked as a musician."

"A musician?" The surprise came from Deputy Garland.

"Charlie played harp. For a child, she was all business and professional."

"Played harmonica?" Garland said and looked to the sheriff, confused." We didn't see no harmonica on her."

Presser ignored Garland and asked Mama, "Was she any good?"

"Yes, and she played slow blues."

"Slow blues—is that important?"

"It is, if you want respect. The way she squeezed a note would make an angel cry."

"Good enough that another musician was jealous enough to murder her?"

Mama answered, "Bluesmen don't mind women talent, Sheriff, though a gal has to prove herself. Nothing new to us women, regardless of race. Murder, though, I doubt it."

"Rob her then?"

Mama thought about it. "Money is scarce."

"How 'bout rape?"

"Rape is another form of robbery to a woman, Sheriff."

"Did she carry anything to protect herself?"

"Only thing she carried was herself and her harmonica when she was playing, but inside my juke she was safe and sound. I'm the law inside Mama Raye's. Whatever happens outside, at the crossroads, is between God above and the Devil below."

"What kind of harmonica?"

"Hohner Marine Band Classic with a custom comb, and made before the War."

"Custom sounds valuable."

"I bought it for her, since she couldn't afford it."

"As a gift?"

"No, as an investment. She was worth it. I don't wish to sound abrupt, gentlemen, but I have errands. If you have any more questions, please come back later or call me."

As they approached their Ford, Grady the butler accosted them and Mama stood at the window for a moment before she disappeared. He asked that neither the sheriff nor the deputy tell anyone that he worked for Mama Raye. He said his wife and family didn't know. They thought he worked as a traveling bank inspector.

The sheriff stopped before he opened the door. "Grady, a question for you, and your answer will be held in strictest confidence." Grady consented. Presser asked him, "Mama used to sing, right?"

Grady nodded. "She did, why?"

"Hear her sing?"

"Around the house, yes."

"Describe her voice to me, please."

"I'm no expert, Sheriff, but if I were to put words on her, I'd say, like smoke and dark chocolate."

Inside their Ford, Garland asked Presser why he had asked about Mama Raye's voice. Sheriff Presser said he had a hunch that it was Mama Raye who had called Campion and varied her voice to skirt identification.

"What now? Garland asked.
"Off to see the doctor."
"Campion?"
"Not him; the Coroner."

Presser and Garland traveled the single asphalt road left untouched by Governor Horton and his corrupt cronies. There was talk that federal dollars would arrive for projects, such as roadside parks and pull-offs for motorists, but most folks in Trinity thought that was about as likely as the Devil on his knees before Jesus.

They found the Coroner, a distinguished man of fifty, with white sidewalls for the color of his hair around his ears, and an absurd toupee on the roof that matched the dark and waxed Warren Williams moustache. Presser gave Charlie's name, and the pathologist escorted them into a refrigerated room, adjacent to where he worked, because Charlie Taylor was 'separate but equal' like the court case.

At first, neither the sheriff nor the deputy said a word, they listened.

"Negro female, fifteen years of age." They were told that Charlie was indeed a virgin; had been strangled and sodomized; that she had struggled and fought off her attacker before he overpowered her and killed her. As they listened to the description of the sequence of wounds that she had sustained in the last minutes of her life, without a word, both Presser and Garland removed their hats.

"No need for you to take your hats off for me, gentlemen. It's cold in here."

Presser said, "Not for you; for the dead. A question for you. Is there any physical evidence that could identify her killer, such as blood, semen, or the like?"

"There is proof the perpetrator orgasmed, but I can't tie semen to an individual."

Garland said, "What about her personal effects?"

"Clothes. Nothing unusual. Wait, there was one peculiar item."

The medical man walked over to another table and pulled open a drawer, and withdrew a small bag. "There's this."

Presser and Garland looked down at the table. They saw a clamshell case, labeled Hohner Marine Band Classic 1896. The doctor said, "Box, but no harmonica inside."

On the drive back to Trinity, Sheriff Presser and Deputy Garland discussed the case while Benny Goodman's "Moon Glow" played on the radio. Presser was perturbed that his original assessment about rape and robbery had been wrong. They seemed to go together. Garland said that what disturbed him was that the thief had taken the harmonica, but not the case. Both men agreed their criminal may have panicked and forgotten the hard-shell case.

Presser was the first to see Campion's house, and pulled the car off the main road and brought it to rest inside the doctor's driveway. They found their man in the front yard, on his knees clearing weeds, cursing the rabbits who had raided his garden. So absorbed was he in his yardwork that he didn't hear the lawmen until they were behind him. He greeted them and stood up.

"Quite the show you've got here," Presser said.

"The thirteenth labor of Hercules, if you ask me. This is an unexpected visit."

Garland squinted since the sun punished his eyes. "Sorry to have disturbed you. We were at the Coroner's. Seems you were right about rape and how Charlie Taylor died."

"It's not something I'd gloat over. I wish I were wrong, and she were alive."

The sheriff surveyed the scene. "You look like you've accomplished a lot."

"I've been at it since I returned," he looked to the strewn

weeds and the wheelbarrow of manure. "I'd intended an early start, but with the phone call and all."

"Up early, your work clothes on, and then the phone rang."

"Why do I sense there's a question behind this social call."

"Only one," the sheriff said. "When you looked at the body, you saw defensive marks?"

"I did, yes."

Garland added, "And Charlie's state of undress?"

Campion nodded. "It's how I surmised that he'd been raped."

"She," said the sheriff. "You suggested rape and robbery before we looked at the body, but did you check her pockets?"

"No, I have an aversion to putting my hand in someone's pockets. I saw the way the body was positioned, the eyes, and I deduced what had happened. You asked me my theory, and I gave it to you."

Garland asked, "Were you at Mama Raye's that night?"

"Yes, but the question, gentlemen, is who wasn't?"

"See Charlie play?"

"Heard a set, and I mingled like other folks did, but I never stepped outside, if that's what you're implying."

"Not implying anything, Doc. I'm sure others can verify it."

"Don't you mean corroborate? Talk to Mama Raye. I talked with her for the better part of the evening about a singer named Billie Holiday."

"Good to know. Anything else you remember?"

Campion approached the lawmen and pulled off his gloves. "Most of the town was present, most of them doing things they shouldn't, but I meant what I said earlier, gentlemen."

Presser said, "And what part was that?"

"I didn't know he was a she, and I know people talk and comment as to how I dress and act, but one thing I am not, gentlemen, is a pederast. Correct my pronouns all you want, Sheriff, but no child deserved what happened to Charlie. Now, if you'll excuse me, I have zinnias that deserve my attention."

* * *

As the day drew to a close, the sheriff said he'd wanted to visit Mama, to ask her about Billie Holiday. Both men agreed that they didn't like the idea that the homicide might go unsolved. The more time that elapsed, the colder the trail to a killer and conviction.

As they neared Mama's property, they wondered how long Grady had conducted the charade with his wife. Traveling bank inspectors were a despised lot, hated by the banks and looked upon with suspicion by everyone else. Banks failed and people were destitute, mistrustful of the government, despite the president's fireside chats in the evenings.

On the porch, they found the door ajar. The sheriff reached for his revolver. Hand on his weapon, Garland said, "Hear that? It's music."

"Coming from the Victor inside, the sheriff said.

The door swung wide with the slightest touch. The air felt heavy, and not from the melancholy melody of the singer's voice. Each man kept close to a wall and proceeded through the foyer he walked through hours ago. Garland noticed some shattered glass on the floor. A framed photograph had fallen from its place on the wall.

The sheriff was the first to see the corpse. Grady lay there, a harmonica next to him. He'd changed out of the butler's uniform into his street clothes. A bullet had slammed into his chest, blown him back and killed him.

The sheriff looked to the fireplace and saw the Winchester rifle missing, and didn't dare enter the room without announcing himself first. "I know you're armed, Mama. We don't want to have to shoot you."

"Pay me no mind, Sheriff. Mama won't shoot you."

"Will you lower your weapon?"

"I will if you will."

Garland asked, "Tell us what happened?"

"He wanted to kill me. He must've figured out I called the doctor and you."

The sheriff peeked around the door's edge and saw her sitting at her desk.

"Why don't you enjoy one of your cigarillos, and we'll come in, and you tell us what you think happened, between Charlie and Grady."

"He raped and killed her is what happened."

"Any idea as to why? Garland asked.

"I thought it was because he feared she'd tell someone he worked here."

The sheriff glanced to his deputy. "But you think there's another reason?"

"I know there is, Sheriff, but he didn't have to rape her."

"No, he didn't," the sheriff said. "He didn't have to do any of it."

The sheriff eased into the room, and Garland followed. The rifle lay on the desk. Garland kept his revolver drawn and the sheriff moved the Winchester away from her.

Mama Raye explained that she would keep the harmonica locked up, on account of its being valuable. Most weeknights she kept it under lock and key there at the house, which is how Charlie had become aware that Grady worked as a butler. Come Friday night and the weekend, at the juke joint, Charlie kept the instrument on her, case and all.

Sheriff Presser said, "Grady knew it was valuable."

"He must've seen her with the case and assumed the Hohner was inside of it."

"He somehow gets Charlie alone, intent on stealing it. Figured he was a child."

"And discovered he was a she, and assumed he had the right. I'll have that smoke now, if that's okay with you."

"It's your house."

"Am I under arrest, Sheriff?"

Presser looked to Garland. "I think my deputy and I see this as a stranger breaking into a home, and the owner defended herself and her property."

"But I killed a white man."

"But he's a traveling bank inspector, a liar, a thief, a rapist, and a murderer."

Mama sat there, cigarillo in hand. "But a grandson of a Klansman."

Presser said, "His grandad is long dead, Mama."

"But, his friends ain't, and then there's the rest of his kinfolk," Mama said. She smiled and then sighed, "Look like I need to decide whether I stay or go, for what's comin' next."

They sat there for a long time, long enough to hear the first cicada, and then another, and then the chorus before the darkness fell.

ONE LUCKY BREAK

Erica Wright

A Strike Three Records executive discovered me crooning at a rundown honky-tonk on Broadway, bought me three shots of tequila, and wrote out my contract on a cocktail napkin. I signed my name, a little wobbly, and started recording my debut album a week later. They gave me a stack of proper papers to sign eventually, full of phrases like "liquidated damages" and "alternate dispute resolution," but I kept the napkin. It's framed above a shelf that displays my Grammys and CMAs. It looks authentic even, little water ring and all. And that's the story I tell when I'm asked about how my career began. The real one's a little more complicated and involves a single-barrel shotgun, a Chanel purse, and felony charges.

This was 90s Nashville, when the streets tenderized newcomers, and the blood that leaked out was twang-filled and sincere. Better for its sweetness. Singers and songwriters arrived every day, believing that they'd be the next Reba or Garth. The city would chew them up, enjoy their tears as a chaser, and not worry once about heartburn. But I was made of tougher stuff, gristle and bone you might say. Nobody was going to make a snack out of me. Plus I was local enough. My middle-of-nowhere hometown was only a thirty-minute drive to Music Row. I didn't make that drive at first, though. No, I called and wrote and called and wrote again, enjoying the rejections for a while. They would make my story better when I finally made it. Nobody likes a star who hasn't struggled a little. I needed to be relatable to my future fans. But after four months of hang-ups and a few snidely whispered insults, I was ready for some action. I looked it, too, as I put on a final coat of waterproof mascara and surveyed the results in the bathroom mirror. I was fixing to turn thirty, and my momma had threatened to throw me out if I didn't get a real job. You know my song "Now or Now?" That moment right there, staring at my own face, inspired it.

> You gotta believe it's now or now
> ain't nobody gonna grieve ya
> unless you make it somehow.

I knew better than to wear sequins, looks like I was trying too hard, but rhinestone boots felt appropriate, especially when pulled over my tightest jeans. I wore a white crop top to show off my tan belly then added a leather blazer. I slathered some vanilla-scented lotion on my exposed skin, hoping I didn't have a reaction to the new brand. I had a decision to make. Would the six-shooter be too much, or would it make me look authentic? I'd recently picked up a silver, leather holster at a flea market.

If you know me at all, then you'll know I like being authentic. I'm quick to bring up how I learned to ride horses from one granddaddy and shoot from the other. I figure if God gave you two grandaddies, you might as well make the most of them as you film a segment for *Sunday Morning*. They wouldn't have minded. They liked a good joke as much as the next man.

I clicked the holster on, and it seemed to approve, disappearing underneath my jacket, not a line in sight. I checked the safety then the chambers: five bullets. My granddaddy told me to always leave one space, give the unlucky fellow a fighting chance. You can even believe that if you want.

My Camry had a full tank, but I took the pickup truck. Lord knows, the term "gas guzzler" was created for that hunk of metal, but it looked the part, half-rust and half-mud. My jeans were so tight when I slid behind the wheel, that I undid the top button. Nobody was going to pull me over. Not that day. If you'll forgive me for quoting myself, that day was *mine for the winning.* I slid on my sunglasses and put on my own CD. I sang along to my favorite lyrics while I wove in and out of traffic on I-24. I even left the truck running when I stopped at the pumps, risking a fire, but enjoying the appreciative glances that flicked my way. I'm telling you, I knew something good was going to happen because I was going to make it happen.

Me and my truck glided through downtown like a cottonmouth on a creek, past the neon sign for Robert's Western World then onward toward the chain restaurants cozied up along Second Avenue. A riverboat churned through the Tennessee, sun glinting off the wake. I didn't need to take the scenic route, but I wanted to survey my kingdom. It was mine for the taking, if only I had the courage to claim it. *Hang your heart on the hat hook,* I sang. *Right next to mine.*

I rolled down my windows for the chorus:

> *I got an empty place*
> *in a you-shaped space*
> *on the hearth in my home.*

There was a parking spot out front, another sign in my favor, and I paralleled into that sucker, barely bumping the car behind me. I jumped down to the sidewalk and looked up at my new home. Strike Three Records wasn't the fancy, seven-story glass fortress it is today. No, it was more like an overgrown brick house, but it had a bronze plaque out front that told me I was at the right place. The lobby, too, proclaimed the company's success with platinum and gold records lining the walls. There was a red, leather bench on one side as if sometimes visitors sat down for no other reason than to bask in the glory. Or maybe they were overcome, got a case of the vapors, and needed to rest for a spell. I had no interest in that sort of weakness and more or less skipped toward the reception desk. I daydreamed about the documentary that would be made about my life.

"She was so bold," the graying producer would say. "A sight for sore eyes sauntering through my office door."

"I wanted to sign her before she opened her mouth," another producer would add, then the two men would share a little laugh at their own genius. They deserved at least a little credit, didn't they?

"Excuse me," I said when I saw that the desk and chair were empty. There wasn't a bell to ring like at the bank, so I raised my voice instead. When nobody responded, I tapped my foot in frustration. When I was a star, I'd make sure they hired somebody more reliable. I reached over for the sign-in list, recognizing a couple of names from the day before, but not being intimidated. I grabbed the blue pen and wrote my name, clear as John Hancock, then headed for the elevator. There were stairs, too, but I didn't want to be winded when I made my dramatic entrance.

When the door dinged open, I whipped my sunglasses off my head, putting one end in my mouth. I wanted to look casual, almost uninterested. They were lucky to have me there, not the other way around. When I gazed around the floor, though, my jaw dropped, and my sunglasses smacked against the wood floor.

"What in holy hell?" The words came out in a whisper, but the gunman closest to me heard, jerking in my direction with his shotgun. Pump-action with a magazine. Maybe a Remington or one of the Italian models. See? I wasn't all hat, no cattle. I was, however very, very irritated.

The man gestured with his gun toward the center of the room, and I stepped forward without thinking, my boots crunching my sunglasses as I passed. *Twenty dollars down the drain,* I remember thinking. There were a few huddled groups. Three women were crouched low behind a desk, but I could see their hair sticking out, shaking. Another trio held each other by the bathroom entrance, and I swear I could feel them wanting to duck inside, which is a nice way to get yourself good and trapped. "No Dead Ends," that's my motto and the title track on my second album. The other group really caught my eye, two men in black suits, one with a solid yellow necktie and the other with pinstripes. The bosses. The decision makers. The whos-I-needed-to-impress.

"Move," said a low voice at my ear. "You got cotton in your ears?"

Apparently the gunman had been addressing me, and when I felt his shotgun on my back, it took every last bit of self-control not to tell him to stuff his plans to heck and back. But I can imagine what a shotgun does to a body at close range. Good-bye, world. The lowlife tried to corral me toward the desk women, but I had the executives in sight and stepped that way. Let them think I wanted men for protection. What did I care?

When I reached my destination, I turned around to survey the room again. No, it didn't look how I had pictured it. The windows were nice enough with views of the tree-lined street outside. And I rather liked the paisley wallpaper. Otherwise, it was a run-of-the-mill corporate office, not a place where dreams come true. The only smells were the new carpet and my own sweet lotion. Then there was the problem of two gunmen running around. Well, one was running at least, going back and forth like he was warming up for the Olympic trials. He didn't seem to have a gun either, so I revised my original impression of the situation. He swung a baseball bat, tried to look menacing. This was a holdup, but what exactly did these losers think they were going to steal? The only computer in the place must have weighed about fifty pounds. Idiots aren't necessarily less dangerous than geniuses, though, so I kept my trap shut at first.

"Here's what's gonna happen," the shotgun wielder said. "Everybody's gonna hand over their wallets and purses and jewelry and whatever to this little volunteer right here."

"Who me?"

I made an expression like I'd just been named a finalist for Miss America. Little ole me was going to help these criminals? I didn't think so. The gunman grabbed my arm and flung me onto the floor. I'm not going to lie. It hurt my hip a little when I landed, but mostly, I was mortified when I noticed that I'd forgotten to button my pants back. This was my day, darn it, and they were ruining it. An idea tickled at the base of my skull, like when I got a new song lyric going. No matter what, I'll stop whatever I'm doing and write. If I don't got paper, I'll write on my arm. If I don't got a pen, I'll borrow one. Nothing can stop me. It felt like that, but instead of a catchy riff, I saw a vague plan. Vague or not, it was better than looking around slack-jawed like everybody else.

"You heard the man," I said, slipping my six-shooter out and pointing it at the woman closest to me. Now that I could see her face, she was pretty, even with makeup running down her face. Younger than me, twenty at most. Not old enough to know about the magic of waterproof mascara. "Hand me everything, or this pretty little raccoon gets it."

The woman gasped, wiping at her cheeks, which only made the situation worse. After her efforts, she had black circles on each cheek. Lord have mercy, this one needed a big sister. I leveled my gaze at the gunman who'd prompted me, and his eyes looked confused inside his mask. I'll say. He was stunned, and I had a moment to study him. Small build with love handles, visible from where his t-shirt rode up. It was one of those Guns n' Roses signature black ones with the flowers and guns. Now that I noticed, those guns looked a lot like mine, and I giggled. This was destiny after all. My laugh made the woman in front of me cry harder, though, so I reigned in my amusement.

"Please," I said, and when the gunman took a step toward me, I pulled back the hammer until it clicked into place. The man's confused expression skidded into fear, and bingo, this was my game now. He hadn't wanted anybody to get hurt. Well, too late for that, pal. My feelings were good and truly hurt. "I got five bullets, and I don't think anybody's feeling lucky today except for me."

The wallets, purses, and watches dropped at my feet. Black and gold, big and small. I clocked a nice little Chanel clutch and an elaborate, pearl-encrusted cross. I've never felt more like a goddess, except for maybe that time I played sold-out shows at Madison Square Garden. Three nights, fifteen gowns, and my faithful band. They don't know this story either, so you better not tell them. Gabriel's a real stick in the mud since he had the twins. Doesn't even like booze in the dressing room, as if he don't get performance jitters like the rest of us.

Anyway, there I was, threatening the life of some innocent intern, throwing the bad guys off their offensive, and shuffling through plays in my head. I'd knocked everybody off-balance, myself included. For kicks mostly, I aimed at the ceiling and pulled the trigger, shattering a ceiling tile. Plaster rained down like soft, January flakes, and I smiled into them. If somebody had been taking pictures, that's the one I would have printed. Offerings at my feet, arm raised like I was the blessed Statue of Liberty.

"That's everything," said one of the producers in a crisp, even voice. I could imagine him giving a handsy reporter the what-for, and I was already grateful for how he'd guide my career. It was Peter Kingsport, but you've already guessed that, haven't you? He took this story to his grave, the dear man.

I could have let the gunmen—gunman and bat boy, I should say—waltz out of there with their loot, but they'd had enough fun, and I told them to get lost.

"Excuse me?" said the one closest to me.

"Get lost. You got cotton balls in your ears?"

The shotgun barrel was on my forehead before I could say "boo," but almost as quickly, I had my arm pointed at his chest. I'd never named my gun before, but decided she was Delilah. Call her a hussy or harlot all you like, she gets the job done. I wrote a song about her, but never recorded it. Still, I play it sometimes at home by myself, think about the day I signed my record contract.

"Don't shoot her, Darryl." The other man spoke at last, taking steps toward us. He was taller and had better taste in music. His Willie Nelson t-shirt looked new and proclaimed "Old Row Country" on the front pocket. His ski mask was olive green instead of black. The color made him look more like a hunter than a burglar. He got close enough that I could smell his pine deodorant, volume up to ten from the stress hormones. These fools wanted a quick buck, not a murder wrap. But Mr. Love Handles had adrenaline kicking through his system. I could almost taste it, sharp and acidic. But that could have been mine. My arm was steady as an oak tree, even when the metal pushed farther into my forehead, threatened to leave a permanent circle. But I wasn't exactly calm. My stomach started to itch and without glancing down, I knew the lotion had given me hives.

"Don't use our names, you dumb shit," Darryl said in response, pushing me another centimeter.

"Trouble in paradise?" I asked, baiting him. He moved the barrel a few inches away, and I know it's impossible, but I could see everything all at once, unfolding before me. How he planned to knock me square in the face, break my nose or jaw or both. How he'd scoop everything into his backpack and run down the stairs and out into the afternoon while I hollered and bled all over that brand-new carpet. The stains would never come out. What else could I do? I pulled the trigger.

The gun popped, and everybody in the room screamed. The woman at my feet grabbed my legs, and at first I thought she was trying to take me down, but she just needed a hug. Bless her heart, you know? Bless mine, too, while we're at it. If I'd shot Darryl, the afternoon would have taken a different turn.

"Well, aren't you today's lucky bastard?" I said, clicking the hammer into place again. The robbers took off for the stairs, their sneakers squeaking and voices loud as they rushed down and out the front door.

The applause was nice, I'm not going to lie. Today? Today, I might not even notice the sound. I'm used to roaring crowds. But that day, eight palms slapping together was music to my ears. When it stopped, I grinned at all of them, my new team.

"I've got a demo," I said, walking toward Peter Kingsport. "And nobody's been returnin' my calls."

I'm telling you, it was an honest mistake. I was hyped up, on cloud nine, ready for my gosh-darn career to get started, you know? I didn't even notice that the gun was still in my hand, and that my arm was still out-stretched. She cleaned up nice, my little six-shooter with four bullets left. I wondered why I ever kept her holstered and hidden away. Elk horn grip and a nitre blue trigger. If you turned it a little, the fluorescent lights popped off the polished steel, made her shine. Made her sing, I might say in a poetic mood.

"Yes, ma'am," said Peter Kingsport, holding up his hands. "Whatever you want."

I liked the sound of that. New lyrics slid into my head, and I asked for a pen:

Whatever you want today, no sense waitin' around
until your hair turns gray. Pick up that crown
that was always yours anyway, always yours anyway,
ooh, ooh, ooh, ooh, ooh.

AFTERWORD

Beware!

Bouchercon, as we all know, is the premiere World Mystery Convention.

But beware of a deep, dark bit of Tennessee lore—the Tennessee Terror! It may be a terror of the Tennessee River, but we all know that tributaries turn and twist just about everywhere.

Once upon a time, this creature brought with it a terrible, life-threatening curse! Those who saw it had less than a year to live. Rumor has it that the fisherman who first encountered the creature died shortly thereafter of fright. First spotted in the early 1800s, it was a monster like no other, the size of an elephant, with a shelled coat, talons on its feet, fire in its eyes and fire-breathing like a dragon. This Tennessee cryptid, known as an 'aquatic,' was twenty-five feet long and snake-like in appearance, except for its size, talons, fiery eyes and breath!

It disappeared for a while, and people began to seek it, searching the rivers, embankments, and other shorelines. And it was spotted! Again and again, as the decades brought us into the twenty-first century.

However, it's gotten friendlier. The curse seems to have lifted. People simply enjoy seeing the creature, snapping pics and posting about him, or her, on social media!

There may be another creature lurking in the rivers, one a bit more popular today. Catzilla! Well, of course, it's a giant catfish, and man, just get one of the whiskers from a little catfish stuck in you, and well, you know...hmm, don't even want to imagine Catzilla!

Then again, catfish can be found around the country...

While you're having fun in the beautiful city of Nashville, remember to keep an eye out if you're by the Tennessee River or any body of water.

Who knows? You might just catch a glimpse of the Tennessee Terror, or—possibly—Catzilla!

We hope you have enjoyed these tales of music, murder, and mayhem with a sprinkling of mystery, thrills, and chills! Thanks very much for supporting the Nashville Public Library Foundation and be sure to seek out and enjoy more stories by the talented authors you've found between these covers! They are truly amazing and an absolute pleasure to work with, and we thank them for joining us on the journey.

Heather Graham
Susan & Kevin Cella

ABOUT THE CONTRIBUTORS

ERIC BECKSTROM is a writer and photographer from Minnesota, now based in Bloomington, Indiana. His stories have been published in the 2017, 2002 and 2024 Bouchercon anthologies, *Black Cat Weekly*, and *Dark of the Day: Eclipse Stories* (ed. Kaye George). One of his first stories, which he adapted for the stage, was produced by The Bloomington Playwrights Project, Indiana's only professional theatre dedicated solely to new plays.

ERIC BEETNER has been hailed as "the new maestro of noir" by Ken Bruen and "The 21st Century's answer to Jim Thompson" by LitReactor. He has written more than 30 novels and his 100+ short stories have been featured in over 30 anthologies. Along the way he's been nominated for an ITW award, a Shamus, Derringer and three Anthony awards. He's won none of them.
For more visit: EricBeetner.com.

VALERIE (V.M.) BURNS is an Agatha, Anthony, and Edgar Award-nominated author. She is the author of the Mystery Bookshop, Dog Club, RJ Franklin, and Baker Street Mystery series. As Kallie E. Benjamin, Valerie writes the Bailey the Bloodhound Mystery series. She is an adjunct professor in the Writing Popular Fiction Program at Seton Hill University in

Greensburg, Pennsylvania, and a mentor in the Pocket MFA program. Born and raised in northwestern Indiana, Valerie now lives in Northern Georgia with her two poodles. She is Bouchercon 2024's Cozy Guest of Honor.

Connect with Valerie at VMBurns.com.

EMILY CARPENTER is the bestselling author of five suspense novels, including *Burying the Honeysuckle Girls*. Her next thriller *Gothictown* will be published by Kensington in 2025. After graduating from Auburn University in Alabama with a Bachelor of Arts in Speech Communication, she moved to New York City. She's worked as an actor, producer, screenwriter, and as a behind-the-scenes soap opera assistant for the CBS shows, *As the World Turns* and *Guiding Light*. Born and raised in Birmingham, Alabama, she now lives in Atlanta, Georgia.

A journalism veteran, published author, and aspiring novelist, **HC CHAN** made her fiction debut with "Murderers' Feast" in *Midnight Hour* (Crooked Lane). She has won awards for unpublished works (Sisters in Crime Eleanor Taylor Bland, 1st place work in progress, and Women's National Book Awards SF Effie Lee Morris, 2nd place fiction) and most recently the Los Angeles Review 2023 Short Fiction Award for "These Poor Mothers," available online and in the annual print literary journal. She is based in the SF Bay Area with her husband and his crotchety parrot Hemingway.

Visit her at VeraHCChan.com.

MICHAEL AMOS CODY was born on the edge of South Carolina's Lowcountry and raised in the highlands north of Asheville, North Carolina. He spent his twenties writing songs and fronting a band in Nashville, Tennessee, spent his thirties earning an education, and has since been teaching literature at East Tennessee State University. He is the author of the novel *Gabriel's Songbook* (Pisgah Press, 2017) and the story collection

A Twilight Reel (Pisgah Press, 2021). His literary suspense novel *Streets of Nashville* is scheduled for publication on April 15, 2025, by Madville Publishing. He lives in Jonesborough, Tennessee, with his wife Leesa.

TINA DEBELLEGARDE writes short stories and flash fiction, as well as the Agatha-nominated Batavia-on-Hudson Mystery Series. Her story "Tokyo Stranger" appears in the Mystery Writers of America anthology *When a Stranger Comes to Town* (ed. Michael Koryta) and was nominated for a Derringer Award. "A Good Judge of Character" in *Malice Domestic Mystery Most Traditional* was nominated for an Agatha Award. Her work also appears in several Best New England Crime Stories anthologies. Tina is currently working on a collection of interconnected short stories based in Japan.
Visit her website for more: TinadeBellegarde.com.

MARY DUTTA is the winner of the New England Crime Bake Al Blanchard Award for her short story "The Wonderworker," which appears in *Masthead: Best New England Crime Stories*. Her work can also be found in numerous anthologies including the Anthony-nominated *Land of 10,000 Thrills: Bouchercon Anthology 2022*. She is a member of Sisters in Crime and the Short Mystery Fiction Society.
Visit her at MaryDutta.com and enjoy her blog at Writers Who Kill.

MICHAEL FERRETER is a writer and editor. His byline has appeared in the *Milwaukee Journal Sentinel* and the *Omaha World-Herald*, among other Midwestern newspapers, in trade magazines and other publications. As a communications consultant, he has advised CEOs, CFOs and other executives at Fortune 500 companies. "Music City Row" is his first mystery short story. It was inspired by musicians he has seen perform and talked with after alt-country and Americana shows in and around Chicago. He lives with his wife, daughter and two cats. Find him at MichaelFerreter.com.

BARRY FULTON is a retired diplomat, former Air Force officer, and occasional university professor with overseas assignments in Brussels, Italy, Japan, Pakistan, and Turkey. His latest novel is *East of Pittsburgh: Death on the Eve of the Truman-Dewey 1948 Election.* He writes the Thomas Sebastian Scott espionage series: *The Irish Imbroglio, Behind the Seventh Veil, The Lady is Bugged,* and *Flame: Hackers, Artists, Lovers, and Spies.* Fulton is a member of the Public Diplomacy Council of America, DACOR, and Sisters in Crime.
Check his website at FultonPub.com or subscribe to his monthly newsletter, A Few Good Words, at http://eepurl.com/gllSxX.

HEATHER GRAHAM is the NYT and USA Today bestselling author of over two hundred novels, novellas, and short stories including suspense, paranormal, historical, mainstream, and Christmas family fare. She lives in Miami, Florida, her home, and an easy shot down to the Keys where she can indulge in her passion for diving. Travel, research, and ballroom dancing, and a love of reading—anything, fiction, non-fiction, cereal boxes when there's nothing else—also help keep her sane. She is the mother of five and considers family and friends her greatest assets in life. She is CEO of Slush Pile Productions, a recording company and production house for various charity events. She has been honored with the Romance Writers of America Lifetime Achievement Award, a Thriller Writers Silver Bullet for charitable contributions, Distinguished Author Award from the Southwest Florida Reading Festival, the Strand Lifetime Achievement Award, and the Thriller Master Award. She is grateful every day of her life to be writing for a living. Heather is Bouchercon' s 2024 American Guest of Honor.
Look her up at TheOriginalHeatherGraham.com.

A native of Los Angeles, **M.G. HALL** is a university student and fitness instructor and thrift store fanatic. This is her first published short story.

RACHEL HOWZELL HALL is the author of twelve novels, including the upcoming thriller *What Fire Brings,* and *The Last One*, the first romantasy in her new series. She is also the author of bestselling novels, including *What Never Happened*, *We Lie Here* and multiple award-nominated *And Now She's Gone* and *These Toxic Things*. Rachel is a two-time nominee of the Los Angeles Times Book Prize. She is a former member of the board of directors for Mystery Writers of America and was a featured writer on NPR's acclaimed Crime in the City series and the National Endowment for the Arts weekly podcast. Rachel is Bouchercon's 2024 Toastmaster.

SARAH ZACHRICH JENG grew up in Michigan and always had a flair for the morbid and mysterious (for her dad's thirty-fifth birthday, she wrote a short story entitled "The Man Who Died at 35"). After a brief career as an aspiring rock star, she now writes cross-genre novels that combine suspense with the speculative, most recently *When I'm Her* (Berkley, 2024). Sarah lives in Florida with her family and two rescue dogs.
Find her on Instagram and Threads @sarah_ezj or visit her website at SarahZJ.com.

D.P. LYLE is the Amazon #1 Bestselling; Macavity and Benjamin Franklin Award-winning, and Edgar (2), Agatha, Anthony, Shamus, Scribe, and USA Today Best Book (2) Award-nominated author of 25 books, both fiction and non-fiction. He hosts the Crime Fiction Writer's Blog and the Criminal Mischief: The Art and Science of Crime Fiction podcast series and is co-creator of the Outliers Writing University. He has worked with many novelists and with the writers of popular television shows such as *Law & Order, CSI: Miami, Diagnosis Murder,*

Monk, Judging Amy, Peacemakers, Cold Case, House, Medium, Women's Murder Club, 1-800-Missing, The Glades, and *Pretty Little Liars.*
Website: http://www.dplylemd.com.
Outliers Writing University: OutliersWritingUniversity.com.

JENNY RAMALEY draws on her experience in the worlds of science, safety, and cybersecurity to create contemporary thrillers and mysteries for adults and teens. Jenny was a Rutgers One-on-One mentee, and her work placed in the Academy Nicholl Fellowships in Screenwriting and Chesterfield Writer's Film Project competitions. Her short story, "A Long-Term Plan," was chosen as the first tale in the Florida Gulf Coast Sisters in Crime anthology, *Paradise is Deadly.* A good day includes a hike in the woods thinking about stories and jotting down plot points in a dog-eared Moleskine.
Visit her website at JennyRamaley.com.

MERRILEE ROBSON's short stories have appeared in *Ellery Queen, Alfred Hitchcock, Mystery Magazine, The People's Friend,* and many other magazines and anthologies. Her traditional mystery, *Murder is Uncooperative,* is set in a non-profit housing co-op. Merrilee has served on the boards of Sisters in Crime—Canada West and Crime Writers of Canada. She is a former member of the Vancouver Police Board, which provides civilian oversight to the Vancouver Police Department. She lives in Vancouver and spends a lot of time with at least one cat on her lap.
MerrileeRobson.ca

After losing their home during a California wildfire, **PEGGY ROTHSCHILD** and her husband moved to a beach community along the central coast—where there are enough trails to keep her out of trouble for years. Her Molly Madison Dog Wrangler Mystery Series includes *A Deadly Bone to Pick, Playing Dead,* and *Let Sleeping Dogs Lie.* Peggy is a member of Sisters in

Crime Los Angeles and National, and Mystery Writers of America. When not reading or writing at her desk, you can usually find her in the garden. PeggyRothschildAuthor.com.

H.K. SLADE is a writer living in North Carolina who specializes in police procedurals with occasional forays into Horror and Science Fiction. When not writing or working, he spends time with his dogs and designing an elaborate custom game each year for Halloween. You can find more of his work in *Everyday Fiction, Mystery Weekly, The Yard, Black Cat Mystery Magazine, Black Cat Weekly, Dark Horses*, as well as at his author website, HKSlade.com.

CLAY STAFFORD is an American author, publisher, filmmaker, actor, composer, educator, public speaker, consultant, reviewer, columnist, CEO of American Blackguard Entertainment, founder of Killer Nashville International Writers' Conference, and advocate for writers, filmmakers, and educators. He has sold nearly four million copies of his books, and his work is available in over sixteen languages. He is Boucher-con' s 2024 Fan Guest of Honor. ClayStafford.com.

KELLI STANLEY is the creator of the Miranda Corbie series (*City of Dragons, City of Secrets, City of Ghosts, City of Sharks*), literary noir novels set in 1940 San Francisco and featuring "one of crime's most arresting heroines" (*Library Journal*). Kelli was named a literary heir of Dashiell Hammett by his granddaughter in *Publisher's Weekly*, and critics have compared her work to her icons Raymond Chandler and Norman Corwin. Her awards include the Macavity and Bruce Alexander and she is a *Los Angeles Times* Book Prize finalist. She was awarded a Certificate of Merit from the City and County of San Francisco for her contributions to literature.

Kelli has also published an award-winning series set in Roman Britain, numerous short stories and essays, holds a Master's Degree in Classics, and is the founder and president of Nasty Woman Press, a non-profit publisher of the Anthony Award-winning anthology *Shattering Glass)*. Kelli is Bouchercon's 2024 Historical Mystery Guest of Honor. KelliStanley.com.

Known for suspense with depth, **J.D. TRAFFORD** is the winner of the National Legal Fiction Writing Competition for Lawyers, has been profiled in *Mystery Scene Magazine* (a "writer of merit"), and written multiple bestselling legal thrillers. This includes *Little Boy Lost*, which has sold over 100,000 copies worldwide and was the #1 overall bestseller on Amazon, as well as *Good Intentions*, also an Amazon Charts bestseller. *Tower Grove*, the third book in Trafford's "Dark River" series, will be published this fall.

MARK TROY writes mystery and detective fiction from his home in Texas. *Splintered Loyalty*, the second novel on the Ava Rome private eye series, was published in 2023. Mark's recent short stories include "Dos Tacos Guatemaltecos y Una Pistola Casera," which appeared in season two of the Guns + Tacos Anthology Series, and "Sundown Town," in *Groovy Gumshoes, Private Eyes in the Psychedelic Sixties*. A visit to Tootsie's Orchid Bar occupies the top spot on Mark's Nashville list. MarkTroyAuthor.com.

GABRIEL VALJAN is the author of *The Company Files*, and the Shane Cleary Mysteries with Level Best Books. He has been nominated for the Agatha, Anthony, Derringer, Shamus, and Silver Falchion awards. He received the 2021 Macavity Award for Best Short Story. Gabriel is a member of the Historical Novel Society, ITW, MWA, and Sisters in Crime. He lives in Boston and answers to a tuxedo cat named Munchkin.

ERICA WRIGHT's latest mystery *Hollow Bones* (Severn House, 2024) takes its inspiration from Shakespeare's *Measure for Measure*. She is the author of seven previous books, including the essay collection *Snake* (Bloomsbury, 2020) and the poetry collection *All the Bayou Stories End with Drowned* (Black Lawrence Press, 2017). Her novel *Famous in Cedarville* (Polis Books, 2019) received a starred review from Publishers Weekly and was called "a clever little whodunnit" in The New York Times Book Review. She is a former editorial board member of Alice James Books and currently teaches at Bellevue University. She lives in Knoxville, Tennessee.

On the following pages are a few
more great titles from the
Down & Out Books publishing family.

For a complete list of books and to
sign up for our newsletter,
go to DownAndOutBooks.com.

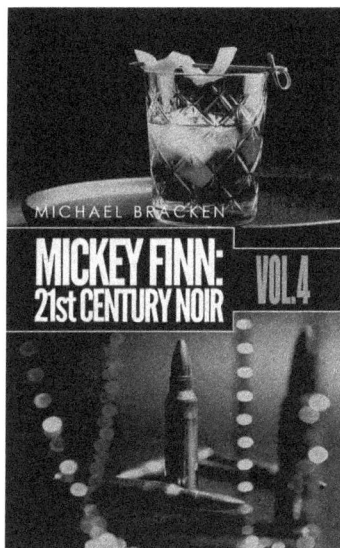

Mickey Finn: 21st Century Noir Vol. 4
Michael Bracken, Editor

Down & Out Books
December 2023
978-1-64396-346-4

Mickey Finn: 21st Century Noir, Volume 4, the fourth volume of the hard-hitting series, is another crime-fiction cocktail that will knock readers into a literary stupor.

Contributors push hard against the boundaries of crime fiction, driving their work into places short crime fiction doesn't often go, into a world where the mean streets seem gentrified by comparison and happy endings are the exception, not the rule.

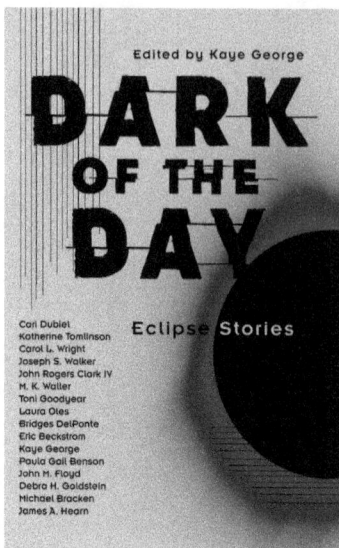

Dark of the Day: Eclipse Stories
Kaye George, Editor

Down & Out Books
April 2024
978-1-64396-395-2

An anthology of stories to celebrate the April 2024 eclipse in North America. These stories are located in various places and are even of various genres and themes. What they have in common, besides featuring eclipses, are that they are all written by brilliant authors and will all entertain you. Read them before the eclipse, to get into the mood, or after, to nostalgically remember it.

Contributors include Cari Dubiel, Katherine Tomlinson, Carol L. Wright, Joseph S. Walker, John Rogers Clark IV, M. K. Waller, Toni Goodyear, Laura Oles, Bridges DelPonte, Eric Beckstrom, Kaye George, Paula Gail Benson, John M. Floyd, Debra H. Goldstein, Michael Bracken, and James A. Hearn.

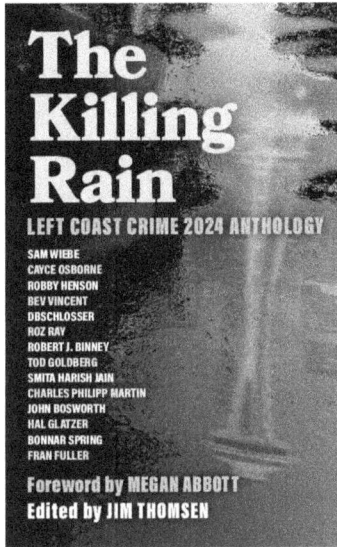

The Killing Rain
Left Coast Crime Anthology 2024
Jim Thomsen, Editor

Down & Out Books
April 2024
978-1-64396-362-4

The Killing Rain is collection of short crime fiction, ranging from the cozy to the hardboiled, with each story depicting the Seattle area as a real or imagine place.

It's in conjunction with "Seattle Shakedown" — the slogan for the 2024 Left Coast Crime conference, slated for April 10-14 in nearby Bellevue.

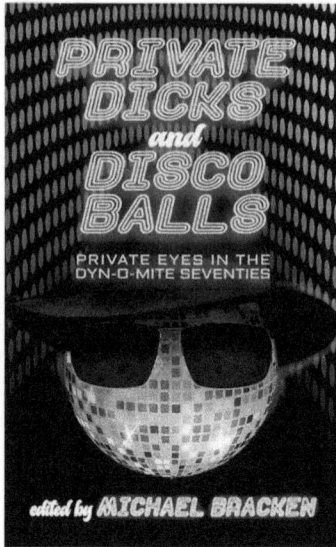

Private Dicks and Disco Balls
Private Eyes in the Dyn-O-Mite Seventies
Michael Bracken, Editor

Down & Out Books
May 2024
978-1-64396-365-5

The Sixties were a time of great cultural upheaval, and that upheaval continued into the 1970s. In the midst of all this, private eyes worked with clients across the generations, from those still clinging to the social mores of Nixon's "silent majority" to those who embraced the rapid societal changes that began in the 1960s.

From old-school private eyes to the Baby Boomers coming of age and entering the trade, these private eyes will take readers on a funky frolic through the Dyn-O-Mite Seventies.

www.ingramcontent.com/pod-product-compliance
Lightning Source LLC
Chambersburg PA
CBHW031137020426
42333CB00013B/422